Infamous
Scars of Lumierna

Pronunciations

Stirling Bakere	Stur-ling Bake-eer
Amiria Rey	Aa-meer-ee-aa Ray
Ignis	Ig-nus
Taika	T-eye-kuh
Calix Gautier	Kay-lix Goe-tee-air
Ealdian Dietrich	Aal-Dee-un Dee-trik
Kinsey Gautier	Kin-zee Goe-tee-air
Giles Bakere	Jeye-ls Bake-eer
Quilan	Kwil-uhn
Aether	Ay-th-er
Dicun	Deye-kun
Quetzecoatl	Ket-suhl-koh-at-uhl
Per'yanny svir	Per-yawn-nee-s-veer
Amphipteres	Am-fih-teer
Wyverna	Weye-ver-nuh
Lumierna	Loo-meer-nuh
Tillfalya	Till-faal-yuh
Uviktiland	Oo-vik-ti-land
Leucasia	Loo-caw-zee-uh
Patu	Paw-too

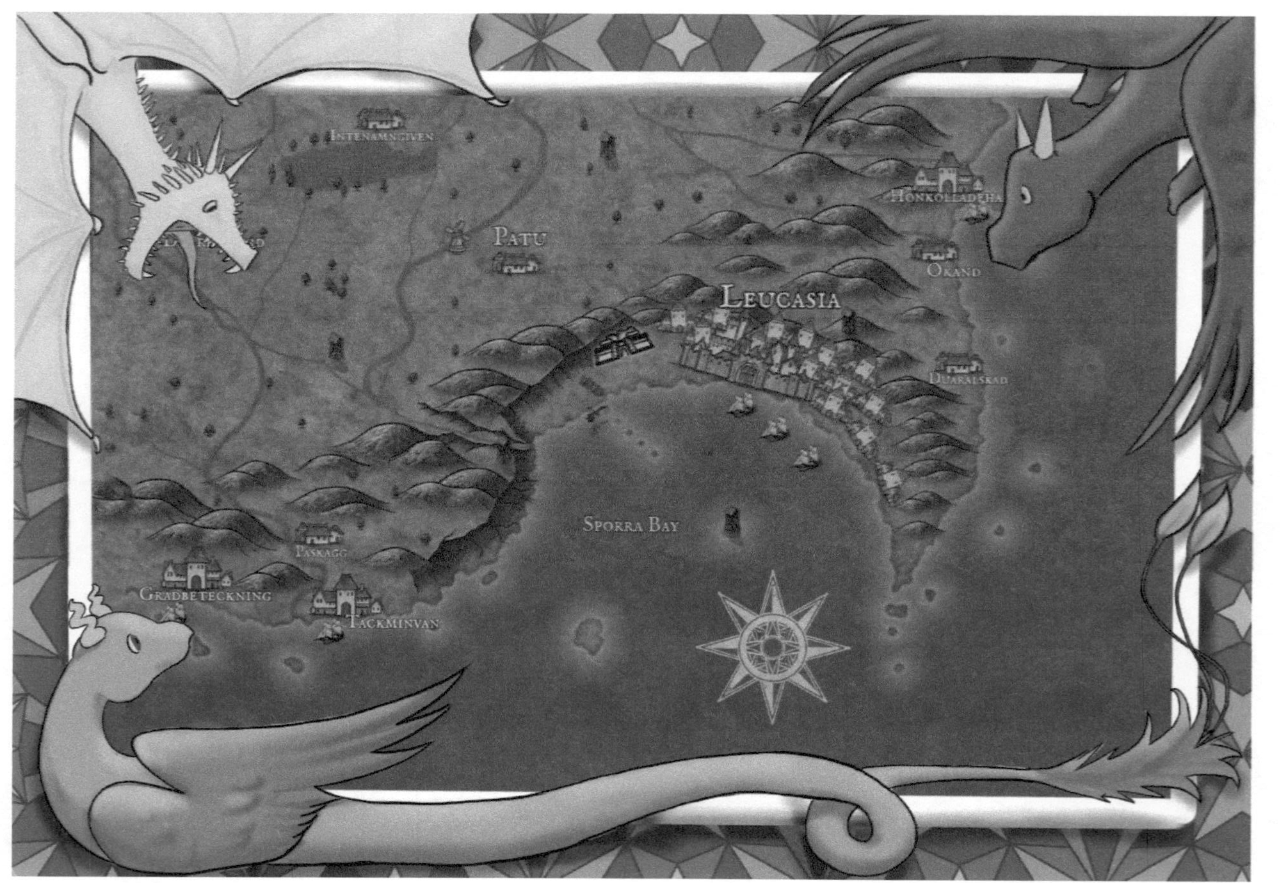

INTENAMNGIVEN
PATU
HONKOLLADEHA
OKAND
LEUCASIA
DJARALSKAD
SPORRA BAY
PASKAGG
GRADBETECKNING
TACKMINVAN

UVITILAND
ISLES OF WYVERNA
AMBER'S PATH
SPELLING'S PATH
KINGDOM OF TILLFALLYA

ISLES OF WYVERNA
Purdy Graveyard
Kicsloo
Koobrict
Milijoel
Monikave
Mishanichey
Villisa
Sophicheno
Fuessdon
Millioaks
durstown
Peterton
Kicsheot
Jamesfield
Iudheaunie
Lumierna
Abram Canyon
N
W
E
S

LUMIERNA
WINGED CAVALRY BASE
THE CAVE

Crystal eyes watch the leaves of the oak tree rustle above him. How long has it been? How long has he been wandering lost in search of the one thing he cares about? The only thing in this god-forsaken world worth living for.

Lying on his back, he dreamily reaches up and traces the outlines of blue sky peeking through the branches. "Oh, my little bird."

One

B aker boy!"

As everyone around him disintegrates into sea foam, Amiria stands above the waves on an island of her own. He sways on the deck of his ship, too astounded to call out for land. She is his personal castle's flag signaling safety, informing him he was home.

Forgetting how to breathe, he puts his hand on a girl's shoulder and gently nudges her out of the way. His mind and body are in a cloud as he floats to her. The pressing fans turn to see who has stolen his attention. Who has captivated their idol? Searching the plaza, they see nothing but a disheveled girl on the edge of the fountain.

"Who is that? She looks like she was dragged through a field by an ox."

"Amiria." His voice is a croaking whisper. "AMIRIA!" he calls, finding his voice. He steps through the crowd with shallow breaths, his soul captivated by her presence.

Her soul cartwheels with joy. She has found him. After all this time, she finally found him!

The crowd of girls lean to him as if by a gravitational pull. *What is this?* Amiria clenches her jaw as she watches them. She has spent months unable to close her eyes, constantly checking over her shoulder for the fear one of her teammates will be there—unable to sleep without seeing herself strung up at the gallows. She has been traversing the unknown world, bartering everything of value she owns just so she can survive.

While she was dying, trying to find him, he was living a grand life of—of fame?

The crowd finally parts a path from Stirling to Amiria. Silence lays heavy in the air as everyone waits to see how the story will play out.

Amiria hops down from the fountain. Her toe almost catches on the lip of a tile as she restrains herself from running into his arms. To breathe in the smell of familiarity while lost in this foreign world. With the warmth of his arms around her, she will know she is no longer alone. As if the ghost of a person stands between them, they stop an arm's length away from each other.

She doesn't need a keen eye to see his tremors. Anyone who knows him knows what the tapping of his fingers means. She follows his arm up to his jaw as it twitches with anticipation of all the words he wants to say. Amiria's face is unreadable, a scroll without a label.

"I—" He rasps. Nervously, he clears his throat.

How does he convey into words everything he is sorry for, everything he has learned, and how he feels? Sweat begins to coat the palm wrapped around the flower stems, his other hand tapping anxiously at his side. Casting his eyes down to their shoes, he thrusts the boutique out in front of him. Amiria keeps her sight on him as it hangs idly in the space between them.

"Amiria…" His voice is despondent, he can't meet her eye. "I'm sor—sorry for everything I did."

Purple, her favorite color. It floats between them waiting for acceptance. She has traveled across the world to be reunited with him, to ask for his help. So why can't she take the flowers from him, take his hand in hers? Their audience is fixated. Everyone is straining their ears for her reply.

With her head held forward, she scans the faces around her. Did he even miss her? Did he think of her while these girls cheered his name, or is she another part of Wyverna he has run away from? Permanently put into his past? Are these flowers for a real apology, or is this a show for *them*? With her mind running to conclusions, anger boils up inside of her. Everything she has been through is rushing to the surface.

"YOU'RE SORRY!?" She slaps the flowers from his hand. The petals tear free from their beds and scatter into the air like confetti.

The spectators gasp in unison.

"You abandoned me and you're sorry!" she screams, shoving him in the chest, hard enough to knock him back a step. "The kingdom, and my life went to turmoil, and you're sorry!" She shoves him again. "The one person I trusted! You broke it and you're sorry!"

She shoves him again, her voice wavering as she holds back any tears from forming. She takes his jerkin in her hands, the fabric crushing between her fingers. Her body is visibly shaking with rage.

"Someone, stop her! She's going to hurt him!" a girl yelps.

Amiria pulls Stirling closer to her, their chests almost touching. "I HATE YOU!" Her voice tears from her throat.

Distraught, she sees nothing except the green fabric crumpled in her fists, but she can feel him. She can feel the warmth of him standing there. She can feel him watching, waiting for her next move. She can feel the solid of his chest as it rises and touches her fingers with each breath. They're steady.

"I hate you," she whispers to the decorated stone of the plaza. "I—hate…you." Her voice is barely audible.

Her eyes widen as strong arms wrap around her and pull her in. Stunned, her face presses into his chest as he engulfs her. With fingers still curled around the fabric, she closes her eyelids and pulls it around her face. She hides from everyone by burying herself in him.

It's warm.

"I'm so sorry," he utters, his cheek resting on the top of her head. He wishes he can speak his thoughts. He doesn't care about any of the people in the plaza. For as long as time will allow it, he will stand here holding her.

She begins melting into him. The urge to slide her arms around him and lace her fingers behind his back as she presses her body into his wavers across her mind. *This feels safe,* she thinks. Her grip on the fabric loosens. *But it's not.*

Pained eyes crack open.

Throwing out her arms, she shoves him away from her. Stirling, unresistant stumbles a couple of steps back. Her sight darts around to the spectators surrounding them. She sees the crowd outside the butcher's shop, but this time, she is in the center. She touches her chest and the imaginary blade protruding from her sternum.

You are a Winged Rider, she chastises herself. She stands corrected. *You* were *a Winged Rider. Compose yourself.* Tilting her chin up, she flattens her wild hair and pushes it back over her shoulders.

"Forgiveness comes with time." Her dark irises blink up at him. "Stirling, I need to speak with you." She motions her hand to the people around them. "In private, please. You appear to draw a crowd of people who need to…" She grumbles the rest. "Mind their own business."

Girls whisper in groups around them, "He has a girlfriend?"

"She talks like him."

"I want to talk like him."

"Is she from the same poor village?"

"She's crazy. She doesn't deserve him. He's so sweet."

As if he had forgotten they were there, Stirling scans his usual audience. "Yeah, I, uh, know a good place to go."

With the inn Stirling spent an entire month of his life in sitting in the distance, he leads Amiria down a path to a quiet spot at the harbor shore. A spot away from everyone where they can hear their own thoughts.

Amiria kicks pebbles in random directions as she walks with her arms crossed. She stops beside him where the land drops off into the deep harbor. Leaning forward, she takes a peek at the rocks disappearing through the clear water into the dark bottomless depths.

Staring at her reflection, Stirling watches her face ripple on the water's surface. "You wanted to talk. So, let's talk."

Amiria presses her lips into a thin line in sudden defiance to speak.

Stirling lets out his frustrations with a sigh. "Amiria." He draws out her name as a parent would a child. "Don't give me that. I know for a fact you have a lot to say because you always have a lot to say. There's a seven-month-long scroll of things you want to say."

Amiria whips her head to look up at him with daggers in her eyes. "Yes, and you've become *real* popular in those seven months."

Backing off, Stirling hops down the ledge to the first rock. They're level now. "I know what it looks like. I thought of you, Amiria." He meets her eye. "Every day. Those people, that attention—I hate everything about it."

He turns away to the water. "The first time I passed over those mountains and saw the city I—I freaked out. My mind overran with those nightmarish memories of Lumierna. Every time I stood in front of the crowd, I swore I could hear the sirens again." He shuts his eyes, forcing the images from resurfacing now that he is admitting it. With a sigh, he hops down to the bottom of the rocks with the water lapping at his feet. "After some rough encounters with the locals in the beginning, I came here to this spot. It was the first time I stood on a beach, able to touch the ocean." He reaches into the water. "Well, besides when we exit from the underground lake."

Amiria watches through her lashes as Stirling reaches into the water. *What is he doing?*

"It helped me reflect on myself." Stirling climbs back up to the shore. "Have you ever seen a starfish before?"

"A what?"

"This." Stirling holds up a purple starfish smaller than the pink one he had initially seen. He shoves the creature bottom-first up to Amiria's face.

"EEP!" Amiria squeals, her face contorting into revulsion. She backhands the starfish, casting it back into the water with a plop.

Stirling bites his lip, holding back his laughter. "Did you just 'eep'?"

"Shut up! Tell anyone I did that, and I will cut out your tongue," she threatens.

"That's it? You won't kill me? Aw, you do still care," he says, smirking.

Blushing, Amiria hardens her facial expression and reverts back to the subject of her original intent. "How could you?"

"With what? The starfish?"

"NO!" she yells, her emotions taking over.

Stirling flinches at her eruption.

Amiria continues, "You didn't just abandon me. You abandoned your father, you abandoned your people." She jabs her finger into his chest.

Stirling puts his palm out, catching her hand and shakes his head. "I never wanted to hurt you, and I can't explain how sorry I am. But the rest of those *people*, they abandoned me long before you and I even met."

Amiria is appalled and with a yank of her hand and a stomp of her foot she criticizes, "Your father loves you!"

"My father tried to kill me!" Stirling raises his voice to match hers.

"He didn't know it was you!" She pauses, realizing her volume is only growing. Bringing it down, she continues, "He's changed. The citizens are changing, and it's all because of you."

Stirling turns his head away, but she sidesteps to stay in view.

"Stirling, listen to me. People are dying back home."

"What do you mean dying?" Dread sinks to his bones.

"They were told you died that night. That you were shot down from the sky and were lost to the dark waters. You're a martyr, Stirling."

Stirling begins to shake his head in denial.

"They saw what you did. They aren't listening to King Dietrich anymore; they are all following you. Now hundreds of people are dying because of *you*." She lays the last word out between them.

Stirling refuses to pick up the word, to accept that responsibility. "I never asked to be a martyr. I didn't tell any of those people to do anything. Whatever it is they are doing, that's all on them. What is going on in Wyverna is not my problem."

Amiria becomes flushed with emotions as she screams, "THAT IS OUR HOME!"

"THAT IS YOUR HOME! This is my home! I have made a new family. Even these city dwellers. They looked down at me at first, but they still had their eyes open to watch me. By the end of the games, they no longer cared where I came from. They instead saw the racer I became. Out of everyone, I thought you would understand?" His shoulders move with his heavy breaths as he finishes, his eyes linked with hers as he waits for a response.

Her eyes are cold and analytical. "You defector. All you ever care about is yourself," she berates with a raised lip.

"You—" He points, biting his tongue. He holds back the words he knows he will regret saying. Waving her off Stirling begins to walk away then spins back around grinding his heel in the gravel. "You know what, why did you even come here? You should have stayed there if you love it so much."

Calix holding his hand out to her for support. A wedding. Them in charge of the Winged Cavalry. Maybe she should have stayed and fought against Wyverna's laws from within. But, King Dietrich's lusting eyes, her father's betrayal, her birth mother's truthful words, the looming noose.

She subconsciously touches her neck. "They were going to catch on to me eventually. I can't keep up with their Miss Perfect act forever."

Stirling is becoming increasingly aggravated. "So, is that why you chose to run away? Because you didn't want to when I asked you to come with me. You said you had a duty to abide. Tell me what changed, Amiria."

"I'm not running away. I don't *run* away." She clenches her fists. "I came to you for help Stirling. King Dietrich needs to be condemned. We need to stop him from killing more innocent people."

"Is that the only reason you looked for me? To get me involved in some revolt against King Dietrich?"

"No—" Amiria shakes her head.

Stirling grits his teeth. "Then why did you? Because—" He lowers his mouth to her ear and growls, "I am no one's hero."

She tilts her head to see into his summer irises. "I'm not asking you to be a hero. But maybe you being there can help inspire the people to rise up. I want you by my side again. I need you."

Stirling's shoulders relax from the fighting tension, and he takes her hands in his. He scans up her arms lined with thin white lines from years of battle. His wet eyes meet her damp ones. "Forget Wyverna. Stay here, stay here with me. Amiria, please. It's safe here. We can live in the home that I built."

Amiria's heart sways. This is what he had asked her the night he ran away. He offered his hand to guide her into the unknown. He asked her to explore a new world with him and find somewhere they could live without fear of being strung up in the gallows. Her body, her heart, they wanted her to go. To leap into the sea of stars with him and never return—but she refused. She stayed put like the good little soldier she was. What was she rewarded with? A never-ending slew of misfortune? How would life have changed if she had just said yes? Would they have both been living here in Patu? Would her name be known as a famous racer?

Now here, the opportunity to change her answer has arrived.

She pulls her hands away from his. Her trained mind can't let the people of her home suffer while she lives happily ever after somewhere far away. She is unable to disassociate herself from them as Stirling has. Her life has been sworn to protect them. The reason she was born was to give her life for the people of Wyverna. Going home will be not only tying the knot of her noose but Stirling's too. Whose lives are more important to her, Stirling and hers or the people of Wyverna?

"I need to go back. I need to stop King Dietrich."

Stirling's eyes turn cold. "You mean kill, King Dietrich."

Amiria peers up at him, her loose hair tossing around from the coastal wind. Her voice wavers. "Drastic times call for drastic measures."

Stirling takes a revolted step back from her. "You ever take into consideration the king is no different than you and me? He is only a man doing what he is told to do. If you kill him solely on that fact, you are no better. Those are old laws deeply seeded into that kingdom. Killing one guy won't change anything. The next heir will step up, you will be stopped, and they will continue on."

He can't lose her, not again. Not forever. Money and fame mean nothing if there is no her. Before he was able to live believing she was at least safe no longer risking each visit to him in the mountains. If she goes back to Wyverna now, he knows he'll never see her again and there will be no hope that one day he can. He would give it all up to live quietly with her, but he can't go back. They can't go back. He cannot let her become nothing more than a name on a parchment. Another document signing away her existence.

"Please Amiria," he begs, tears forming in his eyes, "Stay here with me."

Amiria can't look him in the eye. She can't think straight when she looks into those golden eyes. What compelled her to run after that fight with the bandits? Was she seizing the opportunity? Did she truly think Stirling would return with her to fight against an entire kingdom? She knows Stirling is not a fighter, he is a survivor.

Who is truly telling her to go back, Amiria or the Winged Rider? Does she, herself, want to save Wyverna, or is it the deeply seeded training ordering her to do so? Her heart thumps. Or honestly, did she run to him because she desired to see him again? To see his smile. To hear his laugh.

She had convinced herself she was going to only visit him. She will ask him to come back with her, and if he refuses, she will return without him. Can she leave her best friend's side again? No, she must. Her happiness is not as important as the lives she was born to protect.

Around his neck are the goggles she had given him, and the bag slung around his shoulder. He could have bought new ones. She remembers what Giles had said, *In that moment, you chose what matters the most to you.*

What does matter the most to her? Stirling doesn't need her anymore. He is successful here on his own. The people back home are reliant on her to help them. How many lives have been taken since she left? She must go back to them. She must return to them. But what truly matters to *her?*

"One week."

"Huh?"

"I'll stay one week to rest and restock provisions. It'll give me time to devise a plan to stop King Dietrich." *Just one week. One week and I'll go home. One full week with…* Her heart picks up. *Stirling.*

Stirling's spirit lifts. "Really?"

"Sure." Amiria takes on a nonchalant act. "Let's see this village you love so much you changed your name to it."

"Yeah, they don't have surnames here." He rubs the back of his neck. "So, that happened. But you are going to love it! It's also the perfect day to arrive. It's an important Saint's Day," Stirling says hyped.

"What Saint's Day?"

"One that isn't back in Wyverna," Stirling informs, then calls out to Ignis *"It's time to head back."*

"Oh? So, you survived the encounter? Did you kiss and make up?"

"*No.*" Stirling blushes. "*Just get over here.*"

Amiria smiles to herself knowing Stirling's twitching expression is him talking to Ignis. She lifts her whistle and summons Taika.

Landing beside them with a giddy bounce to his step, Ignis hops over to Amiria wagging his tail like an excited puppy, "*AMIRIA! AMIRIA! I'm glad someone who actually thinks with logic is here.*"

"*She can't hear you.*"

"*Oh, trust me. I know.*"

Stirling frowns.

Amiria laughs, "Still rambunctious as always, I see. I missed you too, Ignis."

Ignis pauses at Stirling, "*Who do you think she missed more? I think it was me.*"

'Shut up Ignis."

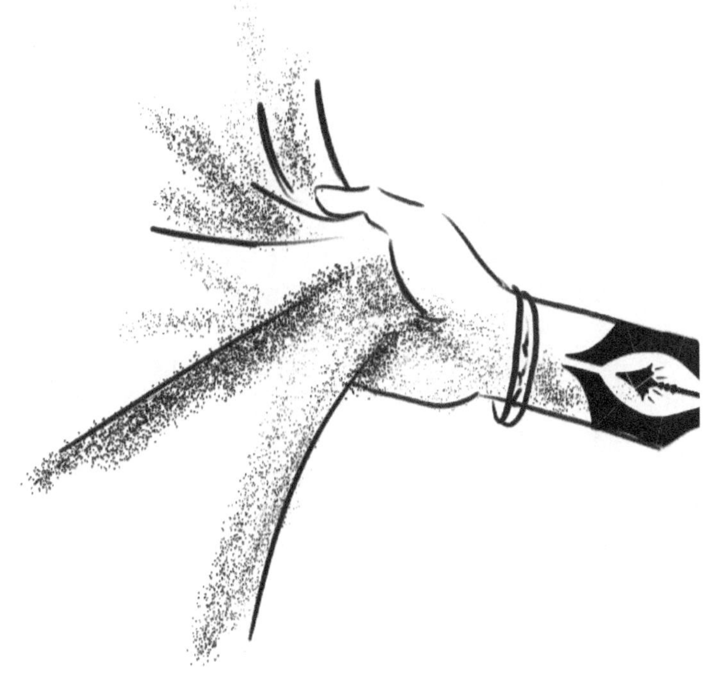

The people scattered across the village look up as their neighborhood dragon flies overhead. They would normally pay no mind to Stirling; he is part of their family. They've seen him almost every day since he moved to Patu except for the small number of times he traveled to compete. What raises their eyebrows is the second dragon flying behind him. It isn't normal for Stirling to be accompanied by another racer and one they have never seen before.

Amiria follows Stirling over the village she had passed on the way to the capitol and lands in front of a quaint half-timber house beside the river. *In a house, I will build.*

Stirling tumbles off Ignis effervescently, his body gyrating with eagerness, "Come look! Come look! This is my house!" Facing Amiria, he spreads out his arms with pride slapped across his face.

Amiria can't take her eyes off the home as she dismounts. Her jaw slacks with awe, "Stirling, you built this?"

"Well, not just me. The villagers and Ignis helped, of course," he answers humbly before using his long legs to take his stairs in two leaps. He twirls back to Amiria who is inspecting the outside of the house.

"Is that a garden?" she asks, catching a glimpse of a fenced area with tomato vines growing up it.

"Yeah, I also have a couple of chickens and a goat around back," he exclaims.

Amiria stops at the first step looking up at him, "You're allowed to own all this?"

"Well yeah, I bought it. Out here you need to be self-sufficient. You can have a specialty if you want or two or three. But you can't rely on others, they've got their own mouths to feed."

"Is it difficult?" she asks, finishing the last steps of the short staircase.

Stirling backs up to the front of the door. His focus remains on Amiria as he opens it, "What? Independence? It's like living in the cave but, um, fancier. It's basically my own little castle."

He holds the door open and motions for Amiria to enter. She stops just past the threshold as the cozy home tells its story.

Afraid to touch her, Stirling squeezes past her into the house allowing the door to close softly behind him, "I don't really have much because I'm not completely sure what a home needs."

Amiria reads the single room home. Her eyes scan across its pages. A kitchen taking up the left corner consists of thin planks of wood running along the wall as a countertop with crates of storage below. She can almost hear the chopping of vegetables on the well-used cutting board with deep imprinted grooves. Cluttering the counter within reach of the board there's several clay jars holding different spices, herbs, and grains, as well as baskets with freshly picked vegetables from his garden, and a bowl with eggs.

She steps over to a dining table with two bench seats and lets her mind wander to a place where she is sharing a meal he has prepared. Reaching out she touches the table and runs her fingers down the grains. She smiles to himself, he really has built himself a life here.Distracted by her thoughts she glazes past the only other door in the room just beside the edge of the kitchen on the left wall.

On the opposing side of the room, there are windows overlooking the river on either side of a large cobblestone fireplace overflowing with ash. Laid out a safe distance from the fireplace is an orange rug with threads woven to resemble the scales of a dragon. Placed on top of the rug is a piece of furniture Stirling had invented to allow him to lounge more comfortably by the fire. A wooden plank with pillow cushions tied down to it makes up the base, with sturdy branches extending up vertically at each end and once down the middle. Heavy fabric stretches across as a backrest with a small amount of flexibility.

She pinches her lips holding back the smile curling at the corners. On display above the fireplace is her old bow. It's mounted to hold its original shape, but the break is held apart just enough to make the damage still apparent. She steals a glance at Stirling whose reddened face tells her he didn't put it up expecting her to see it.

Amiria nods her head in the direction of the other door, "What's behind there?"

"Oh, the bedroom," Stirling answers.

"Is that not what the loft is for?" Amiria questions pointing at the ladder leading up to a small loft able to fit two people on the wall across from the entry.

"It is, but I didn't like being so far from Ignis."

Stirling opens the door revealing steps into a ground-level room. The room is a rendition of his life in the cave.

He has remade his old bed with planes of wood set across the pyramid logs and a goose feather mattress instead of fresh pine. The bed has been disregarded to the side of the room and taking up the entirety of the space is a large heap of straw with a woolen blanket thrown into a crumpled pile.

"You haven't changed much, have you? Even with your new rise to glory?" Amiria states looking over the simple room.

"I like to think I have, maybe a little."

"How so?"

"I don't know, I just feel as if I've grown in a way," he says with a lop-sided grin. "Though it appears you haven't," Stirling levels his hand out with the top of her head.

She bats at it as if it's a bothersome fly, "Will you cut that out." Her face turns flat, smoothing out the sharp edges, "It's wonderful by the way…your home." She looks over his shoulder at the one-room home behind her, "It really is perfect."

"Well, I wouldn't go as far as saying it's perfect. But it suits its purpose. It's just nice to call it mine. Thanks though," he says awkwardly fiddling with his hair.

Amiria wraps her hand around her torso holding her arm at the elbow, "You said there's a Saint's Day tonight?"

"Yeah, the whole village will be there."

Amiria bows her head to examine her attire, stained and torn, "Do you have anything clean I can borrow?"

Stirling cocks his head, "What's wrong with what you are wearing?"

She raises an eyebrow, "I've been wearing this for months now. It's falling apart. This is not the appearance I want to meet your friends as *and* my only other option is armor."

"I think you look—" His words fall short as he catches himself. Amiria's dark eyes hang on him with anticipation of his next words. Stirling swallows the next word and says, "Fine—you look fine."

Amiria's face falls, she throws her eyes off to the side and mutters "Do you have any spare tunics or not?"

"I do, but they will be big on you."

She sighs, "I really don't care. I just need this off."

"Uh…sure…Okay…um," he fumbles his words as he steps back inside the main part of the house and squats down beside a storage trunk just inside the door, and shuffles through the unfolded clothes.

"You go from stitching your only tunic to having a trunk full?" Amiria leans on the door frame watching.

Still kneeling he answers shyly, "Yeah, well no. It's not just tunics, my trousers, jerkins, and braies are in here too."

"Moving on up in the world," Amiria teases.

Stirling pulls out a garnet-colored tunic and holds it out, "Try this on, its waist length on me. There's a leather belt too so you don't have to wear your harness to cinch it in." Amiria holds her hands out letting him drape the tunic across, "You can uh, you can change in the sleeping room."

Nodding, she disappears back into the bedroom clicking the door softly behind her. She holds up the sleeved tunic, *At least the color is nice.* She checks behind her making sure the door is secured. Hesitantly she holds the tunic up to her nose and breathes in the scent.

There is no scent of pine needles.

It smells of straw, rosemary, and nettles. The straw she understands but the other scents are something new. Soap? Is he using soap? Her hands drop to her sides, letting the tunic and belt fall to her feet.

He is no longer Stirling Bakere, her best friend who lives in a cave. This tunic belongs to Stirling of Patu, a famous elite racer.

Stirling leans his hip against the counter while he patiently waits for Amiria to change. Hearing the door creak open, he perks up. His jaw goes slack as he witnesses her step into the room wearing his tunic over her tights. With the long sleeves pushed up to her elbows, she tugs uncomfortably at the hem of the tunic hanging above her knees and adjusts the fabric cinched around her waist by the leather belt.

Entranced, Stirling reaches back to push off the counter as he turns to face her. His palm slips off the edge. He catches himself before falling over, but that doesn't save him from tripping over his words. "You, uh—uh, look…" He mentally kicks himself as he can't find the words. Why is seeing her in his tunic frazzling him to this degree?

Amiria dips her chin hoping he doesn't see the pink on her cheeks pretending to ignore his antics while she ties her hair into a knot at the top of her head. "Do you have any string?"

Clamping his mouth shut Stirling bites the side of his tongue. "Mhm." He pulls out a small box from under the counter and rummages through it. Turned away, he hands her a scrap piece of string.

"Thank you," she says, securing her hair in place.

Tugging at his collar he steps around Amiria towards the front door, "You ready? They're probably already making the bone fire." Amiria checks back at her blades still laying in a heap with her harness and cotehardie. "You won't need them," Stirling assures, opening the front door.

She does a double take between Stirling and her weapons, the overwhelming sensation of being naked without any source of weaponry on her ensnares her. Kicking free, she follows her favorite smile out onto the trampled pathway leading to the village.

Trailing behind Stirling, she signals to Taika to stay and can see in the direction of the village Ignis is already over there. She startles at a flock of birds emerging from the tall grass and taking into the sky. She watches them as the coastal wind blows down from the velvet mountains and out across the prairie.

The geography is a stark contrast to the looming peaks and dense forests they grew up in, but the ambiance is the same. The air is clean and free.

"What's the legend behind the Saints Day?" she asks, catching up to his pace and walking beside him.

"It's about the first time they tamed a dragon. It's the legend of how they became domesticated," Stirling begins.

"Is it not because of mutual bonds or earned respect?" Amiria questions.

"No, they are more like horses out here. Bred and sold to the rich. In a nutshell, the story is about a city that was in fear of a lake dragon. A name would be drawn from a bowl once a month and they would be sacrificed to the dragon to keep the peace. One month the princess' name was called, and the king was going to have to sacrifice her because he was not above his people. A knight showed up from out of town as they were getting ready to sacrifice her. But he didn't fight the dragon, instead, when the dragon arose from the lake's depths to devour the princess, he threw a rope around the dragon to catch it and used his fastener to tie a collar around the dragon's neck. He then traded his horse to the city and rode the dragon out of town."

"Kinda anti-climactic." Amiria scoffs.

"I guess, but they enjoy the story. So now they make a huge fire and burn animal bones to remember those who perished to the dragon." He peers down his shoulder at her as she thinks the story over.

"STIRLING!" A shrieking girl's voice penetrates the space between him and Amiria.

Ignis pauses from playing with the children to look over at Stirling. *"Oh boy."*

Hair tied into a crown of braids for the occasion, Eve prances over from where the village men are stacking logs in the middle of the dirt road just outside of the village to keep clear from anything flammable. She stops just short of reaching them. Her feet plant into the ground as if she suddenly grew roots.

"Who's this?" Eve's voice is a sharp blade.

Eyes so dark they are almost black analyze the warm brown skinned girl in a yellow gown, diagnosing whether a friend or foe.

Oblivious to Eve's tone, Stirling grins wildly. He grabs Amiria by the shoulders and pulls her in front of him, "This is Amiria, my friend I always talk about."

"Oh…I see," Eve cranks out with a rusted smile, "It's nice to finally meet you."

Amiria leans back into Stirling, uncomfortable with meeting the new girl, "And you are?"

"Eve, Stirling's *closest* friend here," her honey eyes leer down the brim of her nose locking with Amiria's.

The heat of the tension rises in the air up to Stirling's height, finally cluing him in, "We should find Bernard. I've got the items he asked for—Bernard!"

Eve leaps to Stirling's side, latching onto his arm as soon as he releases his hold on Amiria's shoulders. Amiria folds her arms, closing herself off as she becomes the third wheel.

"Bernard!" Stirling calls out.

Bernard leans a waist-tall log onto the pile and squints through his bristly eyebrows, "Oi! What took you so long? Too busy conversing with fans to help with the hard labor?"

"No, well, something unexpected happened. Look!" Stirling motions to Amiria, "It's the real Amiria! My best friend Amiria!" Amiria smiles politely as Eve rolls her eyes.

"Nooo," Bernard drags out the word in disbelief. "The famous Amiria."

Conducting herself properly. Amiria sticks out her hand to shake but is taken off guard as Bernard crushes her in a tight embrace and lifts her up from the ground swinging her in a circle. She squeaks like a small toy as the air is squeezed from her lungs.

Bernard holds her out in front of him. "Never did I believe you would show up at our doorstep."

"Wait, what?" Stirling cocks his head.

Bernard sets Amiria down, shrugging off Stirling. "Sorry, boy, the odds were not in your favor."

Stirling blinks blankly as he mulls over the statement.

Amiria smooths her tunic then holds out her hand, "It is a pleasure to meet you."

"No, the pleasure is mine. Stirling has become a son to me. So, I'm honored to meet someone he holds as dear as you." Bernard smiles through his beard. Disregarding her held out hand, he throws his arm around Amiria's shoulders making her walk with him. "I bet you have some fantastic tales. Let me introduce you to the village."

Amiria glances over her shoulder for reassurance as she is guided away.

Stirling watches with his hand half raised partially reaching out to her.

"Oh, she'll be fine." Eve waves her off. "We've still got a feast to prepare."

Still holding on to his arm, Eve drags Stirling in the direction of the tables set out in front of the ale house where several other villagers are already chopping vegetables and removing the feathers from the chickens Stirling had purchased for the entire village.

Amiria peaks over her shoulder grasping one last glance at Stirling as they are guided away from each other.

"ROESIA!" Bernard calls to his wife who is kneeling beside their son Gregory. She puts what she was telling him on hold and looks up as Bernard tells her, "You'll never guess who Stirling brought!"

A smile barely has time to break as Amiria is wrapped up by an overbearing motherly hug.

Three

The fire begins to creep up the tower of logs as the sun falls from the sky. For a few moments, both will be a burning light resting on the grassy plains. Stirling mindlessly watches Amiria from the food prep table. He keeps one eye on the baking bread and the other on her as she continues to theatrically tell her adventures to a mostly male audience.

He begrudgingly skewers the seasoned vegetables, the corners of his lips pulled down to his chin. Why do they get to hear her stories before he does? Shouldn't he have been the first person she told the tale of her escape from the Winged Cavalry to?

Amiria holds two sword-length sticks, the right raised above her head and the left pointing directly at her invisible opponent. She slashes down while stepping forward, and with a dragging foot, she spins swinging her sword backhanded.

Twirling the sticks through the air, her feet dance across the compressed road. Half the village lost in her one-man show.

"You might be light on your feet, but how could a woman beat a man in hand-to-hand combat? You don't have any raw strength," Stirling can hear Miller Edward say as he steps forth from the audience. His biceps defined beneath his tunic from years of manual labor.

Stirling can't hear Amiria's soft response, but he witnesses her step up to the broad man like a prowling cat. He puts his hands on his hips mocking their size difference.

Amiria pounces forward grabbing Edward by the arm. Stepping behind him she pivots, driving his arm into the ground and sprawling him out into a prone position.

Fingers snap in front of Stirling's face. "STIRLING! HEELLOOOO!" Eve says, stripping his attention away from the action. "Can you check the bread? We're going to set the chicken up to roast on the fire soon."

"Yeah…Okay," he grumbles.

He turns to head around to the back of the alehouse where the stove is located when a sudden burst of excitement slams into the inside of his skull like a migraine.

Ignis.

Stirling rubs his temples as Ignis lies in the deep grass surrounded by children climbing and sliding off him, but his attention is aimed at the sky. The throbbing in Stirling's head matches the drumming in Ignis' chest. Stirling applauds Ignis' self-discipline because, despite his excitement, Ignis tenderly stands allowing the children to safely slide off without injury. Already knowing what will be at the end. Stirling follows the string of Ignis' gaze to a ribbon of blue fluttering in the sky from the hilltops.

"Oh! He made it."

"Who made it?" Eve asks, peering around Stirling. Her nails dig into his arm in surprise when she realizes. "Quilan! You invited Quilan! And he showed up!"

Stirling shrugs. "How is that weird? We're close, were together all the time."

Eve dances on her feet as she decides what to do with the news. "No—You two are together all the time. Um, okay—okay—okay. I'll go check the bread and you go greet him," she instructs more than offers, shoving Stirling in Quilan's landing direction. "EEE, Quilan's here!" She runs off toward the oven before Stirling can reply.

Shaking his head at Eve, Stirling begins walking to take his place beside his spirited orange dragon.

Extending her hand out to help Edward to his feet, movement catches Amiria's eye. Her eyes instinctively dart to inspect the incoming arrival.

"Is that a dragon?" she utters out loud.

A serpent-like creature with angelic wings back flaps casually lowering its coiling body to the ground. Stirling holds his hand up protecting his eyes from the gales of wind. Next to him, Ignis's tail wags back and forth. If he was shorter his whipping tail would be cutting the tall grass like a scythe harvesting rye.

Bernard speaks up. "That's Quilan. The kingdom's dragon prince. He's not really a prince though. Always acted like he was too good for the other racers, never cared for them, but he seemed to take a liking to our Stirling. Whoever is Stirling's friend, is my friend. Well, the children are going to love this unexpected guest."

Amiria watches the blonde boy dismount the peculiar dragon, his porcelain features matching the elegance of his dragon. Even from here, she can see his beautiful bone structure overlaid with a stoic expression. The painting was an accurate depiction. The corners of his mouth twitch but his deadpan eyes remain the same as Stirling wraps his arms around him in a welcoming embrace, his face brighter than before.

Quilan points to a hardened leather storage strapped to his dragon. The two boys gently remove the box, each one taking a handle and working together to carry the apparently heavy cargo toward the ale house. Stirling's hair bounces with his hopping steps while Quilan holds himself steady enough for both.

The village children appear from thin air walking shyly in huddled clans as they behold their famous guest.

"Aw, look at that adorable sight," Roesia says, morphing out from behind Bernard. She holds her two children by the scruffs of their tunics to keep them from sprinting toward the two dragons. Ignis and Aether, the Quetzalcoatl, twist their elongated necks together, wrapping around each other in a warm embrace. Mimicking tiny kisses, Ignis gives Aether several playful pecks as they fluff their feathers and snort a laugh. Lifting their long feather tail they tickle Ignis' snout then wrap themselves tighter around him.

Amiria gasps. "What else have I missed?" She turns her sights back to Stirling who has his arm slinked around Quilan as they meet up with the girl Eve. The image punches her in the gut. "Seriously, how much have I missed?"

Stirling cups his hands over his mouth and calls, "AMIRIA!" He waves his free arm beckoning her over.

Bernard and Roesia raise their eyebrows in unison as they read Amiria's mixed expressions. Rosia lets Gregory and Delilah slip from her grasp and they take off sprinting to join the other children.

Crossing and uncrossing her arms Amiria is unable to decide what to do with her arms as she crosses the way to Stirling's small group. She arrives as the fair skinned boy hugs the tall ringlet haired girl.

"Evelina." His voice is deep with a hint of a smile on his lips.

Not hiding her excitement, Eve grins madly as she returns the hug. "Haven't seen you since the race a month ago. How have you been?" They pull back.

"Fine," he replies before Stirling spins Quilan to face Amiria.

"Quilan, Amiria. Amiria, Quilan. This is my—" He pauses, his eyes catching Amiria's, "My friend, that I told you about." Stirling's hand slips free from Quilan's shoulder to stop halfway down to hold his elbow. "The one who would give you a run for your coin. I've never been able to win anything against her."

"Doesn't mean much," Quilan says, eyeing Stirling's lingering hand. His leer shifts over to Amiria analyzing her like an equestrian inspecting the quality of a horse, "The Wyvern yours?" His voice is low and monotone.

"Yes," she answers short and brief.

"Interesting." The word rolls off his tongue. He pauses, holding their eye contact as she stands tall under his crushing gaze. The corners of his mouth twitch. "Racing would be an honor." An ember sparks deep in Quilan's eyes before cooling back to coal.

"Uh, yes, the pleasure would be mine. Apparently, you're the top."

As if he met his quota of words, Quilan only responds with a humble shrug.

"Excuse me, Sir Quilan. It looks as if you have some fans waiting," Eve interrupts.

Quilan turns around to several small faces peering up at him hypnotized by his existence. Their eyes are wide trying to take in every aspect of their hero as if he will disappear in the blink of an eye. It doesn't go unnoticed by Amiria as Quilan's personality alters like an actor changing costumes. All to give the children a presentation they can leave talking about. With an ear-to-ear practiced grin, he kneels to their eye level welcoming them to him.

Stirling informs Amiria, "Quilan brought wine. As soon as we get this food roasting over the fire, we can start this Saint's day."

Leaving Quilan to his adoring fans and Eve inspecting the wine, Stirling helps several of the villagers carry metal bars skewered with a dozen chickens to place over the enormous fire.

Eyeing all the villagers Amiria now clings to Stirling like a lost puppy. "Ignis is enjoying himself."

Stirling glances over to the snuggling dragons. "Yeah." He smiles with the glow of a proud father, "I'm really happy for him."

"Yeah, me too," she replies softly, her lingering gaze skipping from Ignis over to Stirling and the soft bounce of his freshly washed curls.

"Okay!" one of the village men calls out. Stirling and the others carrying the bar halt beside the raging fire. "Place the first one!" With men on each side of the fire, they lift the bars, placing them on the handles suspending the chickens over the blaze. The charring flames crack sending embers into the air as Eve arrives with three tankards filled to the brim with plum red wine.

She holds up her tankard. "To the best little village."

Stirling joins her, holding up his. "To never quitting."

Amiria stares deep into the tankard, her reflection wavering in the dark bloody liquid. "To what lays ahead."

With the sun gone families sit on blankets surrounding the fire at a comfortable distance and others clutter the ale house's outdoor tables. Cross-legged, Quilan watches with a half-raised lip as Stirling pulls the chicken wing picked clean out of his mouth.

"Disturbing," he proclaims then delicately nibbles at his chicken leg. Stirling shrugs and tosses the bone into the fire now roaring with life. Its peaks reach higher than Amiria is tall. The group of four sits crowded on a single wool blanket.

Squatting down beside Stirling, Bernard taps his leather bag. "It's time for the show." Stirling nods with eagerness. Taking a long swig of wine, he wobbles with tilted vision to his feet. Amiria, whose arms are wrapped around her legs, watches him suspiciously. Delighted, Eve knowingly claps her hands with amusement.

With an oof of his cracking knees, Bernard stands up straight and bellows out to his extended family. "Oi! Who wants to see something magical!"

The blistering fire of orange and yellow blaze dazzles the area around it as if it was daylight. The villagers already seated close to the fire remain on their blankets while the ones near the tavern make their way closer. Stirling stands staring into the dancing flames as they reach up to the stars. Through his blurring vision, the flames are a lie. They appear as if they would be silken to the touch. He rubs the scars on the back of his hands; out of everyone, he knows firsthand the truth behind the fire.

Facing the village, Bernard enacts his speech, "Here and now, you will witness magic before your very own eyes. I would like to thank Stirling for providing the feast and our soon-to-be show, but I will also extend my gratitude to Sir Quilan for the outstanding wine and for choosing our quaint home to celebrate the most important Saints Day to racers. These children will never forget this day. And now." He points at the band who have already brought the ale house instruments outside. They begin an upbeat song instantly making the listeners bob their heads and clap their hands along with the tune.

Stirling pulls his focus from the captivating fire as Bernard gives him the go-ahead. With a quick single nod, Stirling reaches into his bag and removes two random rocks. He examines the magical stones in his palm, one a mixture of white and purple and the other appears like a regular rock integrated with teal. With the fire's glow in his eyes, he tosses them into the fire.

Villagers gasp as the flames in the immediate area turn pink and green. He circles the fire spreading out the stones and turning the fire shades of purple, blue, green, and pink.

Amiria leaps up to Stirling's side in bewilderment. "How are you doing that!?" She grabs his wrist, twisting it to look at the orange mineral in his hand.

"There's something in them that changes the fire's color, neat right?"

Amiria laughs overtaken by amazement. Like steam popping the lid off the pot allowing the contents to boil over, her laughs appear to have a mind of their own. She wipes the moisture from her eyes as she watches the rainbow of colors reflect off Stirling's sandy hair like an iridescent cloud.

The children immediately become infatuated with the sight of the sorcery and leap from their parents' side to run and dance around the fire. Their contagious energy is an avalanche that only gains in size as it plummets out of control. Caught up in their momentum Stirling links his arm with Amiria's and begins to spin. Without stopping he tosses another mineral into the fire creating more blue flames.

They come to a pause at their blanket where Quilan and Eve still sit. Stunned, Quilan's dark eyes reflect the colors of the fire like a mirror as he stares at Stirling's extended hand. His eyes walk up Stirling's arm to the beaming face. Staring into Stirling's excited eyes, he shows no emotion as he accepts the offered hand.

Whisked to his feet by the overly energetic boy Quilan reaches out grabbing Eve's hand, stealing her away with him.

Stirling steps and turns whipping his chain of friends as they dance around the rainbow fire lighting up the area like a mosaic window. The world falls away as the four dance together.

Quilan's eyes strain to see past the abnormal colors, the world outside the fire's glow is lost to the dark of the night. The world spins around him as he holds hands between Eve and Stirling, both of whom are overwhelmed with childish laughter at the edge of his vision. He can hear the joyous music playing through his soul. It's as if they are in a tale told to children, where mystical creatures dance at the end of rainbows.

The muscles of his face strain as the corners of his lips pull back into a grin.

"That's the spirit!" Stirling shouts to Quilan.

Unanimously the group of friends slows their dancing chain while clutching their stomachs from the cramping laughter. They fall into a heap on their blanket. Eve, who is lying sideways across Quilan's stomach, wipes the tears from her eyes. Amiria untangles her legs from Stirling's and lifts her tankard to her lips as she eyes Stirling over the brim.

Quilan, who is lying flat on his back, closes his eyes as he catches his breath. He digs his fingers into his tired cheeks rubbing out the strained muscles. Eve shifts to hover over him and places her hands over his. Stifling her drunken giggles, she smooshes his cheeks. She quickly covers her mouth as she practically spits her bursts of laughter. Quilan's face relaxes into a light smile.

"Come on, let's dance some more," she tells him while dragging him to his feet without leaving any time for an objection.

Stirling watches as his two friends take off hand in hand, leaving him alone with Amiria. He finishes the last sip of his wine and asks, "Did Bernard show you the map in the alehouse?"

Amiria shakes her head, suddenly overly aware that they are alone. Her top knot has fallen loose and now flops to one side of her head. Strands of hair stick to her perspired face—flushed from both the heat of the fire and the wine. Unsteadily, he pushes himself off the blanket and turns to her with his hand extended. Amiria bites her lip and hesitantly reaches up to him, placing her always cold fingers into his warm calloused hand. He lifts her to her feet. The two of them stand idle staring at their intertwined fingers. Stirling's throat bobs as he swallows hard before releasing his grip.

"It's, uh, this way," Stirling's fingers curl into his palm at his side.

"Yeah, okay," Amiria crosses her arms and follows him.

They shuffle through the door of the ale house. For the first time since Stirling has arrived at Patu, it is quieter inside the building. Amiria sees the map before Stirling points it out. Taking slow deliberate steps, she crosses the room beheld by its detail. She has flown all over this Kingdom and even tried to read several of their maps. They were useless to her when they only showed towns over a certain population. Patu not being one of them. This map here is an entirely constructed map of the known world. The Kingdom of Tillfalya and all the surrounding kingdoms.

Just how big is the world?

She scans the canvas from right to left, passing over the names of rivers, mountains, forests, and villages to the large empty portion of the Kingdom of Uviktiland that sprawls along the entire western coast. The autumn-colored bracelet slides on her arm as she reaches up to touch the newly painted channel of islands, one significantly larger than the rest.

"Does this say Isles of Wyverna?" she asks, feeling the textured paint beneath her fingertips.

Stirling isn't looking at the map. His eyes waver briefly on his mother's bracelet before moving on to Amiria as a whole. He can't bear to take his eyes off her as she stares in bewilderment. He's afraid if he blinks this moment will disappear and he will wake up alone.

"You can't read it?" he asks.

"No, the characters are different from ours." Her words fade to a whisper as her fingers slide down the canvas. "We're so small."

"Bernard explained that several hundred years ago, Uviktiland conquered the coast and secluded us. No one here had ever heard of Wyverna until I arrived."

Amiria gasps as a revelation comes to her.

Stirling is lost in her. Amiria, his best friend Amiria. Amiria, who he thought he would never see again. Nothing but a page in the calendar of his life he can't turn back to. Amiria, who he left behind as his only haunting regret. He wants to touch her. His fingers twitch remembering the feeling of her hand in his. He needs to feel her again. His vision blurred around the edges from the wine, he needs to know this isn't a cruel dream.

She spins around to face him, her tangled hair finally falling out of its knot. Her face is bright with news. "I think I understand! We used to be one nation! That explains why we speak the same language but have different accents and written language because time apart we developed separately—" Amiria stiffens.

Stirling's hand cups her cheek. She stands immobilized, spooked by the unexpected touch. He caresses her soft skin with his thumb.

"I missed you."

With her body relaxing, her face settles perfectly into the curve of his palm. She holds his hand against her cheek and leans into it, letting the warmth of his hand seep into the depths of her filling in her broken cracks. A remedy no one else can concoct. A cure to mend her soul back together. She stands there in silence letting the moment burn an image in time. Closing her eyes she opens her mouth to speak.

Eve and Quilan come crashing through the entryway. Eve's drunken laughter is a splintering sound across the fragile moment. Stirling quickly drops his hand to his side and jumps to face them.

"There you are! We came in here to get more wine!" Her voice is a volume too loud for their current surroundings.

Quilan leans his shoulder against the door frame. His eyes soften at the sight of Stirling and Amiria, his bottom lip hanging partially opened.

"Come on, come back to the bone fire!" Eve insists.

"Actually," Amiria speaks up first, "I'm exhausted from all my travels. Eve, Quilan. It was a pleasure to meet you both."

Quilan nods in response.

Eve pouts at Stirling. "Awe, are you going too?"

Amiria looks up at him from the corner of her eye as he answers, "I can't let her walk back alone on her first night. I'll see you tomorrow, Eve. Quilan," Stirling pauses as he makes eye contact with him. "I'll see you next week."

"But—but the party isn't over yet," Eve counters.

"Let them," Quilan tells her.

Eve looks back at Quilan and mopes. "Fine," she grumbles before falling back to his side. Both of their eyes follow Amiria and Stirling out into the night.

With the rainbow fire and the village full of chatter left behind them, Amiria walks side by side with Stirling. She can't help but stare down at his hand which only moments ago felt as if it could keep her from ever wanting to leave and return to Wyverna. Without the distraction of earlier, she notices a small difference in Stirling's appearance.

"Why are you wearing your sleeves down?" She asks curiously. He used to always push them up and this weather is warmer than back in Wyverna.

Stirling is caught off guard. It's been months since he has spoken of his scars hidden beneath the cotton, "Because."

"Because why?"

"Just because."

"Stirling," Amiria says firmly, "because why?"

"Because it scared people all right," he states defensively. "You didn't want to leave because you were tired, did you?"

"Yes, I am tired. But no, that is not the reason I wanted to leave."

"Why did you then?"

"You didn't answer my question." She shakes her head, staring up at the stars. "So much has changed in your life." Her gaze drops to the path through the long grass. "And in mine. I want to know what has happened to you these past months." Her eyes travel back up to him.

"Not much to tell." He picks up his speed.

Amiria doesn't buy it. "Stirling!" She matches his pace. throwing her hand out at their surroundings. "Looks like a lot to me." She grabs his hand, digging her heels into the soft earth stopping them both. "Like how did you get these new scars?"

He rips his hand from hers with a snap as if she was the one who burned him. "Take a guess." He steps away letting his long stride take him toward the house.

Amiria purses her lips, knowing exactly what he meant. She bites her tongue, shackling down to keep herself from snapping back at him. Her weak point has always been diffusing situations without resulting in physical contact. There was no training to talk people down, only training to physically bring them down.

She releases her breath slowly through her nostrils as she watches the lightning bugs wink in and out of existence. Lightly jogging, she catches up to Stirling. "Those games you participated in?"

"What about it?" he grumbles.

"It wasn't all fun and glory like everyone thinks, was it?"

Stirling pops his jaw and refuses to look at her, this isn't the conversation he wanted to have. Amiria probes further digging at the bruises that have barely healed from the surface of his skin.

"Stirling, just tell me. They hurt you, didn't they?"

"Yes. Okay." His voice is sharp.

"Why are you shutting me out?" she says, glaring up at him, his eyes dart down to hers then back ahead at his home. "Let me in so I can understand you again. Or is it *Eve* you tell all your troubles to now?"

Breaking, Stirling throws his hands up and steps in front of Amiria, halting them at the bottom of the stairs. "Why do you need to know?!"

Amiria scoffs. "I don't *need* to know. I'm just concerned."

"Yes, yes you do," he jabs. "I can see it. It's eating at you."

"You're wrong. I just don't know why you are keeping it from me?"

"It's not just you, Amiria. I haven't told anyone the full extent of what happened, not even Eve."

"Then tell me!" she pleads. He is her best friend, her only friend. The single person she could confide anything to. She thought she was the same to him.

"Fine! Fine. You want to talk, then you tell me. What new traumas have you experienced?"

Her face grows cold as the innocent lives dying replays in her memories. "If you must know, I've witnessed countless citizens hang. My father offered my hand away without my consent. I found out my mother is actually alive and never wanted me. And I have the blood of bandits rusting my armor, men I killed so I could see *you* again." Her voice is a grizzly growl as she jams her finger into his chest.

Stirling stands, lost for words. "Betrothed?"

"Yes." Amiria shoves past him, knocking him aside as if he was no more than a swinging door. She is halfway up the steps when she turns and says, "Well are you going to start a fire and tell me what happened or not?"

And so, he did. He told her everything he experienced since he last saw her in the cave. How his father thought he was a demon. How he almost died escaping. How he had long-lasting effects he can't shake off. The way his body would panic, making his stomach curdle when he is in front of crowds. How he suffocates when they surround him. How they ridiculed him in the beginning; how they tried to tear him down physically and mentally.

Amiria clears the cobwebs around the lock on her mind and lets Stirling in on everything he had missed back home and the heavy toll it took on her. How the world around her was falling apart and the only people keeping the seams together were his father and the man she was engaged to. She tells him everything except Calix's name.

$\mathcal{F}$our

The neglected fire, burned down to coal, lays cold in its ashen bed as the late morning shines through the opened shutter windows. Stirling stirs awake to the sound of singing birds. Even sleeping on the hard ground, he has never felt more rested. Amiria had pried the lid off the box and emptied the contents that weighed him down.

He tipped over and spilled like ink across the ground staining everything within reach and the more you desperately try to wipe it away the more it spreads. Amiria didn't mind the black staining her hands when hers were already red. A load is lighter when you have someone to share it with.

Stirling sits up leaning on his elbows. He doesn't know why, but somehow the world seems brighter. They had talked till the early hours of the morning. Until their words turned into rhythmed breaths of sleep.

He twists his lanky body stretched out on the floor to take in Amiria who is curled up on the pillows of his lounge chair. Her long-tangled hair covers her face like a veil. Instinctively he reaches over and brushes the black strands behind her ear. The muscles of her face twitch at his touch. She pulls her arm in close, snuggling her face into it.

Stirling's insides flutter. This is the Amiria only he gets to see, or— he thinks of the man she was engaged to. It was only a month-long engagement. He couldn't have seen her sleeping. Was he someone she barely knew or someone she's grown up with? She didn't mention a name. What if it was Calix.

No, Stirling shakes the thought from his mind, *Don't let your mind go there.*

He lets her be and strolls across the room and opens the door to the bedroom. Poking his head inside he checks on Ignis who is still sound asleep from his late night. He wonders what time Quilan went home. He and Eve seemed to have hit it off which makes Stirling happy. Quilan needs more friends who will care about him, Quilan, and not the Number One Elite Racer Quilan of Leucasia.

A sudden knock on the door sends Stirling jumping. He checks over his shoulder to Amiria who groggily sits up while rubbing her eyes. Unsure of her surroundings, Amiria scans around the room for the source of the noise. She lands on Stirling as he answers the door.

Roesia stands with a basket resting on her thick hips. The wicker basket is filled with bath supplies like what she had provided Stirling months ago. "Good afternoon," She pokes Stirling's face mid-yawn, "Or should I say good morning? Is Amiria awake?"

Stirling turns his head peering over his shoulder. Amiria with her hair in a knotted mess stands in the center of his home with a dazed expression. Without the belt on, his tunic hangs loosely around her exposing the bare skin of one of her shoulders.

"Amiria!" Roesia pushes past the stunned Stirling, "Sweetheart! Look what I have for you."

Spine stiffening, Amiria pulls back defensively as the overbearing Roesia rushes up to her. Amiria hooks a single finger on the edge of the basket with uncertainty. She tips it forward to examine the contents inside, "Bath stuff?"

"Yep, we're going to get you all washed up," Roesia says, with a motherly pinch of Amiria's cheek.

Amiria winces at the gentle touch, "Where are the bathhouses?"

"Oh honey, we don't have bathhouses. We use the river," Roesia waves her hand nonchalantly, "Don't worry, the cool water feels nice in this heat and it's calm and clear."

Her eyebrows coming together, Amiria takes a moment to wrap her head around it, "River? Like the one right outside?" She points at the windows facing the river.

"Yes, it's actually a perfect spot right here," Roesia smiles oblivious to Amiria's disturbance.

"But what about?" Amiria's eyes run over to Stirling who is watching the conversation with a disconnected expression.

"What?" he asks, ignorant.

Roesia waves him off, "Don't worry about him. He's going to the city to get you some new clothing."

"I'm doing what?"

"Either listen fully or not at all. None of this halfway," Roesia lectures. "Also, take Eve with you. I don't need you wasting time with your fans."

Stirling blinks.

"Stirling?"

"Yeah?"

"Now," she draws out the word, saying it slowly for him to understand.

"Oh, uh, yeah okay." Forgetting the layout of his house, Stirling steps back and forth before disappearing into his bedroom.

Amiria can hear the begrudging groans of a stubborn dragon as Stirling argues with him to wake up. She opens the front door as Ignis trots towards the alehouse with Stirling on his back. Stepping out onto the porch she can see her dragon basking in the warm sun. A pang of forgotten jealousy awakens. Will she ever get to have a relationship with Taika as Stirling does with Ignis?

Roesia steps up behind her. "Come on, dear, let's get you all washed up."

His sleeves are rolled up. Eve notices as their bodies rock with the motion of Ignis' chest while he climbs the subtle incline of the mountain. It didn't occur to her earlier when Stirling picked her up at the alehouse on Roesia's orders. She was still in dreamy bliss as she swept the old rush out the door. Her mind replayed the night of magic, those unforgettable hours she got to spend being Quilan of Leucasia's friend. Now she can see around his shoulder to the scars and symbols of his past that are exposed to everyone. He has removed the veil over the side of him he wanted to keep secret. Is this because of *her*?

"How was the rest of your night?" Stirling casually asks Eve to fill in the time.

She nuzzles her face into the space between his shoulder blades, her loose ringlet curls catching on his, as she replies, "It was really fun. I wished you had stayed. Quilan and I ended up catching lightning bugs. He's nothing like I imagined. Never would I have guessed he was so humble. Total opposite of how racers are."

"Hey!" Stirling's head nearly turns all the way around. "I'm humble."

"You don't count."

"Thanks," Stirling rolls his eyes.

"I had a great time too. Not like you've asked or anything," Ignis speaks up.

"My apologies, how was your night?" Stirling coats the words in sarcasm.

"Wonderful! Because unlike you. I know how to make a move when I like someone," Ignis slaps.

"Shut up, Ignis."

Ignis accepts his victory as Stirling's thoughts grumble about how humans are more complicated.

Sitting shoulder-deep in the water, Amiria enjoys the cool current slowly flowing around her. The crystalline liquid is a refreshing relief from the harsh sun pounding down upon them. With Amiria's head tilted back, the ends of her long hair flow along with the stream. Roesia sitting directly behind her sets her hand on Amiria's forehead, shielding her eyes as water pours from a bowl rinsing the cleansing remedy from her long dark hair.

With the last of the water poured, Amiria opens her night eyes. The sun's rays shining down glint off her tanned skin. She watches the wispy clouds pass over with a sigh.

"You don't have to worry about Eve. Stirling isn't in love with her," Roesia says seemingly out of nowhere.

Amiria whips around, "That wasn't on my mind."

"Honey." Roesia inclines her head. "I was young once too and people don't cross the world for just anyone."

The trained Winged Rider lowers herself till only her eyes sit above the water. Furrowing her eyebrows, she blows a strain of bubbles.

"Aren't you just the cutest thing? So rambunctious and covered in armor, but inside you are still a young girl in love," Roesia adores.

Amiria dunks her head completely under the water, choosing to drown than admit anything.

This time Eve isn't clinging to Stirling's arm as they walk the slender path to the tailor's shop in silence. Packs of prowling girls watch from their posts as Stirling, and she passes them by. Nevertheless, Eve can read what each of them is thinking. It's not every day a wild girl makes a spectacle in the gate plaza and the very next day Stirling isn't dressed with the doting girl in yellow.

"Brings back memories, huh?" Eve stops in front of the opened door. The shop hasn't changed a single decorative flower on the windowsill since the first time Stirling had bought his new attire during the games.

"Yeah, it does," Stirling reaches up and taps the hanging sign above their head letting it swing. He had been back numerous times, but he hadn't required Eve's assistance after learning his trick of traversing the roofs.

"Oh my, isn't it my prized customer!" Tobias yips with a clap of his hands. The silver bangles on his brown wrists chime with his excitement.

"Hey, Tobias, how are you?" Stirling smiles at the familiar face.

"Better now that your bright face is in my shop. I see you have Miss Eve here with you today. Are we doing a lady's gown today?" Tobias curtseys his tall, elegant frame. "Or did you just need her to tell you what you look good in, because I can do that." He winks making Eve roll her eyes.

Stirling blushes. "Actually, I'm here to pick up some new clothes for a close friend of mine."

"He or she?"

"She."

"Oh?" Tobias tight dark curls standing on end bounce as he peers around Stirling to Eve's scowling face then back to Stirling, "Do you know her adjustments?"

"Her what?"

"Her size, what is her size?"

"She's, um, about this tall." Stirling holds his hand flat in the air then checks over to Eve. He leans into Tobias lowering his voice. "And she's, you know." He makes a gesture at his chest with flat hands.

Eve presses herself into the conversation. "She's about the size of a twelve-year-old boy."

"Hmm, we can sift through the young girl's gowns," Tobias says, rubbing well his manicured goatee.

"Actually, do you have a boy's doublet? Preferably in any shade of purple, then a small pair of black tights."

"That's a peculiar request for a young lady," Tobias cocks his head but trots over to a table with neatly folded clothing.

"She's a peculiar one all right," Stirling agrees.

Eve crosses her arms and scoffs. "Well, I wouldn't use the description lady."

"Eve," Stirling warns.

"What?" Eve plays ignorant. "Ladies don't show up with shredded clothing and bloody armor strapped to a *Wyvern*."

"What is your problem?" Stirling snaps.

"Nothing!"

"Apparently, it's something. You've been abnormally quiet this whole trip and now you're insulting my friend."

"I said it's nothing. I'm going to wait outside." She stomps away.

Tobias lets out a low whistle after Eve disappears through the shop entrance.

"What," Stirling bites, turning his frustration at Eve in the direction of the tailor.

"You don't see it, do you?"

"See what?"

Tobias rests his hands on his hips with a sigh. "Oh, sweetie. I'm talking about the jealousy."

"Jealousy? Of what? Clothing?" He raises a light-colored eyebrow.

"Oh, to be young and naïve." Tobias directs his focus back to the fabric. "I don't really have any vibrant purples since that is a noble color. I do have this purple made from prunes. It's a muddied purple, so not popular with the upper class." He holds up a small doublet. "I can change out the tie string from brown to gold, to make it more feminine. Will only take me a minute."

"Sounds good," Stirling states with a distracted mind. He glances back at the door.

Tobias pulls the string free from the front of the fabric, "I know what you are thinking. The answer is, don't ask her."

"Huh?"

Tobias looks him in the eye, "Don't ask her, let her tell you when she is ready."

Stirling lowers his gaze. What did he do this time?

Lightly kicking her legs, Amiria lets her heels bounce off the layered stone porch she is sitting on the edge of. Behind her, Roesia straddles a stool with a thick tooth comb. The sounds of the prairie are the only thing speaking as the comb glides seamlessly through Amiria's dark hair. Amiria rests her eyes, letting herself enjoy the tingling sensation on her scalp.

An uplifting tune falls in sync with the singing of the birds nesting in and around the home. Roesia's humming soothes her mind and soul.

With a whisper of a smile, Amiria continues to swing her legs through the air. "Hey, Roesia?" She chirps.

"Yes?" Her voice is practically a song.

"Can you teach me some of your household chores?"

Roesia holds Amiria gently by the shoulders, "Why does an alpine swift want to learn to be like us common quail."

"Because," Amiria stares up at the endless sky, a ceiling to most but a road with infinite destinations to her. "What's the point of flying forever, if you're alone?"

Soft arms fall around Amiria as she pulls her into a hug from behind, Roesia leans down nuzzling her cheek onto the crown of Amiria's head, "Even though I just met you, I already adore you. You precious girl, no wonder why Stirling never stopped talking about you."

Stunned by the parental affection, Amiria lifts her hands, placing them over Roesia's embarrassing arms.

Five

Stirling?" Eve speaks up, her voice muffled by the fabric of his jerkin. She doesn't want even the blades of grass to see her face as she buries her face between his shoulder blades.

Stirling's muscles betray him as they stiffen at the sound of her voice. She has sat gripping his jerkin, silently brewing for the entirety of the ride home. Now with the village in view, her quivering voice comes at him like cold water running down the back of his neck.

Reluctant Stirling asks, "Yeah?"

"Are you in love with her?"

"*Oh boy,*" Ignis comments.

Stirling's heart flips, "It—I—it's not like that."

"Don't lie to me, okay? Please? I saw the way you look at her. I've never seen you look at anyone like that, except for—" Eve breaks off. "It was never me no matter how hard I tried." She says as the tears begin to soak through the fabric, "I tried to be there for you, I tried to be beautiful for you, worthy to be on your arm. But she showed up; dirty, grimy, and her hair a rat's nest. Yet despite that, you watched her as if she was the last sunset you'd ever see."

"Eve…"

"Please don't," she pauses, sniffing back the tears. "To be honest, I envisioned us getting married one day. I believed I had a chance. I never thought she would show up. I feel like such a fool."

"*Way to go. First Amiria, now Eve. Aren't you just a heartbreaker?*" Ignis injects.

"*I'm not trying to do this on purpose. Ignis, what do I say?*" Stirling asks.

"*You dug this grave. You pull yourself out,*" Ignis shrugs.

Stirling curses in his thoughts. Letting a few heartbeats count the time he finally tells her, "You're not a fool, Evelina. I stopped believing she would show too."

Eve lets a woeful gasp escape through her crumbling barricades, "Can you tell Ignis to slow his pace…I want to enjoy this one last time." She closes her eyes memorizing the feeling of the warmth of his body with her ear pressed to his back as she listens to his unsteady heartbeat.

"Of course."

Eve's emptied tear ducts have evaporated from the back of Stirling's jerkin. Her red-rimmed eyes are the only evidence left of her confession. With her ear still pressed to his back, she hears his heartbeat pick up and his shoulder muscles spasm under her soft cheek.

Lifting her head, she blinks through her stinging eyes to see they are already in front of the ale house. She pans her view from her home across the back of Stirling's head to Bernard's place on the other side of the road.

"Oh," she says under her breath, "Of course."

Stirling sits idle in the middle of the road, his vision locked on Amiria. His face falls slack as if he was blind until this moment and the first thing he has ever seen is her. He can't look away from her and her newly washed hair tumbling in thick waves around her shoulders. His tunic still draped loosely over her thin frame is now overlaid with a borrowed apron that she holds up, creating a large pouch filled with chicken feed.

Howling with laughter, Amiria watches as the hens cluck around her bare feet. She reaches into her stash and tosses out another handful of feed with a pitter-patter of dancing feet. She reacts with the excitement of a child helping their mother with chores for the first time.

"STIRLING!" she exclaims, finally noticing him. Her grip on the apron fails, releasing the feed to cover the tops of her feet and the surrounding space. The hens immediately swarm her, her toes disappearing into the mass of feathers.

Roesia peaks around a blanket she is hanging to dry to see what the commotion is about. Her round cheeks plump up as the corners of her mouth curl up, in a motherly 'I told you so' smile.

His trance broken, Stirling chuckles with a shake of his head. "I guess you're enjoying your time."

Ignis carefully lowers himself to the ground. Dismounting quickly, Stirling turns back and offers a handout to Eve, but is met with her leaning away from his extended hand. His face drops as she shakes her head.

"It's fine," she grumbles, refusing to make eye contact.

"*Ouch,*" Ignis says.

Stirling retracts his hand, pulling it back to himself with the sting of her words. Without acknowledging the approaching olive-skinned girl, Eve slides off the opposing side of Ignis and heads to the alehouse with her head down.

How is she to compete with a girl who fought and slashed her way across the world to take back what's rightfully hers? No, she will not let herself feel as if she was no more than a temporary replacement. She developed a deep bond with Stirling. She knows she has become someone Stirling can never leave behind for good. This is not a delusion. Their relationship is real. Even with Amiria here, she and Stirling will always be friends. As long as he is happy, so will she be.

Ignis watches tentatively as Eve disappears into the alehouse as Amiria steals Stirling's attention.

"Did they have any cotehardies?" Amiria inquires, ignoring the trail of chickens now following their new mother hen.

"No, I got you a sleeveless doublet. It's like the cotehardie that you tore the sleeves off. I thought that look fit you. Plus, it's warmer here," He tells her, pulling the new outfit out from his bag, "If you like it, we can always pick you up some extra ones for your journey. Or if you don't, I can find you a cotehardie."

"Thank you," accepting the fabric she hugs it against her chest.

"What made you decide to do chores while you wait?" Stirling asks, curious why someone would choose to do chores for a home that isn't theirs.

Amiria shrugs suddenly shyly, "Just wanted to help. We tended to your chickens and goat first, I collected some eggs and Roesia showed me how to milk the goat."

"Really! Thanks for that! Guess we were gone longer than I thought. If you really like helping, you can help with supper. The garden needs tending to, you know, checking for weeds and stuff," Stirling states as they begin to head in the direction of his home.

Ignis gallops through the lazy river, his massive weight sending tidal waves to the normally steady shores. Stirling's top is discarded on the bank and his drawstring trousers are rolled up to his knees while he dips his toes into the river testing the chill before he wades knee-deep into the water following the woven reed fence of his fishweir. Below the water's surface is a funnel basket tricking the fish into a path with no exit.

Hunching over, Stirling reaches into the water to pull his trap free from the fence. Ignis, too involved with his antics, jumps only several human steps away from Stirling. With his head still close to the water a wave crashes over him.

Amiria stares vacantly at the garden in which she can't configure what is a weed and what is an herb. Her ears perk. Behind her, she hears a slew of profanities aimed at Ignis. She turns from where she is kneeling to see Ignis hopping away from Stirling who shakes his shaggy hair dry.

For a moment she forgets the damp soil and the confusing plants as she watches Stirling push his damp curls back from his forehead. Her gaze falls to his bare chest, to the defined lines of his stomach, finally, her eyes dip to his waistline where his wet trousers cling around his hips.

Flushed, she quickly diverts her attention back to the garden. *What am I doing?* She scolds herself, but unable to control her eyes she finds them sneaking back to Stirling who grins widely at her. He is already halfway to her from the river as he raises the fishing basket triumphantly over his head.

She rolls her eyes, that grin. That stupid, stupid grin.

"Can you pick some parsley, sage, and dill? I caught a big one!"

"Will you put a tunic on?!" she blinks up to see him standing over her, his wet curls dripping onto his bare collarbone. She pauses, her eyes stuck before her senses return to her. With her temperature rising she quickly finds a random weed and focuses on it.

"Eventually," he shrugs, dropping the funnel basket beside her with a trout large enough to feed two flopping inside. Stirling squats down to eye level with her and cocks his head with a one-sided smile, "You don't know which ones those are do you?"

"I'll figure it out," she snaps, turning to him. She immediately regrets it. The months of manual labor have treated him well. She swallows the lump in her throat and stares at the freckles covering his shoulders unable to meet his hazel eyes.

With a playful flirt in his voice, he tells her, "It's okay, it's fine if you don't know. It's not like Miss Prodigy needs to learn how to garden. You *are* only a guest here."

Her voice is hesitant, "Yeah, a guest." Clenching her hands on her knees she stares down at the garden.

"3 sprigs of parsley, 4 leaves of sage, and 3 sprigs of dill." He names off as he briefly points at the herbs. Picking up the basket, he stands up, "I'm going to stoke the fire and clean this trout. When you're done, dice up several potatoes to roast."

Amiria nods, eyes still locked on the garden. Once Stirling fully removes himself from her vicinity by turning around the corner of his home, she follows the orders. Her mind remembers the list perfectly.

"See, told you I'd figure it out," she mutters to no one.

With the sky still pink, thin pockets of fog move across the top of the tall grass like steam. Stirling sits on the steps of his home watching Amiria tighten the straps of her double scabbard over her new doublet that hangs past her hips over her new black tights. After he had taught her how to cook a trout they spent their night discussing the Skylit Endeavour in what Stirling thought was excruciating detail. By the end, Amiria was convinced she would have no issues knocking everyone out of the competition.

He enjoyed the light-hearted conversations about each of the races. It reminded him of when they would go to the subterranean lake. How they would float on their backs watching the glowing blue dots as they had conversations about nothing, but they felt like everything.

"Why are you bringing those?" he asks with a yawn.

Amiria, ready to take Taika out to stretch her wings, waves for her to crawl over to her. She shrugs, "Old habits die hard I guess."

With an exaggerated nod, Stirling leans back on the stairs, half-awake as Amiria grabs hold of Taika's harness.

With his eyes closed, he mutters sleepily, "I'm gonna do my morning chores then head over to the alehouse." He opens his eyes into half slits as she hooks her harness to Taika's saddle. "Will you meet me there?"

"Yeah, sure thing," she tells him. Lifting her whistle to her mouth, she lets out a single tune.

Stirling watches the always impressive show of Amiria. The grass flattens and the steam-like fog is cast away by the invisible force as Taika takes off into the sky. With a summersault, they set off in the direction of the prairie.

"You're drooling," Ignis says, poking his head around the side of the house.

Stirling involuntarily wipes his mouth. "No, I'm not."

"Then why did you check?" Ignis chuckles.

"Shut up, Ignis."

With his chores completed Stirling sits chatting at a table in the ale house with Bernard and Eve. Bernard sitting across from Stirling slaps the table laughing at a story he was telling. Eve is beside Stirling. She is close enough that their elbows touch as she tucks a ringlet behind her ear.

"I still don't know how they got the goat on the roof." Bernard leans in, "Little nuisances children are. Well, I wouldn't trade them for the world. On another note, how is Miss Amiria? Does she like it here? Enjoying the village life?" Bernard asks, genuinely interested.

Stirling sits on his hands, "I think so." He glances at Eve then turns to focus on Bernard as he talks, "She appears to be happy. I just wish I knew some way to convince her to stay."

Eve purses her lips, "*Well…*you shouldn't force someone to do something they don't want to."

Bernard frowns at her through his bristly beard as Stirling hangs his head. Distracted, they all turn to the window as gusts of wind can be seen blowing across the dirt road.

"Well look who it is," Bernard can hear Roesia calling Amiria's name from across the way.

Stirling smiles pointing out, "Roesia seems fond of Amiria."

Craning his neck, Bernard peers out the window to his wife, "Roesia has a knack for becoming everyone's mother whether they need one or not. That's why she's practically adopted you." He nods to Stirling.

Roesia slips into the alehouse holding a basket of fresh eggs and vegetables, "We're making lunch. Well, I'm going to teach Amiria how to make lunch."

Running her fingers through her tied-back hair, Amiria combs out the wind-blown strands as she trails in behind Roesia. The sharp edges that distinguished her as the Winged Rider have softened out like the wrinkles, she is smoothing from her doublet now the harness is gone. Catching Stirling's eyes, she gives him a small smile of greeting.

Eve drops her head letting her forehead hit the table with an audible thump, "Ugh."

"Aw, what's wrong Eve," Bernard pats her curly hair.

"She's beautiful," Eve tells the wood grains.

Amiria stops beside Roesia at a counter space next to the open coals. Roesia leans over and pulls out a bowl from under the counter and picks up an egg. Tapping it gently on the lip of the bowl she cracks the egg spilling its contents into the container.

Following her lead Amiria picks up a single tan egg with dark specks, *That doesn't look so hard.* She convinces herself. The delicate shell, a representation of the beginning of life, sits in her palm as she weighs the egg. She hovers it above the rim, and with a light tap she aims where she wants to make the crack.

SMASH.

The egg splatters. Yolk slowly dribbles down the sides of the bowl half inside and the other half onto the counter.

"Gently. You need to tap it gently," Roesia instructs. "Here, I'll guide you," she holds Amiria's hand with the next egg in her palm guiding her through the motion, "Understand?"

Amiria nods and repeats the fluid motion. The egg crushes in her grip before it even hits the bowl. Yellow yolk oozes through her fingers, *Stirling can do this, I've seen him crack two eggs at the same time. Why is this so hard?*

She takes in a deep breath through her nostrils and slowly releases it out of her mouth. She can't let a mediocre task get to her. She tried a third time. The egg again splits entirely in half on the rim, her force almost knocking the bowl over.

Grabbing another egg with a snarl, Amiria turns away from Roesia, reeling her hand back preparing to trebuchet the egg across the room. Quick to respond from raising an energetic son, Roesia plucks the egg from her hand. Amiria, still holding her hand ready to throw, turns back to her.

"We do not throw eggs, we do not waste food," Roesia lectures in a calm but frightening manner, "Do not take your frustration out on lunch." Amiria drops her hand. "Eggs are not your metal armor, eggs are porcelain," Roesia holds the egg up to eye level, "They are fragile and should be handled with care."

Stirling watches as Amiria shatters another egg and slumps in defeat.

Eve rests her hands on her folded arms grumbling, "At least I know how to cook."

Bernard scratches his chin through his beard, "I don't know about you, but I like a wife who is loving and nurturing, someone who can make a house a home."

Eve's eyes twitch, darting over to Stirling waiting eagerly for his answer. Stirling remembers how Amiria held out the costrel to him the first time she found him in the cave. How she kept him from dying there, allowing him to make that his home instead of his crypt. How she watched over his father even though she didn't have to. She can be ruthless and braising when called to by the Cavalry but that is not who she is. Even when she isn't wearing the Cavalry's emblem, she is compassionate and selfless. She'd risk her life to save yours because she wants to and not because she is ordered to.

"I think she is perfect." Stirling finally says. Eve buries herself in her arms with a groan. Stirling continues, "She's trustworthy and caring. She is my best friend. No matter how deep of a hole I dig myself into, she is always there to pull me out."

Bernard dips his head to Stirling, "You should tell her."

"Tell her what?" Stirling plays ignorant.

His eyes roll under his bristly eyebrows, "You want her to stay here? With you? Why not tell her the truth about how you feel. Tell her how your whole world is contained in that tiny frame. I can see it in your eyes, the idea of losing her again is killing you." Bernard pauses, "I have absolutely no clue how you managed to leave her in the first place without destroying yourself."

Stirling breaks eye contact to fold into himself. He knows why. He had convinced himself he was doing it for her. She told him she wanted to stay, and he didn't question it. He chose what he *thought* she wanted, but it wasn't. How was he supposed to know what she wanted if she misled him?

"Well," Bernard's voice breaks through Stirling's thoughts, "I don't think you need to worry. I can see there's one thing she wants above anything else."

"What is that?" Stirling questions, he would give her anything. He looks back over to Amiria as she successfully cracks an egg. She spins to meet his gaze with a prideful grin.

"You," Bernard declares.

Seven

Stirling doubles checks the bag tied to the back of Ignis' harness for the fifth time since he has left his home. His paranoia running high by believing the outcome of his evening relies solely on these contents making it. It didn't take much convincing for him to get Roesia to distract Amiria so he could pack it in secrecy.

"Why didn't you tell her the whole plan? You only told her you were going to show her the gorge." Ignis questions.

"Because…it's less pressure," is all Stirling can come up with.

How does he explain his irrational fear that she would reject his plans, even though they've done this once a week for three years? He doesn't want to admit to Ignis the idea of her reading through his paper-thin walls and decoding his intentions caused bile to lodge in his throat.

Stirling inhales slowly, letting the unrest in his stomach settle. He glances over at Amiria who flies just off to the side of him. With her eyes closed, she lets herself succumb to the sensory deprivation of the weightless world.

Opening her eyes to take in the sight, Amiria stands as much as the saddle allows, "This is magnificent!"

They've passed the tower check mark and are approaching the gorge. The web-like pillars are finally in view. She doesn't want to blink; she doesn't want to miss a single moment of the surreal architecture. Bewildered, she follows Stirling into the deep shadows as the sun falls to the west of the south-leading gorge.

They bank around pillars and dive beneath bridges. The experience is exhilarating as if they are leaping from branch to branch in the dense forest back home. No stopping. No hesitation. Forward is the only option. Flying faster and moving free. There is no one else in the world. It is only their two souls twisting and swirling around each other.

She copies Stirling and Ignis' backflip looping around one of the bridges. She giggles as the world reverts, the ground the sky and the sky the ground. She never wants this gorge to stop. They split, taking opposite directions around a thick pillar. Her mind and her body are overwrought with pure euphoria. Here with him forever, she could fly forever. Two alpine swifts never landing. As they come back together, she sees the goggles she had given him three years ago still on his face. He could have bought a pair designed and styled after him. He now has enough money to replace her old leather bag from any craftsman he desires.

But he didn't.

They are back in Wyverna, back in their canyon. They are back to how they were as if the past half year has never happened. She remembers what future the Isles of Wyverna had written on parchment and stamped with the king's seal for her.

The pass narrows to the size of a single dragon.

Leaning over, she peers down at Stirling who is dodging the obstacles below her. Deep down in her, there is no desire to be a leader. Not if it means standing alone. What she wants is to be a partner. She longs to stand side by side with someone she trusts. Someone she cares for. Someone she—

Stirling turns up to her with his signature grin. A child playing a game with their closest friend.

They emerge out of the passage over the high tide lapping at the sea wall. Amiria lowers Taika to fly steadily over the shifting turquoise waters. The setting sun hits the rippling water with dazzling effects.

Leaning far in her saddle she examines mysterious dark shadows swimming just beneath the surface. She can't help but be curious about their odd and abrupt motions, zigzagging through and around each other. Amiria lets out a yelp of surprise as a bottlenose dolphin leaps from the shimmering sea, then another, then a third, and a fourth. They continue to jump, playing along with Taika's flight path.

She catches Stirling watching her with an expression she has never seen. Before she can configure what it means, Stirling shakes it away. He masks the mysterious emotion that he had let leak to the surface and waves his hand, signaling up to the plateau at the top of the cape.

Taking a sweeping turn, Amiria let's Taika's wingtip skim along the water as she catches one last glimpse of the family of dolphins.

At the top of the plateau, Ignis lands in a slow trot as Taika lands hard skidding across the gravel. Her talons tear gouges in the ground. Once slowed to a stop, she rears her head back like a cobra ready to strike. Stirling slides off Ignis, his already palpitating heart picks up in a panicked frenzy. He pauses holding onto Ignis' harness as his knees go weak.

Breathe. He tells himself. Taking a few shallow breaths, he turns his head only enough to peek at Amiria then immediately presses his face back to Ignis, *Be calm Stirling. Be calm.*

"*Let go of me already so I can lay down,*" Ignis tells him.

Internally pumping himself up, Stirling pushes himself away from Ignis with a nod. "*I got this.*" He tells Ignis but more for himself as he spins on his heel to face Amiria.

"*Stirling, hold up,*" Ignis blurts.

"*What is it?*" Stirling twists his spine to look back at Ignis.

"*You are forgetting your bag,*" Ignis reminds him.

Stirling hops back to Ignis' side with a slap to his forehead, "*Right, what would I do without you.*"

"*Die, literally not figuratively,*" Ignis responds as Stirling unties the bag.

Stirling chuckles. "Shut up, Ignis."

Amiria stands at the cliff's edge with her toes planted dangerously close to the drop. The dizzying height doesn't bother her as her thoughts are lost out over the water. Her tied-back dark hair is a stark contrast to the topaz and amber sky. She holds out her hands as if to catch the last of the sun's rays before it disappears, the harbor below now taking the role of the sun as its reflective surface begins to glow.

Tucking loose strands of hair blowing in the coastal wind behind her ear, she closes her eyes. She breathes in the salt air deeply, letting the smell of the ocean fill her lungs.

"I missed this," she says, her eyes still closed.

Stirling's voice comes from directly behind her asking for clarification, "What? The ocean?"

She smiles inwards letting the simple moment sink in and store away in her memories. Her eyes flutter open, and she pivots to face him. Her eyes trail down the empty air of where he should be standing to find him sitting on a spread-out blanket. He digs through a bag pulling out: grilled octopus and asparagus; a saucer of wine to dip dried dark bread, with chopped olives, garlic, and tomato to scoop on top; and a ricotta cheese sweetened with black currant. Each of the contents is protected in its own container made from tightly woven reeds or clay.

"A picnic? When did you make all this?"

Stirling diverts his gaze and attempts to sound heedless but fails, "I just threw some things together while you were with Roesia."

Amiria raises an eyebrow recognizing his bluff. She stares at the curls on the top of his head as he refuses to look at her, "Only you can just *throw* together a gourmet meal."

His eyes flick back to hers.

Crossing her legs, she plops herself on the blanket. She can see Stirling's cheeks blush from her compliment as he bites his lip, suppressing a smile. Suddenly distracted, she picks up a small red ball with a long thin stem, "What's this!"

"A cherry and the orange ones are apricots. They're more on the tart side but still really good," Stirling explains, "Just watch out for the pits."

Amiria, who had already popped the entire cherry into her mouth, bites down on the hard center. Using her teeth and tongue she removes the pit from the cherry and spits it out over the ledge. "It's delicious!" She exclaims, now eagerly excited about the rest of the food.

Stirling pours a dark liquid with trembling hands. Raisin wine splashes from a wooden cup as he offers it out to Amiria.

She raises an eyebrow at the rippling liquid, "Are you okay?"

"Yeah, just famished," He lies.

Amiria nods once slowly as she brings the cup to her lips and tastes the wine.

Stirling leaps to a new topic, "If you joined the games the people wouldn't know what hit them. You'd roll through like a hurricane."

"You've said this before in theory, but in reality, I thought women can't fly dragons here," Amiria points out as they begin to dig into the prepared supper.

"Has anyone tried to stop you yet? There aren't any rules *against it.* Just like there weren't any rules against me flying," Stirling says slyly.

Amiria tilts her head at him. He's right, women flying isn't a social norm here, but there is no actual *law* against it. People might not believe it is right, but they can't legally stop someone who wants to stand out from the rest.

Fiddling with her food she lays forth, "Maybe one of these times I can show them who really owns the sky." Her eyes zone in and lock onto him, studying and analyzing as she says, "I do enjoy Patu. Country living is a nice change of pace from the castle life, and the people there are wonderful."

Stirling's heart drops from his chest landing on the blanket between them. The only sound now is the updraft breeze whistling from inside the gorge as she waits for him to respond.

Tell her. She laid out an opening for you. Tell her everything, tell her how you feel. How she haunts your mind. There isn't a day you haven't thought of her, a night you didn't dream of her. No matter how many people called your name, you yearned for the day to hear her voice again, to hear her call you baker boy.

"Well, you are half peasant" Stirling teases, reverting to the safe blanket beneath his fidgeting fingers.

TELL HER!

"And you've become a lord in peasant's clothing. Oh, how times have changed," She smiles devilishly. She twirls the wine in the cup and takes a sip while eyeing his nervous tick. Acting as if she just thought of the idea she says, "Oh! By the way, I was thinking of extending my time here. I haven't devised a plan yet. It would be a smart move if I could use some more time to prepare for my travels back."

"Oh," he barely musters. The door is open. The door has been propped open with a warm fire inviting him in from the cold.

Shifting awkwardly with his legs crossed, Stirling shoves the entire piece of bread in his mouth. His mind is running rampant demanding his heart be heard. Becoming light-headed as he chews, he tries to internally tell his heart to calm down. It's as if it's rattling around in his ribcage and knocking into every one of his organs. It leaps up, lodging in his throat and blockading the path. He tries to swallow the bread but is unable as his mouth fails to produce saliva. Coughing, he takes a sip of his wine.

It doesn't help.

"Amiria, I—" The words hit the back of his teeth, falling short before they can be pronounced.

TELL HER!

"Yes?" She leans in closer to him, her dark eyes round and searching.

He can't look into them. He's afraid of what details he might read. Gulping, his gaze lowers to her slightly parted lips.

Ba Dump

He wants to run away. He wants to stay.

Ba Dump

He longs to hold her close, but fear wants to push her away.

Ba Dump

He wants to tell her. He needs to admit to her what he finally understands. He mentally kicks himself. Why can't he tell her? Why can't he just say the words? Why? Why! WHY!

The sound of the crashing waves counts the seconds between them. The knot grows larger with each surge of the ocean.

Amiria tilts her head, "Stirling, you look like you're going to pass out. Are you sure you're feeling all right?" She reaches across brushing his bangs away and presses the back of her hand against his forehead.

Her touch sends a burning shockwave through his body. He leans into her hand, "Amiria, I—."

"Stirling, you're worrying me. What is it?" She says, trying to look into his dodging eyes.

He focuses on Ignis who is watching as he gathers his thoughts. He turns back to Amiria who is peaking over his shoulder following his gaze to Ignis.

"Is he saying something?" She asks.

"No, uh, Amiria, will you please stay here, permanently, with me, because," he can't get out the last part.

Ba Dump

TELL HER!

His heart is about to burst out of his chest. He wishes he can backtrack his way out of this predicament he has gotten himself into. He wants to leap from this cliff and submerge himself in the reviving waters below.

Her eyelashes flutter. She leans in, closing the gap further. "Because why, Stirling?"

His body stiffening, he holds his spine up straight. He can't breathe. "B-because, my life is better when you are around. I—you are my best friend." Screaming. He is silently screaming. His mind and soul, betrayed by their own tongue, cry out in desperate wails that can be heard in the heavens.

"Oh." She sits back with a disheartened sulk.

He blew it.

"*Ouch.*" Ignis can see the self-inflicted wound beginning to bleed and soak into the blanket.

He can still fix this, he can still tell her.

Amiria's voice is flat with a tactical word choice. "You're my best friend too. Friends till the end, *right?*"

The last words are a punch to the gut. Her fist burrows into his stomach as her eyes dig into his mind, calculating every facial twitch.

"Right?" Her voice prowls.

"Right," he chokes out regretfully.

"*Brutal,*" Ignis says.

"*You're not helping,*" Stirling pushes back.

Amiria can feel the change in the atmosphere around them. Unspoken words hang heavy in the air like an incoming storm. This isn't what he wanted to tell, and she knows it.

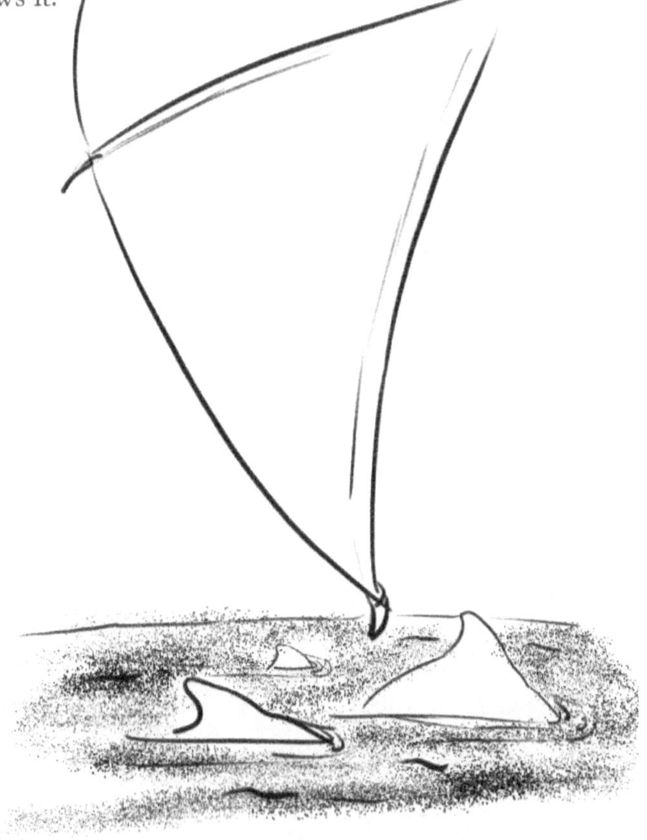

Eight

I can't believe I messed it up," Stirling complains, lying on the hay beside Ignis. The feather mattress he never used has been pulled up to the loft for Amiria. He drags his hands down his face, releasing the control of his muscles as his arms flop down to his sides. "I'm such a coward. I panicked and went the safe route."

"*I know. I was the poor soul who had to witness it. I'm absolutely traumatized,*" Ignis says, annoyed, his head resting on the bedding ready to fall asleep.

"Thanks, like I'm not already ashamed."

"*You know. It's not too late,*" Ignis tells him, his eyelids beginning to droop over his golden eyes. Ignis yawns as he talks. "*She's just upstairs. Honestly, from my perspective, she was at least hoping you'd ask her to stay again. She laid out obvious bait,*" Ignis uses his wing to roll Stirling in the direction of the door. "*Go on, she's probably still awake.*"

Lying on his back Stirling stares up at his rafters. He saw the moments Ignis mentioned, he knew they were there but deliberately chose to ignore them.

"Okay," Stirling says more to himself than Ignis. Rolling to a standing position he repeats, "I can do this, I can do this." All the way to the door. He glances back over his shoulder at Ignis who has already spread out across their bed. With one more reassuring nod, he opens the door and steps inside his home, "Amiria?"

"Yeah?" She peeks over the side of the loft in nothing more than a white undertunic and knee-length braies. The room is lit with the soft glow of the still burning fireplace.

"I—" He is cut off by a knock on the door.

Spinning to face the door Stirling stares at it utterly confused about who would be knocking at this time of night. He listens intently for a verbal sign of who is on the other side of the door. They remain silent and forgo announcing themselves as they stand there waiting in the dark of night. There's a second knock on the door, no urgency, only a light rap of their knuckles. Stirling looks up at Amiria and shrugs.

"It better not be Eve," he says to no one in particular and casually walks over to the front door.

Hanging halfway over the edge of the loft, Amiria strains to see who is outside. She watches as Stirling only opens the door ajar enough to fit his frame. The hair on the back of her neck stands as she witnesses the blood drain from his face.

Her body reacts to a low grumbling voice with a nerve-prickling shiver running along her spine. Her breathing halts stopped halfway sucked in, as the voice asks a question. Stirling is as rigid as a board, his joints locked into place. The muscles in his neck barely manage a nod before a metal fist appears from the crack in the door connecting with his eye with an audible crunch.

"STIRLING!" Amiria hollers as his body crumples to the ground. She dives from the loft. The soft thud of her crouched landing is barely heard over Stirling's half-conscious groans. She keeps her center of balance low and is prepared to fight their hostile guest.

The well-oiled hinges of the new door open with a ghostly whisper. Amiria's soul goes cold, her body growing stiff and frozen under his icy eyes. Stirling's sluggish hand finds its way to his face covering his already swelling eye. His now single good eye blinks awake through the blood seeping from the open wound above his eyebrow.

"Calix." Her voice is a hollow grave.

"Amiria, it's been a while." A silken tone that would be a caress on the cheek if it wasn't for the one-sided grin smug on his face.

"Calix?" Stirling repeats, regaining his cognitive thought. His mind concludes who and what is happening. "*This* is Calix."

"In the flesh." Calix's gleaming smile shows the entirety of his straight teeth as he looks down at Stirling. Signaling with a jut of his chin he tells Dicun. "Apprehend him." Dicun raises his lip into a snarl as he flips Stirling onto his stomach with ease and wrenches his arms behind his back.

Amiria's voice wavers with uncertainty, "You release him." She slides a foot forward, gaining half a step.

"Aw, where's the fierce Amiria I know and love?" Calix plays.

Amiria skips from Calix's deceitful grin to Stirling struggling beneath Dicun's knee jammed into his spine, then back to Calix. She raises her chin, meeting his eye level. "You cannot arrest him. Stirling Bakere has renounced his citizenship from the kingdom known as Isles of Wyverna. He has the king of Tillfalya's seal finalizing his immigration. The person formerly known as Stirling Bakere no longer exists. The Winged Cavalry has no authority over this man, Stirling of Patu."

"I assumed that would be the case, but don't fret, we aren't returning to Wyverna empty-handed. You, my dear, are our main priority," Calix says matter-of-factly as if he was no more than talking about a hangnail.

Amiria's frozen soul melts, draining from her body as it seeps through the cracks in the floorboards.

"Amiria Rey, you are under arrest for harboring a fugitive, mutiny in the Winged Cavalry, and treason against King Dietrich," Calix tosses an old pair of goggles that Stirling had given her the first day they met. The beloved goggles land with a deafening sound and slide in her direction stopping at her feet, "But I assume you are well aware of the fact."

Without notice, Amiria bolts across the room rushing towards the fireplace. Calix, with his long stride leaps after her, his hands stretching out like talons, an owl swooping down to catch his prey. Amiria snatches the iron poker and whips around swinging.

She can feel the vibrations shutter through her as the rod clashes against Calix's dark vambraces. Without hesitating, she retracts her weapon and thrusts the pointed end aiming it at the eye that she can finally see his lies through. Calix takes hold, stopping the incoming demise, the tip only a blink away.

"Tsk, tsk," He clicks, "That really hurts, Amiria."

"You don't know hurt," she hisses, using her entire body weight to push the poker closer to his eye. Calix holds it steady; the iron poker hangs in the air suspended in time.

His eyes weigh down on her more than his strength, "Oh, but I do."

Amiria twists unexpectedly changing from a push to a pull, yanking Calix forward and off balance. Taking this small advantage, she darts around him and sprints for the bedroom door.

"IGNIS!" She hollers desperately reaching out for the door handle.

She never feels the cool of the metal handle as Calix grips the collar of her night tunic and jerks her backward with the sound of tearing fabric. Her shoulder blades slam into his chest plates with her arms pinned to her sides trapped beneath his control. Her legs kick and thrash at the empty space beneath her. Her body wriggles in his grasp like a hare trapped in a snare that leads her nowhere except this enclosure tightening in on her, his edge armor digging further and deeper into her skin.

She can feel his lips graze the back of her neck as his face nuzzles into her. The warmth of his breath sends pinpricks across her skin as he whispers, "If you had just stayed mine... I would have continued to protect you."

Running on survival instincts, Amiria drives the back of her skull into Calix's mouth in two rapid motions. She falls to the ground as he drops her, his hands reflexively jumping to guard his split lip now dripping with blood. Handsome features contort as he runs his tongue along the inside of his cheek.

"What? Can't you handle a single girl?" Dicun criticizes still pinning Stirling down whose eye is now completely swollen shut.

Calix spits in Dicun's direction. A small ivory object stained in red tumbles across the floor leaving behind tiny ruby prints. Wiping the blood from his mouth along the back of his gauntlet, it smears from his lips to ear in a half smile. He doesn't need to respond to Dicun. Dicun knows who they are dealing with is no ordinary girl.

Stirling struggles under Dicun's weight. Craning his neck, his fading vision wanders, searching the room for Amiria. There. He sees her crouched like a feral animal. Her eyes dart frantically in every direction.

What to do? What to use? How to survive?

She leaps backward dodging the charging Calix. Her light frame is more agile, but his built physique is stronger. She cannot let him take control of her again. He won't make the same mistake twice with how he held her.

Playing this game of cat and mouse will only buy her moments of freedom. She needs to fight, but she can't bare knuckle strike armor. Her mind climbs the ladder to the loft where her blades reside. How could she have forgotten them in her haste to defend Stirling?

Backing into the kitchen, she picks up a jar and whips it at Calix. Ceramic explodes in the air as he blocks with his forearm. Keeping her eye riveted to him, Amiria hurls every item her hand touches. Unflinching, Calix deflects the missiles and stalks Amiria into a corner. She kicks a storage crate from under the counter knocking it into the space between her and her perpetrator.

Anything, anything to slow his advancements on her.

Past Calix, Amiria can see the thumping on the bedroom door from Ignis. One latch holding back her salvation. She has no doubt he is calling out to Stirling wondering what is happening. Is Stirling even coherent enough to respond?

She risks a glance in his direction. With his head pressed to the floor, he stares up at her with one panicked eye.

"IGNIS! HELP!" she howls.

With his claws digging into the wood, Calix lifts the crate blocking his path. Taking advantage of the small distraction, Amiria dives under the table. Her bare knees skid across the wood as she slides. She halts catching herself before emerging and nearly misses the crate crashing to the floor directly in her escape route. The wooden frame cracks open, spilling its contents out.

She jumps as Calix slams his hand on the top of the table.

He stoops down to peer at his prey hiding in her rabbit hole, "Give up Amiria. You can't win this fight."

A puff of white fills his vision. His eyelids snap shut as particles contaminate his eyes. He bolts up straight, ferociously clawing at his eyes.

Amiria reaches through her cloud of weaponized flour. Hooking her hands around the backs of his knees, she yanks his feet out from under him.

Calix topples backward.

His helm is knocked off his head as the back of it clips the counter clattering to the floor beside them. Amiria leaps to his chest straddling his ribcage. Pinned to the ground Calix blinks the stinging flour from his eyes. His sight returns in time to see Amiria's fist jab down at him, striking him in the bridge of his nose. Through watery vision he grabs the hand hammering down for a second blow and casts the light frame to the side with ease.

Amiria gasps as her body is flung through the air and slammed into the floor, reversing the rolls. She growls up at the man of many faces. Blood drips from the mouth and nose of his current mask as he hovers over her.

Amiria can barely recognize him, purple already beginning to appear around the brim of his nose and under his eyes. The blood smeared into a permanent smirk. This is the monster he's been hiding beneath his gentle cloak.

She can hear the pounding from Ignis urgently growing louder.

Bunching the front of Amiria's night tunic in his fist he reels his hand back prepared to repay her for the pain she has caused. Something flickers behind his eyes. He hesitates, his eyes stuck in hers.

The door to Stirling's room bursts from its frame. Splitting in half, it falls to the floor crunching the broken ceramic beneath it. Splintering shards and fragments of the wall and framework erupt across the radius surrounding the door.

Calix huddles over Amiria, shielding her from the impact of the blast. Shrapnel ricochets off his armor as an orange dragon head roars into the room.

Calix doesn't waste time. He scoops Amiria up by the neck forcing her to her feet. Dragging her heels, he backsteps away from the snarling fangs.

"Ignis...Help," she coughs, Calix's forearm sawing through her throat to touch his brigandine on the other side.

He holds her hands bound behind her back with a single hand, securing her place against him. "Call off the dragon," Calix demands.

"Or what?" Amiria chokes out.

"Or I'll burn this building down with your boyfriend in it," Calix threatens.

"I'd rather burn here with him," she spits.

Knowing Amiria is true to her word, Calix's eyes widen as they fixate on Dicun, begging for help.

Dicun pops his jaw, annoyed at the younger rider's failure. His fingers lace through Stirling's curls, snagging them by the roots. Sliding a dagger from its hilt on his waist, he yanks Stirling's head back, exposing his neck to see his pulse throbbing beneath the thin skin.

Stirling's face contorts from pain as hairs are torn from his scalp. His breath hitches as the stinging sensation of cool sharp metal presses into his jugular.

Ignis immediately snaps his attention from Amiria to Stirling. Blood trickles down Stirling's neck from the wound forming beneath the dagger's recently sharpened edge.

Dicun's lips curl demonically as he stares into Ignis' dilated eyes, "Let us take the girl, or I'll slit his throat."

"*Ignis, don't,*" Stirling begs, tears forming in his eyes.

Ignis looks back and forth. Stirling, Amiria, Stirling. He doesn't know what to do. What option does he have that doesn't lead to Stirling's death? Go to protect Amiria and he dies. Go to protect Stirling and he dies.

"Don't let them take her," Stirling cries, *"Please, Ignis. Don't let them take her."*

"What's your choice, dragon!" Dicun roars impatiently.

Ignis' eyes bore into Amiria hoping she can hear his heart lamenting his apology, *"I'm sorry."* He lowers his snout.

"Good choice," Dicun states, lightening the pressure of the blade but not removing it entirely.

"IGNIS! NO!" a tear slips from Stirling's eye.

Amiria screams and kicks as Calix drags her resisting feet in an arc across the room, avoiding the submissive dragon who did what all dragons do: choose the life of their master over anything.

Causing the dagger to slice deeper into his skin, Stirling regains his energy and struggles under Dicun's weight. With hands that had been freed from Dicun's control, Stirling attempts to push up from the floor.

Dicun feels Stirling's shoulders rising beneath his knee. Removing the dagger, he places it back into its hilt and smashes Stirling's face back into the wood grains now stained with his blood. He retakes one of Stirling's hands and twists his arm so he's touching his shoulder blades.

Stirling cries out in agony, his free hand gripping Dicun's wrist still entangled in his curls. He kicks and bucks with a surge of adrenaline. He needs to stop them. He needs to save her.

"AHHHH!!!" Stirling howls in frustration trapped by the older man, weighed down in dark polished armor. Straining to see with his face shackled to the floorboards, Stirling's one eye watches Calix struggle to contain the thrashing Amiria.

No. No! NO!

They can't take her, not now. Not now that he finally understands what she truly means to him. How fame and fortune mean nothing if she isn't in his life. He would give it all up. Give them everything he has if he gets to grow old with her. He can't lose her again. What a cruel world to tease him with the possibility of a life together only to tear it from his grasp when he's barely got to hold it.

"AMIRIA! I LOVE YOU!"

The room pauses. Two men in armor, a fierce woman, and a surprised dragon all focus on the weak and injured boy.

Amiria's mouth drops open. *Did he?*

Calix breaks the silence, "Aw, isn't that sweet." He transfers his arm around her back to clamp her face from under her jaw. He leans down forcing her face close to his. Locking eyes with Stirling he gives the hissing Amiria a peck on the cheek leaving behind a red stain, "You know we were betrothed."

Calix lets that weigh on Stirling as he holds Amiria's face in place. She bares her fangs ready to bite if given the chance.

Calix continues, "Tsk, sad it had to come to this. She could have lived a fine life, but you drug her through the rut. You tied her noose."

Calix's eyes narrow as he smiles down at Stirling, showing the fresh gap in his once-perfect smile.

Stirling stares up in disbelief. It was Calix. He was who she was engaged to? Is that why she left out the name when she told him the story? Dread begins holding him down with more weight than Dicun. Is it true that he tied her noose as he always dreaded he would do?

His mouth gapes like the trout he catches in the river, mouthing words that never come out.

"Let's go." Calix glares down at the boy who has caused all this disruption in his life and instructs, "Make him sleep."

"Gladly." Dicun smirks.

The anvil holding Stirling's head down is released. Feeling weightless, his head floats off the floor to fully take in the person he holds above all others one final time. Heartbroken dark brown eyes meet his. Her face twists in anguish as she screams, "NO!"

An impact strikes Stirling's jaw, turning off the lights.

Nine

S tirling?"
"Stirling?"
"Stirling?"

His eyes sluggishly open to a half lid. Through his clouded vision, he can barely make out a female figure. "Amiria," he slurs, his mind succumbing to the unconscious realm once again.

"Stirling?" the girl says, her familiar voice as soothing as the cool relief of the damp cloth being pressed to his temple.

"Eve?" Still lethargic, he awakens to his head in Eve's lap as she leans against the wall with her legs out straight. With a groan, he shifts to lift himself.

Eve presses her hand down on his shoulder, "It's okay. Don't get up."

The room gradually comes into view. From the orange light coming in at an angle he assumes it must be dawn. Bernard leans his shoulder against the fireplace. His arms crossed resting on his pop belly.

He doesn't move as he speaks, his voice a low graveling sound, "Ignis came and woke us up. He led us here to find you unconscious, bleeding, and missing half a wall. Stirling, be honest. Who did this? Where is Amiria?"

"Her dragon is still here," Eve points out.

Stirling speaks through clenched teeth, unable to move his stiff and swollen jaw, already a deep purple, "Took 'er."

"Took her? Who took her?" Bernard deciphers.

"Cava'ry," Stirling manages to say. His eyes dance across the room envisioning the night before. The shattered clay pottery, broken crates, his blood, the missing door, and frame. "I'nis?"

"He's off sulking, I think. He's definitely upset about whatever conspired here." Eve lifts the cool towel to check the swelling of Stirling's eye then presses it back down. "Just rest for now. Okay?"

Bernard removes himself from the wall and squats down beside them, "You can tell us all the details when you're feeling up to it. We don't want you straining your injuries."

"No." Stirling fights through his throbbing head and attempts to sit up again. Bernard lays his hand on Stirling's chest stopping him. Stirling looks up into his soft brown eyes beneath the bristly eyebrows. "I nee' to sa'e 'er."

"Not in your condition. Besides if Amiria couldn't fight them off, it would be suicide for you to chase after them. Stirling, you're part of our family. We don't want to lose you."

Stirling lays his head back on Eve's lap as she speaks, "Bernard is right. Rest for now and we will think the situation over."

His vision begins to cloud and this time, not from his consciousness. Rest? How can someone rest during a time like this? The only girl he has ever loved is going to die, and he did nothing to stop it. He was useless. No, if he was useless, it would have been because of a situation he had no control of. What he is, is a level below that, he implemented it. At the bottom of everything, the single root cause of this disaster is him.

Eve watches as the man who stood tall through his fears in the stadium shrink into a small boy. He's breaking into tiny pieces, and she doesn't know how to put them back together. It tears at her heart to see him in this state. As her closest friend, someone she has fallen in love with, she wants to see him happy. She closes her eyes holding back her tears. She would rather see him smile because of someone else than not at all.

Mindlessly playing with his curls she begins to hum the tune. The same healing melody she did to calm his nerves before his interview.

Stirling shuts his eyes pushing free the built-up tears. They run from the corner of his eyes, blending in with water from the damp cloth.

Calix's heavy lids creak open. His armored leg beneath his wool blanket is jostled as Dicun kicks his boot. Leaning against his dragon Calix rolls his head and draws out the word, "Yes?"

"It's your turn for watch," Dicun grumbles. He doesn't wait for Calix to remove the blanket tucked around him, before heading to plant himself against his Wyvern for the rest of the night.

"Great," Calix says under his breath.

On the other side of the flames Amiria sits with ankles bound and wrists tied behind her back. Staring into the fire she can feel the heated energy that can release her from her restraints, but all her mind can call forward is how the scent of the smoke would linger on Stirling's clothing.

The flames that flicker and dance in the pit between Amiria and Calix reflect perfectly in her dark eyes.

Amiria's trance on the fire finally breaks as a blanket is strung around her shoulders. She jerks away from him to stare off into the night with a set jaw. Only her eyes shoot back and track his movements as he retakes his place on the opposing side of the fire. She smirks at the dark circles under his eyes and the swelling of his broken nose.

He reaches behind him and pulls his travel bag closer, "Are you hungry?" he offers, looking at her sympathetically. "Do you need anything? Water?"

"Hmph." Amiria turns, giving him the cold shoulder.

They're several days into the two-week-straight trip home to the Isles of Wyverna. Through day and night, she has held her tongue, refusing to give them a single word. During the day Calix is as cruel and cold as Dicun, but at night, after Dicun has gone to bed, he drapes his blanket around her. The ice in his eyes will melt beside the fire and the man she had grown to care for during that month together will ask her how she is holding up.

What she has learned the hard way was to not refuse every water offer. Refusing too often leads to Dicun force-feeding her and almost drowning her to make her drink. She has already concluded they are instructed to bring her back alive.

This realization makes her more nervous than if they were to let her die during their travels. She can barely keep her mind from wandering off and seeing the images in the shadows of the night of what the king might have planned for her.

"Dammit, Amiria!" He tosses a small branch into the fire, spitting up sparks. Amiria flinches. "Are you going to be like this the entire way back?"

Like the glowing specks coughed into the air by the branch this comment ignites her, "Oh? I'm sorry. How is a prisoner supposed to act?"

"A prisoner! You're a prisoner because you chose mutiny, over, over—" He cuts himself short.

Amiria rolls her eyes, "You mean I chose him over you." She runs her eyes over Calix, he is already seething after only one comment. His temper is as flammable as this wool blanket. She continues, she's never been afraid of flames, "You knew what I did, but you only chose to ignore it because you had me."

Calix's reaction is not what she expected. His face twinges, hurt from a deep pain. "I would have given you everything." He hates this, hates seeing her like this. Someone so beautiful and strong reduced to a bound criminal laying in the dirt in her stained nightwear.

Amiria doesn't let it get to her and pushes deeper. "Instead you took *everything* from me." She holds his gaze, the color of the sky staring into the color of night.

They don't speak. The only sounds come from distant crickets and the crackling of the fire between them.

Amiria finally talks first. "You're bringing me to my death, so act like it."

Calix grimaces at the cutting words.

The night pricks her skin as she shrugs the blanket from her shoulders, letting it crumple in a pile around her. Kicking the blanket away she lays on the grassless ground, rolling onto her side to face away from the fire and Calix.

Ten

"Thanks, Roesia," Stirling says without opening his swollen jaw.

He was lucky it wasn't broken, trying to aim through the small space of the ajar door had lessened the severity of the punch. That didn't stop the entire left side of his face, from the cut above his brow to his jawline, from swelling up and turning various shades of purple. Now, he sits straddling the bench seat at the table in his house. Roesia stands beside him fiddling with the bandage around his head.

Tying off the new bandage she says, "It's no problem, hun." She double-checks the bandage around his throat. "Anything to help such a sweet boy," she tells him with a squeeze of his shoulder. Tugging on one of his curls, she watches it spring back. "Have fun with your friend."

Stirling's blushing cheeks blend in with his bruises. With the tips of his ears feeling warm he looks over at Quilan, who is sitting across from him on the other side of the table. Quilan remains unphased by the overly mothering Roesia as she coddles Stirling, but his opaque eyes study her.

Even when Roesia kisses Stirling on the top of the head, Quilan's gaze remains expressionless, or when she tells him, "If you need another bandage change or if you're having difficulty eating let me know."

Stirling turns away, knowing Quilan is watching. "Okay."

Roesia turns her attention to Stirling's quiet friend. "It's nice of you to stop by Quilan. Watch over him for me."

Quilan nods in response.

"A man of many words," Roesia laughs as she gathers up the old bandages. Halfway to the door, she turns around to add one last thing. "I'll be back tonight, Stirling, to check up on you. Bernard is worried about letting you be alone for too long. Have fun boys." She heads out the front door, leaving Stirling and Quilan alone.

Quilan's dull eyes roll back to Stirling, who had corrected his seating to sit facing the table. "So?" he asks, gesturing to his face in reference to Stirling's.

When Quilan arrived, Roesia was already at Stirling's helping him eat breakfast. He sat patiently while Roesia talked and tended to Stirling's wounds. The bowl of uneaten almond milk oats she forced upon him when he joined them now sits cold between them.

He received a letter the night before in the words of Stirling requesting him to come over as soon as he was able to. Quilan, who hadn't left his house since the bone fire, finally put clothes on and escaped his home as the sun started to rise. He didn't know what to expect when he showed up but this, he looks into Stirling's one good eye, this is not what he expected. He did not expect Roesia to open the door. He did not expect to see his friend in a shattered state, physically and emotionally. The voice in his head ceased to speak as his mind and heart broke at the sight, but his face revealed none of that.

With his left eye swollen shut, Stirling fumbles blindly patting the top of the table. Quilan leans forward nudging the wooden cup of water to tap Stirling's searching fingertips.

"Thanks," Stirling whispers, picking up the cup.

Quilan watches as half of its contents run down the corners of Stirling's mouth, wetting his tunic.

Stirling skips Quilan's question and asks his own. "Have you ever been in a relationship?"

"Plenty."

"Oh," Stirling says, taken back with an unknown pang in his chest. Why is he surprised? Quilan is two years older than he is and has been the number one racer since he was sixteen. Stirling has been antisocial in Lumierna and was living in a cave at sixteen. "How many?"

"Too many," Quilan replies with his eyes never leaving Stirling.

Stirling sits wondering what that had to be like. He thinks of all the girls and boys screaming at him from the crowd. None of them really know him and none of them will ever get to know the true him. Especially if he jumped from one short relationship to another. They wouldn't understand him and his past on the level Amiria does. No one will. Even Eve spends every day with him and barely knows below the surface level. She knows stories of his past but she didn't live it. She doesn't know the full extent of the scar it left in his core. She knows he fears standing on a stage, but she doesn't know he can still hear the creaking of the rope from the garden lady's, Faerydae Rhoslyn's, hanging body, or how he still has nightmares that it's him instead.

It dawns on Stirling. Maybe that's the point.

"Did you love any of them?" Stirling asks.

Quilan's eyes linger on Stirling before switching to look out the window. He watches the two feathery dragons of orange and blue play in the river. His dark eyes return to Stirling's, "No."

Stirling's entire posture drops, "I might not have been with anyone else, but I know I love Amiria." His chin touches his chest as he hangs his head. Relentless tears follow the trails stained before them and begin their journey down his swollen face, "and now she's gone."

Engrossed in his emotions, Stirling doesn't realize Quilan gets up from his seat across the table. He is oblivious until he feels the pressure of a hand soothingly rubbing between his shoulder blades. He peaks up to see Quilan sitting beside him to his right. Quilan uses his free hand to take Stirling's resting on the table and lays his head on his shoulder. Feeling the calming warmth of his friend around him Stirling rests his cheek on top of Quilan's hair.

Quilan continues to draw lines across Stirling's shoulder blades, but his eyes are lost through the hole where Stirling's bedroom door once stood. He is alive because he wanted to hear Stirling's story and now is his chance, "From the beginning?"

Stirling shifts uncomfortable, but he wants Quilan to know everything about him, "Well, back in Wyverna."

Eleven

There's no more resting. It's been almost two weeks. If he leaves now, he can still make it back to Wyverna to help her. Stirling pulls the last strap of provisions and gear strapped to Ignis tight. He knows it's the right choice. Why else would Taika have let him strap Amiria's armor to her.

Ignis gripes, *"Can we leave next week?"*

"What!? No," Stirling says, appalled.

"What about in the morning, I want to say bye to Aether. I don't want them to worry, and—and you can say goodbye to Quilan. You like Quilan, you can't leave without a goodbye. Stirling please," Ignis begs.

"No, we need to leave now. We should have left days ago, but Bernard kept me on house arrest being spoon-fed by Roesia," Stirling pushes.

"How is your not-so-pretty face?"

"It hurts."

"Then we should stay, you need your beauty sleep," Ignis tries another tactic.

"Do you want to tell Taika?" Stirling points his still bruised jaw at the cream-colored dragon watching them with intense eyes.

Ignis pulls his head back in apprehension. "*Ehh, noooo.*"

"STIRLING!" Eve's voice calls out from the night. Her black curls are a new moon amongst the dark grass sky filled with firefly stars.

Stirling exaggeratedly sighs before facing her. "It's not going to work Eve." He blinks through the fuzzy vision returning to his half-closed eye.

She slows stalling a dozen steps away. "I'm not here to stop you."

"Then why are you here?" He disregards her and returns to checking the straps.

Ignis twists his neck behind himself, "*NO! Eve! You were my last hope. I don't want to go back there! I want to stay here!*"

"Ignis, we have to save Amiria. Remember you didn't help any more than I did when she fought them," Stirling snaps.

"*You didn't have to bring that up,*" Ignis lowers his head.

"Look, Ignis. I'm sorry, I—" Distracted by Ignis, Stirling is taken by surprise. His heart jumps from his chest as Eve wraps her arms around him.

Her honey eyes look up at him. "Please come home to us."

"Evelina…" His voice trails off. She fits her head perfectly against the curve of his neck like she was built to be there. He lifts his arms pulling her in tighter.

He can hear the tears in her voice. "Even if it takes what feels like forever. We'll be waiting for you. You're part of our family, we all love you. So, promise me, promise you'll come home?"

"*Aw. How sweet. I say make the promise. I'm on her side,*" Ignis interrupts.

Ignoring Ignis he holds her tighter, memorizing how she feels in his arms. "I promise."

"Stirling?" Roesia calls from outside his front door, her small voice echoes through the empty house alongside her gentle knock. "Stirling?" The fireplace sits cold. "Bernard and I have come by to check on you." The straw in the bedroom lays undisturbed without a gentle giant. "Eve seems to have hogged you the last couple of days." The cupboards sit with doors hanging open, empty of food.

"Maybe he's sleeping," Bernard mumbles.

"Stirling, we're coming in," Roesia announces as she pushes open the door. "Stirling?" She steps cautiously around the slow swinging door. "Stirling?" She slows to a stop in the center of the home and glances around. "Stirling?" Confused, she turns to Bernard for insight. "Where—" she cuts herself short as she looks down at Bernard.

His stricken face turns to her from his knelt position beside the now empty storage crate Stirling kept his clothing in. He leaps up, throwing his hefty body out of the front door. Cupping his mouth with his hands he calls to the clouds. "STIRLING!"

He bounds down the steps. Turning the corner, he hollers across the river. "STIRLING! STIRLING! STIIIIRRRLINNNG!" He drags out the name as it wears at his throat.

Dropping his hands, his knuckles bump into something at his side. With his cheeks and beard already glistening with tears, he peers down at Roesia. Her small hand curled around the hem of his brown tunic.

He swallows hard and barely manages to choke out, "He's gone." He turns back to the clouds hoping to glimpse them emerging from the floating hilltops. "He's really gone." The mountain-sized man crumbles to a heap as he sinks to his knees.

Roesia leans over wrapping her arms around him and pulls his head to her chest. "But he's not gone forever." With tears rolling down her cheeks, Roesia comforts Bernard, her fingertips petting his thinning hair, "Believe in him as we've always done. He's doing what he knows is right. If he loves us as much as we love him, he'll come home."

Bernard wraps his arms around his wife's hips holding her closer as he weeps.

Twelve

A child's squealing laughter fills the royal solar. King Dietrich, dressed down in soft comfortable robes sits slouched in a plush chair. His hips slid down to the end with his legs crossed wide, his ankle perched on his knee. With his arm propped up and resting, he leans his temples into his finger, while half-lidded eyes watch the boy around the age of four play by his feet.

With wooden men lined up, the boy is the ruler of his make-believe land. Taking a carved dragon, he crashes it into the cluster of staged men.

Uninterested, King Dietrich turns his attention across the room. His wife only by marriage sits at a round white table with his two daughters of seven and nine. They make girlish sounds as they drink clarea of water, spiced honey water, from small cups.

Useless, all three of them. A queen is supposed to be a trained dignity. Someone to substitute and uphold his duties if he was to fall ill or pass before the boy at his feet is old enough to rule. This *woman* spends her days acting as if those children of hers are her personal dolls. His face turns sour as he thinks. Always playing dress up, having sweet drinks accompanied with desserts, and prancing around the castle as if it were a field of daisies. She's always pandering to the nobles as if their opinion matters.

He is not an elected official, and neither is his son—the son it took her years to provide him. She was at least able to prove herself useful with one of her Queen's duties, producing him a suitable heir, but she should have given him his son first and then had her daughters to play with.

He has no need for daughters. He has no other Kingdom to barter a princess with.

There is *one* thing the woman can do right. It is coordinating the balls, banquets, and ceremonies in the castle. At least she's not completely worthless. The balls are grand.

Barely using the energy to move his head he glances at the door with the sound of a light tapping knock. The servant he swore was a wall ornament opens the door ajar enough to peer out. He steps back allowing Major Gautier to step inside.

King Dietrich sits up, dignifying himself. The queen and her princesses remain unfazed as they giggle over almond cookies.

"Is there an emergency Major Gautier?"

"Depends on your definition." Major Gautier swoops across the room, his face giving no indications of what news he's come bearing.

Stopping beside King Dietrich, Major Gautier side glances at the other people occupying the room. The view of the corner of his eye stopping on the servant still standing beside the door. He leans down whispering into King Dietrich's ear.

King Dietrich's eyes widen. He can feel it bubbling up inside of him. Holding back his elation, he dismisses Major Gautier. "Your son has done well. Summon Field Marshal Rey. He is instructed to meet me in my cabinet at noon. Now excuse me, Captain, for I need to freshen up for this special reunion."

Major Gautier bows. "Yes. sire."

Barely containing his grin King Dietrich looks over at the round table at the sound of giggling girls. *Right, they are still here.*

Standing up from his chair, King Dietrich orders, "Oriana, take the children. I have business to attend to."

With an overly powdered face and hair pinned into curls, Oriana sets down her cup of clarea of water. "Ealdian, this is family hour. The one time of the day you see your son." She motions to the small boy at King Dietrich's feet.

King Dietrich scowls. No one, not even the queen, has authority over him. "You listen, my duties as a King do not stop so you can play pretend. The younger he learns that, the better of a king he will be. Now remove yourself and these children from this solar."

Oriana huffs and passively plucks the cups from her daughter's hands, setting them down on the table. "Come on, let's get some sun. Your father is being cranky."

King Dietrich rolls his eyes as the small copies of her trail behind at the extended hem of her gown. She stops in front of Ealdian Dietrich and holds her hand out to the boy sitting at his feet.

"Come on, Aramm." She smiles at the young prince. "Come with Mother."

Looking back and forth between his parents, Aramm doesn't question where he is going. Leaving his toys behind, his small hand wraps around his mother's fingers. With a turn of her nose, Oriana leads her children out of the room.

Before the door can shut behind the long hem of her dress King Dietrich motions for the servant to exit as well. At the click of the door, he begins to beam.

Finally, he thinks, tilting his head up to the ceiling as if he was a flower soaking in the sunlight. She has been brought back to him.

His right side will no longer be empty. His perfect purebred warrior. His beautiful knight. She is an immaculate display of what a soldier should be.

His robes swaying as he spins and dances across the room, Picking up an apple from an overflowing fruit bowl. Turning the red crisp fruit in his hand, he closes his eyes picturing her standing beside him in her red brigandine as he sits upon his throne.

He doesn't care anymore that she tried to run from her duties, run from him. What's the point of having your trophy if you didn't play the game to earn it?

The crisp apple crunches as he bites into, the juice running down the sides of his mouth and through his closely trimmed beard. So, brazing. So feisty. So deeply fascinating unlike...he looks down his nose at the table where Queen Oriana sat. He raises his lip. He turns away from the table, the sight of it souring his sweet dream.

This has turned out better than he could have ever planned. Before he was only able to command his little warrior to be placed at his side. Always in his line of view.

Now... He grins. *Now I will own her.*

Thirteen

Square beams of light break through the burlap sack she has been donning since arriving back home to Wyverna. She lets out a small grunt as an aggressive hand shoves her forward, her bare feet slapping the cool granite floor.

There is no reason they need to roughhouse her. She has been compliant the entire length of travel. She's held back her words and followed their directives, seeing no reason to waste energy on a fight she can't win.

Is this what she has been degraded to? A faceless prisoner? A criminal to parade through the castle halls with her hands bound together with rope? The braies she's been wearing for several weeks are no longer white; instead, they're stained from dirt, grass, and sweat.

Is there anyone in these halls watching her? Are there nobles hiding their disgust behind their fans and shirt collars as she is made an example of?

Where are they taking her?

From the sounds of the boots of her escorts and the roughly guiding hands, she has one on either side of her and one behind.

The one on her right grabs the linen of her night tunic signaling her to stop. She can't make out more than shadows through the burlap, but she hears the latch of a heavy door slide open. Another shove on the center of her back staggers her across the threshold. Disoriented from her lack of sight, her feet trip over one another as she finds her balance. Her bound hands jut forward in a feeble attempt to counteract the offset of her weight.

She cocks her head from side to side, straining her ears to search for some clue of what room she has been forced into. She stands blind in the vacuum of space.

Jagged nails dig into her shoulder as a strong hand pushes her down to her knees. She bites her lip suppressing a gasp as her kneecaps are jammed into the hard floor. Her eyes clench shut as the bag is ripped free from her head.

The bright afternoon light streaming in through the windows assaults her now sensitive eyes. Rapidly blinking against the harsh light, her eyes slowly adjust, bringing the room into view.

King Dietrich's personal Cabinet. Her heart rate spikes. She has been in this room only a handful of times during her three years of working beside him. Nothing ever good comes from having to speak to King Dietrich in his Cabinet. A room where no one can hear what is being said, private matters, secret dealings, and information that will die along with the occupants are contained inside the room.

Her eyes hurtle around the room, frantically leaping from the wall lined with bookshelves, a timber-framed window, and her escorts on either side of her. Armundus and Everard stand in ready position front facing with their hands crossed behind their back in their silver armor and red brigandine. Eda stands behind her with a smirk curling all the way back to her ear. She drops the hood on her polished armored boots.

Amiria's eyes skip over Dicun and Major Gautier to finally land on Calix. His eyes, no longer black and blue but a mix of yellow, are locked straight. A muscle in his cheek twitches as he refuses to meet her gaze.

Closing her eyes, she inhales deeply. Opening them slowly she stares straight at the massive desk made from strawberry trees. The expensive wood is a striped mixture of maple and birch, then stained with crimson streaks like blood spewed across the hardwood.

King Dietrich hasn't bothered to look up at her yet, his eyes scanning a parchment. Her eyes reluctantly climb to the man standing beside the king. Her face hardness, her physical state composing herself at the sight of her father while her mind screams. His brown eyes are cold and analytical. His stoic face leers down at her as if this is no more than another chore added to his busy day.

Amiria is surprised the sun hasn't set by the time King Dietrich sets his sights on her. He pushes the parchment aside and takes a sip from his gold chalice. Slurping the contents, he watches the girl with stained underclothing and matted hair over its rim. He sets the chalice down carefully with a satiated exhale and leans back in his chair.

"Get on with it already!" Amiria cries out in frustration.

He sucks his teeth and makes a faux concerned face, "Eager, aren't you?"

"Just get it over with," Amiria's head hangs.

He absorbs the site, taking in all he can of the young Rey, forced to her knees, her life in his hands. The insufferable man who had created her is forced to watch the first of the belongings he will be losing. "You who is knelt before your king. Do you identify yourself by the name of Amiria Rey?"

"What?" Amiria asks, confused, he knows who she is.

"Do you go by the title of Amiria Rey?" he repeats as if he is talking to a subservient stranger. As if she was a nobody dragged from the streets of the lower district.

"Yes?" She asks in a form of a question, her voice rising with a twist of her face.

"Then we shall proceed," King Dietrich lifts his parchment, glossing it over once again.

"*What is he doing?*" she wonders. He knows what she did. He is only prolonging her humiliation for his own amusement. He just needs to sentence her to death already.

A voice replays in her mind, "*Amiria, I love you!*" A small smile shines through her mask as she thinks of Stirling. *We almost were, Baker Boy,* she thinks.

Her wandering mind snaps back as King Dietrich begins speaking again, "Amiria Rey, you have been found guilty of mutiny against the Winged Cavalry and treason against your kingdom. Evidence has been discovered that you withheld knowledge of the existence and whereabouts of the boy now known as Stirling Bakere, who had been found guilty of illegally possessing and riding a dragon—a crime falling under high treason. He had already been found and held accountable for his crimes."

Amiria cocks her head in confusion. Is that a lie they've spread to the people?

King Dietrich continues, "After purposefully harboring the fugitive you deliberately gave the Winged Cavalry and your king false and misleading information resulting in a substantial amount of time lost. You proceeded to lead your team in the wrong direction and then deserted them during an ambush. You were then discovered with said fugitive." He pauses to announce to the room, "Amiria Rey. For the unforgivable acts of your heinous crimes…"

Here it comes, she thinks mentally preparing herself.

"It has been decided that you will be brought to the great keep. You will remain locked there until you are ready to be a personal servant to your king."

Field Marshal Rey's head snaps from Amiria to King Dietrich, his marble features fissuring.

Amiria shakes her head. She must have heard him wrong. The stress and lack of proper sleep from travel must be playing tricks with her mind. She can't help but steal a glance at Calix. Maybe his reaction will clear up what has been said.

She regrets it. Her entire body pales at the sight of his once tan and vibrant skin now turned a sickly gray. He catches Amiria's gaze. With a horrified expression, he drops his eyes to his boots. She scans the spectators in the room. The ambiance in the room changes as no one wants to meet her eyes. She makes it back to King Dietrich. His smile is a revolting sneer.

She had heard him correctly, but she wished she didn't. She, for one, would have chosen death. Time begins to slow. Her chest heaves as she sucks in and dispels the air. The sound of the blood flowing in her ears is as loud as roaring rapids turning her vision red.

What does she have left to lose? Amiria leaps to her feet and before anyone can react she charges the king. Armundus and Everard reach out snatching at the wild girl. Their hands miss as she dodges by, rolling under their arms. King Dietrich leans forward resting his head on his interlaced fingers. A genuine smile as slow as molasses spreads across his face.

The golden handle jams in the scabbard as Field Marshal Rey fumbles to unsheathe his sword. Amiria twists, evading another gauntleted shackle around her wrist. She's almost to the desk. She can make it if she just—

Amiria pounces.

Her body flies through the air, prepared to land on the desk that cost more than the bakery itself and stomp the precious documents the king loves so much.

"Umph." The oxygen is knocked out of her as a strong arm snags her out of the air. She screams and pounds on Calix's back with her balled fists of furry as he throws her light frame over his shoulder. The sound of shuddering metal echoes in the frozen room.

King Dietrich, satisfied with the response, sits himself back properly in his chair, "Oh what a prize you are."

Field Marshal Rey's perfect posture sags. His hands falling limply to his sides. His lips disappear into a fine line as he watches.

Amiria stops thrashing as Eda fills her vision with a chaotic grin. "Bye, bye little girl." She throws the burlap bag back over Amiria's head.

The door to the Cabinet closes, leaving Field Marshal Rey alone with King Dietrich. Neither of them takes their eyes off the last place they saw Amiria as Field Marshal Rey speaks up, "Sire?"

"What is it, Sir Rey." The corner of the king's mouth twitches, his eyes still glued to the door.

"Servitude? Can you elaborate on the reasoning? Why not execution, as planned?" Field Marshal Rey questions through his teeth.

King Dietrich tilts his head sidelong, glancing up at him, "tell me, is there something wrong with my punishment? Field, Marshal?"

"I believe there is, Your Majesty. This is not the set punishment for Ami— The girl's crimes. You are not following the decree we wrote. Execution is the standing punishment on the original ordinance we still follow," Amiria's father chooses his words carefully to tiptoe around committing treason himself.

King Dietrich picks up the decree Field Marshal Rey was referring to and tears it in half, "Have you forgotten our titles, Rey? I don't have to follow anything." He turns the parchment and tears it again, "What I say is law. I am the king. Remember this, Field Marshal, because over the years it appears you have forgotten. You are in control of the Cavalry. I am in control of this Kingdom. You work for me, Field Marshal." King Dietrich drops the torn paper on the ground behind him, "Since you've shown a disdain for my decisions and you don't deem it fitting, I want you to oversee it. Make sure the orders I give are followed through properly. If there are any transports of the detained for any reason, I want you to personally attend them."

Field Marshal Rey takes in a deep breath, the creases in his face deepening, "Of course, Sire."

Fourteen

Amiria skids across the dusty floor of the Main Keep, the most fortified tower of the castle, sitting at the southeast corner of the grounds. Her body smears a path in the rotten straw and old rush of her derelict cell.

Eda clings to Everard's arm laughing as Armundus slams the bars shut. Calix standing behind them flinches at the rattling sound.

Everard slides the lock into place. "The only sad part of this is the loss of a good fighter."

"I never liked her anyways." Eda glares down her powdered nose.

"Traitors get what they deserve," Armundus grumbles as he heads to the exit.

Ignoring her other ex-teammates, Amiria sits staring Calix in the eye. "You finally out of things to say?" He can't hold her gaze and sends his blue eyes to the corroding ground.

"He finally did this team some good, that's all he needs to say," Everard answers for Calix, then turns himself and follows Eda to the exit. He waves without looking back.

Calix is the last to leave, slowly backing to the door. He comes off as if he wants to say something but doesn't. Fumbling for the door handle, he's hesitant to leave her behind. Bringing his heart to his sleeve, he casts pleading eyes to her before slipping out and closing the heavy wooden door with a small, barred window at the top behind him, leaving her alone for the first time in weeks.

Ignoring the pain, Amiria rams her heel several times into the door of her cage letting the clanging metal reverberate through her bones. Sitting up, she grabs the bars pressing her face between them. The bars are just close enough to keep her from sticking her head out

The Main Keep. No one has ever been held up here. King Dietrich has never needed to keep a prisoner. Why would he want to waste manpower keeping a criminal alive when the gallows are easier?

From what she can see, the room is small, consisting of only a few cells. The entire damp and dark crypt is lit by one single forge already sweltering with heat and the light from the brick-sized window is too high up to see out of.

She stands to get a better view of the table beside it. Rusted iron tools and shackles clutter the table and hang from the wall. Dread fills her as she sees a decaying chair with leather straps occupying a corner of the room.

"Hello?" she calls out, straining to see the other cells. "Hello?"

Sighing, she limps back against the wall. Using it as support she slides down the damp and crying stone. She wraps her arms around her knees and leans her head back watching the dust move across the sunlight, imagining they are flocks of birds, clans of dragons, and stars in the heavens.

The castle's corridors are like catacombs as Calix's hollow corpse floats through the hall. He chastises himself, muttering under his breath. He feels like he is nothing more than a bag of dirt being carted out of a tunnel on a set track.

What has he done? The rage and jealousy he had felt were overpowering. She had run away. Not just from the kingdom but from him. She had run away straight into *his* arms. He had always known the obvious. He just refused to admit it. He could see something was amiss. She frequently visited the market. How she reacted the night they were called to action when *he* was discovered. Her peculiar behavior at their meeting. Then the goggles in her room tied the knot.

He would have kept it a secret. He would have lied for her, protected her. He was willing to do anything for her. He had her. He looks at his empty hands. He had her.

He only knows in hindsight what King Dietrich had planned for her. If he had known the sentence was changed, he would never have brought her here. The idea of another man having her, even the king, makes him ill.

Stopping, he leans against the wall weakly. His body is already devouring itself from the inside as he recognizes what he has done. How can he live a life where he sees her every day but can no longer even speak to her? He had broken through her iron-plated walls and saw the smiling girl hiding within. He should have built his around her while he could, now she's been taken away and he will never see *her* again.

"Calix!" Major Gautier calls bounding down the corridor.

"Yes Sir!" Calix corrects his posture, pulling his shoulders back. His father, now within reach, extends his arm out. Calix holds his posture firm but his face flinches anticipating what is to come. But it doesn't.

Stunned, he looks at his father. His arms wrapped around Calix's shoulders in a tight embrace. Calix says confused, "Sir?"

Major Gautier holds Calix out in front of him to take a good look at his son. "I am, so, proud of you."

His eyes fall from his father's matching set to his father's shoulders, to the wall, then back to his eyes as he tries to transcribe what he had been told. His mouth gapes open. His mind is trying to remember how to form words. "Permission to ask for the reason?"

"The reason!" Major Gautier shakes his son, grinning wildly. "Not only were you the only one to configure the truth about the Rey girl, but you personally tracked her down and brought her to the king. That's true loyalty, Calix. Loyalty to the Winged Cavalry, to Wyverna." He drops his hands. "I know how you felt about the girl. You made the right choice. A leader's choice." He exaggerates the words with a pointed finger. "Now that there is no heir to the Field Marshal." He winks. "Someone who works personally at the king's side would make a good candidate."

His father is proud of him? "Th-thank you, sir," Calix manages to say, too afraid to say anything more. Afraid it will break this moment like he has broken everything else in his life.

The bear rug leaves a clean imprint on the floor as the dark brown fur is rolled away. A package crinkles as Mairead hugs the treasure Amiria had left for her close to her chest. The helping hands of the servants worked silently to make the girl Mairead had grown to know and care for disappear. Amiria had never come home from her deployment, not on her own accord. But she isn't supposed to know that. Now, she is questioning everything she does know, because apparently, she didn't know the real Amiria.

She was assigned to the Rey family, as were her mother and her grandmother. Where will the Field Marshal send her to work next now Amiria is gone? Will she luckily be brought back to the Rey manor to continue serving?

Standing against the wall by the fireplace she watches as the furniture is stripped of the personality Amiria gave it. The color and life she brought were carried out and given away to distant relatives or sold to any willing buyer. The room now shows the dreary cage it truly is.

She looks over at the two guards overseeing the job leaning by the doorway. She averts her gaze quickly before they notice. Her ears stay on their whispering conversation.

"I wonder why she did it?"

"Did what? Help the fugitive?"

"Well, yeah. I heard she had known about him before that night."

"Who knows."

"Then she runs away to be with him." The younger guard chuckles to himself. "Like some star-crossed lovers."

The older guard rolls his eyes with a shake of his head. "You watch too many plays."

The younger opens his mouth to rebuttal but looks to the ceiling pondering for a second. "Yeah, maybe you are right."

Mairead removes herself from the wall. "Permission to return to the servant's quarters?"

The two guards who have forgotten she was there turn to her in unison.

"Who? Oh right, the handmaiden. Yeah, sure, whatever." The older one waves his hand, dismissing her.

Ducking her head, she watches her golden slippers as she shuffles past the guards into the hall. She looks up at the door where Amiria's name is no longer labeled. Biting her lip, she continues down the empty hall. Safely away from the Cavalry's rooms, she sits in the narrow stairs, never seen by any noble leading below the castle and through the walls.

Peeling back the wrapping, she reveals a yellow bliaut. She picks up a note in Amiria's scribe.

"To match your slippers.
Thank you, I wish I had more to give you."
-Amiria

The gown unfolds as Mairead holds it up, the itching of her current wool dress suddenly prevalent as she pinches the soft fabric in her fingers. A heavy object falls from the unraveled dress landing on the step beside her feet.

Struggling to see around her legs in the dim light she pats the step until her fingers brush velvet. With a raised eyebrow, she picks up a deep and vibrant blue drawstring bag. Jingling sounds echo down the stairs as the coins in the bag shift. A second note is tied to the string.

"Be happy. Be Free."

With trembling hands, she pulls open the drawstring. Peering inside gold and silver coins stare back. She will never have to work again.

A pang stabs her heart. Choking back tears, Mairead hides her face into the yellow fabric. Her ears perk to the sound of distant footsteps. Hastily, she hides the coins and takes off with a new urgency in her gate.

Fifteen

Amiria startles awake. The sounds of clunking metal resonate deep in her chest. She had fallen asleep sitting up against the wall. She rolls her shoulders. Her muscles ache and are stiff from the cold.

Her mind already groggy and slow, yawns awake before taking in her surroundings, she squints at the three silhouetted men backlit from the forge. She recognizes one of them. "Clyde?" she says with a graded voice.

The fire lights the whites of his eyes and the glint of his smile, "Hello Amiria. It's good to see you again."

She ignores the happy reunion of her old classmate to inspect the two other ones, barely older than herself, on either side of him. Guards in their patrol armor—soft blue gambesons beneath chainmail hauberks. One has dark black hair like hers, slightly above average height, and the other slightly below with swooping auburn hair that hangs close to his eyes.

Clyde, wearing a navy-blue gambeson, notices her wavering eyes, "I didn't mean to be rude. Let me introduce my men. This is Robert and William. If you cared to remember, I was demoted from the Cavalry to lead Lumierna's Guards. So, they work for me personally and they are here in case you put up a fight."

"Fight?" Amiria grows defensive. "Against what?"

"This," Clyde informs.

Robert and William seem to fly across the room. Amiria blinks and they are above her. She has nowhere to escape as they each grab an arm and rip her from the floor. She digs her heels into the stone floor in simple defiance. Their faces are grim as if they lock eyes over her head. Nodding they both reach down and grab the cloth at her knees and lift, suspending her in the air as they escort her unwillingly from the cell.

Her dilated eyes widen as she runs through scenarios in her head. She doesn't know what they have planned for her, but it can't be anything good if they are afraid of her fighting. If a fight is what they want, a fight is what she will give them. Like in the King's Cabinet, what does she have to lose?

Thrashing her body like a fish out of water, Amiria kicks out, striking William in the side of the knee, contorting his limb. William's knee buckles, giving in before it pops. Falling, he releases his grip on Amiria to catch himself in a kneel.

Robert's already secure grip around her arm squeezes her bicep. Using this to her advantage, she stabilizes herself by leaning into him and putting both of her heels into William's cheekbone and jaw as he lifts his head to find them. William's head snaps to the side with the force, throwing him over.

The once meek boy from her class, now filling out his armor, snags her by the roots of her matted hair. She yelps from the strands of hair being pulled from her scalp as Clyde pulls her from Robert's hold. She uselessly claws at his leather-gloved hands while her body is dragged the last several steps. Her spine slams into the back of the chair as he drives her into the restraint chair that had been staged in the center of the room.

Her head, following the lead of her hair, is forced back against the rest. She blinks dazed up at the moldy ceiling. She can't let them do this. Her hands reach out, grabbing for anything to help her. Panic taking over her emotions she raises her hips up from the chair as she refuses to sit. If she can just get her head free.

Robert looms in front of her. "Nope," he says, as he drives his knee into her hip bones forcing her to sit back in the chair. With his knee still in her lap, he grabs one of her wild wrists and traps it to the armrest.

William massages his jaw and grabs her last free limb and punches it down onto the second armrest and quickly secures the leather restraint. Robert sighs with relief as he finishes strapping the arm he had trapped, and William had secured the lap band. Together they lock her in place with restraints around her ankles. They take a step back from their work. The taller one, Robert, pulls William in close to inspect the swelling, no longer concerned about the girl in the chair.

Amiria flails in her seat refusing to give up even if she knows she will lose in the end. If she is going down, she will go down fighting. The leather straps begin to dig and slice into her skin as she pulls. Her head pops up, suddenly weightless as Clyde releases his hold on her.

Exposing her fangs Amiria lifts her lip and snarls at the men around her. Clyde tilts his head back, peering down at Amiria through the slits of his eyelids. The girl who never even had a strand of hair out of place glares up at him with wild eyes as she fights against the restraints. Her tattered clothes are beginning to hang loose around her thinning frame and her mangy hair is stuck to her sweating skin.

He used to be jealous of her. The look Instructor Aldred used to give him. How he was nothing more than a disappointment. With her in his class, a prodigy, everyone appeared pathetic in comparison. Even with a tutor, he couldn't keep up. It wasn't fair, she was never at the arena practicing like he was. Everything just came easy to her.

Then to salt the wound, she was chosen by the king to personally guard him. King Dietrich wanted her by his side while he himself was demoted, and outcasted from the Winged Cavalry, but he is a captain now. Even if it is as one of Lumierna's guards, he is still a captain. He stands here in charge, not her.

His gaze is like spider legs as it crawls from her eyes down to her insignia. A smile stitches across his face. "I'm going to enjoy this."

"Clyde?" Amiria's voice is thick with fear. "Clyde what are you going to do?" Her eyes lock on Clyde. From her peripheral, she sees Robert put his arm in front of William guiding them several steps back giving Clyde and Amiria space.

Clyde doesn't remove his eyes from Amiria's insignia as he backs up to the forge. "It's best if you try and remain still."

Her breathing begins to pick up as terror envelops her. "Clyde! What are you going to do! Clyde!"

With his heels against the forge, he turns his back to Amiria. His face glows a hellish red as he picks up an iron rod from the lit coals. A bead of sweat forms on his brow as he inspects the brand. The glowing X reflecting in the center of his expanded pupils.

Amiria thrashes in the chair. "CLYDE! CLYDE! DON'T DO THIS!"

Calm and collected, he steps up to her. The branding iron is his paintbrush, and she is his canvas. She whips her head back and forth holding in begging tears. Throwing herself to one side of the chair, she is unable to escape while her arm remains strapped in place. Never meeting her eye, Clyde pushes her bracelet down and out of the way, steadying his hand.

She watches in horror as the red-hot iron is lowered just above her insignia. She can feel the hairs singeing and the skin flushing and turning pink like a sunburn.

Biting her lip, she searches for Clyde's eyes, for his humanity. Composing herself, hiding her horror, her voice is sad and broken as she begs, "Clyde, please."

Clyde doesn't respond. He doesn't lift his gaze from her arm.

"NOOOOOO!" Her screaming word cracks and changes into an inhuman howl as her voice tears from her throat. Her soul desperately tries clawing its way out to escape the pain her body is enduring.

She throws her head back, the tendons bulging in her neck. She jerks her arm, the brander pulling her melted skin as it drags across her arm leaving behind a second outline of the X over her insignia.

She doesn't feel the brander go from her burning skin, her still intact nerves in overdrive send the hellacious pain signals to her brain. Her spirit collapses in on itself and her torso slumps forward. With her eyes half-lidded, she stares numbly at her lap. Her mind is empty except for the pulsating beat of pain from her arm.

Clyde squats down in front of her and lifts her face up by her chin. He sucks his teeth, "Tsk, Amiria Rey, Winged Cavalry prodigy, King Dietrich's pet. What has become of her, they wonder?" He exaggerates an "Aw" and pushes back the sweat-soaked hair from her face but finds it impossible to meet her eye. "You peaked too early. Now it's my turn to shine."

Her face is feverish with sweat, she opens her mouth letting the words slither out, "I'd rather rot with this seat than live a life as a subservient puppet to a merciless Kingdom."

Clyde frowns. He opens his hand, releasing Amiria's chin. Stepping back a step he straightens himself, "People who disobey the laws don't deserve mercy anyways." He turns away, no longer wanting to watch the girl now pressing her forehead to her arm. Her ragged breath heaves as she barely weathers the pain he had inflicted. He nods his chin at her cell commanding Robert and William, "Lock her back up." The two young men share a glance.

The leather restraints fall free from around her. She has no more energy to put up a fight. Her head is barely able to lift from her arm for her to see the back of Clyde's head.

With Amiria now putting up no resistance, Robert grabs her uninjured arm. She sucks in a sharp breath as she is hoisted from the chair. He keeps his hand gripped around her bicep holding her up and assists her walking back to the cell.

Robert's hand disappears from her skin as he stops at the entrance, and she takes several more steps on her accord to the center of the cell.

Rolling her shoulders back, she faces Clyde who is leaning against the exit. She finally catches his eye. "You're wrong Clyde. You're wrong."

His face is unchanging as he receives her message but his hand crawls up to grip his insignia beneath the sleeve of his gambeson. The door to her cell clangs shut and he finally blinks with the clicking of the lock. Releasing the grip on his arm he opens the door and holds it for Robert who is assisting the limping William to pass through. His eyes start to tiptoe back across the room to observe the raven he had clipped the wings from. Shaking his head, he closes the door.

Amiria flinches as the slamming door echoes through her heart. Pulling her arm to her chest, she cradles it like an infant and huddles to a corner of the cell in a crouch.

With the smell of cooked flesh still pungent in the air, a whimper escapes from deep in her throat as her leather bracelet slips down her arm, touching the burnt remnants of her insignia.

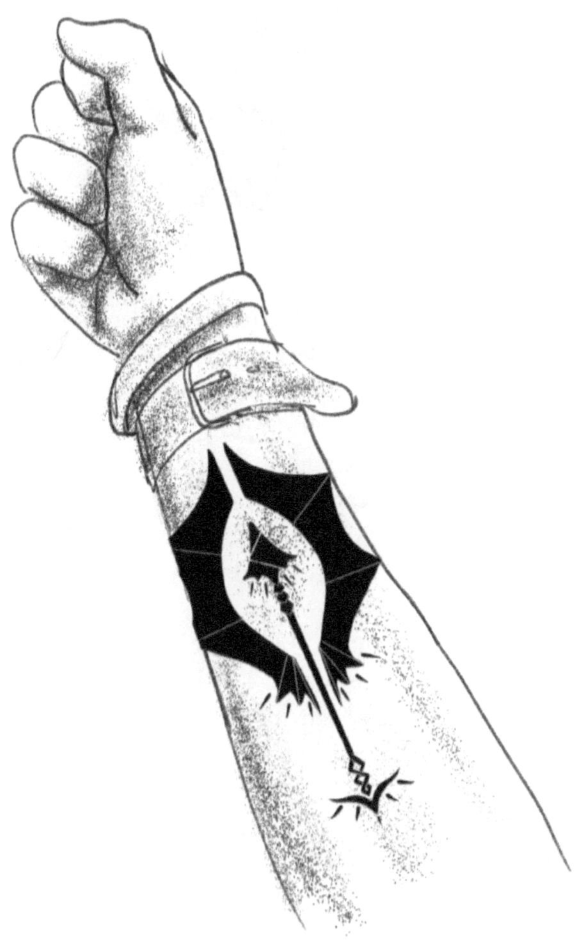

Sixteen

Water ripples from the air streaming below the two dragons hidden in the cloak of night. The looming peaks of Wyverna rise from the ocean like the jagged teeth of a titan unhinging its jaws to swallow them whole. The island skyline is a black absence of space against the galaxy of stars.

Stirling folds over, clutching at his chest. His forehead, beginning to perspire, presses against Ignis as Taika follows close behind. He can't do this. He can't do this. He can't do this. He's dying. He's already dying, and they haven't even reached the island. His heart is going is going to continue to beat harder and harder until it bursts like some kind of spell was placed on him if he ever returned.

"Stirling?" Ignis notices Stirling's shift. *"Hey, hey, you're going to be fine. It's like the first time we saw Luecasia. Nothing is going to happen, okay?"*

Sirens. Fire. Falling. Falling here. Falling into this ocean. He can't breathe. He can't breathe. He's suffocating.

"Stirling!" Ignis yells. *"We're going to the safety of the cave. Nothing will happen to you. We're here to save Amiria."*

Amiria. The cave. The cave only Amiria knows about. The place they could relax worry free. It is safe. The cave is safe.

Breathe, breathe, breathe. Stirling reminds himself. His body is reacting as if he has already been shot down by the Cavalry, though they are nowhere to be seen.

He never wanted to return to Wyverna, he had no intention of returning to a place that wanted him dead. Now here she is, towering before him and promising him nothing but hardship and death.

Ignis pops his shoulder up, bouncing Stirling back to attention, *"Hey, you're going to be okay."*

Rolling his head, Stirling looks at Taika and the empty space on her back, *"For once it's not me I'm worried about."*

Ignis doesn't respond. He doesn't know how to respond. They've spent the couple of weeks it takes to travel to Wyverna avoiding the topic. Stirling acted outwardly as if they were only on a trip, sightseeing the land while avoiding cities. Below his paper-thin surface Ignis could see what was really scribed across his face.

"Up we go," Ignis states as they reach the bottom of the coastal cliff with the high tide. Staying close to the wall, they climb vertically through the air until the mouth of the cave opens before them.

The two dragon's claws grip the remnants of Stirling's past life as they climb inside. Still on Ignis' back Stirling scans the cave, thick in shadows barely lit by the moonlight.

He mumbles in a sullen tone, "Home sweet home." With movements heavy in remorse, Stirling slides off Ignis and shuffles his way to where he remembers his fire pit being. Feeling through the dark he finds an old log that never got its chance to warm the home and tosses it into the middle of the pit with the others.

Ignis leans over Stirling's shoulder breathing life into the dead wood. Flickering light cascades around them, bringing definition back to the cave's features. Stirling searches around for the belongings he once left behind. Three years. He spent three years living in this cave. Even longer if he counted the years he spent running away here.

His eyes fall to the old windshield that had fallen and crushed his old bed. *There must have been a storm.* Kneeling he slips his fingers under the wall and lifts it enough to slide it off his old bed. In his haste, he had forgotten items precious to him. He runs his hands through the dried pine. Coming up empty handed he sits back on his heels disappointed.

A coastal wind curls around him tugging at his sleeves. With a sigh, Stirling slumps, already missing the warmth and comfort of his new home back in Patu.

Reminding himself of why he left it all behind to come here, he instinctively reaches up and runs his finger along the fresh pink scar over his eyebrow matching the thin line across the front of his neck. The muscles in his jaw quiver with incoming tears.

Laying his head beside Stirling, Ignis nudges the curly-haired boy's leg with his snout. Stirling tips over and buries his face into the soft spot behind Ignis' jaw. *"I know,"* Ignis consoles. *"I know."*

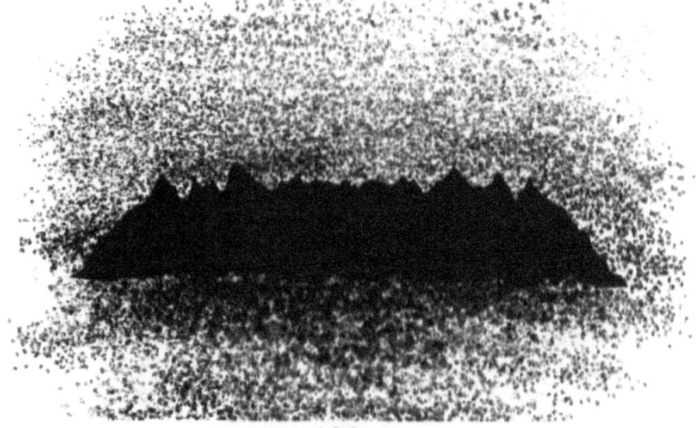

Seventeen

Crusted eyes struggle to open. Blinking the sight back into her eyes, Amiria squints at the vibrant figure sitting in a chair outside of her cell.

"Ah, you're finally awake."

Amiria recoils at the sight of her king leaning forward in his chair like an orchid blooming inside of a crypt. With a pained grunt, her shoulder reminding her of her old injury, she drags her tired and useless body into the corner of the cell. She curls into herself wishing she had a blanket to hide beneath, like when she was a child and needed a shield against the monsters in the night.

"Oh, don't be like that," King Dietrich complains. He sits back in his cushioned chair, unimpressed by his new possession. "Amiria, I am your king. You, my dear girl, of all people should not cower from me. Remember I personally chose you; you should have been honored. Why weren't you honored?"

With her knees to her chest and her spine aligned with the corner of the wall, Amiria hides her face in her arms. She wishes he would go away. Wishes he would burst, poofing into a cloud of color like the paper canons Stirling had described to her.

King Dietrich huffs, "Is there any Amiria Rey left, or did you break that fast?" A wad of spit lands in the rotten straw before the bars. King Dietrich glows, his posture straightening, "She lives."

"Why."

"Why what Amiria?" King Dietrich leans his cheek on his ringed knuckles.

"Why not just kill me." She glowers.

"Where's the fun in that?" He smirks.

Amiria speaks with earnestness, "Is this all a game to you?"

King Dietrich runs his finger across his lips as he stares up at the ceiling recalling, "Ah, have I ever told you about my strong hatred towards the Reys."

"I've witnessed you and my father feuding."

"The Reys, a lineage of field Marshals. A family who has *forgotten* which name rules this kingdom." He gets up from his seat stepping up to the bars. "Ever since I was a prince growing up beside your father, I thought of ways to end his reign. You don't understand how elated I was when his wife died and he never remarried. He had a single heir. A single girl who would not carry his name. One small girl between me and my dream. I had prayed for a son for you to marry, to give you my name, but my queen had failed me. Then I thought of ways to possibly have you killed, but you grew up so beautiful, so astonishing." King Dietrich runs his hand down the metal of her cage landing on the lock he lifts it, "I knew I had to steal you." He lets the lock fall with a thunk, "When I watched you at your exams, I was thrilled. Why? Because you did all the work for me. You were a perfect candidate for Unit Larua.

With this, I had you in some form, with you on my team. I would train you until you were only Rey in name.

But God must truly exist because your father doomed himself by engaging you to the young Gautier. I was jealous of Calix, yes, jealous I couldn't marry you myself or one of my offspring, but he was the next best thing. It meant the next Field Marshal would be a Gautier. A family more concerned with the title and status than actual power, they are controllable, even their crazy offspring are raised to take orders without question."

"Why are you telling me this?" Amiria shakes her head in confusion.

"Because Amiria," He leans into the bars, dirtying his silken robes. "I had all these ideas to make you mine, but it's as if God wants me to have you. You, my precious thing, you wrapped yourself up like a present and threw yourself at my feet. Mutiny. Amiria Rey committing Mutiny. Not even the stars could have predicted this. Everything I have done for these people has blessed me with good fortune. Tell me, Amiria, how does it feel?"

She stares idly at him, not wanting to play into his game.

"This is where you're supposed to ask me, 'Your Majesty, how does what feel?'" He pauses, waiting for her to respond, but she continues to hold her tongue. He grinds his teeth, "Say it." With Amiria still refusing to speak, King Dietrich bursts, "I SAID, SAY IT!"

"How does what feel?" she forces out.

"Ask me properly!" He strikes the metal bar with the palm of his hand.

Amiria flinches and stammers, "Your Majesty, how does what feel?"

A shadow falls over King Dietrich's face with a devilish grin as he whispers, "To lose."

Eighteen

The jade green cloak snags on a gnarled shrub. The thin twigs snap, freeing the wool fabric as Stirling continues to walk, his fingers tapping rapidly at his side. He takes in a deep breath, his lungs no longer used to the thin mountain air overwhelming his senses with the fresh aroma of pine and cedar. It feels cool on his body after half a year in the more humid weather of Patu. His shoulder brushes Ignis' wings as he hugs close to him, as if he was a child clinging to their mother in the market streets. He was raised by this forest, but these trees are no longer his family. The evidence that this was once his home, the trails created by his feet, are now reclaimed by the forest. Now hidden beneath the overgrowth and beds of moss and needles.

"*Are you sure this is going to work?*" Ignis asks, stepping over a falling tree, "*I don't know about you, but I don't want to reenact last time.*"

"I believe so. This time he knows I'm alive. Amiria had explained everything to him." Stirling searches for a reason to proceed, "He's my father. I want to see him. I want to show him who I've become."

"And what about the reason you are here?"

As if he was knocked in the gut by a branch, Stirling stumbles hunching over as he is reminded about the pit chewing away at his core, "I should tell him. My father cares about Amiria after all these years. But I honestly don't even know where to begin in rescuing her. I'm not her. I can't charge head-on. I'd be killed instantly, and that will get us nowhere."

The layered stone wall, turned green with moss and ivy, is the only thing separating them from the city as they breach through the last of the forest. Ignis mentally slaps Stirling, *"What if she is, already, you know?"*

Stirling's knees go weak at Ignis' implications. They are bending beams no longer able to support his weight until he is sitting on his heels. Hugging his arms, Stirling's fingers dig into his sleeves at the idea of Amiria at the gallows before the entire city. A city he thought he would never have to return to.

He can already hear the alarms ringing across the rooftops and he can feel the hounds nipping at his heels. He thought he was over this. He's been dealing with cities for the past half a year. He's been to cities all over Tillfalya. His mind shows him the prediction of himself standing beside Amiria with matching rope necklaces. Stirling shakes his head to keep the memories he's labeled as nightmares from coming back. His tense hands run up from his biceps to his throat and close around the delicate skin. *No—no—no no no nonononono.*

His breathing picks up as he jumps back up to his feet and begins pacing. *They won't recognize you, they won't recognize you, they won't recognize you. You have to help Amiria, Amiria, Amiria. This is for Amiria.*

He sits on a rock half buried in the earth. His stomach-churning, Stirling curls over, his face hiding in his hands. "Just give me a moment," he retches as he struggles to quash his fears that will lock his feet in place and keep him from proceeding.

Letting Stirling have his moment, Ignis passes the time watching a woodpecker hop from branch to branch listening for his next meal. Stirling breathes in sharply and throws his hands down to his lap, "Okay, I'm ready—" Fear stabs him in the chest. "No, I'm not." He hugs himself and refolds in half. Without lifting his head, he asks. "Maybe my father knows—if she's been sentenced—or not."

His father, his father who tried to kill him last time. He's about to go into a whole city that tried to kill him last time he was there. *They are not going to kill you. They are not going to kill you. They are not going to kill you.*

"Okay." Stirling stands up abruptly. "I'm ready."

The hole in the wall made long before his time is now showered in a thick coat of ivy. No one has been through here to disturb the growth. It is no longer used by those who wish to escape. He takes one step, then another. His heart beating out of sync in his chest.

The wall wavers, billowing and rippling in his swaying vision, "I'm not ready." U-turning, Stirling begins to retreat to the safety of the forest.

"Oh no you don't," Ignis says, using his muzzle to guide Stirling back around to face the wall. Stirling stares blankly at the cage barred with ivy. Ignis nudges him forward, *"Go."*

"I wish you could physically come with me." Stirling's fidgeting fingers pull the wool fabric tightly around him.

"Yeah, let me borrow your cloak. I'll blend right in," Ignis jokes light heartedly.

Stirling lets out a small breathy laugh, his fear making it hard to find solace in the humor. Frowning, he stoops before the ivy curtain, hesitantly, he weaves his fingers through it.

Ignis says impatient, "*You dragged me all the way here against my will. You can handle being on your own for a night. Plus, I'm only a thought away. I'll be here waiting when you come back.*"

Closing his eyes with a slow and steady breath, Stirling pulls back the curtain and enters the reality he had abandoned almost four years ago.

His existence is barely noticed as he wanders down the upscale neighborhood bordering the outskirts of the city. With his vibrant green cloak synched together with a golden clasp and a hood pulled down to his eyebrows, no one bothers to acknowledge the young man. His clothes are no longer worn and frayed; he appears to be another average nobleman out for an evening stroll to enjoy the natural beauty of the setting sun.

Being invisible, brings ease to his panicking heart, but that doesn't calm his twitching fingers beneath the fabric.

I am nobody here, he repeats in his head *Nobody knows who I am.*

Turning at the end of the neighborhood, he begins down the main dirt road that leads to the center of Lumierna. He, along with several other pedestrians, step to the side as a cart heading out of the city rolls by. Stirling's hazel eyes stand out below the green hood as he watches the passenger, a teenage girl in a yellow gown cradling a blue drawstring bag who is consistently checking over her shoulder. She feels him watching her and turns her attention down to him as they pass.

She has never met the boy on the side of the road. She has barely been outside of the castle grounds or away from the Rey manor. She corrects herself in her seat and faces forward. She can't describe it but for some peculiar reason, those eyes were familiar.

The wretched aroma of the city assaults Stirling's airways. He holds back the urge to cover his nose. He must present himself as the local he once was. Someone unaccustomed to the foul scent of the city will stand out as an outsider. The people living in this city will never understand the condition they are living their lives in until they experience a new way themselves. The city doesn't have to be decrepit, unwilling to change and fix the old. A vibrant and sanitary city is possible, he has seen it with his own eyes. An entire kingdom that molds and changes with time.

Pretending his heart isn't spasming in his chest, Stirling walks anonymously past the few people still congregated on the bakery's street. Most shops are already closed or closing for the night with families settling down for supper.

The bakery.

His father's bakery. Where he was born, his original home.

Stirling pivots spinning around and begins walking away. *No. I have to go in.* He turns back and takes several steps before spinning back to the opposite direction.

Two women on their way home watch the young man argue with himself as he walks back and forth.

Grinding his teeth, Stirling slows to a stop in the center of the road facing the bakery. His fingers tap nervously below his cloak as he forces the imagination he has only been out playing in the woods for the day. His mother will open the door with a friendly smile welcoming him home. She would pull him in and kiss the top of his head so many times as if she is trying to kiss each curl. He wouldn't resist as she squeezes him and tells him how much she loves him and what a great man he will grow up to be.

You can do this. Stirling bounds up the stairs but stops at the door, his fist hung in midair in front of the wood.

His fingers unfurl and run down the patched-up hole in the door created that fateful night. Breathing in deeply in hopes to ease his mind, Stirling suppresses the urge to run. He has escaped death, traveled the world, stood in front of thousands of spectators, and held his own against elite racers. If he can do all that, he can face his father.

Ignis pushes his thoughts into Stirling, *"I swear. If you don't buck up and go in there, I'm leaving you here."*

"You wouldn't," Stirling calls the bluff.

"You want to bet? Your girl might be here, but I've got a beautiful Quetzalcoatl waiting for me back home and I'm the one who can fly."

"Fine," Taking one last gulp of air, Stirling holds it deep in his lungs and focuses on his tapping fingers *index, middle, ring, pinky, ring, middle, index*. Releasing his breath, he gently knocks on the bakery's door.

Washing down his bread baked with cheese, Giles hears a light knock at the door. He sets his wooden cup down, perturbed. He isn't expecting Grace tonight and it is too kind of a knock to be a guard. There haven't been any unexpected visitors to his home since the day Amiria left on her deployment and never returned. It's not like she ever knocked anyways.

When the mystery of her disappearance causes him to toss and turn at night, he imagines she found Stirling. She had flown far away, and they are living happily in a place only they know. He will admit he misses her. Misses her barging in at any hour of the day. Misses the little girl inside the Cavalry armor and misses the daughter she had become.

Another knock slow and dying on the door gets him out of his chair, "Hold on now. I'm coming." Giles swings open the door to a well-dressed man with a green hood hanging low over his eyes, "May I help you?"

"Y-yeah." The man's young and stuttering voice doesn't match the confidence of his attire.

"What is it I can do for you?" Giles requests thinking this nobleman must be lost on his way to the castle.

"Don't freak out." The man blurts.

Giles takes a step back uncertain of what he meant by that statement. The man reveals his arm from under his cloak and displays his insignia for Giles to see. A wave of emotions capsizes Giles and the world starts to tilt. Releasing sandy blonde curls that bounce free as the hood falls back, the man lunges forward stabilizing his dazed father.

Jannell's curls. Jannell's hazel eyes.

"Stirling." It comes out as a whisper, the expelled air barely forming the syllables.

"Yeah. Father, it's me."

Stirling's lungs are compressed, rung dry as his father wraps his arms around him. Tears flood from Giles' eyes and wet his beard. His hands bunch and grip Stirling's cloak like a lifeline, "My boy, my son."

Taken aback, Stirling is delayed in returning the embrace. Confounded, he finally raises his arms and hugs his father around the shoulders.

"Oh, my son." Giles sobs, his legs giving out to the emotional stress. Stirling is dragged down to kneel with the weight of his father. The same father who believed a son should stop being coddled once they can walk on their own. The father who acted as if a child is nothing more than someone to pass their business off to.

"My son, my son." Giles repeats as his body trembles with the repairing of a broken heart. "I'm sorry, Stirling." Giles' voice is thick and catches in his throat.

"For what?" Stirling asks, his emotions lagging behind reality.

"For everything, for how I treated you, for how I'm acting now—" He breaks off making a sound somewhere between a laugh and sob. "I never thought I would get the chance to tell you how much I love you." Still gripping the cloak, he squeezes Stirling tighter, afraid this is all a cruel dream.

Stirling chokes between the loss of air in his lungs and the emotions catching up. "I love you too."

Smiling, Giles releases Stirling from his constricting wrap and wipes his red-stained face with his sleeves. He chuckles at the mess of a state he is in and sits back on his heels. Slapping his hands on his knees he says, "Let's get a better look at you."

Moving for them to stand, Giles takes a step back from Stirling who throws his cloak behind himself letting it hang like a cape. A deep timber green long-sleeved doublet that he's wearing for the first time is still crisp and clean with an unstained white tunic underneath. His worn out turnshoes are replaced with ankle high slip-on leather boots that are sized perfectly for him and his once unruly curls fall softly around his head.

Giles covers his mouth choking back another wave of tears. This man standing before him is not the boy he lost four years ago. He had thrown out a child he could not control, and a dapper man had returned to him. His son grew up without him, without his help. He stands here with the clothing of success, something he would never have obtained staying here.

"You look good." Giles finally says. "You seem like you no longer need this old baker's help."

Stirling deflates, the cloak slipping back over his shoulders as they hunch forward, "But I do. I do need your help…Or at least some comfort only you can provide."

Giles dreads the answer but asks anyways, "It's not Amiria, is it?"

Stirling raises an eyebrow. "It wasn't announced?"

"What wasn't announced?" Giles presses.

Stirling opens his mouth, but he can't say the words directly. He begins to ramble "Amiria…Amiria, she found me. It's my fault she committed those crimes. She found me in a world where we could be free. Free to be whoever we wanted to be. The Cavalry… they also found us. But I was no longer their target. Not compared to her." The tears finally catching up spill out of him as he talks. "They took her. They took her right in front of me. They took her and I couldn't do anything to stop it. I don't know what to do. Father please. I love her."

Giles internally crumbles. His heart tears into fragments that litter the floor. It's not only the news destroying him, but the sight of his only child crippled in despair. When Jannell, his mother, had died he did no more than tell him they will get through this. He never helped Stirling learn to cope with living without his mother, only taught him to carry on with a missing piece of his heart. His son is now shattering before his eyes. If he loses Amiria like this, he won't emerge the same afterwards. He will only be a husk of the boy he once was. The words *we'll get through this* are obsolete now.

Large palms press into the sides of Stirling's face, pinching his head between them. Giles leans in closer to his son. "Stirling, look me in the eye. Amiria is a tough girl. There's no way that ball of fire will let people like them snuff her out. What you can do is believe in her like she believes in you."

Stirling acquiesces and nods. Shutting his eyes, he pushes out the rest of his tears.

Giles pats Stirling's curls then pulls him into another hug. The hug is not the same as the one he had received moments ago. The hug of a person having a lost loved one returned to them. This hug is an embrace only a parent can provide. A temporary shield against all the troubles the world can use against him. Tears now soak the worn wool tunic where Stirling's face presses into his father's shoulder.

Stirling's voice is barely audible through the fabric. "I love her."

Soothingly, Giles rubs Stirling's back. "Did you get a chance to tell her?"

Stirling pulls away, digging the heels of his hands into his eyes. "No, yes, sort of—I'm an idiot."

Giles sighs with a smile. "You're not stupid. You're just young." Giles pulls out a chair. "Here sit, tell me, do you know how to help her?"

Stirling slumps his body into the chair letting his forehead bounce on the table. "No." He grumbles.

Giles rubs Stirling between his shoulder blades. "Let's take an emotional break, you hungry?"

"No," Stirling says stubbornly, his stomach protesting with a growl.

Giles rests his hands on his hips. "Let an old man feed his child. Plus, I want to hear everything."

"About Amiria?" Stirling looks up with his head still resting on the table.

"No. Not yet. I'm going to make you a snack and I want to hear all about this dragon of yours. I want to hear about this new land you live in and any friends you made." Giles turns to the pantry and begins pulling out ingredients.

Stirling lifts his head with a raised eyebrow. "Really?"

Peering over his shoulder, he says, "Well, yeah. I want to know about your life." He touches the bowl in front of him and frowns, "I had refused to participate in it. I barely even know you." Stirling stares at his father's hunched shoulders while Giles stirs the bowl's contents in a prolonged silence.

"His name is Ignis," Stirling begins, his words slow and deliberate. "My dragon, his name is Ignis, and he is my family. We crossed paths when I was ten." Stirling sped through his time training on the island, skipping to how Amiria almost killed him the first time they met. How close they grew over the years. How he asked her to look after his father for him. How he wished he tried harder in convincing her to run away with him. If she had disappeared with him that night, they might never had been able to follow her.

A new spark flickers in his eyes as he tells him about Eve, Bernard, and the rest of the village. Involuntarily, Stirling stands from his chair as he talks. His hands move wildly as he explains; describing the village's ale house and the group singing and dancing, the festivals, and the saint's days they love to celebrate, how close they all are.

His feet dance across the floor with twirling arms as he reenacts the games. How he outraced each person, the outlandish move he pulled off in the trick contest, the complexity of the agility run, and exhilarating fun of dogging the color projectiles.

He doesn't hide the troubles beneath wins. He describes the downfalls as much as the highs.

He pauses, staring at the empty staircase, with a new longing in his chest. He tells him about Quilan, the number one racer, and how he believed him to be a pompous jerk. But in reality, he was an exploited soul, created to appease the masses, but he is also more than that. He is someone who is more focused on listening than talking. Someone who will never judge you. A friend who will always stay by your side no matter what. A person he wants to keep in his life forever now.

Stirling smiles as he tells him how, yes, the village believed in him, but so did Quilan, and rightfully so as he took the number two racer spot.

Giles hides the tear escaping here and there as he listens in wonder. His defiant child. His reckless and disobedient son. This is Jannell's masterpiece. He did not raise this child. He could never have raised someone like this. This child grew up to become who he is today because his mother taught him to never stop dreaming.

Stirling slows his excitement as Amiria reappears into his story, making her debut in his life once again. How they almost were together in a home he had built.

He stops, his head falling back so he stares up at the rafters as if the rest of the story is transcribed in the wood grains. His neck bobs as he swallows. Rolling his head, he looks to Giles. "Father."

Giles hides the food he had prepared behind his back and answers, "Yes?"

"Thank you."

Giles is taken aback. "Thank you?" His eyebrows knit together. "For what?"

Stirling turns his whole body to face him. "For everything, raising me, teaching me how to cook, giving me a roof over my head…until I was sixteen. But if you didn't push me out… There's a chance I would never have become friends with Amiria. I would never have run from this island, never found a place where I truly belong. Living in those mountains." Stirling swipes his hand in the direction. "I didn't just learn how to survive. I learned what it's like to live. I sometimes think about who I would have been if I didn't leave that day from this bakery. Would I have given up on everything? Or would I be dead. Would Amiria have continued on her straight path with the Cavalry, or would she still have deviated on her own?"

"There is no reason to dwell on the what ifs. Now eat up." Giles slides a plate full of fresh gingerbread on the table.

Stirling laughs back his swelling emotions. How did he not smell this cooking while he was absorbed in his memory trail? He sits down at the table across from his father and shares a loaf of gingerbread.

Nineteen

I'm already tired of doing this every night." William, the shorter of the two with copper hair, complains. His face is still bruised where Amiria's heel had struck him.

"It hasn't even been a week yet," Robert refutes, holding a small basket containing a scarce amount of food and a clay bottle with water.

"An incredibly long week." William sags.

Robert sighs, "It's been a long year."

The candlelight in the hall wavers as a heavy presence weighs down the air. Slowing to a stop under the immense pressure they turn inward facing each other. They pause breathing in the air between them before continuing to find Calix at their heels. His pale eyes glow in the shadows of his eyebrows from the torch's light.

"Ss-ir Gautier," Robert stutters, nearly dropping the basket. "Is there something we could assist you with?"

Calix's eyes disappear into the shadows of their sockets as his lips curl upwards, "I'll take the provisions to the girl. I have words from King Dietrich to pass on to her. So, it won't be any bother to me."

William and Robert exchange glances.

Calix continues, "You two can run along and do whatever it is you guards do."

"Y-yes sir," Robert manages, the basket still tucked in his arms.

Calix's fingers curl around the rim of the basket. He leans in closer, his voice ghostly, "Go."

Robert weaves his fingers through William's and tugs him back from Winged Rider, leaving the basket behind in Calix's clutches as they turn heel and scamper off.

Steading his breathing, Calix pushes upon the door to the main keep. He fumbles to hold the basket as his heart is ripped from his chest and thrown to the floor. His decaying body numbly carries him to the cell where the girl's paling features are beginning to blend in with her tomb. Her dark hair that once flew feather light in the wind now shrouds her face in a mangle heap. A single thinning hand lays out reached through the bars.

His feet slip out from beneath him. Caving in, he crumbles to his knees before her. Setting the basket down to the side, he scoops up her hand, cradling it in his own. Her skin is cold and gray against his. He thumbs the bracelet her father gave to her as a little girl around her wrist. The autumn colors standing out in the orange light from the forge, "At least they let you keep this."

He rotates her arm so the inside faces up. He covers his mouth with his free hand in revulsion as he takes in the site of the burned X over her insignia, now red and festering.

Still holding her hand as if it is as delicate as a butterfly's wing, he reaches over brushing the hair from her face. Even in this state she is breathtaking. A stunning masterpiece only a higher power could create. She is a fallen angel. Her wings stripped from her back as she lived in the clouds with nothing and no-one to catch her as she fell. She is a creature of the heavens doomed to lay wasting on the burning land.

He tried to be the one to catch her, to save her. He wanted her more than anything. He still wants her more than anything. She consumes his heart and mind. She has overthrown the free space in his head and has planted her flag. The beating of his heart seizes, sending a last pulse through his body as he stills.

Amiria's eyes flutter open. Her lips hang partially opened with her soft and shallow breaths. Something is warm around her hand. The calloused fingers of a working man. "Stirling?" She whispers weakly.

Calix's eyes dull and his nostrils flare. He clenches his jaw along with his grip, tightening it around her small hand. Amiria winces, the bones in her hand beginning to shift and pop under the constriction. Wondering what is causing her pain, she looks up. The whites of her eyes show as they open wide and panicked. The instinct to flee takes command. Mustering up all the energy she can, she pulls back on her arm.

Calix holds firm on his control of her hand, trapping her in his snare. His face now wiped of all emotion.

She grips the bar with her free hand, her cheeks flushing with rage while she stares her hunter in the eye, "What more do you want from me!"

Calix's voice is colder than the cell, "I want everything from you."

"You've already taken me from my everything," she growls.

He pulls back on her arm forcing her face to press against the bars, "It isn't enough."

"Ah!" She gasps, unable to fight back. Her shoulders on the verge of tearing from its socket as the rest of her body remains stuck on the opposite side of the bars.

He leans in with snarling words, "Why do you haunt me? Why can't I carry on with my life? Why do I want you more than air "

Digging deep inside of herself Amiria finds a smile and puts it on for display, "Till death do us part."

The smile on Calix's lips never reaches his eyes, "I can make sure of that." Already leaning in, he closes the last of the gap pressing his lips against hers. Amiria jerks her head fixed against the bars. He removes his lips and throws her hand to the floor.

Amiria reels in her hand before it can be taken captive again. Calix barely notices as he picks up the basket. Removing the canister of water, he uncorks the lid. She watches in horror as he turns it over, dumping out the contents.

Her eyes tracking his movements she follows him as he backs up to the forge.

"Goodbye Amiria," he drops the basket into the infernal coals. The wicker basket immediately ignites into flames. With a perfect smile Calix disappears from the main keep.

Furious, like a lion trapped in a cage, Amiria rattles the bars belting a roar no one but her, Calix, and the moon can hear.

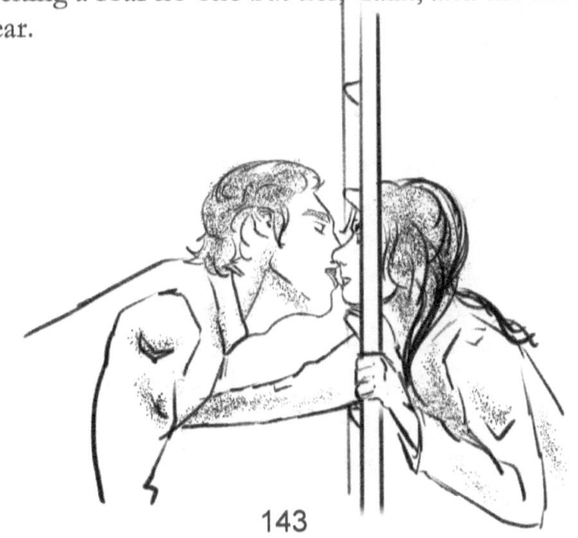

Twenty

I t's like he was transported back in time. Stirling rolls over on his old mattress, opening his eyes to his childhood house. Now in hindsight, it was a simple time where his only worry was the next time, he would see Ignis.

For nostalgic purposes, Stirling slides himself out of bed and stands at the window. A timber frame of his old escape. Raising an eyebrow he reaches down, picking up a wooden dragon worn smooth from years of exposure in a cave that sits perched on the windowsill.

"Amiria?" He wonders aloud.

He thinks back to the state his home of three years was in when he arrived back in Wyverna. The picture finally becomes clear, it wasn't a storm. Well not a storm formed by nature. He rubs his thumb over the dragon and sets it down. Brushing the four years of dust off the stool he takes a seat.

"*Good morning.*" Stirling wishes to Ignis. His vision skips past the old thatched and wood shingled roofs of the wilting city to the mountainous peaks. A monstrous beacon emerging from the pine riddled forest.

Stirling tilts his head examining how the mountains resemble fence posts around a corral, keeping the farmer's sheep within his land.

"Why do you have to wake up so early?" Ignis responds with a yawn.

"Why are you complaining? You've got nothing to do today but sleep."

Ignis bobs his head to the truth, *"When are you coming back? Taika isn't the best company, you know?"*

"I don't know. I've got no information yet. There's been no word on the street about Amiria."

"Is that good or bad?"

"I honestly don't know…Wait hold on." Stirling turns from the window as his father calls his name from downstairs. *"Hey, my father is calling me."*

"Boy, does this bring me back."

Stirling stands up from the window as Giles calls his name again, "Yeah!"

"Come downstairs. There's someone I want you to meet." He calls up.

Confused on who his father would want him to meet without jeopardizing either of their lives, Stirling throws on his long-sleeved doublet, keeping the arm pieces down. He calmly travels down the stairs but halts on the bottom step. Stirling's eyes flit back and forth between his father and a woman with fair skin, red hair, and green doll-like eyes.

"Stirling, this is Grace. Grace, this is my son Stirling." Giles introduces.

Grace covers her mouth with her hands as it drops open. Her eyes waver, seeking some form of affirmation from Giles, unable to find the words on her own. Stirling cocks his head eyeing her suspiciously.

Taking a step closer to Giles, Grace asks behind her hands, "So it is all true?"

"Yes." Giles nods. His eyes are still reading Stirling's reactions.

Locking his eyes with his father, Stirling points at Grace, "Who exactly is she?"

Giles rests his hand on Grace's shoulder as she drops her hands to her side, "Grace and I are seeing each other."

Stirling's heart falls to his stomach, "You're what?"

"It's an honor to finally meet you." Grace holds out her hand. Stirling stares at it like it was covered in barbs. Grace retracts her hand but continues to talk in nervous banter, "I've never seen Giles glow like this before. I almost didn't believe him until you came down the stairs."

Stirling's eyes flip from her to his father. He steps back with a slow and steady shake of his head. "No." He spins on his heel to face the stairs, "No. No."

Grace bites her frowning lip as her clouding eyes find Giles. Stirling's repeating "No's" carry up the staircase as he retreats up them.

"Let me talk to him." Giles reassuringly squeezes her shoulder before following his son up to the second floor. "Stirling?" He says at the top of the stairs.

Shaking his head, Stirling paces the small room. His long legs cover the short distance in only several steps before having to turn around.

"Stirling." Giles reaches out to grasp Stirling's wrist, "Stirling, stop."

"DON'T!" Stirling yanks his arm away before Giles can touch him. His voice still straining, he lowers his volume, "Don't—touch me. I just." He turns his shoulder to his father, "I just need a moment." He rests his hand on his hip and aggressively rubs his eyes with the other.

Giving Stirling a wide girth of space, Giles steps over to the table and leans his hip against it. Stirling pinches the brim of his nose, watching his father out of the corner of his red rimmed eyes.

"What?" Giles shrugs.

"What?" Stirling repeats showing anger in his voice. Stirling throws his hand with a frustrated laugh, "What? How about mother? That's what."

"We're not doing this." Giles rolls his eyes along with his head.

"Do what?" Stirling bites.

"Argue." Giles says as plain as day, keeping his voice steady. The muscles in Stirling's jaw pop as he grinds his teeth. He refuses to look at his father. Giles sighs, closing his eyes he takes the time to breathe then says, "I still love your mother."

Stirling scoffs.

Giles glares, his voice firm, "Stop your antics and listen to me."

Stirling rolls his shoulders.

"Are you done?"

Stirling opens his mouth with contempt.

"Are—you—done!" Giles emphasizes each word to drive it through his son's thick skull. Stirling clamps his jaw biting back his tongue. Giles eyes him momentarily, letting the silence hang between them. Testing if Stirling will speak over him or not. Satisfied, Giles continues, "I still love your mother. I will never stop loving her. But as much as you don't like to admit it, she's gone. And while you went gallivanting in the woods," Stirling hides his face from his father. "I remained here. Days turned into months that turned into years in this empty house. Stirling, I'm not replacing your mother, but just how you found a new home, and new family. It didn't replace Wyverna and us here. Good or bad you hold the two places in your heart separate. I have found love again, but the love for your mother will always remain."

Love again? To love again means there's no soulmate. There's no person you are meant to be with over the others. Stirling looks out at the window, the sound of the morning market beginning to arise. Could he love again? If there is no Amiria, could he find another friend that understands him on the deepest level to fall in love with. His heart beats with a,*yes,* but he pushes it away. h

Stirling hangs his head, "I need some air."

"Stirling, talk to me," Giles persists, stepping forward.

Stirling glances up for a moment, "I-I don't really know what I think." He pauses suddenly concerned with the floorboards. He doesn't lift his gaze as he speaks, "I should head out before they realize who I am." Stirling picks up his cloak folded on the table, "I'll try and stop by again." He stops at the stairs and looks back at his father, finally making eye contact, "I love you."

"Stirling." Giles says as his son disappears down the stairs.

Stirling stops at Grace's hope filled eyes staring up at him from the table. "It was uh-nice to meet you," he mutters.

Her face falling, Stirling exits out the front door, closing it softly behind him. Disheartened, Giles stops at the last step and slumps down. Grace gets up from her seat and settles herself next to him. Holding out her hand supportively, Giles accepts it.

"Ignis." Stirling calls out. His leather shoes pad along the dusty city road.

"Yeah? Wait. Let me guess. You and your father fought. Surprise to no one."

"I'll admit I started the argument. But he didn't have to spring he has a new woman on me like that. He could have told me he was in a relationship before she was standing in the bakery." Stirling is numb as he wanders aimlessly. Following the direction of the flowing crowd.

Ignis questions Stirling's excuse of his actions, "*How would that have made a difference?*"

"*Well first, less of a surprise, so I would have… I guess it could have… Shut up, Ignis.*" Stirling ends deflated.

"*Hey, you wanted to talk about it with me. Are you sour because your father also made some good points?*"

"*You're supposed to be on my side.*" Stirling pouts as he is ganged up against.

"*Oh sorry. How could he ever love again.*" Ignis' voice over the top.

"*Hold on, somethings going on.*" Stirling changes the topic noticing the traffic he was following like a school of fish had led him to an overflowing town square.

Stirling almost doubles over as panic wracks through his body. He doesn't know the faces with the ropes around their necks, but someone does. To someone that is their father, mother, brother, sister, or friend. To someone here in this crowd that is their Amiria.

He sees her face in all of them. They hold their heads up strong, standing for the time high above the crowd. The guards who stand watch shift uneasily on their feet. None of them can look at the condemned. They struggle to hold their emotions neutral as they find items in the town square to occupy their attention.

Bile rises, climbing its way out of Stirling's stomach to the back of his throat. He slaps his mouth holding back the rushing contents. Backing out he desperately shoves his way out of the still forming crowd. Barely clearing the last of the bystanders, he leans his forearm against a shop and spews his stomach's contents.

"HEY!" An authoritative voice calls out from behind him, "You can't be shoving people like that." A guard in a navy-blue gambeson and freshly cleaned chainmail grabs Stirling's shoulders, whipping him around to face him.

Stirling's hood slips from his head, his curls springing to life. The young guard with red rimmed eyes full of fury clasps his gloved hand around Stirling's wrist and pushes up his sleeve revealing his scarred insignia, his eyes soften and flick back up to Stirling's hazel ones. Stirling witnesses the recognition reveal behind the guard's broken eyes. The young man's face twists at the sight of Stirling as if it deepened fresh wounds and yanks Stirling's sleeve back down.

The guard releases his grip, letting Stirling's quivering hand fall dead at his side. Stirling flinches, sucking in a sharp breath as the guard reaches forward. He slowly exhales as a shadow shades his face, his hood obscuring his eyes, but his body stays rigid against the wall.

"You better watch where you are going, or you might end up in the main keep." The guard says under his breath.

Baffled, Stirling stands idle against the shop, unable to grasp what is happening.

Rolling his eyes the guard grabs Stirling's arm shoving in the direction away from the town square, "Go on get!"

Stirling restrains himself from running as he leaves the peculiar guard and the horrific scene behind. He doesn't dare look over his shoulder, *"Ignis I'm—uh—I'm on my way back."*

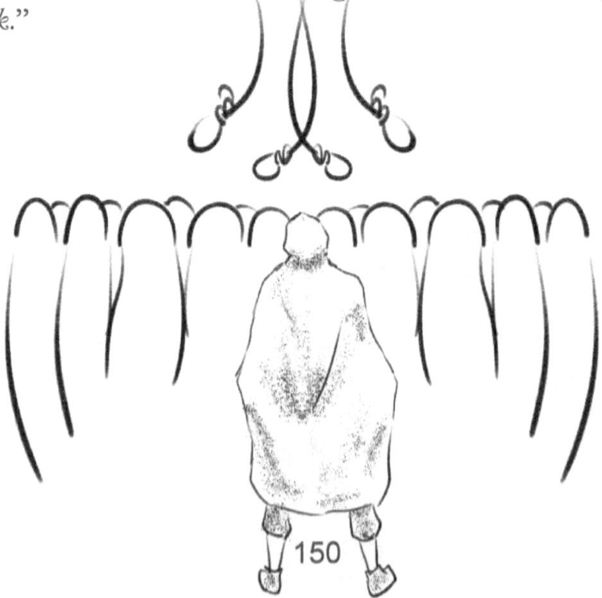

Twenty-One

"You still alive?" The apathetic male voice wakes Amiria up.

How long have I been sleeping? Her eyelids pry apart, exposing the dull and lifeless irises. Blinking several times, the cracking ceiling slowly comes into focus. Without moving her head, her eyes roll in their sockets to Clyde standing at the bars of her cell.

She twitches her shoulders in a barely noticeable shrug, "Perhaps. This could be the underworld for all I know, and you are the devil." The words sting her dry and coarse throat, but she still ends her comment with a smile. With a grunt, she rolls up onto her left side shielding her oozing right arm.

Clyde scowls, "You always have something to say, don't you?"

"Yes." She scoots back leaning against the wall to support her weakening state. The King doesn't need her healthy, he just needs her alive. She peers past Clyde, "You don't have your helpers this time."

He crosses his arms scanning the frail girl. Her olive skin paled to a grayish tint, the heavy purple bags under her eyes, "I don't need them."

"Ha." She lets out, "You're as wimpy as ever. Only willing to face me alone when you think I'm too weak to stand." Amiria insults, discreetly tucking her legs under her into a low squat in a disguise as only getting comfortable.

"I'm not afraid of you anymore." Clyde throws out. "I'm the stronger one now."

"You wanna bet?" Amiria leaps to her feet and across the room.

Fear on his face Clyde almost trips over his heels as he backsteps away from the bars. The metal rattles as Amiria rams her entire being into them. Her mutilated arm reaches out clawing for Clyde.

His heart is pounding as he stands out of reach. Her gnarled fingers a thread away from grabbing his navy-blue gambeson. With her face pressed to the bars she drops her arm and bursts into a frenzied laugh. Her teeth clack together halting her laughter, her facial features turning as cold as the stone around her, "You're not strong. You only prey on the weak to make yourself feel big."

Clyde, eyes red and puffy, hides his shaking hands behind him as he grips his right forearm, "At least I'm not fighting alone in a battle I already lost. Give it up Amiria, you look pathetic."

"At least I'm fighting. Pathetic is someone who continues to follow orders to keep his life comfortable at the cost of others." Amiria spits not only her words but a wad of saliva on the ground between Clyde's feet.

Clyde's face falls flat his body sagging with the weight of something Amiria can't see. His gaze skips to the small window at the top of her cell wall, "Is it true?"

"What?" Amiria's face twists in confusion.

"The rumors." He hops back to Amiria, his voice unusually small, "About you and the fugitive."

Amiria's lips curl inwards until they all but disappear into a thin line. Her fingers gripped around the steel bars turning white.

"I see." Clyde backs up several steps. So, he *was* correct this morning at the hanging. Clicking his heels together he turns about face. Holding his shoulders back he composes himself and steps out of the main keep leaving Amiria alone once again.

The sound of the door clicking shut slaps Amiria. Releasing her hold on the bars, she staggers several steps back and collapses in the middle of the cell.

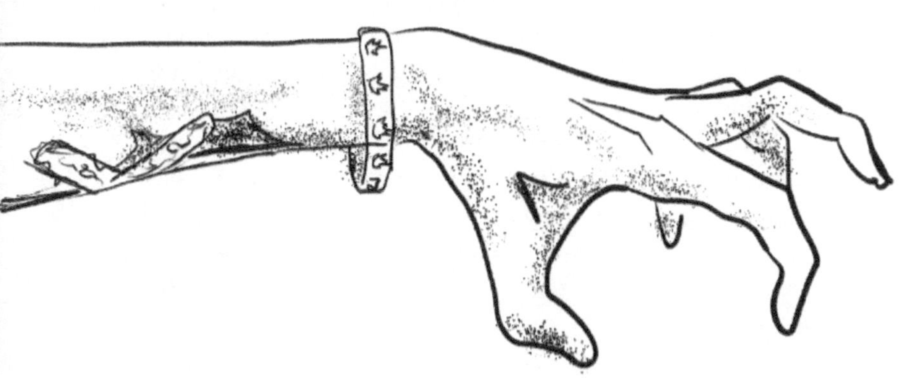

Twenty-Two

Seagulls flock around the single harbor in Wyverna. They surround the ships rocking in the port waiting for scraps to be tossed. The buildings of the port town Kitlsbo line the sea wall and are built on top of each other in apartment-like terraces. Some of the more lavish homes stand solo on stilts over the lapping water for ship captains to flaunt their wealth.

Up the catwalks connecting the homes and spread along the carved foot paths of the cliffside, hides the Winged Cavalry. They watch from above, camouflaged against the stone. Each member is chosen for a keen eye that can see far out into the sea for ships or for trouble down on the dock.

Half-lidded, Nellie lazily watches the pestering birds squawk as they are disturbed by a fisherman shooing them away from his morning catch. She was sent to the only coastal town in Wyverna, so she made the best of it by fixing herself a hammock from an old net. The corners are securely hooked to the saddle of her dragon that is perched on one of the hand carved walkways. She hangs with a leg free, suspended over a deadly drop to the chimneys and tops of warping roofs.

She hates the rotting fish town she's been forced to live in. Everything in this town looks and feels as if it is being eaten away by the salt in the air and from the water thrown over the town during each storm. The harsh cyclones that rush across the ocean always stop to clean its shoes and leave its worst at Wyverna's doorstep before entering over the pass.

Several months ago, when she was deployed across the waters to Uviktiland, she was ecstatic to see more than the seaweed of this harbor and the ever-expanding field of blue. She was back with Garret and Warrick from her old class. They were going to see a new land. They were going to be real members of the Cavalry. They were going to do something with their careers.

Who would have thought. Amiria the relentless prodigy. The perfect soldier. The girl bred to become the Field Marshal; hand sculpted since birth. The last person she ever expected to even dismiss an order, would be the root cause of it all.

She closes her eyes thinking back to her class days. How she hated Amiria. Everyone in the class did, everyone in their surrounding age group did. She made them look deplorable in comparison. No matter how hard they would practice they couldn't compare. They were nothing but straw dummies in the eyes of their instructor, just objects for her training.

Nellie laughs. I guess you never really know who people are on the inside.

Maybe one day another offer will come along again, and she will no longer be subjected to the smell of low tide.

"Hmm?" She cranes her neck as movement catches the corner of her eye. A man on a small paddle boat follows the rock shore away from the harbor to another cove out of sight. "Now what could you be up to?" She wonders.

Climbing back on to the saddle of her dragon, she reels in her netted hammock. With a click of her tongue, she steers her sandy colored dragon along the walkway. It scampers the narrow and vertical path with ease as its talons pierce the rock wall until she is above the cove.

Silently, she watches as the man pulls out a line winder, a two-prong fork carved from bone with a hemp line. He drops in the hand line, slowly unraveling it as the weighted fishhook sinks into the shallow depths.

She doesn't confront him. Something in her gut tells her not to. She sits back in the saddle and observes. He can't be one of the fishermen, they all go out together on the larger vessels. If he had a fisherman's insignia, he would not be hiding in this cove discreetly fishing.

Pulling a salted meat from her pack Nellie nibbles on her snack. He won't be going anywhere soon so neither will she. This is her job correct? To watch the ocean and the people in it.

Nodding off, her body jerks awake. The man is reeling in his second catch. With the flounder flopping in his boat, he swiftly stashes it under some canvas rags with the first. Winding up his line, he hides the small line-winder in a pouch on his hip and picks up his oars.

Above the port town, Nellie ties her dragon to the stable's posts. Keeping her eye on the man, she leaps down the multitude of rickety staircases with rusted points that groan at each of her impacts. Reaching the ground level, she becomes a shark in a school of fish as the people of the town muddied together move in unison as if an invisible force surrounds her. No one, not even the man, knows who she is tailing. Everyone lowers their gaze praying it isn't them.

They leave behind the water view homes belonging to the fisherman, mariners, and ship chandlers. They pass

the buildings at the entrance of the pass where the sun
light still shines belonging to the specialized harbor
merchants like the fishermen, salt makers, net weavers,
and fish salters. They don't stop at the homes of average
workers every town has, grocers, bakers, glovers, roofers,
and the carpenters who built the contraptions climbing
the walls of the town.

Deep into the pass where the sun only shines at high
noon are dock workers, the people who clean up after the
fish gutters, and the ones who clean the barnacles from
the ships.

Several children run out of a one room house that is
thrown together from the scraps of other buildings. The
small children orbit around the man she's been
following's legs. They jump and skip excitedly that their
father is home while a pregnant woman with a swollen
belly greets him at the door with a kiss.

Like a predator waiting in the tall grass, Nellie watches
the family disappear inside. She checks up the pass to the
harbor town. No one walks down here unless they are the
transporters carrying the cargo into the kingdom. She
emerges from the shadows and steps up to the dilapidated
home. Hardening her features, she knocks on the door
with a closed fist.

The man opens the door ajar enough to peak out with
a single eye. Nellie touches the door with the tip of her
index finger and pushes. He doesn't resist her as the door
slowly swings open.

"Please, not in front of my children," he begs under
his breath.

Nellie's lips remain sealed as she closes the door
behind her. Her thoughts are preoccupied on the
pregnant woman paling at the single table top in the
entire house with the two fish laid before her ready for
cleaning. Her eyes scan the small and empty space. The

three children sit huddled on a woven seaweed mat that must be their bed.

Her eyes drag away from the children back to the man, "I could kill you here on the spot. You have been caught committing two acts against the kingdom. You have been seen fishing without a Fisherman's Insignia and you have stolen from King Dietrich. I should remove your hands before you're hanged."

The man's throat bobs as he gulps. "I understand, ma'am, but please spare my wife. Our children need a mother, and she has another on the way."

Her eyes skip back to the wife and children, each of them with sunken cheeks and visible bones beneath their paper skin. "I said I could, and I should. Not that I would."

"Pardon me?" The man's face was already sunken in with fear.

"I'm only citing you with a warning. Next time you might not be so lucky." Her voice lowers. "I will not defend you against another member of the Cavalry, but today I will not be turning you in."

A clatter comes from the table as the pregnant woman drops the cleaning knife. Her face turning red she doubles over covering her mouth as she weeps openly. Her husband stands staring at Nellie astonished.

"W-what do I owe you?" he stammers.

"To be more careful and take care of your children." Nellie nods at the faces huddled in the corner. Turning on a coin she leaves the bewildered family behind.

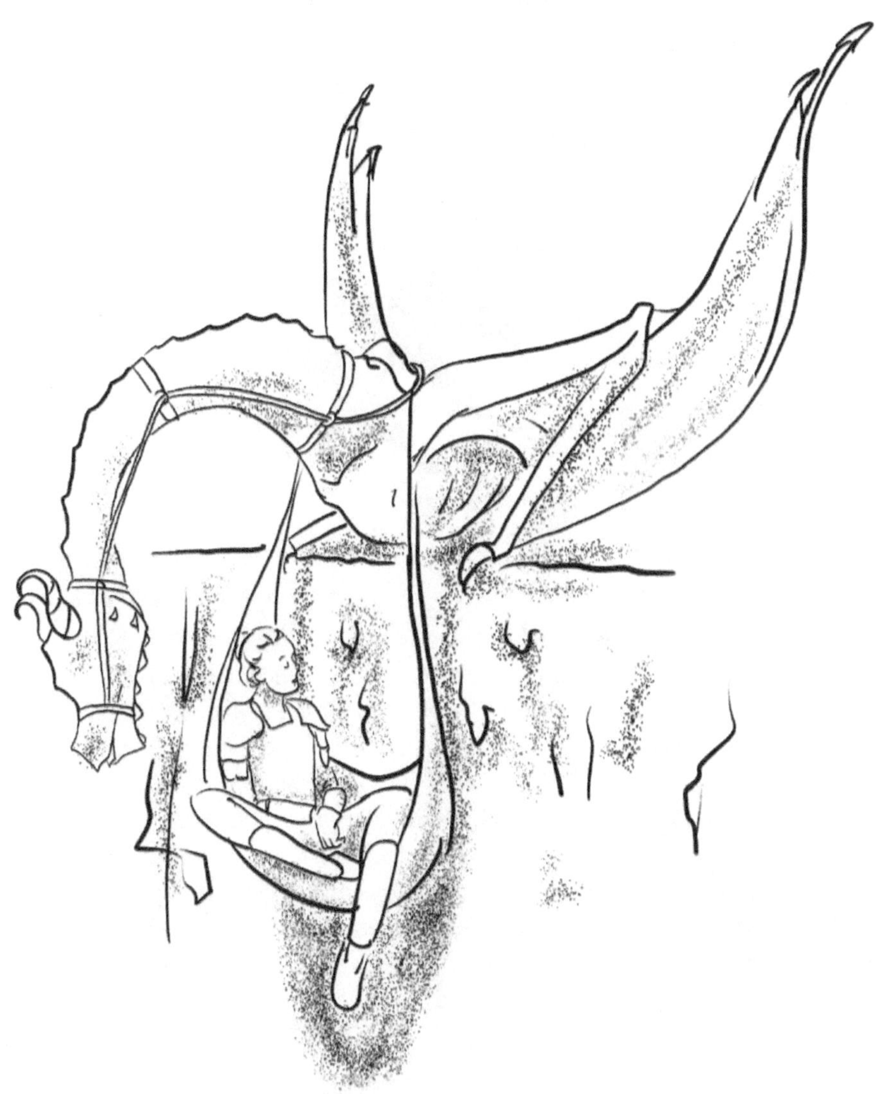

Twenty-Three

In in the silence of the night, Ignis swoops undetected over the castle grounds. He's an owl flying out from the trees, invisible to the mice below. Stirling's curls flop in the wind as he swings from the bottom of a rope attached to Ignis. He scans the ground past his foot hooked through a loop at the end of the rope.

"Good. No one guards the back." He says. They will be in and out before anyone even knows they were there.

Back flapping as they reach the lonely tower, Ignis hovers Stirling in front of the minuscule window. Stirling stretches out his arm reaching for the bars. The more he leans the more his foot counterbalances keeping him the same distance from the window.

Ignis rolls his eyes and gives Stirling a boost swinging him closer to the window. Stirling's fingers slip around the cool metals as he finally takes hold.

With her cell lit by moonlight, Amiria sits up as she hears a whispering voice, "Amiria, psst. Amiria."

Her black silk hair is neatly pulled back and her mauve cotehardie is only lightly ruffled as she peers up at the narrow window. "Stirling!" She yelps, leaping to her feet.

"Yeah, I need you to stand back." He instructs.

"Okay." She agrees. Stepping back, she presses her back against the cell bars, unable to retreat any further. Her hands shoot to her face blocking the light as if someone turned on the sun. Metal melts and stone cracks from the fire chewing away at the base of the window.

Holding onto the side of the tower, Stirling loops the rope he was swinging from around the weakened window and uses his teeth to pull the knot tight. He shimmies safely to the side of the window on the perfect foot and hand holds of the uneven stone structure. Ignis begins to pump his wings, straining the rope. With a boom, the barred window burst from the tower. It rips from the frame, nearly taking out Stirling.

Shaking off the close disaster, Stirling climbs up to the now open window. He ignores the rough edges as he drapes his arms through and pokes his head inside. At the sight of him, Amiria leaps up wrapping her arms around his neck. Her feet dangling in the air as he holds her up.

"I knew you would come for me," she cries. "I love you, Stirling Bakere."

"Hold on tight," he tells her.

He reaches back, grasping the rope once again. Ignis slowly backs up, sliding Amiria free from her doom. Her arms wrap tighter around Stirling's neck as the inner bailey threatens their demise ten stories beneath their feet.

"Take me home," she says, burying her face into his neck, "so we can live together in a home you built."

He rests his head on hers, "As you wish."

"What if?" Stirling says, coming back from his daydream.

"Not going to work," Ignis, already having seen what Stirling is going to say, stops him from saying his outlandish idea out loud as they hide on a bluff overlooking the south towers of the castle.

The last time Stirling observed Amiria from a bluff she was a stranger to him. He saw her on a surface level, the character she was written as by her father, by Wyverna. She cut her strings and rewrote her scenes, refusing to be the Cavalry's puppet.

"I didn't even say the idea." Stirling pouts, scanning the luxurious architecture of the castle. It is a maze of wings, towers, and bridges. He doesn't know which one, but one of these windows contains the girl who became his best friend and the woman he fell in love with.

"You don't need to. Every idea you've had will get you killed."

Stirling scoffs, "Not...*every* idea."

Ignis rolls his head to look him in the eye, *"Us flying to the castle, dead. You climbing that wall, dead. You waltzing in there asking for directions, let me guess. Oh yeah. Dead."*

"I had other ideas," Stirling grumbles, his words dragging and dying off.

"Okay, let's hear them," Ignis sits back prepared to listen.

"Well—we could—" Stirling talks with his hands, "Or how about—"

"Waiting." Ignis sings.

"Shut up, Ignis."

Twenty-Four

King Dietrich waves his hand impassively. "You're dismissed." Behind the strawberry wood desk that's red tinted grains resemble spilt blood, King Dietrich leans back in his chair.

"Yes, sire." Clyde leans forward in a deep bow. He had finished giving his daily report of Amiria's health and state of mind.

King Dietrich's face never changes during these meetings in his private cabinet. Clyde will provide him with his intel then be dismissed. He still has never been told why the king insists on keeping her locked in there instead of hanging her and being done with it.

Most days, but not today, Calix Gautier is standing beside the king. Unlike King Dietrich, Calix's face isn't disinterested, it's as cold and sharp as a sword. Clyde is never able to manage more than a quick glance at the unsettling features with eyes that are slicing him apart. He much rather keeps his eyes forward on the king who always acts as if he has somewhere better to be.

Stiffly, Clyde retreats from the cabinet but not before catching General Gautier's eye as she enters the room.

Her narrow face leers at him, making him instantly regret meeting it as a shiver runs down his spine. He hops aside and bows respectfully to her before escaping through the doors.

"Is he always so timid?" General Gautier's voice is sour as she stops in front of King Dietrich's desk.

"I don't get to know *guards*." He raises his lip at the idea. He sits up straight. "What I do know is you've decided something was important enough to enter my cabinet without notifying me beforehand. What emergency can you be having, General, that warrants this intrusion?"

"Your Majesty, I know you are aware of the Reys' predicament. The fact they have no heir?" Her smile cuts across her face.

"I'm aware. What are you getting at," King Dietrich steeples his hands and presses it to his mouth as he awaits the answer he is wanting.

"With Sir Rey on a noticeably cognitive decline after the arrest of his daughter, I am unsure of how long he can uphold his position. I have two healthy children who are fit to take over the duties of field Marshal at this moment and a third who will be ready soon." She explains, unknowingly feeding into King Dietrich's wishful plans.

"You believe the Gautiers are suited to take over as the highest ranking in the Winged Cavalry?"

"More than suited. I am looking out for the Cavalry's best interest and my family is ready to make that sacrifice."

King Dietrich struggles to keep his features placid. Life continues to fall in perfect place for him. He has to do nothing but let fate guide the people and world around him and everything lines up perfectly. It's as if he has the powers of a god. Whatever he wishes comes true. "I understand the benefits regarding the Cavalry but explain to me what I, your king, will gain from this?"

"I predict under a new field Marshal, the king will have his entire hand on the Cavalry." General Gautier smirks.

King Dietrich smiles knowingly.

The cool evergreen breeze rolls down from the mountains filtering out the pungent aroma of the city, forcing the wretched cloud back down to the lower districts. Calix breathes in the fresh air as he strolls across one of the several bridges connecting tops of towers of the castle. The intermittent shadows of the pillars holding up the bridge's roof temporarily casts over him as he passes through.

Dark braided hair that starts in two French braids down the sides of her head whip through the air. Kinsey stands one foot on the hand railing, the other suspended out several stories up as she spins around a pillar in the center of the bridge.

"Hello, older brother," her voice is artificially high pitched. She plops herself down on the railing sticking one leg out.

Calix slows to a stop before reaching her barricade. One side of his lip raises and he forces air to hiss through his gritted teeth. His eyes slide up the leg blocking his walking path to her smiling face, "I could walk around—or—I could tip you over."

Before she can reply, Calix snaps out his wrist seizing her ankle. Kinsey doesn't flinch, her top lip tucking into her bottom as she pouts, "Yes, you could, and you wouldn't feel an ounce of regret." She lifts her leg while leaning back. Eight nimble fingers hook around the railing keeping her from diving to the castle gardens as she teeters over the edge.

She closes her eyes, embracing the floating feeling. Pinky, ring, middle, she removes all fingers but the index to hold her up from an inevitable death. Calix mutters a series of slurs beneath his breath and pushes down on her ankle seesawing her up to a standing position.

Her lips curl into a foxlike smile, "Aw, you do care."

"What do you want?" Calix grunts, pushing past her.

Like a contortionist, her spine bends backwards, her head rolling to look behind her following her brother, "Father has been boasting about you."

He doesn't slow his pace as he speaks over his shoulder, "And?"

Each of her limbs move loosely in their joints, her spinal cord flexing like the top of a tree in the wind as she stalks after Calix, "Heard him and mother talking. Guess their game is to make you Field Marshal."

"That isn't new." His voice is bland.

"Now they don't need you to marry the Rey girl to do it, not after you've handed her on a silver platter to the king." Kinsey nips at his heels. "Your perfectly, imperfect girl." She slinks around practically walking underfoot. "Did you do it on purpose?" She's a nagging itch in his conscience. "Bait her with your smolder then filet her in the back?"

Throwing an elbow Calix spins around. Kinsey's boneless body dodges, pouncing away to a safer distance.

"Aw did I say something?" Playing coy Kinsey puts her hand to her chest.

Calix scowls, unenthused by her gimmick. Without saying anything, he carries on nearing the end of the bridge.

Kinsey skips after him. Wrapping herself up in his feet as she circles him to obtain his undivided attention. "Sad for you really. Did your relationship even make it two months?" Stopping in his path. "That's a record." She skips backward, matching each of Calix's steps forward as he doesn't slow his approach. "You should keep it to single nights." Her face scrunches "Best to not let them get to know you."

"I should have let you fall," he growls.

"But you didn't," she sings to him. They reach the end of the bridge; her shoulder blades barely touch the door leading into the tower.

Calix's movements are a flash. Nothing but a blur until his hand stops on her throat. His long fingers encase her neck as he slams her back against the wall. Kinsey winces as her head hits the solid wood, her hands dangling loosely at her sides.

Her head lobs to one side as she cackles, the muscles of her neck tensing under his tight grip. Her laughter stops abruptly, her teeth clicking shut. The uncanny smile still plastered on her face. "You still can't do it. You're weak! WEAK, WEAK, WEAK!" She giggles. "You won't make it as a field Marshal. But it's okay, dear brother of mine. As general, I will take over for you." She looks at him with hollow eyes. "Because, when it's my hand, I won't hold back."

Calix recoils, his hand snapping back to the safety of his side. Kinsey hops to the side giddy, she sweeps her arm accompanied with a bow of her head as she shows Calix the door. Calix wastes no time in flinging the door open as he flees his sister.

Twenty-Five

If I ever get free, you two are the first on my list." Amiria threatens, her voice a rash whisper. The exhaled air scratches at her parched throat.

Robert and William each hold an arm, their hands wrapping around the entire circumference of her bicep. Amiria's useless feet drag along the unfinished floor of the servants' tunnels. "Yeah, you tell us that every time.".

"Just making certain you don't forget." Amiria growls, "You know what? I'm feeling generous. I'll kill you both at the same time since you can't be without each other."

"Thanks." William, his face still partially bruised, states.

Amiria cocks her head. "Say Robert, where's the ex-Rider Clyde? You two are trusted to transport me alone?"

Robert keeps his eyes forward as he speaks. "We've got someone higher up over seeing the transport."

"Must be a slow night," Amiria utters, her voice slowly dying under the strain.

Using their free hands Robert and William push open the small servant door while maintaining control of Amiria. The chill of the night air prickles Amiria's skin through her braies and undershirt, worn thin from the consistent use.

The inner bailey?

The main keep blocks the moon above them as they exit the back of the castle to the most innermost ring of the castle's property, coating everything in thick shadow. While the inner bailey contains some of the noble's homes and the castle's private trades, no one besides the stable boys come to this segment of the castle ground. With the stables around the corner, this area possesses nothing more than forgotten crates, broken carts, and excess building materials.

Her surroundings become obsolete as her eyes lock in on the figure standing in the open, his frame unevenly lit by the single torch in his hand. The orange hue only emphasizes the creases on his face making him appear worn out and weathered.

She can see the grays in her father's hair highlighted by the fire's golden glow. Her body uselessly jerks in the guard's grip. *NO!* She screams internally as her toes grapple at the dirt, searching for traction, something, anything to hook onto and stop her approach.

She curses her legs, unable to do the basic task of holding her up. He can't see her in this state. Not like this, not weak and broken down. She refuses to let him see her as anything less than a fighter. She desperately pleads for her legs to listen to her, for her muscles to respond to their commands. If only she could bring forth the energy to hold herself up.

Field Marshal Rey squints through the bright light in his hand at what used to be his daughter being dragged from the night's shadows into view. Anger twinges inside of him, but the father side of his life comes second to his responsibilities to the Cavalry. Clenching his hand into a fist, he suffocates his instincts as he watches his only child struggle to even lift her head.

Through matted clumps of hair falling over her eyes and a grime-streaked face, she locks eyes with her father. Holding his gaze steady, he sucks his lips into a straight line, digging the creases around his mouth deeper.

Loosening his jaw so his mouth falls open, the practiced and artificial words fall out landing between them, "In here gentleman."

Amiria's eyes bulge as the realization hits her as hard as a warhammer crunching her armor. She bounces from her father to the lid already propped open exposing the small entrance into the oubliette.

The dark hole is an absence of space as if part of the ground has been eaten away. Robert and William release their hold on Amiria's arms, dropping her to the dirt. She reaches out instinctively to catch herself. Air escapes her lips as she lands at the lip of the opening and her skidding palms slip into the dark pit.

Amiria stares into the abyss in a state of shock as William holds the scruff of her fraying tunic, stopping her from falling headfirst into the hole. She feels the hands grip her biceps, but she is too physically drained to fight the two guards as she is lifted into a sitting position. Doing the only thing she can, her chin lifts and her eyes fixate on the dark. She can hear her father's boots crunch in the gravel as he takes several steps back. The lines of his face darken as he extends his arm out further to keep the light on them as Robert and William tie a rope harness around Amiria's chest and shoulders the connecting across her shoulder blades creating a secure harness.

There is no way out of this. She can't even stand; how will she manage an escape without coming off as pathetic in front of her father when the two guards overpower her easily? She keeps her eyes locked on the outline of a shed overflowing with straw. Nothing in there will help her. Not in that one, not in the next one. No one will help her. She protests her fear, negating the panic raging inside her ribcage. The only evidence is the subtle tremble of her bottom lip.

Using the tip of his boot, Robert nudges Amiria's useless legs over the lip where they swing into the oubliette. With her jaw set, Amiria is a lifeless doll with unblinking eyes. A ragged toy unable to function its designed purpose anymore.

Her father squeezes his eyes shut. The muscles of his body trained to obey someone other than his mind fights back against his instincts. The closing of his eyes is the only command his body follows, saving himself from witnessing his child, his daughter, his once little girl, being lowered into the void. He won't admit his current thoughts, but it would have been easier watching her being lowered into a grave.

Amiria's legs fold underneath her and sink into the deep mud as she reaches the bottom. With her calves deep in the muck, her body slumps to one side and she rests her shoulder on the damp wall. Rubbing her eyes, she strains to see the inside of her new cage. Grated moonlight decorates the wall far above her head, unable to reach her at this depth. The blood in her veins begins to rush as her heart beats fast. She sits up and reaches out blindly running her hands along the roughly cut rock wall while she mentally builds her surroundings.

She is in nothing more than a large underground cylinder, the area barely large enough for her to lay down and be absorbed into cold and puddled earth.

"Hold it together." She whispers, encouraging herself.

Palming the wall, she searches for grooves to help pull herself to her feet. Finding a lip in the rock barely able to fit her fingertips, she tells her legs to stand in unison with her pull.

"WORK!" She berates punching herself in the leg. With her will still strong, she analyzes the grated lid above sealing her in. The rope they used to lower her is tied to the bars. She reaches above her head and tugs on it, they've left her enough slack to lay down.

How courteous of them.

She yanks on the rope. It appears secure. Gripping it she lets out a grunt of frustration as she musters all the strength she can. Hand over muddy hand she climbs. Exhausted, muscles on fire, and her shoulder giving out, her hips are the only part of her that has been lifted from the ground. She loses her grip, her hands sliding on the brown slime now coating the rope. She fumbles to secure the effort she has made but the rest of her stored energy sputters its last and drops her back to the ground.

A fever flushes her skin as her breathing becomes shallow and ragged. She wants to punch; she wants to kick. She wants to break something to alleviate the pressure building up inside of her by transferring it into the destruction of an object.

She fights back the tears by slamming the heels of her hands into her eyes. They are the reinforcements to the thin-skinned dam holding back the flood. The fury in her head, unable to be contained, bursts to her limbs; she thrashes, slaps, and claws at the wall. Throwing her head back she lets out a howl of a scream, the call of a lost wolf searching for her pack.

When you are trained to protect everyone, raised to sacrifice and be the hero, who will be yours?

Resting her forehead against the wall she limply pounds it with a single fist. "Taika." She utters. "Taika." Her voice cracks as she screams. "TAIKA, HELP ME!"

She chokes back the tears; a Winged Rider doesn't cry. Her words falls soft. "Taika, please, can you hear me? I need you."

"I hear you," a melodious voice reverberates in her skull.

Twenty-Six

His head resting on his crossed claws, Ignis takes a long deliberate blink as he watches Stirling run over another one of his useless plans. The cave is lit by the soft fire's glow as Stirling bites his bottom lip, deep in thought as he moves his twig people around his rock buildings.

Ignis releases a sigh through his nostrils, blowing a light cloud of dust into the air.

Ignoring him, Stirling continues verbalizing his plan, "Then I'll hop the wall here."

"*Guards are posted on the walls,*" Ignis reminds him for what feels like the hundredth time. "*And on the grounds, and in the halls, and well everywh—*" Suddenly his pupils constrict, and his head shoots up in alarm. His full attention on Taika who is sitting up alert.

"Are you even listening?" Stirling asks still holding his display props. "Ignis—"

"*Shut up,*" Ignis snaps. "*I'm listening.*"

Stirling crosses his arms dumbfounded. He mumbles under his breath, "Don't tell me to shut up."

"It's about Amiria," Ignis blurts, turning his head back to Stirling.

This grabs Stirling's undivided attention, his heart sinking into his stomach. "What do you mean it's *about* Amiria."

"Well, I guess, somehow, she's communicated with Taika."

Stirling raises an eyebrow, "She what?"

Ignis continues, *"Like how you and I do."*

"WHAT!" Stirling springs to his feet. Tripping over his display, he scampers over to Taika, "How is she? Is she all right? Is she hurt? Where is she?" Stirling desperately wishes he could hear the mind behind the beige dragon's brown eyes. He wishes he could understand her. He wishes he could hear Amiria through her.

Turning on a swivel his eyes jump back and forth between Taika and Ignis.

"So?" He makes a motion with his hand signaling for Ignis to clue him in, "What is she saying?"

"Amiria is unconscious."

Stirling's hopes drop.

"But she was able to relay her location and some helpful details. She said they are keeping her alive but just barely. She only ever sees the same two guards and they moved her in the middle of the night to the oubliette, so she suspects she will only be given water at this hour to continue the secrecy."

Stirling runs his hands through his curls tugging them back from his face. Sucking in a deep breath he drops his hands back to his side, "Okay, all right. This is better. We can work with this. She is easier to get to, you know?" Stirling swallows hard, his jaw trembling. "Right?" He looks to Ignis for reassurance.

Ignis doesn't answer.

Knees buckling, Stirling drops down into a squat burying his face in his hands. "I don't know what I'm doing." He confesses his secret to his palms. Removing his hands, he gestures to his display model half scattered from him tripping over it, "This is backward. It's all wrong. Our roles are reversed. I'm in way over my head, I'm not some prince or warrior. I'm not a hero."

Ignis lowers his snout to the pretend castle grounds, blowing hot air, he turns the twigs to ash, *"Well look at it this way. You're not Amiria, so stop trying to be. Be Stirling. Do what Stirling does best, act without thinking, follow the wind and let luck carry you along."*

"Yeah?" Stirling's confidence lifts.

"Or you die."

Stirling tips back, falling onto his butt defeated. Lying back, he stares up at the uneven ceiling. Flecks of mica reflect and dance with the light.

Don't be Amiria, be Stirling.

Amiria is ruthless when it comes to combat. She doesn't fight with strength; she fights with technique and wits. Stirling can't fight at all. In Wyverna he is a commoner, another face in the crowd. He has no power here.

Stirling's eyes widen, cranked open by the turning gears in his mind. A commoner might be exactly what is needed. Why make a grand spectacle of your rescue when you can hide in plain sight?

Forgotten by the nobles lounging on velvet furniture is a series of tunnels. Like mole-tunnels beneath the farm, the servants' quarters are a labyrinth under the castle leading to passages in the walls. They have some privacy, rooms designed to sleep a small family or four single adults' shoulder to shoulder.

A woman in her fifties, dressed in an undyed hemp dress, sits in the hall outside her glorified closet after a long day of work. The lively hall is packed with chattering servants back from their daily jobs, only several remain maintaining the castle through the dead of night.

They have rooms to disperse to, but they crowd the hall with family laughter and smiles. Baskets of yesterday's bread, the cheese too hard for the noble's teeth, and fruit that is no longer pretty enough for decoration get passed along the hall.

"My lovely Lady Lorelle." A man with strawberry hair plops himself down on the ground beside her, "Want some?" he offers a wine skin.

"Yes, *Sir* Henry, don't mind if I do." Lorelle sips the warm wine that was meant to be dumped after the last large banquet.

Henry leans his head back on the wall deep in thought, "I wonder what they are going to do to that poor Rey girl."

"Our soldier who said no more? I don't know, but it's nothing good with how they are keeping her." Lorelle takes another sip of the wine, passing it back to Henry.

"It's bizarre to me. The castle life is always buzzing with gossip. It's what they wake up each morning for. But when it comes to her... There's not a single word."

"Are you talking about Amiria Rey?" a young girl joins them sitting beside Lorelle. Lorelle nods in reply. "The servants who saw her get put into the oubliette said she was still holding strong."

People standing near them in the hall overhear the conversation topic and join in.

"That's because she is stronger than anyone in the kingdom," a teenage boy adds.

A girl around his age crosses her arms as she investigates her thoughts. "True, because if it was me, I would have married Calix Gautier. There's no way I would say no to that perfect face." The boy nudges her with his elbow. She playfully slaps him back on the shoulder.

The girl next to Lorelle clasps her hands and presses them to her cheek dreamily, "I want to know what this Stirling Bakere looks like. If beautiful Amiria Rey left handsome Calix Gautier and deserted her entire Kingdom for him, he must be dashing."

Lorelle shrugs, "All we know is he has curly blonde hair and hazel eyes."

Sighing the girl mopes, "I wish I could find a gorgeous guy in the lower class." She looks at the men standing around her with a raised lip, "Yeah, I meant what I said fellas."

Lorelle furrows her brow, "You know what I've been wondering. Whatever happened to the boy? We know the statement of him being dead is false. Rumor has it, Amiria Rey saved him that night Lumierna saw him fly. So..." she looks up at her family in everything but blood, "Where is the baker who flew?"

The evening light colors the wattle and daub houses of the city gold. With his hood concealing him from the neighbors, Stirling lightly raps his knuckles on the bakery's door. He hears his father call from inside, "It's open!"

Stirling nudges the door open. He had stayed up the entirety of the night tossing and turning on his pine bedding. The sun rays finally distract him from the dread of what he will be voluntarily putting himself through. His brain shows an exhibit of potential outcomes—all leading to his blood being spilled.

He is a lamb willingly waltzing into the lion's den.

Shrugging his hood off, Stirling gently closes the door behind him.

"You've returned." Giles says, pulling out the old charcoal from the oven and letting it coat the ground at his feet.

"I'm sorry for the way I reacted, but not for the way I felt." Stirling pauses, "It was a lot to take in. I was a bit overwhelmed. I am glad you are happy, I just— I just miss her you know?"

"I miss her too." Giles grabs Stirling by the shoulders, pulling him into a tight embrace. Stepping back, Giles holds the sides of his son's face between his palms. He watches a tear form and fall from the corner of his son's eye. He wipes it away with his thumb. The scar above Stirling's eyebrow catches his eye. He was too engrossed with seeing Stirling again, he hadn't noticed the first time he was here. His gaze drops down to the white scar on his neck, "You're not just here to talk with your old man are you?"

"Yes and no. I do want to spend one more night talking with you. Because if I live through this…I'll be going back home."

"And home…isn't here." Giles' face falls. He grips Stirling's shoulders and gives them a squeeze, "I'll miss you. I'm proud of who you've grown up to be."

Tears leak down Stirling's face, "You can come too. I can build you a new bakery and everything."

"I don't know about that." Giles face softens, he mindlessly rubs his beard.

"It's safer. You can make a new home there. You can be free there."

"I can't leave this old bakery. It's part of me. I'll be fine here, don't worry about your old man. You worry about saving Amiria and protecting yourself. Now, what can a father do to help?" Giles puts his hands on hips, setting his decision.

Stirling reveals a set of folded, quality fabric he had tucked under his cloak, "How about we make a trade."

Twenty Seven

The carefree giggles of two freshly graduated Cavalry members fills the empty shadow pockets of the night. The young boy walks with his arm around the girl's shoulders as they follow the trail back to their homes near the castle ground from the Cavalry base.

The girl nuzzles herself in closer, taking in the boy's warmth. Breathing in his scent, she blinks up at the stars, "I used to aspire to be like Amiria Rey. She is absolutely perfect. A beautiful warrior, a brave soul."

"Used to? I thought you are her biggest fan." The boy teases giving her a tight squeeze.

The girl looks over her shoulder, checking her surroundings. "Even more now," she admits. "She's shown us what true courage is. It isn't how well you can follow orders, and if you will fight when told to fight. But will you fight of your own will." The girl swoons. "What a tragic love story, isn't it though. To be given power, wealth, AND to be engaged to someone deemed *perfect* and to throw it all away for the true love of a poor outcast." She cups her hands together, pressing the back of her hand to her cheek as she bats her eyelashes. "I'm going to tell the tale of her to my children one day."

A frown sets on the boy's face. "More of us should follow her example, we all know what is happening in this Kingdom, we can see it's wrong."

"No one has the guts like she did," the girl points out.

"We can, we can start small—like—like not turning people in. So, when the day the world finally changes we can say we were there. We were part of the change." The boy dreams.

Jumping giddily at his side, the girl gives him a peck on the cheek. Slipping his hand into hers, they continue their path.

Slowing to a stop as they reach the side gate of the castle grounds, they see a figure leaning against the gate. His pale eyes reflecting against the moonlight are striking against his tan skin.

"Funny how well sound can travel downhill."

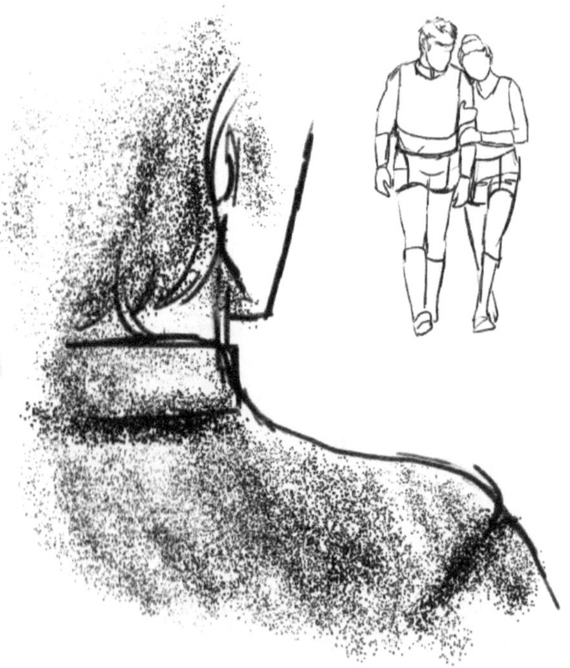

Twenty-Eight

Stirling's cloth-wrapped feet feel every pebble as he joins the morning group of servants. They follow a path on the outskirts of town leading away from the castle to a river flowing down from the mountains. It'll pool into a lake near the farmlands supplying the crops with water from manmade irrigation consisting of small streams flowing through the farmlands.

Patting his coif, Stirling checks all his curls are tucked away. He tugs at his sleeves, keeping his insignia hidden and approaches a woman who must be older than his father by ten years. She is hooking two wooden buckets of water to a carrying bar that lays across the shoulders with a half circle cut out to fit around the neck comfortably.

"I'll carry that for you," he tells her.

"Oh, what a nice lad," she smiles, showing the wrinkles in the corner of her eyes. "Your mother raised you well." She straightens her crooked back with a crack and pop.

Stirling squats down, lifting the wooden bar over his head and stands up steadily, trying to keep the water from sloshing and spilling.

The older woman leans to look at Stirling's face, "I don't recognize you, are you new?"

Stirling falters searching for a lie, "Uh, yeah. My old lord needed more females to take care of his home, so they traded me."

The woman raises an eyebrow, "I haven't noticed any of our girls being traded."

Stirling can feel the sweat forming on his palms as he holds his expression neutral as if he has no idea what she is talking about. Her eyes digging through Stirling's lie shift about him as if trying to read his contents.

The woman plays off as if she didn't see through him, "Guess there is an abundance of us, maybe I didn't know them." She smiles sweetly, "My name is Lorelle."

Following the trail with Lorelle back to the castle, Stirling shifts the heavy buckets on his shoulders, "Quilan. I'm Quilan." Another lie.

"It's nice to meet you Quilan." She ponders for a moment, "That's a nice name, Quilan. What does it mean?"

Stirling blinks thinking of the real Quilan. How the aloof boy is hiding a kind soul. How receiving his rare and genuine smile feels like receiving a heartfelt gift.

"A friend," he answers with a small smile.

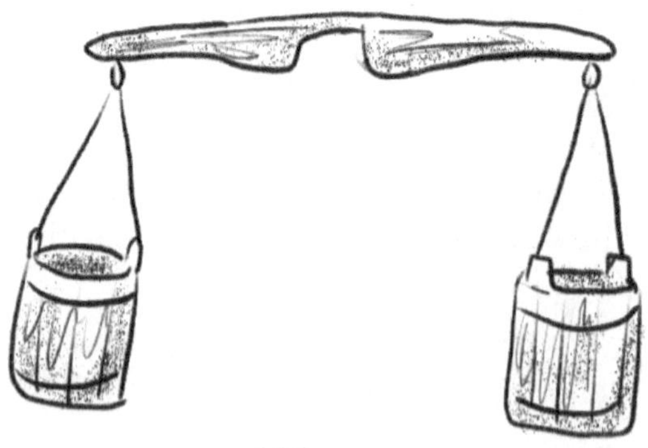

Twenty-Nine

The metal badges on his golden brigandine with wyvernite buttons are knocked crooked and uneven by trembling hands. Frustrated, Field Marshal Rey releases a ragged breath and runs his hand through his hair, slicking it back. He looks over at a light knock on his open office door.

"Sir?" General Gautier stands poised. Her hands laced behind her back; she holds her chin up as if the top of her head was being pulled up by an invisible string. Light brown hair Is pulled back into a tight knot on the back of her head and her almond-colored eyes stare dully at the flustering Field Marshal.

When she speaks, she manages to not move a single muscle in her face except her lips, "The court martial is waiting on your presence to begin."

His eyes narrow, "This isn't a court martial. This is an execution. The King didn't sentence his people, he sentenced mine."

General Gautier's lips pull back like a smiling snake, "Would you like to tell him that?" The next words come out as a hiss, "Is the saying true? Like father, like daughter?"

Field Marshal Rey is across the room before General Gautier could flick her split tongue, tasting the fear in the air. With a puffed chest, he threatens through his gritted teeth "Silence yourself, before I make sure your jaw is incapable of speaking, General."

She slithers forward a step matching his gaze, her voice silk like a new gown with the tailor's pins still holding it together, "Such a Rey response, all fangs and claws."

"Could be worse, General. I could have the Gautier sneer." He throws on a charming smile.

He pushes forward, General Gautier pivots on her heel like a door swinging open as she allows him to exit. With pursed lips she takes her second in command place and follows the Field Marshal. The tips of her boots practically clipping his heels as they travel to the place of arms in the castle.

A scaffold has been erected for the special occasion. The new wooden structure sits on display to one side of the expansive room with arched and vaulted stone ceilings. A skeleton crew guards the island as the majority of the Winged Cavalry stand in orderly sections in parade rest, their feet shoulder width apart and their hands behind their backs. Perfect rows of Winged Riders stare forward with stoic expressions, ordered to stand witness to the repercussion of disobeying orders.

The entirety of the room, in synchronized unison, stand at attention, the clap of their boots coming together echoes in the hollow hall, a single applaud to begin the death march. Field Marshal Rey looks out at his men and women. They don't meet his gaze as he scans them. Their eyes fixated; their bodies unmoving. They will not twitch;

they will not flinch. Blinking is the only movement that will differentiate them from a statue.

His brave men and women. *His.*

The other command rankings below him, including the Lieutenant General, Major General, Brigadier, and Colonel, stand in their own group to the side of the gallows. Field Marshal Rey's boots are the only noise as he crosses the short distance from the entrance to where the command stands. They nod their heads in respect as he takes his position in front of them.

The room has acknowledged who is their leader. Everyone except for the only person above the Field Marshal.

King Dietrich sits on his perch behind the Winged Cavalry, a balcony built for the intended use of giving commands to a large group. A cushioned seat had been lifted to the balcony. He sits comfortable in a position designed for leaders to stand and speak as he watches the deaths of subservient children.

Calix stands at attention beside King Dietrich. He betrays his stance as his eyes shift across the room. In the back corner of the formation stands his team. He leers down at the back of his father's head. His lip twitches with an underlying scowl.

He moves on, his vision glossing over the insignificant heads of riders up to his mother and Sir Rey himself. He snickers, even from here he can see the light dying behind the man's eyes. He won't be able to endure much more of this. He'll soon be nothing more than a hollow husk of the man he used to be. After that he will crumble at a subtle breeze.

Field Marshal Rey turns about face to look up at the gallows. He closes his eyes counting his breaths he swallows and opens his mouth to begin.

His voice bellows, resonating in the domed ceiling and coming back down as if he had the voice of a god, "PRISONERS TO BE EXECUTED! MARCH UP!"

In a two-person wide line, perfectly spaced apart the young couple, a man in his twenties and Nellie march in order with their hands shackled behind their backs. Beside them, marching in step, are four masked Winged Riders.

No ropes attach the four as they are escorted without resistance up the wooden stairs of the gallows.

"PRISONERS! HALT!"

They halt center stage facing the side of the room. The rope scarves hang menacingly between them and their assigned executioner. Riders, people, chosen at random to follow their command orders.

"RIGHT! FACE!"

All eight of them turn their right foot towards their audience, having the left follow behind. Without moving their point of place, they face out across the Winged Cavalry. Tears slip down Nellie's reddened face. A whimper escapes from the girl, a quiet sound echoing all the way to the back of the crowd.

Field Marshal Rey pops his jaw loathing the words to come out of his mouth knowing what he says will come to play, "PRESENT! NOOSE!"

The executioners take control of the noose hanging in front of their faces behind their prisoners. They step closer, almost breathing down their necks. Keeping the rope taught they move it around the prisoners' head to the front.

"MAKE READY!"

The boy breaks formation to look at the girl he had gone through training with. He can hear the other rider, Nellie, weeping past her. They were going to be in the same unit. They were going to be married one day and have a family. His hand shifts in the shackles behind his back wishing to hold her hand during their final moment. The braided hemp tightens against his throat. His girl, with her rope collar, turns to meet his eyes.

"EXECUTIONERS! DROP!"

"PACK YOUR STUFF!" Field Marshal Rey hollers as he barges into Arietta's home.

"Excuse me?" Arietta stands in her kitchen with a hand on her popped hip.

He shuts the door in a hurry and yells across the room, "Your stuff! Pack it! You're moving in with me!"

Arietta drops her stance, his brigandine half opened, and his metals disheveled, she searches his paled face, "Derek. What's wrong?"

Derek looks past his fury and the sinking feeling in his gut to the woman grounding him to a life outside the Cavalry. She holds onto him like a kite as he soars through the skies so when the weather gets bad, she can reel him in to safety. In this room, he doesn't have to be Field Marshal Rey. Who she sees standing in her home is Derek. She doesn't see the brass on his chest, she sees the man she has loved for over twenty years.

Derek collapses onto the stool at her spinning wheel with a hunch in his spine. Veins bulge from his hands as he grinds his face into them to hold back the explosion. His body rattles the old furniture. In a blind fury, he grabs a spool of wool and hurls it across the room. It smacks the wall with an audible crack. It falls to the floor, rolling until it catches on its newly cracked edge.

"Derek Rey! You stop this right now and you use your words!" Arietta screams at him. "Tell me what is happening!"

Derek's face hardens as he regains control of himself, his voice hollow, "No one is safe."

"Well, that's obvious, have you been to the town square lately." Arietta comments.

"Arietta listen to me for a moment. I mean *no one* is safe." He buries his face in his hands, "They were children, just children." His shoulders heave with his heavy breaths. When he looks up from his hands his eyes have become red and swollen, "He forced me to march my soldiers to their own execution." He chokes, closing his eyes he inhales slowly, he releases it in a whisper of a voice, "One of the girls was from Amiria's class."

The color drains from Arietta's face at the mention of Amiria's name. She can barely form the words, "Is she still…"

Derek's fingernails dig into his palms as he clenches his hands. Feeling the sharp pain, he uncurls his fingers, a small number of red lines form crescent shape cuts. He stares at the blood on his hands. His voice eerily calm, "Just pack your stuff please."

Arietta nods with no further questions.

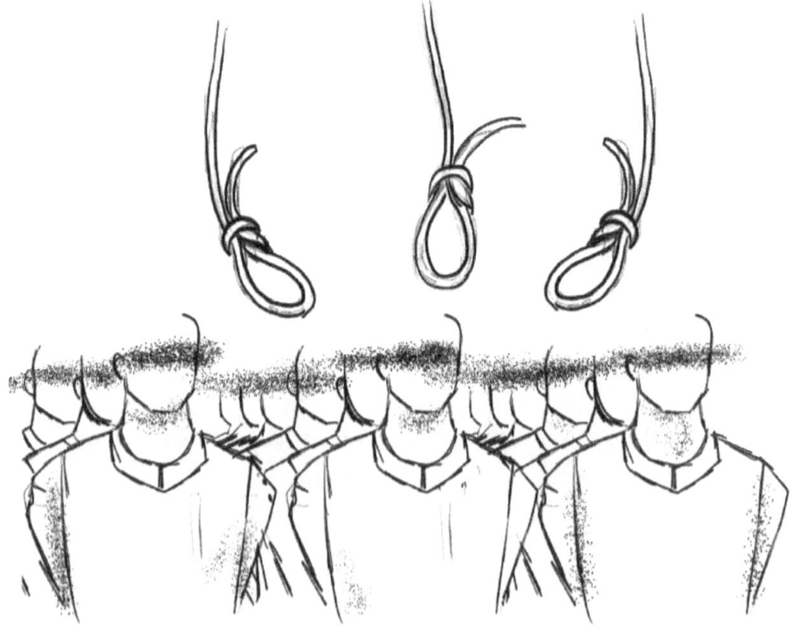

Thirty

Avoided like social pariahs, Robert and William stand patrol in the inner bailey. The nobles who reside in the vicinity of the castle carry about their days as if life is normal, but on the inside, everyone is on edge. They keep their voices low and their pathways distant from the patrolling guards. Trust is as common as a rainbow at night. Everyone believes the other is a shark in the water.

William scuffs the dry dirt with the toe of his boot, digging a shallow hole. They've been instructed to keep an eye out for nobles or other guards speaking negatively about the court Marshal earlier that day. Robert reaches up and fixes William's collar of his gambeson.

"Thanks." William puts up a weak smile for the only person he truly trusts in the kingdom.

Robert nudges him, concerned, "Are you doing all right?"

"Well." He stops himself. With skittish eyes, he checks their surroundings. They stand off to the side of the bailey near one of the wall's buttresses. Keeping his hands tensed at his side he nods motioning to the corner shadow. Discreetly. they step backward until they are hidden from sight.

William's voice is barely audible, "What they did today, to, to, to the Cavalry. There's a guard being walked tomorrow with several upper-class citizens. We're out here spying on nobles." He hugs himself as if he is suddenly cold in the warm and sunny weather, "What we've done to Amiria Rey." He thinks about how they strapped her to that chair. How they watched as she shrieked in pain. They dropped her down a hole in the ground and give her water once a day, all due to orders by King Dietrich. How much longer can he keep committing these horrendous acts under the safety blanket of 'he is only following orders'.

Robert clamps his hand over William's mouth, "What I'm getting at is you're just exhausted and need a night off, am I right?" He lifts his eyebrows insinuating the protective lie.

Nodding, William drops his gaze as the hand falls free from his mouth, "Yeah, that's what it is. I'm just in need of a good night's rest to perform my duties efficiently."

"Good, now let's get back to work." He shakes William's shoulder with encouragement. William's body shakes loosely under Robert's grasp.

"Just as assigned?" His voice was somber.

Robert's eyes drop to William's neck. He watches the pulse of his beating heart through the thin skin. He gulps, his Neck bobs bobbing, he can already feel the noose tightening. "Exactly as ordered."

He redirects William to the castle grounds and gives him a nudge forward. "Come on, let's get out of this corner before people start talking."

"They already do," William utters under his breath.

Stepping out into the light, the two guards wipe the residual emotions from their faces. Taking out their masks, they hide who they are and become the guards Lumierna expects them to be.

Thirty-One

"Did you hear?" replays over in crawling whispers throughout the servants' quarters. Stirling lays on his matt with several layers of blankets pulled to one of the four corners of the shared room. The bed he made in the cave was more comfortable than this. Beside him is a wicker box to keep all his possessions in. Even this small of a box the servants find hard to fill.

He has inserted himself as a servant and no one besides the other servants have noticed his presence around the castle grounds. He has been following Lorelle around as she shows him the ropes. He has helped replenish the fresh water around the castle by spending half a day bringing it up from the river to be switched off for an empty bucket with a different set of servants or maidens who will disperse the water inside the castle.

The other half of his day was spent removing the debris that is thrown out from all parts of the castle, from the kitchen to the privies. He thanks the callouses on his hands and the muscles on his body from the labor of taking care of his home. If it weren't for that, and the years of flying, he would have collapsed.

He stares at the ceiling with his arms behind his head, *"Being here has really put my life into perspective."* Stirling tells Ignis.

"Being a baker doesn't seem so bad now does it?" Ignis points out.

"It's a grand life compared to this." Stirling pauses, hearing two servants converse as they walk by his room. *"Hey Ignis, I'll get back to you. I want to see what's going on."*

"Don't forget about me when you become a hero. Remember I knew you back when."

Stirling steps between the edges of the other beds, the space barely wide enough to walk, and leans his head out into the hall. The servants' quarters hide beneath the castle grounds with a labyrinth of tunnels weaving through the walls. Like an ant hill, the servants travel through the hidden tunnels to make the day run seamlessly, an invisible thread holding the elegant fabric of events together while being hidden from view.

Stirling watches with curiosity as the other servants dip in and out of each other's rooms talking in hushed voices. He turns to look down the other side of the hall. He sees the elderly woman who has been guiding him.

"Lorelle!" He calls out to her.

She pauses in the threshold of her family's room, "Yes?"

Anxious to gain intel and to find out what everyone is whispering about, Stirling practically leaps down the hallway to her side, "Question, do you know what everyone is going on about?"

"Already interested in the castle gossip I see." She plays, "I don't know what it was like where you came from but here, we have a bad habit of hearing what we shouldn't." Lorelle puts her hand to her chest as she justifies her reason, "It's not our fault they forget we're not furniture." Stirling sinks back onto his heels. He has already begun to experience the treatment she is referring to. "Sad truth it is." She lightens up and shrugs it off, "Well, you get used to it."

Stirling brings her back to his question, "What did they overhear this time?"

Lorelle beams at getting to be the bearer of outlandish news. She motions for him to lean closer as if everyone doesn't already know what she is about to tell him, "They are eating their own now."

"What does that mean?" Stirling shakes his head confused.

"The guards, the nobles, *the Cavalry.*" Her eyes shine as she reveals the last group. "The common class is no longer the only ones being sent to the gallows. Maybe they will finally stop this ridiculousness now that it's *their* children being hanged."

Stirling's mouth goes dry, he curls his fingers into his palm to hide their tremble, "Members of the C-Cavalry." He stammers.

"I couldn't believe it either." Lorelle leans against the door frame, "There were four in total. It's hard to feel for the Cavalry after the stigma they've created for themselves. I guess it's still sad though, they were so young." Lorelle pouts her lip as she thinks of her children and young grandchildren, "there was two girls and two boys."

Stirling keeps himself from doubling over from the knot growing in his stomach, "Names? Did you hear any of their names."

Lorelle looks up as she searches her memory, "They were mentioned, but I don't recall what they were. I didn't know who they were." Her voice is calm as if this is a casual conversation about their day.

Stirling leans forward pressing her memory, "Was one of them named Amiria?" His heart is going to explode. It will burst from his chest if he is unable to decipher the names.

Lorelle shakes her head, "Nah. Wasn't that. I do know that name."

"You what?" Stirling's body goes cold as his blood stops.

Lorelle looks him in the eye, she holds his gaze before shouting down the hall, "Hey Henry!"

"Hey what?" A man calls back from an unknown room.

"The girl in the hole, the one you give water to. What is her name again?"

A man in his early thirties with strawberry blonde hair pokes his head out of a room several doors down, "It's that Rey girl. Why?"

Stirling's body wavers. *Rey. Rey. Amiria Rey. AMIRIA.* He takes a couple half steps back to hold his balance. *Amiria, they know where she is.* Stirling composes himself and turns to Henry who has stepped fully out into the hallway, "Can I ask you if you are assigned to give her water again tonight?"

"Yeah, it's every night." Henry tells him. Several other servants pop out from their rooms interested in the conversation.

"Am I able to go tonight instead?" Stirling says in a quivering voice. He looks back at all the eyes watching him.

"I'm going to assume no. The guards were insistent that I don't even tell anyone about her." His eyes narrow on Stirling's shifty movements. "What is it to ya?"

"It's well, I uh." Stirling falters, shifting his weight back and forth on his feet while his thumb begins to tap his fingers one by one.

A look of certainty crosses over Lorelle's face, "Hey Stirling? Your curls are showing."

Stirling's hands instinctively shoot up to his coif. Feeling no free strands of hair, it dawns upon him; she had called him Stirling instead of Quilan.

"Well look at that." Lorelle smiles smugly. "I told you, us servants have ears everywhere."

"Are-are you going to turn me in?" Stirling dreads.

Henry steps up to Stirling, their chests practically touching. Sizing Stirling up, he grins, clapping him on the shoulder. "Nah lad. You two are infamous in the castle, but trail blazers to everyone else. We're going to help you."

"You're what?"

"WAIT!" A girl pops her head out from the room next to Lorelle's, "That is Stirling Bakere!" Her face scrunches as she complains, "But he is so—so—average looking!"

Stirling touches his face self-consciously as the girl returns to her room. He can still hear her griping. "Ugh, this doesn't make any sense!" Bewildered, Stirling stands gaping at the servants around him. *Famous? How? Why?*

"Ignore her." Lorelle waves her hand. "We have a rescue to plan out."

Thirty-Two

Wispy clouds do nothing to stop the sun from beating down on the top of her dark hair, pulled up into a top knot. Eve sweeps the last of the dirt from the porch of Stirling's home. The dust pluming off the edge to be carried away by the refreshing breeze.

She sees the view of the village he had chosen. The small community she grew up in never used to feel dull. The village center she called home is always filled with boisterous laughter of loving neighbors, more family than friends.

Now each crawling day feels sucked dry, absent of life since Stirling left a month ago. He only called this village home for half a year, but he left an impression they will never be rid of, like the tide changing the shape of the coast. Even when the water recedes, the rocks hold their new formation.

She hates how empty his home feels when she sweeps inside, her eyes always avoiding his blood stain on the wood. Sometimes though, she feels as if she still hears the residual laughter of when they used to talk all night.

Pulling her apron up to her forehead, she wipes the perspiration forming at her hair line. Between keeping up with Stirling's home and working at the ale house, she barely finds any time to relax, to think.

To think about him. To look up to the blue sky and search for the orange dragon, for a sign he is coming home. He's on the other side of the world now, and it eats at her heart each time she lets her mind wander to him. She can't walk to him; she can't send him a message. She can instead tend to his garden and feed his goat while the possibilities of what could happen to him run rampant through her mind.

She curses herself for letting her mind slip to the dark thoughts that keep her awake at night. She has to believe in his promise, to believe in him. He will be all right, and he will come home. When that day finally comes, his home will be ready for him. Life will return to order; return to the way they want it to be. The way it should be.

Stirling is family now.

Or? She leans on the broom watching the village carry on with their daily chores.

Or is it only her that feels this way.

Those days he was around were better and brighter. Tomorrow was no longer just another day. She looked forward to each morning, to wake and see him again. She doesn't care if he brings the other girl back with him. She doesn't care if they got married when they returned. She just wants him home. She just wants her friend back. To know the time, he was here wasn't just some dream.

Eve drops the broom, letting it smack the ground. Stepping down one step, she slouches hiding her face in the skirt around her knees.

She's just being dramatic her father would tell her. Stop being such a girl, her brother would scold. She is overreacting, her mother would laugh off.

A strong breeze tussles the loose strands of hair that had fallen from her top knot. Her heart skips. Could it! Her head pops up from her knees. As quickly as her hopes were raised, they were crushed beneath a robin egg blue Quetzalcoatl.

She squints, holding her hand to protect her eyes from the gales, "Quilan?"

She stands as Aether coils up in the grass, their head snapping back and forth as they search for Ignis. Quilan slips off his dragon, his unblinking eyes slither smoothly around the yard before landing on Evelina.

He stops at the bottom step, "Stirling around?" His voice is as monotone as ever.

Eve's mouth moves without words. She hasn't talked to Quilan since the bone fire. There she had Stirling and the ambience of the night to help her along. She stands here with none of those assistances. What does some alehouse maid say to the number one racer in the kingdom?

She manages a shake of her head.

Quilan finally blinks, "When?"

Eve chokes back the beginning of a sob. She desperately wishes she could provide him with an answer. She folds her arms around herself, "I don't know."

"Oh," is all he replies, his face remaining expressionless. But for the first time since meeting him Eve heard a fluctuation in that single word. Hidden under his low voice was recognition of the situation, as if he somehow could read her mind and understand what she truly meant.

Lowering his chin, he turns to leave.

"Wait!" She blurts. She covers her mouth with her hands, surprised with herself. Half turned away Quilan's eyes flick back to her. Dropping her hands, she plays with the hem of her apron as she asks, "Are you hungry?"

He stares at her.

Growing nervous her words start to stutter, "Th-thirsty?"

He continues to stare without replying.

She fills in the awkward silence, "D-do you want to come in and talk, I-I can at least tell you what happened."

Quilan nods and climbs the stairs to Stirling's home.

Thirty-Three

uard?" Henry asks over his shoulder. Robert, who has been assigned the duty with William walks alone behind Henry. He holds the torch in one hand and the other on his hilt as they wind their way through the servant's tunnels.

"Servant," Robert replies unenthused.

"If this is your assignment and that's why I can't tell anyone, then why am I doing it in the first place?" Henry doesn't care about the reason as he makes small talk. He only wants to distract the guard and to divert his attention.

"You haven't told anyone right!" Robert snaps.

Henry puts his hands up, "No, no of course not. I'm a servant, who would listen?"

"Good," Robert nods worried.

"Of course, Sir." Henry smiles, pushing open a small door he has to hunch over to exit.

Ducking through the short doorway hidden behind bales of hay, they enter the inner bailey. "All right, let's get this over with." Robert groans, ready to go to bed.

Captain Mannering trusted only William and him to keep Amiria a secret, but this didn't exonerate him from his regular assignments. During the day they still walk their posts, but in the dead of the night when they should be sleeping so they can wake at morning bells, they must provide food and water to the girl in the hole. This is the real reason Robert and William take every other night off. They only want to sleep through an entire night. Tonight was supposed to be William's shift but he convinced him to take the night off. William has been slipping, and they protect each other. They are all they have.

Henry steps up to a wooden cart deliberately parked over the metal lid hiding the oubliette. Heaving, he curls his fingers through the grate and lifts. The heavy metal makes a scraping sound that echoes in the courtyard as he slides it to the side.

Planting his feet in dugout grooves, he hand over hand pulls the girl that weighs less than the lid up from the unseeable depths. Seeing her come into view, Robert reaches down, snagging the back of her tunic, and lifts the limp body out of the hole. With her legs still dangling he gently sets her rag doll body to the dust and straw.

Pinching her face between his fingers, Robert shakes her head, "Hey, you alive?" His eyebrows lifts with genuine concern. "Damn, we might have to have to pour the water in her mouth again. Get her propped up."

Henry scoops his arms under Amiria, cradling her. He gently lifts her head and shoulders to lean against his chest. He leans down, whispering in her ear, "You'll be all right." Tilting his head up, Henry's face is directed at Robert, but his eyes are focusing past him.

"What?" Robert squints at the servant then a wooden plank cracks against the back of Robert's skull. His vision goes white for a split second before he topples over unconscious.

Stirling blinks. "I did it?" A breathy laugh escapes as he jumps. "I did it!"

Henry rolls his eyes. "Not quite yet. You still need to get her out of here."

Stirling hears Henry speaking but his attention is locked on Amiria. The plank slips from his hand and clatters to the ground as reality sets in. "Amiria." The constriction of his chest barely allows the airflow to form the word. He numbly steps over Robert and drops to his knees in front of Henry.

The pit in his stomach churns, blending concoction of love, sorrow, and horror. "Amiria, what have they done to you?" He runs his finger along her injured arm.

"No time. Take her." Henry thrusts Amiria at Stirling like a disregarded toy and gets back up to his feet.

Stirling can feel each one of her ribs as she slides into his arms, as if she was his missing puzzle piece. Her head lolls back, the nape of her neck resting on his bicep. She doesn't feel real. She doesn't feel like the strong and unbreakable person he used to know. Her limbs feel like the dry twigs he uses for tinder, able to snap between his fingers. Her matted hair is brittle and splitting at the ends. He thumbs her hollow cheek, the skin cold and thin.

He pulls her in closer burying his face into her hair. "You smell awful." He mumbles but doesn't pull his face away.

"Eh hem." Henry interjects the moment. He pats the cart he had moved earlier, "Put her in here. Then change into the guard's armor. I'm going to go fetch you a horse from the stables around the corner. Don't worry, he shouldn't wake for a while."

Stirling nods, scooping his other arm under Amiria's legs as he stands with ease. Henry lifts a canvas covering the cart. Stirling eyes the cart, then down to Amiria and back at the cart. "Sorry" He says setting her down on the lip of the cart and scooting her under the canvas, "Just uh-stay here."

Henry lowers the canvas down concealing her and disappears towards the stables as Stirling moves back to Robert, "Please, please don't wake up." He begs as he squats down beside the guard.

"This is not weird at all," Stirling mutters to himself. Undoing the straps of the guard's duty belt, Stirling lets it fall to the man's side and gripes, "Chainmail, why chainmail." Then with a grunt and several curse words under his breath, Stirling manages to pull off the chainmail and piles it into a metal clump as he moves onto removing the matching blue gambeson and padded chausses, leather gloves, and shoes. Piece by piece he puts the ensemble back together on himself and begrudgingly heaves the chainmail over his head and lets it fall around him. Already breathing heavily from the exertion, he pulls the coif from his head, letting his curls spring free. He can't be the only curly-haired guard.

Trying to not let guilt set in, Stirling leaves the guard lying on the ground in only his undertunic and tights and buckles the broadsword in its scabbard around his waist. The sound of hoofs clopping draws nearer until Henry, leading a horse, comes into view and guides it over to the cart.

Watching as Henry hooks the horse into the harness Stirling mentions, "I don't know how to drive."

Henry shakes his head and finishes buckling the straps around the horse, "Aren't you the baker who flew?"

Stirling stares blankly, "The what?"

"Look, if you can control a dragon you can control the reins of a horse. Pull right, go right. Left left. Back to stop. Flick to go." Henry pats the horse's neck and throws the reins up to the driver's seat.

Muttering to himself, Stirling repeats sarcastically, "Just pull right, it's easy. Can't talk to a horse."

Henry raises an eyebrow then shakes his head with an exasperated sigh. "Okay." His eyes land on the wooden plank. "I'm ready. Just not as hard all right." He holds out his hand to shake, "It was a pleasure to meet you. To have a face to the name."

Stirling accepts his handshake, "You guys saved me. You saved her. I don't know how to thank you enough. I wouldn't have been able to do it without you."

"Yeah, that's true."

"What?" Stirling barely catches the comment.

"I wish you luck, take good care of her." Steadying his breathing, Henry kneels beside Robert.

Stirling picks up the plank. "Thank you," he says before swinging.

The wooden wheels turn, the cart shuddering as they roll over rocks and away from the castle. Keeping his face down, no one pays any mind to the young guard at the reins. In the night with a uniform, he is nothing more than another person performing their assigned work. No one questions authority.

He never turns back as the castle shrinks behind him. His eyes fixate forward, afraid if he looks anywhere else but the ears of his horse, the Cavalry will morph from the shadows and seize him. His heart pounds louder than the horse's clopping hooves through the empty streets.

He won't pass the bakery; he will take a roundabout way if he has to and he won't call for Ignis. There will be no obvious orange dragon coming to assist this time. More than getting caught though, he fears this is only an illusion and the smallest hint of reality, like the bakery steps, will shatter it. He can manage this one task on his own. He will take her away from this city.

His shoulders finally relax as he reaches the neighborhood bordering the wall with the hidden passage of escape. The horse slows to a stop on the deserted road, not a single candle flame can be seen. The only light source comes from the sky, heavy with stars.

Creaking fingers uncurl from the reins Stirling was white knuckling since he sat in the driver's seat. Taking a moment to breathe, he claps his hands onto his knees. He swallows hard and his head snaps over his shoulder to the canvas behind him. Nervously, his hazel eyes begin to dance around the night, searching the shadows, for anyone who will threaten to stop him. His eyes tiptoe back to the canvas.

Sliding off the driver's seat of the cart, he keeps his eyes locked on where Amiria was placed under the canvas. He doesn't know what is louder, the sound of his breathing or the blood rushing in his ears as he drags his hand along the wall of the cart following it to the back. Biting his lip, he reaches out for the hem of the thick fabric, but his fingers hover just over the canvas scared of what he might reveal.

"Please don't be a dream, please be here." He rips the canvas back before he can convince himself not to.

His knees buckle beneath him as he reveals her slumbering face. Holding onto the cart for support he lowers himself down letting his knees dig into the gravel, but he doesn't care about that. The pain of the sharp rocks putting dents into his skin will never compare to the unbearable stress beneath his ribs.

Regaining his courage, he climbs into the cart, careful not to step on the sickly girl. Cupping her under the arms, he lifts her with ease on top of the canvas. He folds it in around her and swaddles her like a newborn, leaving her face exposed with a hood around her head.

He tucks a strand of hair behind her ear. Even now she looks nothing less than beautiful in his eyes. "Just a little bit farther, we're almost free."

He scoops her thin body into his arms, propping her head up against his chest. Scooting to the edge of the cart, he slides off, careful not to jostle her around. He walks back around to the horse waiting patiently for a command.

"Go!" He instructs in a hushed tone. The horse shifts its weight but doesn't move. "Get!" Supporting Amiria's weight with one arm he slaps the flank of the horse who snorts in response.

Stirling throws his head back in frustration, "Please! Go!" The horse takes off in a slow walk following the road into the night. Stirling stares momentarily stunned, "Oh, that worked."

He turns to the mountains that, despite their size, are almost invisible in the night and begins carrying her back to where he first saw her.

Thirty-Four

The moonlight pierces through the overlapping evergreens scattering light to the forest floor. Damp moss and leaves shimmer, highlighted by the soft white light. Stirling's vacant body moves without thinking. His feet follow the familiar path as his mind grows numb to his surroundings. With each step he takes, the canvas sways, brushing his legs. It's the only thing he can feel besides the weight in his arms.

He barely wakes as the one creature on this planet he considers a brother comes barreling through the trees.

"Why didn't you call me to meet you at the wall!"

Stirling's voice sounds lost in the shadows. "I don't know."

Ignis follows beside Stirling, hanging his head over him he looks down at the face exposed in the canvas. *"Is she alive?"*

Stirling glares up at him from the corner of his eye. Ignis retreats a step back, putting himself behind Stirling's periphery.

"You want me to carry her?"

Stirling hugs Amiria closer to him. "No."

"You all right?"

"I don't know," Stirling answers sincerely, ignoring the burning sensation in his muscles, but he knows that isn't what Ignis was asking about. For all the fighting she has done for others, the least he can do is carry the bravest person he knows into the safety of the mountains they once knew together.

Ignis looks around. *"This isn't the way to the cave."*

Stirling's mind begins to open with the familiarity of Ignis by his side, "I know. I just, I just can't leave her like this. I'm hoping some water will not only clean her off but help her wake up.

Ignis bends around Stirling and sniffs. *"Good idea, she reeks. Don't let her stink up the whole cave."*

"Shut up Ignis. It's not her fault," Stirling snaps.

"See, you know it's the truth."

They come up to a babbling brook lined with rocks and crisscrossing logs. Turning, they follow it upstream. The sound of the trickling water soothes his soul as they climb. The trees clear overhead as they come up a series of pools reflecting the moon and the stars.

Small knee-high waterfalls hop down their rocky terrain connecting the pools before turning back into the steady brook. Kneeling, Stirling gently lays Amiria by the water's edge and respectfully unravels her from her canvas cocoon. His heart flutters as she stirs, her eyes moving behind her eyelids.

Is she dreaming?

Ignis hovers over Stirling observing. *"Well at least she is alive."*

At least she's alive. He repeats the words in his head.

Hunching over Amiria, he dips his fingers into the water testing the temperature. He wants to help her, not shock her. Satisfied, and knowing there isn't any other choice, he gladly removes the heavy chainmail. He stretches his sore shoulders now free of the weight and strips down to his braies. Not caring about his lack of modesty, he picks Amiria back up in a bridal carry and carefully wades into the waist-deep pool of crystal-clear water.

At a steady pace, he lowers her feet and then legs into the water. He keeps his eyes on her face watching for any sign. With the water now up to his ribcage, he sits on a large river rock. The water flows around her shoulders as he dips her head back letting the water soak through her hair. The dark strands fan out around her, flowing with the soft current.

He can't help but be enchanted by her presence. Her lips hanging partially open, with the moonlight highlighting her features. Shifting his foot, a rock holding him steady in his seat slips out from its hold.

Twitching his arms to keep his balance, Amiria's head dunks under the water.

"Well don't kill her." Ignis says watching from the comfort of dry land.

Water invades her lungs as she breathes. She gasps, stretching her hand out above her, she can feel the air so why is she drowning? She struggles to sit up with the help of a hand on her back. There is a person, there is a person, and they are trying to drown her. Her half-lidded eyes give her no indication of who her perpetrator is. With blurred vision, she uses the heel of her hand to strike the man in the jaw.

Stirling's head barely moves as Amiria hits him. Her weakened state mutes her deadly hands into cushioned mittens. He doesn't fight her as she struggles in his grasp. Her hands are spread out against his bare chest as she pushes away in an attempt to flee, her frail body unable to uphold her fight or flight instincts.

Stirling finally raises his hands to hold her loosely around the shoulders to keep her from drowning,

"Amiria! Amiria stop! It's me, Stirling! It's safe—you're safe!"

With her arms extended out and her face turned away, her world appears frozen. She no longer hears the small waterfalls or the owl in the tree. She only hears his voice. Opening her eyes, she looks back at the face belonging to the one voice she can never forget.

His chest rises and falls with heavy breaths. She stares wide-eyed at the curly hair and hazel eyes watching her with heartbreak. A face she believed she would never see again.

When you're the hero, who will be yours.

She reaches up with a single hand knitting her fingers through his soft and wild curls. Electrified currents tickle his scalp as her hand runs through his hair to the back of his head.

Her voice is a single breath, "Stirling."

"Yeah." His voice cracks as he holds back his emotions with a grin.

"*Am I intruding? I feel like I'm intruding. Do you need a moment?*" Ignis says while being ignored.

"OW!" Stirling blurts as Amiria uses her hand in his hair to pull herself into him with a cry of overwhelming relief. She buries her face into his neck, her eyes wet with tears that never fall.

With her body quickly running out of conserved energy, her arms fall loose around him. Her head rests on his shoulder, and her hands fall back into the water behind him as he supports her full weight.

"You came for me." She whispers wistfully, her eyelids drooping.

"I had to. If anyone deserves to fly free. It's you." He tells her honestly.

"*Yeah, I'm giving you a moment.*" Ignis turns his entire body to face away from the pond.

Her tired head cradled against him, Amiria uses only her eyes to excavate her surroundings; forest, Ignis, night. "Why are we in a pond?" Her words start becoming slurred and lethargic.

"Um well. Ignis said you smelled bad."

Ignis whips his head around, "*SAY WHAT!*"

"Oh, okay." She says acceptingly. Cupping her hand, she scoops water up to her mouth to drink. Using the residue, she wipes her face smearing the dirt around. Groggily she takes another drink of water. She drops her hand back into the water. Her eyes glaze over as she stares at her insignia. Ignoring the fact her arm is wrapped around Stirling's neck she begins to rub at the scabbing X that breaks open. Red trickles from her arm and flows into the water in miniature eddies.

A compulsion with cleaning her arm consumes her. Pushing back from Stirling again, she is able to shimmy out of his arms without any resistance. Stirling reaches out to help her as she floats back towards the center of the pond.

"No." Her voice is painfully coarse. She lets herself sink beneath the surface, submerging her entire body.

Stirling reluctantly sits back with poised hands ready to rescue. Her frame willingly rests at the bottom. Closing her eyes, Amiria lets the water cleanse her. She scratches at her scalp, pulling apart her tangles before moving back to her body, and scrubs at her arms and legs, each second growing more violent as if she is trying to remove the top layer of her skin.

"*Um.*" Ignis cocks his head.

Stirling snags her from the shallow depths bringing her back to him. Her back pinned against his chest, her hands still ferociously clawing at herself.

He protectively grabs her wrists, "Hey, calm down, calm down."

Amiria freezes. Her vision nailed to the X over her insignia. Stirling uses his thumb to twirl his mother's bracelet around her wrist. His old and healed scars exposed next to her peeled scabs, now open and bleeding.

"Do you want to talk about it?" He rests his head atop of hers.

She relaxes into him. Without answering his question, she asks hers, "Will you carry me baker boy?"

Stirling smiles internally, "Always."

Guiding her back to the bank, he helps her out of the pool. Amiria crawls on her hands and knees and sits beside the pond with chattering teeth. Her body convulses in a series of shivers as the night air pricks through her soaked clothing. Ignoring his goosebumps forming, Stirling throws the dry canvas around her shoulders. She instinctively wraps it tight around herself and bundles up.

Amiria watches with tired eyes as Stirling shrugs on the old worn-out tunic and trousers and ties what she could swear is a guard's armor to Ignis. When he is done Stirling holds out a mauve cotehardie and a pair of black tights to Amiria.

Snatching the fabric, Amiria buries her face into the wool and says with a muffled voice, "A cotehardie."

Stirling spins away, red in the face as Amiria tugs her old, ruined night tunic over her head and changes into her dry clothing. Unable to stand, she shimmies into her tights. "Okay," she tells him.

Cautiously, Stirling turns around. Amiria had pulled the canvas tight around her once again, and he steps up to her holding out both his hands. With her hands still tucked inside the canvas, she reaches up to him. His hands engulf hers, and she is whisked to her feet.

Before her legs have the chance to give out, he wraps his arms around her waist and picks her up. She doesn't care that she is being held like a small child. This is Stirling, her Stirling. Her baker boy. Her best friend who will never judge her. She loops her arms around his neck and her legs around his waist.

He cherishes the moment. Never again will he let something as small as her embrace be taken for granted. He hugs her close, praying he never has to let her go.

"*Eh-hem.*" Ignis interrupts. "*You ready to take this back to the cave, because I'm exhausted.*"

"Exhausted? You didn't do anything." Stirling scowls taking the lead back to the cave.

"*Worrying about you takes a toll, you know. I don't know how Amiria has done it all these years.*" Ignis complains.

Stirling doesn't answer. He doesn't know how worrying not just about him, but everyone hasn't killed her.

It almost did. He realizes.

Stirling can hear Amiria's breathing change to a soft rhythm as she falls asleep to the rocking of his steps.

The beige dragon perks up her head, her senses signaling the return of her bonded rider. Even before speaking, a dragon always knows the proximity of their rider. She could feel each step bringing her closer. Amiria's mind was opened to her for a brief moment. She was finally heard, after all these years of wishing Amiria knew she heard each of Amiria's confessions to her. All those times she felt foolish for confiding in a dragon weren't in vain. Taika heard each of her words, but Amiria had not broken through that barrier; they were not connected on the level they needed for her to hear Taika tell her everything was going to be okay. Amiria's mind is closed for now, but she will be back, and she will awaken stronger.

Clamping a log between her teeth, Taika adds it to the half-burned pile. The weak boy Amiria seems to care about instructs her to have a fire going when he comes back with her because she is going to need it.

There are stronger, more suitable mates all over Wyverna. Even some in the new land they were stationed in for a short period. Taika used to not understand why Amiria settled for this one. She couldn't wrap her mind around it until...

Stirling enters the cave with Amiria asleep in his arms. Containing her excitement, as the only rational one in this group, she lowers her snout to the logs and blows a current of hot air, igniting them. The cave comes to life, the fire yawning awake as it stretches its peaks.

She doesn't move as the clunky dragon she's grown to tolerate lands in the mouth of the cave behind her. Her eyes fixate on Amiria being carried by Stirling across the cave.

"She's back with you again, Taika. Don't worry," Stirling kneels beside the fire, laying Amiria down on one of the quick beds he made from layered pine and moss for padding in a branch frame.

As his hands slide out from under her, leaving her to lie alone, Amiria stirs awake, the warmth of his body heat replaced by the fire. It sinks through her thin and bluing skin, reviving her with energy.

Amiria reaches out with a smile so wide her cheeks block her eyes, "TAIKA!"

Extending her neck out over the fire she nuzzles the tips of Amiria's fingers. Amiria scratches under Taika's chin before curling back in on herself, "I missed you too."

"Are you hungry?" Stirling asks, "Do you want something to eat?" He squats down beside her.

"Maybe in the morning," Amiria says dreamily as she lowers her head down to the pine.

Stirling sets a costrel beside her, "In case you get thirsty."

"Thank you," she says with her eyes already closing again, "Are you going to lay down too?"

Stirling pulls a blanket over her up to her shoulders, "Yeah, I'll be just a reach away." He tells her, motioning to the other bed making a 90-degree angle around the fire.

"Oh. Okay." She says, sullen as if she was wishing for something different. Her mind once again gives into exhaustion, and she falls asleep with her head on her arm.

The embers in the fire glow a dark red, emanating enough light to see the outlines of the two people asleep beside it. With his heart racing Stirling bolts up right, tossing his blanket half off his body. He squints as his eyes adjust to the dim light.

Amiria lets out another painful cry. Frantically, Stirling kicks the blanket twisted around his legs off to the side and crawls to her. He searches the cave confused. No one else is here besides Ignis, who is sprawled out still deep asleep, and Taika, who's light brown eyes watch him instead of Amiria.

His attention is brought back to Amiria as she whimpers. She has broken out into a sweat, the muscles in her face and hands twitching in response to a nightmare.

"Please don't hit me," Stirling says to himself. He reaches out, setting his hand on her shoulder, shaking her lightly, "Amiria, Amiria wake up."

Panicked, Amiria takes hold of his wrist, her jagged and chipped nails digging into his skin. Her eyes are dilated and wild as if her life had flashed before her eyes. Stirling winces as she breaks the skin of his wrist, but he doesn't remove her fingers.

"It's okay, it was just a dream, you're okay," he soothes, rubbing her back.

Amiria's rapid breathing begins to slow with each gasping intake. Removing her claws from Stirling's wrist, Amiria lets out a broken sigh and slips her hand down to lay a top of his. She lets the weight ground her. She is safe in the cave, his cave. Their cave.

Liquid seeps into her eyes, filling them. She doesn't know where it's coming from, but she can't stop it. *No, no, no, don't.* She closes her eyes, shutting the floodgates. *I can't, I've never.* It's too late. The lake built up from years of being stuck behind a dam finally cracks and breaks. Set free for the first time since she was a toddler, the tears pour down her face.

Stirling feels each fiber in his heart tear as he sees her cry. He reaches out, cupping her cheek, "Hey, hey it's okay, it's all right." He brushes his thumb across her cheek wiping away a tear.

Amiria reaches up, taking his tunic in her hands. The fabric bunches in her grip as she pulls herself into his chest weeping.

Stirling protectively wraps his arms around her, and he strokes her hair consolingly, "Shh, it's okay. I got you. I got you."

She lets him hold her, lets him be the support as her walls crumble into a new layer of pebbles and dust on the cave floor. She knows if someone was to attack, she won't have the strength to fight. She has never been more vulnerable, but even in her state, here and now in his arms, she has never felt safer.

Wiping her face with Stirling's tunic, Amiria works on containing her sobs, diminishing them down to free falling tears like the few rain drops still falling after the passing of a storm. Her voice is softer than Stirling has ever heard it before, her words barely audible through the fabric bunched around her face, "Lay with me."

"What?" Stirling says shortly. Did he hear correctly?

Her head turns up, her dark eyes peering through her thick lashes wet with tears, "Don't let go. Lay with me. Please."

"O-okay," he manages to say, finding it suddenly hard to breathe.

Hoping she can't feel him trembling, Stirling keeps one arm held around her as he scoots himself onto her bed and lays them both down on their sides. Stirling pulls the blanket over them, putting a roof to the new walls around her. With his arm as her pillow, he drops the other one around her back, keeping her safe in his fortress.

Amiria shivers into him as she feels the warmth of his body surrounding her. What had terrorized her moments before is now obsolete. She is slowly forgetting what it was. Forgetting the nightmare she had that was too close to recounting actual events. One day she will tell him about that place. What they had done—what *he* had planned. For now she will listen to the sound of his heartbeat filling the silence.

Is there a more beautiful sound?

She edges closer, pressing her face into his chest. She feels a pressure on the top of her head, light and delicate. He had kissed her, and like a magic cure, she fell asleep in his arms.

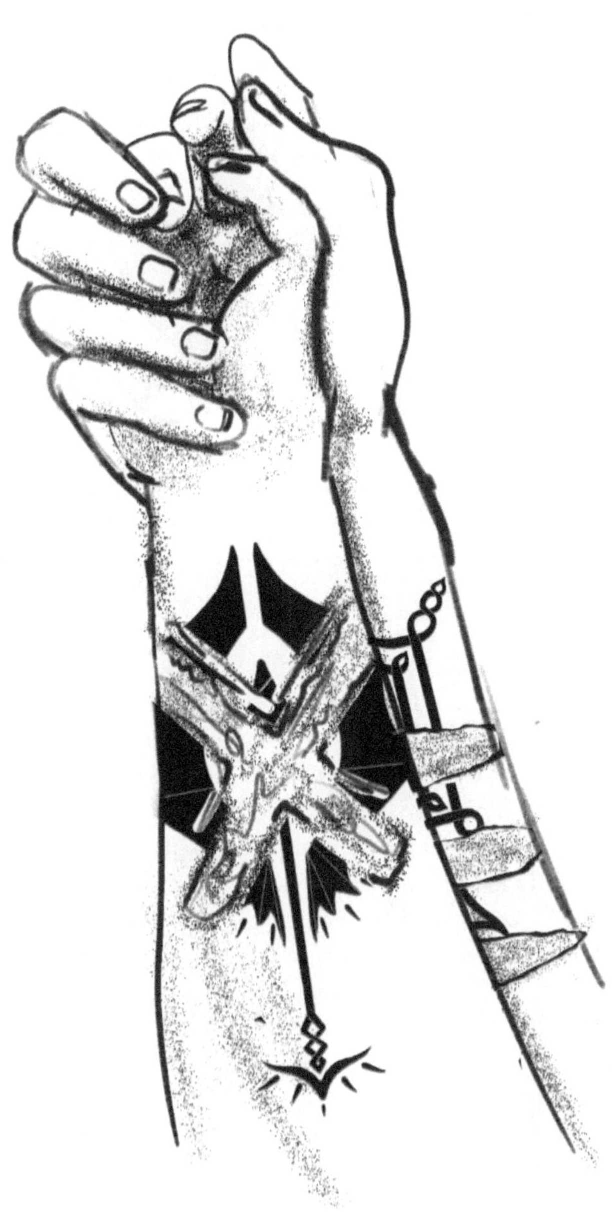

Thirty-Five

Silk covered arms swoop across the long, elegant hardwood of the strawberry tree desk, crashing and dragging all the contents across it. Parchments fly like released doves as he casts all of the items to the side in a fit of rage. Seals, wax, ink, paper weights, all go crashing to the plush rug beneath his feet.

Calix tilts his head as he observes. His handsome features show less expression than the royal paintings as King Dietrich unhinges before him. He stands poised with his hands crossed behind his back, his light eyes reflecting the scene without a readable thought.

Clyde kneels in the same square of marble Amiria was once forced down to. With a great deal of effort, he holds his voice steady, "Someone must have infiltrated us, Your Majesty. Our—" He pauses, throwing in a partial lie. "Guards were both attacked from behind while providing the girl with water. The perpetrator escaped wearing one of the guards' uniforms as a disguise."

King Dietrich slams both fists on the now empty desk. "I understand what occurred." He says through his teeth,

"I don't understand how. How did you allow something so crucial to slip under your little *guard* nose."

Swallowing at the lump forming in his throat, Clyde grinds his teeth at the underhanded jab. He is a guard because King Dietrich demoted him to one. He oversees Amiria because King Dietrich assigned him. But Amiria escaped because *his* guards failed because *he* failed as their captain. His fingernails grip into the fabric over his insignia. He failed against Amiria yet again.

With a cynical smile, Calix clears his throat. What does he gain from watching the punishment of this measly guard? Nothing. He finds some enjoyment at this moment but in the long run, it adds nothing to his plans. Let the fish go, he's hooking a shark, "Permission to interject?"

Top lip raised and still fuming, King Dietrich growls, "Permission granted."

"I might be mistaken but the Field Marshal himself was in charge of the girl, was he not?" Calix casts his line. "If there is a person who should be questioned on these present matters, I strongly believe it should be him. There was a conflict of interest between him and the girl."

The silver pitcher makes a whooshing sound as it whips past Calix's head, crashing into the wall behind him. He stands composed, not a hair out of place, cautiously watching the crazed king still in the after pose of throwing.

"I made the right choice with you." King Dietrich rises to his feet matching Calix's height. Calix bows his head in respect. "Guard!" King Dietrich shouts his eyes still on Calix, "Bring me Sir Rey."

Clyde stares blankly.

King Dietrich's head cracks to the side to face Clyde roaring, "NOW!"

Clyde slides on the smooth ground as he scampers to his feet and out of the King's Cabinet with his tail between his legs.

"She is mine." King Dietrich lifts his chair and hurls it to where Clyde was once kneeling. A muscle twitches in Calix's jaw. "She belongs to me, ME!"

"Sire."

Breathing heavily and his eyes hidden beneath the shadow of his brow, King Dietrich says in a gravelly voice, "What is it?"

"I have two propositions," Calix begins.

"Go on."

"The first is the girl is far from Wyverna by now, but I've tracked her down once before and I can do it again. The second is, if she is the same girl I've come to know. It means she is still here in the kingdom." Calix explains.

King Dietrich spins on him, "What gives you the idea she is still here?"

The younger man resists taking a step back and holds his face unwavering. "Because the Winged Cavalry doesn't run. She wants revenge." King Dietrich raises an eyebrow. Calix continues, "She will hide, regain her strength then she will be coming for you."

King Dietrich searches Calix's face as he calculates his words. Would she come back to him? Fate has brought them together more than once, maybe she is destined to fall into his lap no matter how many times or how far she runs. "Find her."

"She can never run further than I can hunt," Calix's eyes narrow.

King Dietrich smiles, "Good." Calix straightens his back, unnerved at the king's deranged smile. King Dietrich continues after his elongated pause, "Because if you don't find her, I have an empty oubliette up for rehousing." Calix's stomach drops. "But if you do find her, I think the current Field Marshal will be retiring soon."

Be tortured or promoted, Calix thinks to himself. Those are his options, no in-between, but isn't watching the king own Amiria a form of torture in itself? The only difference is one will physically kill him, but what's left in him to kill? He will figure something out, a way to still win. "Understood, Your Majesty. I will devise a small search party and begin as soon as possible"

"Oh." King Dietrich waves his hand adding another minor detail to their deal, "Try and keep that sister of yours out of this. I need the girl returned to me *alive*.

"Yes, sire." Calix bows.

Wool threads through delicate fingers as it's pulled by the spinning wheel. Arietta hums along with the tapping of the pedal feeding the intricate machine. Derek leans back in his chair with his eyes closed, listening to her.

This isn't the home he grew up in, the original Rey manor. But this is the home Amiria grew up in. He had downgraded from the extravagant home with its own towers situated between the castle and the base. He sees no need for lavish items and his family was and still is too small for a mansion.

When his parents passed away and he inherited both the home and the title, he sold it and moved into Amiria's adoptive mother, his best friend, Corliss' house. The cottage-like home with vine-covered stones lined with hydrangea flowers he will admit is still on the noble side of living but he at least has use for all the rooms.

Hidden against the tree line, it had always reminded him of the fairy tale stories he heard as a kid. The ones he knew Corliss had told to Amiria, but he never told himself. The stories where the girl was always saved by the boy.

Derek smiles to himself as distant memories he forgot he has replays across the back of his eyelids. He remembers a rare occasion when he was home, and Amiria had first heard one of the tales. How she questioned why is it always a boy saving a girl? Why doesn't the girl save the boy? He had told her that there was plenty and to ask her mother how many times *she* had saved *him* on the battlefield. Giddy with newfound knowledge, she had taken off in search of her mother.

In this home, he found a place where he could relax the tension in his shoulders without keeping up the heavy weight of his name. The Gautiers had taken the burden of the oversized stack of stone decades ago.

Lost in his memories Arietta's humming begins to lull Derek to sleep. Amiria's young childlike face grows and morphs into a woman. Her eyes, full of astonishment and wonder, turn dead as the night. Empty darkness hiding monsters in her shadows. They stare unblinking as she is lowered into the oubliette.

Breaking out into a cold sweat, Derek's eyes burst open. Arietta pauses her work to turn to him, knowing he had another nightmare. He rests his hand on his chest feeling the rapid thumping of his heart. He knows Arietta is watching him, waiting for the day he confesses what keeps him up at night, but his lips remain silent. They're his mistakes to live with, his trauma to carry. He had promised himself the day he met her that he would not invoke her to the horrors Field Marshal Rey lives with daily.

Arietta never wanted Amiria in the Cavalry. He did, he was the one who needed an heir. He insisted she became a Winged Rider despite her disdain and the fear of watching her daughter march into battle. He now sits here drowning in a pool of reality he created.

If he wasn't broken down inside, he would laugh at the ironic circumstances. Amiria grew up without her real mother because she feared the life of the Cavalry. Yet here they now sit in this main room of his home for another fear. For the first time after over twenty years of being together, they are living under the same roof.

His heart slows and his face falls as he imagines the two of them sitting here like this, watching their daughter grow up. A team approach to guiding her through all the twists and turns life throws at her. Instead, nannies who could not answer life in the Cavalry questions did their best.

He had missed her first steps, her first words, the first day she got her dragon, the first day of training. Who is she? Amiria is a stranger to him, the only thing in common being the blood in their veins.

Derek climbs his way out of the hole he mentally dug as a knock rattles the front door. He scowls. He can't have a moment of solitude, can he? The Cavalry has taken his entire life. Now if only they can find the decency to give him a single day uninterrupted. The sun hasn't even finished rising and they already need him.

Arietta knowingly returns to the tranquility of her wheel as Derek stands up from his chair with a grunt. His overworked body cracks as he stretches his spine back. Hardening his face back to Field Marshal Rey he travels across the room and answers the door.

Field Marshal Rey blinks away the morning light breaking through the surrounding trees and stares at the guard standing on his doorstep while recognition takes place, "Captain Mannering what is the matter with you? Coming to my personal home."

"My greatest apologies Field Marshal for the intrusion but I come on the orders of King Dietrich. He beckons for you," Clyde says, shifting his weight back and forth on his heels.

"Can this wait till after breakfast?" Field Marshal Rey fakes a yawn.

"No, sir. It's urgent matters." Clyde's fingers twitch nervously. He leans forward, speaking in a volume so low he can barely hear himself, "It's about Amiria. She's escaped."

Derek seizes Clyde by the collar, who flinches, pulling his face back in fear of being hit. Slipping out of his role as Field Marshal and back into a father, Derek checks over his shoulder. Arietta has stopped spinning the wool and is watching him with her dark eyes, Amiria's eyes.

Derek releases Clyde with a slight shove. "Carry on Captain, I know the way to his *majesty's* cabinet."

With a shaky breath, Clyde fixes his collar with a nervous gulp. He nods his respect to Amiria's father and backs away into the morning rays.

Thirty-Six

Amiria's face scrunches as the morning sun enters the cave. With her head resting on the soft spot on Stirling's chest in between his shoulder and his collarbone, her eyes blink awake. His arm is still cradled around her with his hand resting on her waist and hers lays across him.

Hearing the soft sounds of his breathing, she watches the matching rise and fall of his chest. Tilting her head up, she admires his slumbering face. Seeing how the sun shines on only half of his face creates a golden outline from her perspective. It runs down the profile of his face and lights up where his lips hang partially open.

She runs her hand up his chest, feeling the curvature of his body up to his neck where she trails her fingertips along his jawline. His eyelids drowsily open.

Rolling his head, he smiles down at her with bright hazel eyes. "Good morning."

Amiria blushes. "Good morning."

Kneeling beside the fire, Stirling checks on the progress of the breakfast he is cooking, an egg cracked into a carved-out potato then reclosed to cook the egg inside with wild chives and garlic.

Stirling glances up from the charring potato skins, "Drink some water."

Amiria, who had been quietly watching him, scrunches her nose playfully before sipping from the costrel he had laid beside her the night before. Pulling her knees to her chest, she wraps her arms around them, "I really did speak with Taika? That wasn't a dream?"

After they had woken, Stirling had spent most of the morning explaining to Amiria what had conspired leading up to her rescue while he bandaged her arm with medicinal herbs. He told her about returning to the bakery, glazing over his argument with his father, and skipping to the gallows and the guard giving him indirect information. He told her about all his implausible rescue plans he was reciting when Taika informed Ignis she had spoken to her. He told her all about Lorelle and Henry, how they came up with the plan and deserve all the credit.

Amiria didn't open herself to tell him what she had been through. Stirling could see it in her eyes that she wasn't ready to talk about it, so he didn't pressure her to. He's learned the more someone forces her to open up the more locks she will create. Like a feral animal, you have to let them approach you.

Pursing her lips, Amiria furrows her brows as if deep in thought, "Is there an on-and-off to it? Like a special trick to hear her?"

A single burst of laughter escapes from Stirling, "Ha! On or off. I wish. It's stuck on as far as I know. No special trick, just talk like you and I do."

Ignis flicks his tail, *"You aren't the only one who wishes there was an off lever."*

Amira adjusts her legs to sit cross-legged, closing her eyes she relaxes her body and mind. She can feel a mental door opening. "Good morning, Taika." She says out loud.

The mellifluous voice she heard during her living nightmare sings in her mind again, *"Good morning, Amiria."*

Pupils dilating Amiria's breath hitches, her soul elated and overwhelmed. Radiant tears fill the edges of her eyes, "That's her voice. *That's* Taika's voice. It's beautiful." She laughs back the tears.

Stirling's eyes remain on Amiria the entire time. He can't help but fall in love with her every day. Witnessing her moments of raw emotions, his best friend exhibiting pure jubilance sends his heart tumbling. Like a drug, seeing her smile releases dopamine through his body, giving him a unique sense of satisfaction. In his euphoric state, he knows for certain he wants to see her smile for the rest of his life.

"Huh?" Stirling asks, realizing Amiria was speaking to him.

"I said, Taika wants to thank you for saving me."

Using two sticks as tongs, Stirling removes one of the potatoes from the fire. He shakes his head, "Remember, I didn't do much. The servants devised the plan, and the guy, Henry, walked me through every step."

Amiria's voice snaps with urgency, "Asking for help doesn't make you less brave or any less of a hero." Her eyes flick across the ceiling of the cave as she searches for the right words to convey her thoughts, "Understanding your faults and asking for assistance doesn't make you weak. It makes you stronger. Stirling Bakere you are my hero and—" her eyes fall back to him, "I'm in love with you."

Stirling fumbles, dropping the sticks as he removes the second potato from the fire. It rolls across the ground by his knees, "You-you-you—love me?"

"*Well, well, well,*" Ignis comments.

"Yes stupid. I've always loved you," Amiria blurts.

Okay, all right, okay, calm down, okay. You got this. He can feel his face growing hot, suddenly very self-aware of every movement he makes. Scrabbling, he picks the potato he had removed from the fire off the ground with his bare hand.

"OW!" He drops the burning potato back on the cool cave floor.

"*Smooth.*" Ignis laughs.

Amiria stifles a giggle at Stirling's sudden—more than usual—foolishness. Her smile fades and her tone become serious, "So, what's next?"

Stirling can't look her in the eye. "Well…" His voice trails off.

She rolls her eyes, "I mean about Wyverna. What are we going to do about Wyverna and her people."

Blushing and embarrassed by his misinterpretation, Stirling hides his face as he shrugs, "Run, I guess. We're only two people. There isn't anything we *can* do."

"*YES! Let's go home!*" Ignis perks up, "*Now that you two are finally an item. I want to go be with my own love.*"

Stirling's eyes briefly flick to Ignis in acknowledgment then return to Amiria, who continues, "When I say Wyverna, I mean King Dietrich, I mean Calix. I mean those who hurt *me*." She flashes her newly rebranded arm that Stirling had bandaged with herbs Faerydae had taught him about, "Don't get me wrong Stirling. I understand I can't dismantle a several hundred-year-old system. But what you fail to understand is, no matter how far I run. Calix *will* find me. This anger, *my* need for revenge is on a personal level."

His eyes drop to the torn cloth used as a bandage over the "X" on her arm. Blood has already begun seeping through from the previous night where she scratched open the scabs. His eyes follow up her arm to where he can see the protrusion of her collarbone past the loose fabric of her cotehardie.

King Dietrich, Calix, the Cavalry, this place. They all had locked her away, they left her in a hole in the ground to wither away until she stopped fighting physically and mentally. But she didn't. Even with all the strength sapped from her body she never let them have her mind. He pictures Calix throwing her into the cell. Anger he has never experienced before boils inside his core.

He has just gotten her back. He can't hand her back over to them. Not again. Especially not after seeing the terror in her eyes last night. Images flashed behind her dark iris of memories she doesn't want to speak of.

"No!" he exclaims. How had their conversation turned to this? They were on the topic of them and love. Not the beginnings of an argument.

"No?" Amiria repeats taken back at his outburst.

"*Uh oh.*" Ignis' eyes dart between them.

"No," Stirling says again with sureness. He pinches the bridge of his nose. "Didn't we already have this conversation back in Leucasia? You can't take on a *king*. Taking on a king means taking on a kingdom." He thought she was past this nonsense. Before she was taken, she had come to her senses and was choosing to stay in Patu with him. Why is she reverting back?

Amiria speaks quickly and irrationally, "Not if I can just slip in, kill King Dietrich, kill Calix then slip out again."

"Do you hear yourself right now? Amiria, I can't risk losing you again. After you escape, you're supposed to run away, not run back. Look what they did to you," Stirling tells her.

Amiria, unable to stand, jabs her finger in his direction, "You think I'm crazy! I know what they did to me and I'm not afraid to go back there!"

"BUT I AM! I am afraid of you going back there!" he yells on the verge of tears. Letting out a slow breath he lowers his voice, "I care deeply about you and if you care about me or about Taika you wouldn't go running to your own funeral."

"I'm not running to my own funeral," Amiria crosses her arms.

Stirling throws his hands, "A lifetime of servitude, same thing."

"Why won't you understand," she's on the verge of pleading, "Stirling, they will *never* let me go. No matter how far I run, he will always find me." She points to the back of the cave in the direction of the castle. Bringing her hand to her face she digs the heel into her eye in frustration. She drops it to her lap looking up to the ceiling. Blinking back the tears, she refuses to mourn what she can never have, "We will never be an us, if there is them."

Stirling speaks to the dusty ground, "I'd rather live on the run together than to leave here alone."

"That isn't living," Amiria says as if teaching a child. "That's surviving. What you have in Patu, that is living. Growing up and growing old in a place surrounded by people who love and care about you." Several tears slip from her eyes, and she wipes them away aggressively. How could her body betray her like that? She's trained to contain her emotions. Is this how it's going to be from now on? Useless human features, she curses.

Stirling does not hide his tears, but his words come out with spite, "If I wanted to grow old without you, then I would never have come here."

They sit in silence; his words linger in the fire's smoke between them like a howling phantom. Stirling picks up the now-cooling potatoes and steps around the fire to sit by her side.

He hands one of them to her, "Let's sleep on this, we should be safe in this cave while you regain your strength. Spending some nights lying low might be good. Maybe it convinces them we're long gone. Then when you're healthy again, we'll come back to this conversation. Deal?" His smile doesn't reach his red-rimmed eyes.

"Deal." She replies with no trace of a smile on her lips.

Ignis groans, *"We're never going home."* He tips over, sprawling out in a tantrum.

"Ignis." Stirling frowns.

"Don't look at me. Just let my broken heart consume me." He whines. Taika rolls her head annoyed.

Putting her and Stirling's conversation to the back of her mind Amiria asks, "What's wrong with him?" She bites into the potato and egg, the starch and protein rejuvenating her with new energy.

"He's just being dramatic." Stirling brushes him off.

Ignis lifts his head. *"Am not!"*

"Yes, you are."

"Not any more dramatic than you act!" Ignis throws back.

Stirling scoffs. "My cases are different."

"Love is love." Ignis drops his head to the floor with an exaggerated thump.

Amiria smiles at Taika. "Thank you for being you."

"I would never behave in such a fledgling way," she says in disgust. *"By the way Amiria."* She says changing the topic. *"I will not tell you, which is the right or wrong choice to make, but I will defend the one you do choose."*

Amiria nods in reply.

Noticing Amiria's listening expression, Stirling swallows a large bite of potato and asks, "What is Taika saying?"

"Huh?" Amiria says blinking with a shake of her head as if her mind trailed off, "Oh, just making fun of Ignis."

"*Rude,*" Ignis says without looking at them.

"It won't be forever Ignis," Stirling says.

"*Even if Taika lit you on fire, you won't burn like my heart does for Aether.*" Ignis laments. "*They are my life, my muse, my new reason for living.*"

Exasperated, Stirling sighs, "Oh, shut up, Ignis. You just think they are pretty."

"*The most beautiful sight I've ever beheld.*"

Thirty-Seven

H ah!" Eda bursts. "You have to be out of your mind to think I'll ever take orders from you." She lies to one side, lounging on a chaise in their team's private cabinet.

"He's already proven that he's crazy on several accounts." Everard, resting against the back of the chaise, supports Eda's claim.

Calix stands in a wide stance with crossed arms at the head of the room, the exit to his back. His eyebrows knit closer together as each of his supposed teammates speaks.

"You're Corporal Gautier, not Major Gautier, not General Gautier. Corporal," Dicun throws out smugly.

"I'm just asking for assistance." Calix bites down his pride.

"Why don't you have your good ol' pa give us the orders himself?" Armundus snarls. "Or are you just trying to pass off *your* assignment?"

"You're the king's lap dog—" Eda makes a shooing motion with her hand. "Go play fetch on your own." Her disdain slides off her tongue.

Dicun sighs at the disparagement he had assisted in turning the conversation into. "Look Calix. You've tracked her across a new world. I watched you. How hard can the mountains we've trained in be?"

Stepping around the chaise, Everard sits beside Eda, who moves to rest her legs across his lap. "I would say the Field Marshal would be proud of all your accomplishments, except he's speaking to the king right now about how he let his wretched daughter escape." Everard strokes the stubble on his chin to fake deep thought. "I wonder if he knows how you are trying to weasel into his position?"

Eda walks her fingers up Everard's arm. "Step by step, the Gautiers are coming, Field Marshal. But—" She drops her hand. "I don't care who is in charge." She narrows in on Calix. "As long as it's not you, because I don't like you, or your face."

"You're one reliable team." Calix rolls his eyes.

Armundus snaps, "Not like you have the best track record for most selfless acts."

Calix throws back his head in defeat, then looks back at his supposed team. "I'll remember the years I spent with you. When I'm sitting in the Field Marshal's seat I'll think of you, rotting in this room with your stale attitudes well past your prime." He raises his arms. "Thought I would share some reward by having you help capture the girl. Guess I'll have to get my own reconnaissance team. Good thing I know the General."

He backs up towards the exit afraid to turn his back to the room. Reaching behind him, he feels the cool metal of the handle. The door pushes open, allowing him to slip out and remove himself from the den.

Standing where Clyde had stood earlier this morning before the sun rose and where Amiria had been forced to kneel in what feels like ages ago, Derek's lips disappear as he pulls them into a thin line. It's his best effort to keep back the onslaught of words he wishes to release on King Dietrich.

King Dietrich's uncanny smile sits painted on his face as he twirls a letter opener tip down, creating a notch on his desk, "Speak Field Marshal. What information do you have to add? Was this or was this not your jurisdiction? While you were sleeping peacefully at home, someone infiltrated the castle and stole the girl."

"The girl is a person, a person cannot be stolen. They aren't property," Derek lets slip from his barricade. He is glad Amiria is out of this man's heavenly jeweled grasp.

King Dietrich stabs the desk, the letter opener sticking straight up from the split wood, "Wrong! She had given up her rights as a human when she committed treason. She is mine to do with as I please. She is royal property and was stolen."

Iron covers his taste buds as he bites his tongue. A muscle in his jaw pulses a morse code of what he wants to say. He fears Amiria hasn't run far enough. He dreads the outcome for who had betrayed the king to save her life. He can see it happening: a captain standing on the quarter deck calculating the changes in the tides, their ship's mast turning to follow a new wind.

He swallows the words and says, "I have no knowledge of the traitorous act, Your *Majesty.*" Derek bows at the waist. "My sincere apologies for not keeping a closer eye on those I assigned the responsibility of something of great importance to you."

Derek keeps his head low, his mind conflicted. He is elated Amiria is no longer confined to this life, but he has failed his duties. His instincts as a father fighting against his trained mentality of high officer of the Winged

Cavalry. He failed an assignment. Reys don't fail, but is this a win?

King Dietrich growls, his crown slips on head as he leans forward, "If I discover the words coming from your mouth are not genuine, I will strongly believe a new Field Marshal shall be required."

Derek, still holding his bow, states, "I understand sire."

Dark leather shoes land on the threshold of the Gautier manor gate. His lean body hangs idol, stuck in the present while his mind is sent back to the past of horrors. Clenching his jaw, he pushes through the air dense with repressed memories, and his feet trudge along the manicured pathway up to the front door.

Stiffly raking his hair back with his fingers, he raises his knuckles to the door. Breathing in deep through his nose, he taps the back of his hand against the sturdy wood.

The soundless door pulls back into the house, a handmaiden with gray hair tucked into a coif and wrinkles in the corner of her eyes stands in the opening. Her questioning eyes turn soft, the soul behind them breaking at the sight of a young gentleman standing at the doorstep.

Her voice exposes the sadness in her heart. "Oh, Master Calix." Her shoulders slump. "It's been years, are you…finally doing well?"

"I'm managing." His smile is warm for the one soul who bandaged his wounds as he grew up. "It's good to see you, Genevieve. Is the General home? She was not in her office."

"Yes. She is in the study." Genevieve steps to the side inviting Calix into his childhood home.

His outer shell, never revealing the contents it contains, holds his composure stoic as he steps into the foyer. His hands clasp behind his back, hiding the ill effects that the oppressive energy still leaking from the walls is having on him.

He nods to Genevieve. "Thanks."

Giving him a sympathetic smile, Genevieve reaches out and touches Calix on the arm. She opens her mouth as Calix turns to her.

"I'm fine." He lies through a smile, his hands turning white in his grip. "Please don't wait on me, I'll be able to show myself out. I know you're busy with work."

Her hand drops. "Yes, Master Calix. Take care of yourself. Remember, you've got more to live for than this."

Calix's smile falters at the comment but he turns away from Genevieve before it falls completely from his face. Without another word to her, he bites his bottom lip and ventures deeper into the house, passing a set of stairs leading to his and his siblings' rooms.

His sister's scream echoing down the hall as she's dragged past his room.

"Don't," he whispers to himself, closing his eyes. "Don't remember." Still walking, he opens his eyes to a tapestry in the main drawing room beside the fireplace.

He's playing hide and seek with his older brother, small feet poking out from the tapestry. It's not his brother who seizes him, but his father's hand. He's ripped and dragged from the room, tears leaving a trail for Genevieve to mop through the house.

"Don't," he commands himself. His fingernails dig into the meat of his hand as his mind is flooded with locked away images. He shifts on his feet, and he can see the well cared for garden out back through the window.

Blisters, split skin, ruby painted rocks. Another lap around the garden barefoot. His muscles are straining and burning. He can't stop, not until he's granted permission.

"What are you doing here?"

Surprised, Calix spins around to face his brother. His mother's double.

With his glowering almond eyes pinpointed at Calix, he crosses his arms and repeats, "I asked you a question. What are you doing here?"

Calix composes himself. "I've got business matters to speak to the General about. It's none of your business."

"It will be mine as soon as you fail. I heard your little prisoner escaped. Good job." Keaton slowly claps. "Really, great job you're doing."

"I lost no one. The Field Marshal did, and now I'm going to clean up his mess. So maybe in the end you will be Major. Below me and—" Calix smiles. "Kinsey."

Keaton rolls his eyes, unimpressed. "Kinsey has a loose spoke in her head."

"She might," Calix agrees, walking towards the hall his brother is standing in. "But General knows Kinsey will do *whatever* it takes to get the job done. So, it's all yours *little* brother, be Major." He stops before their shoulders touch, he looks sideways down at him, "You can spend your days with father." Keaton's eyes widen in fear. Calix's voice carries over his shoulder as he continues down the hall. "And to think, Keaton, you had it the easiest."

General Gautier glares down the long and narrow bridge of her nose at a scroll on the desk in the manor's study. Disgruntled, she carelessly drops the scroll on top of a disregarded stack in the center of the desk as a figure appears in the open doorway. "What do you need, Corporal?" She picks up another scroll and begins skimming it.

"General, I have been assigned a reconnaissance mission by King Dietrich in the surrounding mountains. I am requesting permission to be granted a section of four to carry out the orders," Calix says, conducting his posture formally.

She releases the bottom of the scroll letting it curl up with a snap. Her eyes strike like a snake at Calix. "Tell me, Corporal." She sets the scroll down and knits her fingers together. "Why are you unable to carry out your orders solo?"

Calix had prepared for her opposition. "The order can be completed solo, but time is a crucial factor, and it would be more efficient to have a team. We can cover the ground and air simultaneously."

Her pupils practically narrow into slits as she purses her lips. "I assume this is for King Dietrich's *personal* matters?"

Knowing she has guessed correctly who the search is for, Calix nods.

"I see. That information does sway my decision." She pauses, venomous eyes watching the beating pulse on Calix's neck as he struggles to hold his emotions flat. "Well—" She breaks the leering gaze. "I can find some spare trainees to assist you, Corporal. But this is not from the kindness of my heart. I just want to see Rey's face when you drag that child of his back to the king."

"I understand, General."

"I will have the trainees meet you on the field just before dusk. Let's see if you can prove yourself leading a team."

Prove himself by leading trainees? Children who have yet to graduate? He was assigned a platoon of fully fledged members half a year ago. Was he not worthy then? Had he not proven himself when he had tracked and apprehended the king's most valuable object down in uncharted lands with Dicun merely there for physical backup. Calix clenches his jaw. No, of course that wasn't good enough. That was only a move in her game, a game she has no interest in until she wins. She isn't here for the enjoyment of strategizing; she is only playing to destroy her opponent. Everything before the final move is impertinent.

"Yes, General. Thank you." He nods his respect.

General Gautier waves her hand in dismissal. "Show yourself out Corporal. I still have business to complete.

"Yes, General."

Thirty-Eight

Lorelle's weathered hands dip the water bucket with rotting edges into the river in a line with several other water carriers. A young man with a brewer's insignia who had followed a half-beaten trail from town squats beside her.

They keep their heads down. Their eyes stay on the water running around their already-filled buckets.

Lorelle speaks without moving her lips, "Terrible when a bird gets out of its cage."

"Children tend to leave the doors open," the brewer replies.

"Especially boys," Lorelle states, pulling her bucket to the shore next to her other filled one. Without giving the brewer so much as a glance she hooks them onto the shoulder bar and heaves them up into the air with a grunt.

Taking his pail, the brewer disappears in the opposite direction, heading back to the lower-class district of the city.

Whistling his regular tune, the brewer walks casually through the streets. Shouldering open the door to the quiet tavern, he shuffles past the several guests hunched to themselves at separate tables. The tavern maid continues to count the coin on the counter as the brewer sets the pail of water beside her.

"How's your morning?" she asks, uninterested.

"The same as always, but I did hear the baker was able to save the bread before it burned." The brewer turns away from the maid, occupying himself with the items on the shelves.

"Did you buy any?"

"No, they were all gone," the brewer excuses himself and heads into the back rooms. A smile slides across the maid's face.

A whispering wind travels through the people's mouths. It picks up dust swirling through the city streets and blowing through every opened window, gaining speed through every shopper's ear.

Standing beside the oven, Giles jumps as the wind blows open the bakery door. Grace leaps across the room, taking Giles' hand in hers, the tears already rolling down his cheeks and disappearing into his beard. With a trembling lip, the corners curl up into a proud smile.

Thirty-Nine

Calix's eyes, lit by the setting sun, scan the surrounding mountains. He stands on the training field where he had first seen Amiria. He remembers how when he saw her flying, nothing else mattered. She had him completely captivated and he wanted her more than a starving dog wants a bone.

He turns only his head, speaking over his shoulder to his young section of four undergraduates, "You might be nothing but shadows in your ranks but if you succeed in this mission you will be casting the light." He turns about-face to speak directly to his section, "I want you to work in pairs. Scour the forest for any evidence of human life, and report back to me. If you encounter the threat do not engage unless left with no other option. Send out the signal and I will come to assist you in apprehending the target. Am I clear?"

"Yes sir," they answer in unison.

"Ready the hounds."

With wobbling knees, Amiria manages to get up into a squat. Her fingers spread out tapping the ground as she tries to balance. Focusing on her breathing Amiria starts to rise, her legs straightening out to stand. Straining her weakened muscles, they give in to fatigue and she topples over with a curse.

"Stop pushing yourself—" Stirling kneels down beside her "--It hasn't even been a full day yet. Your body needs time to heal."

"I don't approve," Amiria motions to her frail body.

"Of what? Recovering?" Stirling guesses.

"No. Being weak and vulnerable," Amiria's face falls.

"You're never weak. Even now," Stirling comforts. "That's one of the many things I love about you."

Amiria turns away from him as the heat rises in her cheeks. He can show his heart so easily. It's as if he is native to a foreign land she has never been to and has no map to guide her.

"You want to walk so badly." He holds out both of his hands, "Here."

Raising an eyebrow, she rests her hands in his. He closes his hands around hers, almost covering them entirely. Standing back up, he lifts her to her feet with him and before she can object, he hooks her hands around his neck. Her rubber legs begin to bend as she tightens her hold on him. He slips his arms around to her back to brace her, he's not going to let her fall.

"Step up onto my feet." He instructs. Amiria does as he says, stepping her bare feet on top of his leather slip-ons.

Chest to chest, she peers up at him, her face practically touching his, "What now?"

"We dance." He smiles down at her.

"Dance?" A quizzical look casts over her face.

"Yes."

"To what?"

"To us." Grinning wildly he sidesteps, spinning them around the cave lit by the fire.

Amiria lets out a high pitch fit of laughter. She feels like a little girl dancing for the first time. The time Stirling spun her and his friends around the bone fire was only a month and a half ago in reality but a lifetime ago in experiences. She embodies that carefree moment, the smiles on everyone's faces, the rainbow light twirling with colors. She was happy then.

She is happy now.

Ignis taps his tail along to soundless music drumming a simple beat. His head bobbing along.

Amiria watches the cave spin around them but Stirling watches her. He sees nothing but how crinkles form in the corner of her eyes as her smile takes over the entirety of her face. Her ebony eyes hide behind her thick eyelashes. From here he can count the faded freckles on her nose.

She's so close. Close enough he could lean down—he feels his heart punch the inside of his chest—and kiss her.

Taika leers protectively over Amiria as she spins around with the boy. She doesn't understand the feelings everyone in this cave speaks of, but the boy keeps getting awfully close to Amiria. Closer than he used to dare. She needs to keep her guard up. Taika snaps to attention. "*Hush!*" she yells as she listens intently.

Amiria's mouth snaps shut, cutting off the laughter. Stirling slows to a stop as Amiria's face grows somber. He bites his lip knowing from the look on her face he is about to hear bad news.

Her eyes, filled with terror, find his, "Dogs, two of them. One is far, the other close and gaining."

Wearing the lighter leather armor provided to them during their training Jesse and James, two of the four riders of Calix's section, trail behind their panting hound. They step over another moss-covered log as they travel deeper into the forest than they've ever been.

"You can barely see a stone's throw away in here," James points out.

Jesse knocks off a mushroom growing on the side of a tree watching the fungus tumble to her feet, "That's probably how that baker kid lived out here unnoticed all these years. And to think we've trained not far from here."

They both stiffen at the low bellow from the hound.

"He's locked onto the scent," James says the obvious out loud even though Jesse understood what it meant. She grows pale, her hand resting on the hilt of her sword as they nod and trudge forward.

"Stirling," her voice is a quivering whisper. "I can't fight like this."

He holds her head to his chest, scanning the room he evaluates his options. He won't hand her over again. He will not lay useless beneath someone's knee while she fights for her life.

He skips from Ignis to Taika, and out over the ocean. The light is receding fast, throwing the mountain's shadows out over the water.

They've lost sight of the hound. Jesse walking at James' heels keeps her ears open, listening for any sounds. She focuses on her unsteady breaths. She hopes she doesn't hear anything.

James squints through the dimming light. He questioned why Sir Calix had them start at dusk and not at dawn. They are racing against the sun and will be out here searching blindly soon. The heavy shadows relentlessly play tricks with his eyes. Movement and figures always appear to be in the corner of his eye.

Possibly. His head whips to the side, checking another shadow. Possibly that is the reason he chose it. The average person is settling down for the night. Even fugitives must bunker down when the sun sets and won't be expecting someone to emerge from the dark.

"It's a dead end." Jesse frowns as they step into a small glade against a rock face. The hound they had been following sniffs around the patchy grass with his tail wagging.

"Hold on." James steps across the clearing. "What is that?"

Nearly invisible in the heavy shadows beneath a beech tree with roots clinging to the boulders and mountain face is a tunnel. With his nose to the dirt, the hound follows the scent up to the entrance and lets out a short howl. They listen as the echo plays back the signal that he has discovered something.

James' shaking hands pick up the horn hung around his neck. His eyes lock on the entrance as he feels an invisible force keeping it from reaching his lips.

Jesse notices the hesitation. "Let's check inside. Maybe it's a false lead."

Sitting cross-legged watching Stirling pack up the supplies on his own is driving Amiria mad. They are in a race, and she is sitting on the sidelines while her teammate does the entire relay. She rolls the blankets, but it isn't enough to staunch her feelings of being useless.

Stirling tightens the strap of a half empty bag of provisions, "This is why we should have left this morning."

Amiria churns the ash putting out the fire, "You know I'm not well enough to travel. This just means they have eyes on the mainland, not that they know where we are. They haven't seen us cross the border and are taking a guess we're still here."

Stirling raises his shoulders. They could have left. He could have strapped her to Taika and took care of her while they traveled back to Patu gaining as much distance as they could. But she had refused to leave this morning, and this isn't the time to start another argument, "We'll just change our hiding location…" He sighs and grits his teeth, "if we make it out of here first."

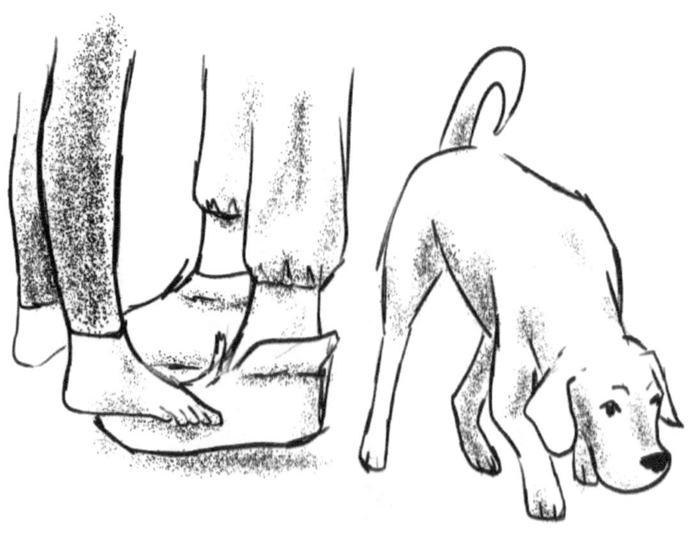

I can't see anything. How long can one tunnel be?" Jesse groans.

"I don't know. I'm just following the sound of the dog's breathing!" James exclaims as his hand drags along the cool rock leading through the mysterious tunnel. His hand drops suddenly absent of stone as they enter the hollow pocket on the other side of the mountain.

"A cave?" Jesse says, scanning the large area. The hounds tail wags as he sniffs the items around the room.

"A home," James corrects, stepping around the pine bedding to stoop beside the fire pit. He holds his hand out to the dead coals feeling the residue of their dying breaths. "I say they must have left almost half an hour ago."

Jesse's eyes skate across the room from the recently slept in beds, to a log carved out to hold water, to a wall built to block the wind. She glides in silence to the wall. Tilting her head observing, she touches the old rope tying the long branches together. Feeling the years of salt and wind exposure eating away at the knot.

James rises to his feet and swiftly matches Jesse standing at the other corner of the half-raised wall. A whisper of a smile blows across Jesse's face, like a summer wind across the grassland. With an understanding nod they push the wall off its stands to the lip of the sea cliff.

With a single thrust of their arms, they send it toppling over the edge. James turns to face the cave looking at the remnants of human life, the ocean wind tugging at his clothing and hair. "Let's hide the rest. No one will know they were here."

Amiria's heart beats like the snare drums leading into battle. She slouches forwards in Taika's saddle as they approach the second-largest island in the isle. Wrapping her arms around herself she presses her forehead to Taika's back. Who has she become? She has never feared the possibility of a fight before. Even outnumbered against an unknown number of bandits she has never chosen flight over fight. The possibility of death is not a new condition to her life's contract.

In the state she is in she wouldn't have been able to defend herself, let alone someone else. Taika and Ignis could have helped but the missing Winged Riders would have only sent waves of search parties and her demise wasn't what she was fearing.

She peaks through her flowing hair at Stirling, who looks as frightened as she feels. She wishes their situation was as simple as running away together. Take his hand and let him guide her to a new life. But what kind of life would that be? Always on the run, always checking over your shoulder, never being able to fall asleep in each other's arms.

King Dietrich will never stop pursuing her. Calix will never let her live any life he doesn't control. She has become a game, a piece of property. Something to occupy their empty lives. Stirling disappears as she closes her eyes. She can see Calix's piercing gaze watching around every corner. A hunter who has spent years studying his prey, able to read and predict its every movement.

A shiver runs down her spine and she opens her eyes to warm herself with the sight of her best friend. He looks back at her with a reassuring smile. Her lips struggle to return the gesture. Pulling away first, she turns her view to the volcanic island rising from the waters in a series of steep terraces.

Her focus switches to the foreground, Taika's spiked head and the reins flapping in the wind, *"Stirling has cheated this whole time,"* she says.

"What do you mean?"

"This is a much more efficient way to fly. A single mind versus using reins," Amiria explains her point.

"Is cheating the appropriate term? Or is learning under different circumstances more accurate? Because as someone who had to teach himself with no guidance, he could see professional training as cheating," Taika counters.

"I guess that's a good point." Amiria pauses, mulling it over in her mind. She used to think how unfair it was that this all came so naturally to Stirling, but she had never given much thought to all the years he spent learning through trial and error. While he struggled on his own, she was having someone show her every detail since she could walk. *"Let's head up to the usual."*

"I assumed as much."

Ignis' claws clack against the hard ground as they land in the familiar pocket between the towering rock walls. It has been nearly a year since the last time he had come here with Amiria. They came as children barely stepping into adulthood to play in the lake and explore the mazes of crevasses to escape for the day. Now Stirling's shoes crunch the gritty pebbles, again escaping for his life, all to live at least one more day with her.

Crouching, Taika lowers her body as Stirling approaches, so Amiria is level with him. She smiles at him with sunken cheeks and dark shadowed eyes.

Stirling touches her arm. "It's not comfortable but at least it's safe."

Patting the dense earth, Ignis shrugs. *It's fine to me, I always nap here.*

Stirling rolls his entire head to look over at him and rests his hand on his hip. "Well, be prepared for me to use you as bedding then."

"Oh? And is Amiria going to use you?" Ignis pesters.

Stirling's face flushes as he turns back around to Amiria, still on Taika's back. She reaches her arms out to him. "What did he say to you?"

"Usual Ignis stuff," Stirling tells her with a shake of his head. With her arms wrapped around his neck, Stirling helps slide Amiria off and into a bridal carry.

Holding her close, he examines the area. He regrets not storing supplies here or making a camp. Never would he have guessed he would be spending the night here. Amiria shivers and turns into him. The pocket is neglected of sunlight far before the sun has set and is cool even on the hottest of days. He's glad he was able to pack the blankets before they left.

Stirling carries the still-shivering Amiria over to Ignis, who has already made himself comfortable. Carefully, he lowers her down to rest against Ignis' soft feathers. He unpacks both blankets, laying one on the ground. Amiria scoots onto it as Stirling unravels the second and sits down beside her, shoulder to shoulder. The blanket is thrown over them both, the edges barely reaching to cover their sides.

Feeling the cool air invading their space, Stirling lifts the blanket holding it open. His eyes meet Amiria's inviting her closer. She stares at him hesitantly.

Embarrassed, Stirling mumbles, "You don't have to. I just want you to be warm."

Amiria sucks in her bottom lip holding back the involuntary smile. Casting her eyes downward, she is unable to look at him as she crawls over his thigh and roots herself in the space between his legs. She leans back resting her head on his chest, his warmth already seeping through her cotehardie and smothering her compulsive shivering.

"*I told you,*" Ignis winks.

Stirling wraps his arms safely around Amiria, his mind already starting to drift off to sleep. "*Shut up, Ignis.*"

Forty-One

*L*IES! Calix jams the heel of his boot into the back of his chair, kicking it with more force than needed. The light framework topples over and skids across the cold floor. Unlike Amiria's room, he has never bothered warming it up and personalizing it with lavish furs and tapestries. There are no vibrant colors in his bedchamber. The only color is the red of his pourpoint, a center point of color like the splatter of blood on polished armor.

He's always thought, why bother if he barely has time to sleep here?

With the buttons already halfway undone, he tears it off. The fabric buttons pop free from the quilted fabric, speckling the ground like crimson droplets. Nostrils flaring, he chucks his pourpoint across the room then stands shirtless beside his unused desk seething. The veins in his arms burst from his skin as he clenches his hands. Grinding his teeth, he replays the earlier events in his mind. He knows his section had lied to him, but he has no proof. He could see it in their shifty eyes. They had found something but weren't telling him. He can read it wasn't Amiria in person. No, it was evidence. They had found some form of evidence she recently resided in the mountains. He doesn't know what or where.

After he dismissed his section, he spent the rest of the night scouring their area. He came up empty-handed. They must have destroyed whatever it was. They are covering for her. He should have searched alone. Everyone is against him. He can trust no one but himself.

Why are people defending her? No one liked Amiria before she was deemed a mutinous traitor. Everyone talked slander behind her back, men were appalled at first sight, and women were aghast at her presence. He was the only one who saw the girl beneath the armor. She was his and his alone.

He stomps over to the slit of a window and looks out over the castle grounds. Why do they all suddenly love her? Why do whispers of gossip flutter as light as butterfly wings through the castle and the city about the soldier who said *no more* and the baker who flew?

Snorting, Calix spits out of his window watching the wad lit by the rising sun fall from view. They see her infamy as heroic. Nothing she has done is *heroic*. She has saved no one. She has only doomed everyone including herself. What she has succeeded in is leading her blind followers to the gallows.

He pushes away from the window and paces across his large barren room. He would have kept her safe from all of this.

Kicking at one of the buttons littering his floor, he stops to look at the gold and lilac ribbon stained with blood tied around his wrist. He can still feel the silkiness of her hair as he tied it back for her. Fixed in the center of his room, his hand begins to turn purple from the braided fabric digging into his skin as he subconsciously twits and pulls on it. He would have run away with her if she had only let him in. He would have given it all up for her. All she had to do was ask. All he wants is her.

His face growing red he digs the heels of his hands into his eyes. He would have been able to defend her. He would never have let someone take her from his grasp as easily as that fool of a boy had. But she has chosen him over and over again.

Who is the fool now?

With a lunging step, he punches his wooden armoire. Ignoring the blood on his hand, he leans his forearm against the fissured door. His free hand pounds the armoire several more times, the cracks splintering further. The muscles in his back ripple as he presses his forehead against the cracked door.

He doesn't lose, he can't lose. He isn't a loser. He can't lose her.

Smearing blood, he runs his hands through his hair gripping the strands at the scalp and drops to his knees. He leans his shoulder against the furniture, the pressure in his head throbbing closer and closer to making his skull explode. He can't let her get away. King Dietrich can't have her. That boy can't have her. No one can have her if he can't have her.

He wants his suffering to end. She needs to be put to an end. The only place she can live is in his memories of how he wants to remember her. He drops his hands to his lap, his legs relaxing out in front of him he leans his head back to stare at the six-candle chandelier hanging above his head.

He wishes he can return to that night they stayed up talking about pointless things. To how for that month, she smiled at him and slid her hand into his, no longer repulsed by his existence. He drops his chin and looks down at his hand, sticky with blood. She had held this lethal hand at the gallows as if they were a lifeline.

Anger surges through him and his fingers curl into claws. He should have wrapped them around her neck when he had the chance. But he can't have the evidence lead back to him. King Dietrich had given him strict orders. Amiria *has* to remain alive.

He can't jeopardize his chances of becoming Field Marshal. To show his Major, to show his General, he isn't worthless. He is a son they will be honored to carry on the Gautier name. He won't be disowned like his older brother. He remembers standing in the window of his childhood room. How he leered down at his older brother as he said his goodbyes to a six-year-old Kinsey. He didn't even give him enough of his energy to wave goodbye. That would be the last time he would see or hear from him. His brother was pathetic.

Calix thumps his head against the wardrobe, upset he let his mind wander to this part of his past. His older brother caused some of his worst childhood experiences issued by his father's hands. He had tried to teach him happiness comes before the Cavalry, but those lessons came with a hefty price.

He thumps his head against the wardrobe again. His brother had failed but he will not. He will show the kingdom the Gautiers are not second-rate to the Reys.

He pops his jaw. How can he be rid of Amiria for good but keep his hands clean? He opens and closes his hand watching the new blood ooze from the gashes on the back of his knuckles. His hand stalls with an idea rolling across the front of his mind. His mouth twitches with jerking movements into a merciless smile.

Kinsey.

Kinsey will be his scapegoat. His little baby sister loves to play games with people. She has mastered the art of deception. Would she catch on if someone turned the table and played her like a pawn? With a crack of his neck, he walks his bare back up the wardrobe to a standing position.

Maybe with the right bait, she'll easily fall for a trap. It's not like a shark expects a hook hidden inside a fish. When you think you are at the top of the food chain you aren't expecting something to attack. She's been desperate to pull one over on him, so why not give it to her?

She specializes in devouring people's weaknesses. Exploiting their flaws for her gain. He can put up a front, a false insecurity of his flaws. With this new information, a vulnerable opening she has never seen from him she will get ahead of herself and snag the hook. She won't realize the meal is too easy until she is ensnared.

King Dietrich won't believe her if she exposes that he coerced her into it. The entire Kingdom knows she is a pathological liar, a manipulator of words. She has no allies.

He strolls across his room in a newfound bliss and throws himself onto his bed. He lays on his back with his legs hanging off, smiling to himself. If he is lucky maybe, they will kill each other in the process.

A man can dream.

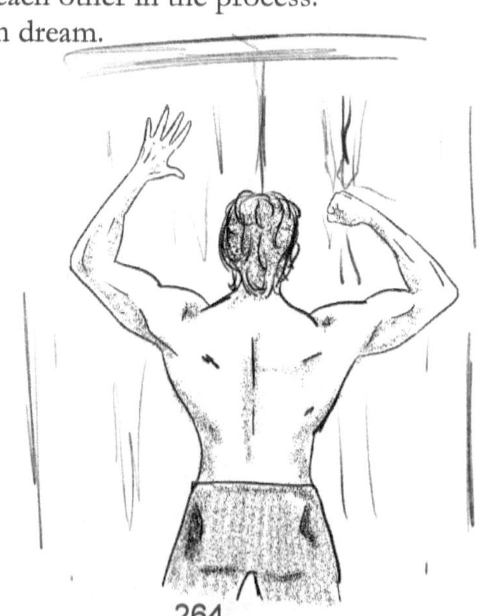

Forty-Two

We're out of water again," Amiria holds up the costrel letting the last drop fall to her parched tongue.

"I'll go get more," Stirling, eager to help, leaps up from a dried kelp mat he is weaving together that is large enough to fit two bodies.

"I can handle it," Amiria insists. "I've rested for several days. I need a good walk." Stirling sinks into his heels with disappointment. Ignis and Taika have left to fish and stretch their wings leaving Amiria and Stirling alone. She fiddles with the leather cord of the costrel, "We can walk together if you want."

Barefoot, Stirling crosses the small distance between them and holds out his hand, "Like old times."

Lifting her to her bare feet, Stirling holds her hand as they approach the passage in the rock. Stirling enters first, the space barely able to fit the width of his shoulders. With his arm stretching out behind him, he feels Amiria's hand slip from his.

Twisting his torso, he checks behind him. Amiria stands planted at the entrance with an uneasy expression, like a person with a phobia of water standing at the edge of a dock.

"Amiria?" His voice is low.

Amiria's attention snaps to him. "I'm fine," she blurts. He offers his hand again and she snatches it.

Amiria lets Stirling's rough and calloused hand guide her forward. She puts her trust in him as she closes her eyes blocking the sight of the crushing walls. She can feel them closing in on her. She can't see them, but she can feel it—the tops leaning in to seal them in their tomb. She can hear the metallic sound grinding against stone as the lid falls into place. Each step her breathing becomes more erratic. Shallow gasps with each brush of andesite stone.

"I'm not locked in," she reassures herself under her breath. "They aren't closing in," she feels the shift and pull of Stirling's hand before he releases their grip. First bumping into his solid form with her face, she puts her hand up laying it on the flat of his stomach. He has turned around.

"Amiria, are you okay?" She hears him ask.

"Uh, huh," she squeaks.

"Then why are your eyes closed?"

Her eyes creak open against her mind's wishes to keep her far from where she is currently. She keeps her vision focused on the dark green tunic.

"This isn't normal for you. Are you sure you're all right?" He hunches, meeting her at eye level. "Be honest with me." His eyes shift back and forth searching hers.

"I'm fine," she forces out.

Stirling's brows knit together, seeing through her lies. Sliding to the side, he presses his back to the wall, opening the pathway. A shock pulsates through Amiria as if she had been falling from Taika. Her eyes glue to the gaping chasm several steps away. The swirling darkness waiting to reach out with inky tendrils and pull her out of existence.

Blinded with fear, her instincts take control. She yelps and jumps away crashing her shoulder into the wall. Clamping her hand over her mouth to stifle her terror, she leaps away from the wall. Stirling snatches her before she slams into the opposing wall, his hands around her biceps.

"Whoa! Hey! Settle down!" He wrestles, holding her in place as she twists and pulls frantically, her wild eyes darting around their cage.

Her heart beating as fast as a hummingbird's, she drops her head back to stare up at the free sky above, her arms falling lax at her side.

Stirling's face hovers over her, shrouding her vision and grounding her. "AMIRIA!" Amiria shoves Stirling off her and turns away hugging herself. He doesn't reach for her, letting her have a moment to gather herself. "Amiria. Talk to me."

She bites her lip, holding back the water resting at the edges of her eyes. Her nails dig through her sleeves and into her arms.

"Please. Let me in." His voice is soft and broken.

"I—" She starts, finding it difficult to find the words to convey her emotions. "I don't know what has come over me." She hunches her shoulders to hide herself, "Is there something wrong with me?"

"No. There is nothing wrong with you. You're just human." He wants to reach out to her. His fingers twitch at his side with anticipation. "It's called fear and we all experience it. I've experienced lots of it and reacted much worse than you." Amiria looks over her shoulder but doesn't meet his gaze. Stirling lets out a long breath, "Don't worry, you're only being normal if you experience human emotions."

"Yeah?" She sniffles.

"Yes." He smiles lightly.

She reaches out, her fingertips gliding feather light down his arm and sending goosebumps across his skin. She lingers at his hand, hooking her fingers around his ring finger and pinky. Summoning enough courage, she looks over at the break in the ground with a shiver.

Stirling laces his fingers through hers and leans down to whisper, "There's magic down there. Remember?"

She squeezes his hand. She does remember. How could she ever forget the wonders to behold in their secret lake.

He moves behind her, still holding onto her hand. "Want to go?"

She tightens the cork on the bottle containing her fear and musters more strength than she has ever needed and steps forward. She can hear the water rushing beneath their feet as her toes inch closer to the edge. Instead of forward, she takes half a step back pressing into Stirling behind her.

"I'll go first," he tells her, scooting around slowly, careful not to startle her. Sitting down, he lowers his legs into the channel. Excitement swells up in his chest as he mounts his arms on the edges and gingerly lowers himself down to the slick rock and the water rushing around his ankles.

Amiria drops to her knees and peers inside, her mind flashing back to the oubliette. The feeling of abandonment trapped and alone in a pit believing no one will find you. No one can help you. A discarded doll thrown away to be broken down and rot over time. A small whimper resonates deep in her throat.

Stirling offers out his hand once more, "We don't have to, but I think it will help."

Dragging in a long breath through her nostrils, Amiria holds it in, letting it burn her lungs before releasing it out her mouth. She grits her teeth and accepts his assistance. He places her hand on his shoulder and she follows his lead by matching with her other hand. Taking her by the waist, he lifts her from the sandy shelf and lowers her down to the water.

A shudder rolls through her as her feet submerge in the cool water. She relishes the massaging feeling around her toes, instantly relaxing her tense shoulders. She takes hold of the ledge as Stirling lowers himself down into a seated position. He palms the smooth wall as he fights the current pushing against his back.

"Ready?" He says behind her ear as she situates herself in front of him. He can feel her nod, her head tapping his chest. "Away. We." He releases his anchor on the walls, "GO!"

The water takes control, guiding them along its curving and smooth path. They slide in silence, their words left behind with the light of day as they flow like leaves in a current. A scream filled with laughter escapes from Amiria as they drop from the chute in the ceiling of the cave and plunge into the reflective pool.

They hang suspended in time. Their clothing and hair flow in a world where gravity ceases to exist. Their surroundings are basked in a shimmering blue hue. Amiria turns to him with an ear-to-ear grin, her weightless hair a halo around her face. Stirling's heart flutters at the radiant sight. Bubbles escape from his mouth as he gapes.

Amiria giggles, adding to the display of rising bubbles. She nods her chin up signaling to resurface. Following her lead, Stirling breaks the surface seconds after Amiria. He breathes in deep, sucking in fresh oxygen.

He is once again captivated by her entirety. Every breath she takes is more magical than the blue star lights on the cave ceiling. The droplets of water on her face and hair glinting like she's made of diamond. She is beautiful as untouched snow but tougher than iron.

"I love you," the words escaping like a breath from his lips.

Amiria looks at him through her long eyelashes, a knowing smile light on her face, "So, what's next?"

Reaching out, Stirling cups her cheek in his hand. She closes her eyes leaning into his touch the warmth of his hand pulling the breath out of her lungs. She shyly opens her eyes, her dark irises seeing into the deepest parts of him. No mask to hide behind when she knows him better than he knows himself.

His heart drums the beat she conducts like a metronome whenever she's around. He drifts to her, drawn in at a slow and measured speed, afraid she might pull away.

She doesn't.

Their noses brush as they tread water. He is painstakingly close to her. With the slightest movement of his head, his lips would touch her. But he leaves it open for her to choose while he desperately asks her if they can take that step. Stirling, her best friend, the boy she loves, wants to kiss her. She has waited so long for this day.

Amiria entwines her fingers into his wet curls and closes the small distance, her lips parting his. All she feels is him. All she tastes is him. All she knows is him.

Consumed in the other, they forget to tread water and their intertwining bodies sink, their heads dipping beneath the surface. Amiria doesn't want air. She only wants him. The feel of his lips on hers and his hands holding her close, so they don't float away. She will drown here in their secret place that is filled with magic. She will die but at least she's got to find out what it's like to kiss someone you're in love with.

Finding his restraint first, Stirling drifts back from her at arm's length. He holds onto her arm, pulling her back to the surface with him.

Breathing in air instead of Stirling, Amiria touches her still-tingling lips. Stirling catches her eye and an embarrassed tint of pink spreads across his cheeks and the tips of his ears. A grin cracks across Amiria's face. Clamping her jaw shut she suppresses the urge to laugh resulting in a small snort. Contagious, Stirling breaks out in laughter with Amiria joining in filling the cavern with joyous echoes.

Stirling arches his back letting his legs rise to the surface as he floats, his laughter slowly sputtering out. Following his lead, Amira floats beside him. They drift side by side in the glowing blue dots reflecting perfectly around them as if they were hovering through the night sky.

His breath hitches at the shock of Amiria's skin as her hand bumps into his. He reaches out with only his index finger feeling for her. Butterflies storm through her stomach as he brushes her hand, their fingers dancing around each other until his hand slips into hers. Their fingers lacing together perfectly.

Forty-Three

Calix's long fingers are curled like talons as he buttons the soft, black armor pourpoint. The knuckles of his bruised hand have scabbed over where they had split open like his wardrobe. His face is cold and analytical as he turns to the window in his private chamber and rests his hand on the cold slab of stone, drumming his fingers as he thinks.

Where is she? What is he missing? How does someone live in the mountains for years with a dragon and not be noticed? What did the reconnaissance team miss four years ago? What was so obvious they skipped over it?

They had scoured the forest from the city wall to mountain peaks. The boy's hideout is within walking distance, and he knows it. All the evidence says so. He leans forward, his head fitting through the narrow window though his wide shoulders do not. He stares at the mountain ridge, the hideout is right there, so what is in such plain sight they continually look past it? His eyes run along the sharp ridge.

Look past it.

It couldn't have been that simple. He grabs his sword belt looping it around his narrow hips as he disappears out his door.

With silver goggles etched with black engravings, Calix sits on the back of his brown wyvern, leaving Lumierna behind. He skips over the triangle tops of the sprawling forest and grazes the low-hanging clouds; he leaps over the island's spiked circular spine of a coiled serpent to the sheer sea cliffs.

Having his dragon fly at a steady pace, Calix scrutinizingly excavates the rock face. Several pelican and seagull nests, a couple of open pockets barely large enough to fit a single person, nothing of significance except...

He pulls sharply back on the reins. His dragon roars back in the air with a hiss. He stares face to face with the mountain's yawning mouth.

An enormous cave able to fit several dragons sits open and inviting. Ripping off his goggles for a clearer look, Calix's sharp features tighten as he takes it in. Steering his dragon to land on the lip of the cave he unhooks his harness and leaps from its back.

His head tilts to the side as he squints into the darkness. His eyes slowly adjusting to the dim light he reads the markings in the dirt. He can see the scene unfolding before him just as he had when he followed Amiria's fight with the bandits. He scans the small piles, the lines, the flattened, the skids, and the shuffles. People moved, people slept, and people lived here.

He squats down to a scorched circle. Pressing his fingers to the soft velvety residue, he pinches the scattered ash between his thumb and index. His eyes run over the rocks thrown around the brushed-away ash. His creaking fingers curl around a rock with a single black residue side.

The veins in the back of his hand bulge as he begins to squeeze the rock like the contracting binds around his heart.

Spinning to his feet, he takes several skipping steps, and his arm is like a trebuchet as he hurls the rock out over the ocean. The coastal wind tugs at his clothing as he watches the rock. It soars along with the sky as its backdrop. Losing velocity, it dips, beginning its final descent towards the cold waters.

With his lips partially separated he tilts his chin to his chest. Looking up with only his eyes, he stares through the rock as it falls past the horizon line. He is transfixed on what he used to see as an insignificant smudge on the horizon. The barren wasteland of the Wyvern's nesting ground. A place the Cavalry only goes to do boring routine work of taking a census of the wild dragons. Somewhere a rider with the ranking Amiria and he possesses would never be sent.

He reaches his hand out as if he could touch her. He strokes the air, imagining her hair flowing between his fingers when he had tied her hair up for her. If only he could touch her one last time. To hold her hand during her final moments. To be the last person she ever sees. To be the last person she ever feels.

He should have been the only person to feel her. When he held her hand in the high keep it was *that boy's* name she said. It was *his* hand she wished to be holding. The vision of Stirling's arms around Amiria flashes across his mind. It was as fast as lightning, but the damage left behind is just as destructive, an unrepairable black scar burned into whatever it struck.

Calix digs the heels of his hands into his eyes. His tan skin turns a shade of red. They are together. He has her.

He should have slit the boy's throat in that worthless village. Why did he leave him alive? He was deemed weak. A worthless tool to persuade her to stop fighting and to come along willingly. She would have fought tooth and nail, most likely killing herself in the process if they hadn't used that boy as leverage. If he only knew what he knows now, what the king had planned. He would have burned the house down with them both in it. That boy has defiled her.

The tendons in Calix's neck pop and strain. Unhinging his jaw, he releases a beast. His scream is something between a furious roar and tortured howl. His knees give out beneath him. They strike the hard ground, and he sits back on his heels impervious to the pain. His spider-leg fingers crawl up from where they lay on his forehead to snag in his hair. Letting out another desperate cry, he yanks on the roots of his hair, throwing himself forward and slamming the backs of his hands into the ground pinched between his head and the mountain rock.

Hunched in a praying position, his body violently shakes. He spent years trying to court her, to get her to spend a moment by her choice with him. He knew she ran somewhere every week. He just didn't know where. But it was to this… this mangy cave. A place where animals sleep. Every week, for years.

What have they done in this cave?

With his face between his forearms and his hands still twisted in his hair, he screams into the dusty ground. Spit strings from his mouth. Images taunt his mind. Amiria's back to the ground. Calix continues to scream. The boy is over her. His voice growing hoarse, he punches a fist into the ground. He's holding her now. He slams both of his fists into the ground. He doesn't care about the pain running up his arm. His body shudders with rage.

He should go there and finish what needs to be done, but if her body isn't returned to King Dietrich it will be him in the oubliette. He can't fail his father. He is not his older brother. *He* is the most capable in his family. *He* will bring the Gautiers into the number one position.

He sits up, twisting like a starved beast to stare at the cave over his shoulder. He snaps his fingers and shoots his hand with his fingers spread out to the back of the cave. The cave ignites in flames. His dragon unleashes a devil's wrath by opening a new gate to hell.

Calix's head lobs to the side. What is that he sees?

He watches the vortex of flames be sucked from the cave through a back entry. His body moving as if put together with loose hinges, Calix crawls up to a standing position and stalks his way across the cave. Without hesitation, he dives into the unknown passage.

The open forest sun is harsh on his eyes as Calix emerges from the cave. He squints, blinking his pale eyes to adjust to the bright light. He glances around gathering his bearings. Step by quiet step he stops in the middle of the clearing. How has no one seen this cave before? There's an empty glade right in front of it. It's not shrouded in a dense pine forest. Surely it must be visible from the sky.

He turns around. His muscles tense as he grinds his teeth. The cave is nearly invisible against the mountain wall. His eyes climb the beech tree clinging to the tops of boulders. It looks as if it's about to fall at any moment. He watches with a glimpse of serenity as the leaves sway and rustle in the wind.

His forehead creases as he scowls. He had seen this tree from the air during his search. He rips his sword free from its sheath. He missed finding Amiria because of this tree. He raises his long sword above his head. With a vein popping and his voice already straining he lets out a rasping yell as he chops down on the clinging roots. Without aiming and with a total loss of control of his limbs, he begins to hack away.

Chunks of bark fling into the air, his swinging blade axes gouges into the tree's supports. He stumbles back as his blade strikes the stone with a vibrating clang. His head rolls as his shoulders slump. With his crystal eyes still on the relentless tree he bites his lip, creating a high-pitched whistle.

His narrowed eyes never leave the tree as his dragon lands beside him. Snapping his fingers, he points at the roots. He steps back and to the side, as his dragon's blazing breath turns the roots of the tree to char and ash.

With the fire reflecting in his eyes, one side of Calix's mouth lifts into a smile as the tree begins to slide. He can hear the cracking of the burned roots snapping under the extensive pressure to hold the tree up. He doesn't take a step back and he doesn't even blink as the tree falls. It rips free from its impossible home and crashes to the forest floor it had refused to grow on.

The tips of its branches touch Calix's boots. He gives a satisfied smile to the roots now blocking the entrance of the cave.

Forty-Four

This is worse than when she used to visit Leucasia with Stirling. The head of every person within sight of them tilts to their neighbors. The murmuring is a white noise like the sound of a seashell held up to your ear.

When she walked along the storefronts with Stirling, his fans would applaud his name with praise, and girls would blow kisses. The majority of them would ignore her presence altogether. The others would gawk at her with jealous disdain in their eyes, but they would keep their thoughts and comments to themselves. She had been Stirling's friend from the start. She had been sitting in the stands rooting for him since his mishap at the opening ceremonies.

She told him words of encouragement while they shouted vulgar phrases from the stands. He was outcasted and beaten down by the other competitors. Quilan was his only inside support but even when he conducted his endorsement to help Stirling along it was without Stirling's knowledge. It wasn't until he began his winning streak did anyone cheer his name and wear his color.

The ridicule coming from them now as she walks beside Quilan is especially crafted to disparage her. They aren't discriminating whispers undetectable by her ears as they discuss her with their friends. They are articulate and pronounced, they are meant to be heard.

Quilan's face is never changing as always. She wonders if he even hears them, his expression says that he doesn't, but this might be from years of training to ignore them.

He answers her thoughts, "They don't matter."

They climb another set of stairs, they are one level from the top layer of the city. This is farther up than she ever imagined traveling in Leucasia. She has never been further than the several bottom levels. The walking paths have thinned out, and the residents living up this far are too absorbed with their own self-worth to pay mind to anyone that isn't for their benefit.

"How long until it stops bothering you?" Eve questions. Her distracted eyes drift across the lavish homes with the number of spare rooms with which they can establish an inn.

Quilan side glances at her, "It doesn't."

Her mouth hangs in the shape of an "O" as she realizes. This surprises her. She expected the few-word sentence, but she also expected some form of wording about never caring about what they say.

She watches him now. What the glamorous homes contain does not compare to the complex mind of Quilan of Leucasia.

The Quilan who has perfected his smile, pulled his shoulders back, and stands with his arms raised to his fans is an actor. He was born and raised for their entertainment. The Quilan she walks beside now is not that person. He has a drag in his gait, his shoulders slump forward with his hands swaying limply at his side. His lips are turned down, heavy from the weight of the fake smile they must hold up.

She prefers this Quilan—as lackadaisical as his personality might be—but he's real. This is the real Quilan. She smiles internally at the fact Quilan of Leucasia is comfortable enough in her presence to be his true self.

Only three homes take up the top layer of the sea cliff above Leucasia. Their expansive sizes are all the summit can afford to hold with each family insisting to have a luxurious garden to spend their days in without having to step foot off their property.

They pass each set of stairs leading to the top tier, remaining on the second. The pathway curves with the horseshoe shape of the harbor until they reach the last house on the street with its own sizable yard.

"Here," Quilan pushes open a metal gate shining with the pearlescent coating of abalone. It swings soundlessly over a pathway made of crushed sun-bleached shells. The white path winds through an immaculate garden of color-coordinated blue and white.

Eve taps the soft petals of a snow-colored rose, careful not to snag her sleeve on the cat claw thorns. She trails behind Quilan through a garden of bluebells and spring gentians swaying in the wind like the waves of the harbor.

She takes in the multi-story home with several balconies jutting out over the homes below that make the one at the inn look like a balancing act with a single plank of wood. The mansion, keeping with his chosen aesthetic of the garden, does not have the traditional red brick roofs of the well-known sea cliff homes of Leucasia. Instead, Quilan took his own approach with a flat roof and blue accents decorating the corners of the buildings, around the windows, and framing the door.

"Do you live here all alone?" Eve asks, imagining how many rooms a home this size must contain.

" mployees," Quilan tells her as they step up the quartz stairs to his front door.

"And your family?"

Quilan points with his chin to the largest home of the three estates consuming the top tier. Eve's pupils dilate as they take in the sheer size of the property, consisting of a multitude of separate structures that can house all of Patu. "You don't want to live up there with your family?"

Setting his jaw, Quilan's eyes slide down to half-slits.

"I'll take that as a no, but isn't it lonely?" She thinks of the crowded ale house she has grown up in. She doesn't know the meaning of the words *personal space*.

With a gentle push by Quilan, the front door to his home welcomes them inside. Their footfalls echo in the empty entryway leading to an immaculate, white-washed room with marble floors. The entire far wall is missing, connecting the main room to the balcony outside it with one continuous sweep. A blue privacy canvas is pulled back, exposing the room to the view of the harbor speckled with fishing boats past the rust-colored rooftops.

Eve steps around Quilan with her mouth hanging open in awe.

"It is," Quilan answers, too low for Eve to hear.

She gingerly steps across the sparsely decorated room as if the ground is made of glass. Dragging her fingertips along the plush velvet fabric of a lounge chair, her eyes are drawn to the striking contrast of the light-colored olive wood with dark swirling grains making up the room's shelves and furniture.

Passing under the archway to the balcony, she leans on the half-wall railing and rests her arms on the smooth stone. She can see everything from here. She can see the wooden bleachers where she had watched Stirling during his first race. The street with Tobias' shop where she learned the truth of how the other competitors were treating Stirling. She can see the fountain in the entrance plaza. The fountain, Stirling told her, was the place he found Amiria standing above the crowd.

Amiria, the girl who swooped in like a typhoon from the sea and tore apart the small village of Patu in only a week. Only one house was hit with property damage, but the emotional damage has wreaked havoc on many lives.

She closes her eyes, feeling the fresh coastal breeze. Stirling could have purchased a home up here. He could have lived beside the other elites, but he didn't.

"You might not live with your family, but they aren't far if you need them. I wonder what it must have been like for Stirling. To leave everyone and everything you ever knew on the other side of the world. The idea terrifies me. I used to want to move out of the ale house and live in the city. But I don't want that anymore." She stays focused forward on the buildings flowing down the mountainside. "I love Patu. I just never noticed until I saw it through Stirling's perspective."

Quilan leans the small of his back against the railing with his elbows propped up. Eve feels the spark of warmth through her as the point of his elbow bumps hers. She ignores the sensation and hangs her head, slouching.

"I just miss him. I worry he's—" She wipes away the tears catching in her lashes, so he doesn't see.

Her heart thumps as warm fingers cup her chin. Eve is only two fingers shorter than him so when she allows his fingers to turn her face, she is eye-to-eye with dark blue irises with depths deeper than the ocean.

Using his thumb, he wipes the tear she missed from her cheek. He drops his hand from her chin and slips it around her shoulders. With a gentle tug, he pulls her into him.

Eve gasps as his arms wrap around her.

He touches his forehead to hers and whispers, "Me too."

Filled with uncertainty if what is happening is reality, her hands slide around his back. With his shoulder blades beneath her palms, she lines her chest to his, holding their bodies together tight like putting pressure on a wound. Her body moves to the rhythm of his breaths as she lowers her head, resting it on top of his shoulder.

Spectators that log every account of activity on Quilan's balcony commentate from below. He hears them now as he always does, and just as he's learned from childhood, he ignores them. Their opinions have never mattered to him. What matters to him at this moment is her.

Forty-Five

KINSEY!"

With rosy cheeks, Kinsey's sweet smile falters as she hears her brother call her name. Wearing a more feminine attire than most Cavalry women, Kinsey dons a form-fitting pink cotehardie that flows around past her knees and is slit down the sides adorned with ankle-height boots. She sits poised on a bench beside a butterfly bush in the courtyard and behind her, Amiria's bench sits cold and empty. The once destroyed primroses have been replanted and are blooming. Scars Amiria had made in the soil of the flower bed are now nonexistent in the perfect garden.

A young man around eighteen breaks from her hypnotizing features to glance around, "Did you hear that?"

"Nope." Her voice is sweeter than the nectar of the flowers around them. Fingertips are feather light as she runs her touch down his arm. "I didn't hear anything," she purrs.

"KINSEY!"

"I swear I hear your name," he persists.

Restraining herself, Kinsey pops her neck. "I guess someone *is* calling for me."

"Kinsey. There you are," Calix announces, entering the courtyard. His posture squared off and determined.

"Calix! My older brother! Is there some sort of emergency?" She mocks being surprised. She turns away from the boy she is courting. Her honeysuckle eyes turn into daggers as she glares at Calix. "Because it's rude to interrupt a lady's outing with a *Lord*."

Calix squints. "My apologies *Lady* Gautier next in line General of the Winged Cavalry. Although, I have Cavalry business to be discussed in *private*." His narrow eyes shift over to the boy.

A scowl flashes across Kinsey's face before turning into a heartbroken pout, bringing a tear to her eye, she turns back around. "I'm so sorry, Sir Kailon. I wish I did not have to cut our time together short, but when the Cavalry calls, I cannot ignore my service to this fine Kingdom." She sets her hand gently on his knee.

Lord Kailon picks her hand up gingerly in his. "Do not fret. We can schedule again. Are you free this time next week?"

"I believe I am. I will have my handmaiden deliver you a note tonight." She smiles bashfully.

"Super cute." Calix rolls his eyes. "Can we speak now?" Calix loathes the courtyard. His eyes flicker over to where he had once danced in the moonlight. Every time he passes through here, he expects to find his begrudging Amiria moping on her bench.

"Yes, brother. Of course." Kinsey lets her touch linger on Lord Kailon as she gets up. Their fingers slowly slide out from each other until his hand falls empty back to his lap.

With plastered smiles the siblings walk away. Neither speaks until they step onto the tiled floor of the covered pathway around the perimeter. Calix speaks through gritted teeth. "I didn't take you for the romantic type."

They turn a corner now out of sight of the courtyard. Kinsey's honey-sweet voice now brash and sour, "He's of royal blood. I'm whatever it takes type."

"Oh, that poor boy doesn't know who he's playing with." Calix feigns sympathy.

"Ha—Ha," she fakes. "Life's a game. Either you play or get played."

"Oh?" Calix raises an eyebrow. Hiding his reaction, he smooths back his hair. "Is power all you care about?"

"Yes," she says matter-of-factly. "Tell me, Calix. Is my lust for power really any different than yours?"

A muscle in Calix's cheek twitches.

"I didn't think so." Her face is smug. "This isn't about the Cavalry, not really," she eyes him watching, waiting for any clue on his face. "This is about that girl isn't it."

Calix hushes her. "Not out here." He checks up and down the empty corridor before ducking into a private solar.

Sighing, Kinsey rolls her eyes and saunters into the solar behind him. Inside, Calix closes the door quietly behind them. Kinsey's lip raises at the décor. Gold and red painted furniture slathered in more golden cloth.

"This place hurts my eyes." She sticks her tongue out. "Yuck."

"Ignore it, we're just here to talk alone." Calix leans his back against the wall beside the door.

Popping her hip, Kinsey examines her nails. "All right then, get on with it."

Calix closes his eyes, leaning his head back against the wall struggling to speak what is on his mind.

Kinsey tosses one of her two long braids over her shoulder, her words backhanded, "Aw, so heartbreaking. My brother is lost for words for his little bird." A genuine smile twitches on Kinsey's face as she watches her words slap her older brother. His eyes open as his breathing stutters.

Like a spider with a fly in her web, she begins to spin her rope around her victim. He should have known better than to let her in on his personal matters. How desperate and lonely can he be, if she is the one, he is turning to for assistance? She tilts her head, "Now tell me what is so important you ruined my date over it? Tell me why I shouldn't paint this ugly room's floor red?"

Calix's face is a grayish pale, his tongue feels enlarged in his mouth, unable to form the correct words. He slides down the wall into a low squat sitting back on his heels. He hides his face from his younger sister, "I need you—I need you to help me. Please, Kinsey?"

"Oh?" She drags out the word with a raise of an eyebrow. "Why should I believe you?" She drops to her haunches in front of him and paws at a loose lock of his hair that had fallen in front of his face, "You never ask *anyone* for help."

"I'm serious," he bites his lower lip and blinks up at her with begging eyes. "King Dietrich wants me to kill her after I find her. I—I can't. I can't kill her."

What a turn of events. Hopping up, Kinsey walks with her hands clasped behind her back as she thinks. She never guessed he was going to play a move like this, playing the victim. Calix Gautier the victim? He must be pretending, though she doesn't know his motives. But if he is not acting there are so many directions, she can take with this. All the different possibilities, all the different strategies. She licks her lips intrigued, treasure laid before a pirate. She can't resist taking what is in front of her. She can't help but skip the warnings and play the game. Acting uninterested. she begins plucking petals off a bouquet of flowers. A smile cuts across her face.

Dancing alongside her words, she twirls up onto her toes and begins walking on tiptoes until she stops at the back of the chaise, dropping the petals in her wake. "Who is *her?*"

Staring at the ground his fingers twist into his hair. "You know who."

Kinsey's eyes glint. "No, tell me?"

Calix pulls at his hair, messing up his perfect locks. "Amiria. I'm talking about Amiria" He puts the back of his hand to his mouth biting on the skin as if her name pains him.

Satisfied with his discomfort, Kinsey spins to the front of the chaise. "And what does my big brother want from little ol' me? What service can I provide you because I know we're not here for a heart-to-heart."

"I need you to chase her away from Wyverna. I can't do it. She won't run for me, she'll fight. I don't want to fight her. I don't want her to get hurt, I want her to get out of here."

She falls back onto the chair and lands poised with one leg up with toes pointing to Calix, "But big brother, what about the king's orders for her to be killed, she's a mutinous fugitive." She uses the swing of her leg to sit up with an exaggerated gasp, her hand shooting to her mouth. "You want to betray your orders! What about becoming Field Marshal!"

Walking his hands up the wall behind him, Calix straightens out. Still leaning against the wall he tells her, "I'm not playing around. I honestly don't care about that anymore." His face pales, his words catching in his throat as he holds back the tears that were beaten out of him a decade ago. He pushes himself off the wall and takes a step toward Kinsey, "Please, I need her to be safe."

Her body like a prowling cat, Kinsey slinks up to Calix encircling him as she speaks, "Has love really changed you? Changed you to such an extent to let the girl you spent years pining for." She stops behind him speaking into his ear, "To run away with that *boy?*"

Calix stiffens at the mention of Stirling.

Wrapping herself around his rigid arm, Kinsey leans her cheek on his shoulder, "The baker boy she loves instead of you? Heart-wrenching, isn't it?" She callously smiles watching what is left of his soul die from her front-row seat. "Tsk," she removes her headfirst, her body following as she slinks away from him. She folds her hands behind her back, "Quite the tall tale they are. A fable of two lovers escaping the king's wrath to be who they want to be."

Calix clenches his fists at his sides. He hates her roundabout way of talking. She can never stay on point. There is never a straight answer with her. Would it kill her to answer with a yes, or no?

She turns back to him, analyzing his emotions, taking note of every time he blinks. Every conversation is a ball of wool, and she is a cat ready to play.

"Will you help me?" His voice is hollow.

Kinsey plops herself back down on the chaise with her legs crossed, "I don't know. You *are* going against King Dietrich's direct orders." She leans back on outstretched arms, "Do you even know where she is?"

Calix stands stoic.

"You do know where she is!" She puts her hand over her heart falling back on the chaise swooning, "Oh Calix, you poor soul. Knowing where she is hiding in the arms of another man yet you haven't driven a sword through his heart?" She throws her arm back down to her side and speaks to the ceiling, "I always knew you were the nicest sibling."

He keeps his face absent, the less he talks the more she feels inclined to compensate. He turns his cheek to her, speaking something truthful, "You know that's false."

Kinsey's face falls, her mind slipping back to the past. She slams the door shut before it can arrive. Her face hardens, "What's in it for me? What will I risk the king's rage for."

"Field Marshal."

She sits up abruptly, "Excuse me?"

"You heard me. I'm offering Field Marshal. I'll decline the offer. I'll be Major and Keaton will be General." Calix says seriously. He is offering her the position instead of him. There is still no heir for the Rey's. Calix knows the General has been speaking to King Dietrich, planting the idea of the Gautier's taking over. That was why his parents wanted him to be with Amiria Rey, but that is not why he had fallen in love with her. They have been grooming him to take the Field Marshal's place.

Kinsey focuses, searching for any intel in his body language and the emphasis in his words, "Field Marshal?"

"Yes, or no? Do we have a deal?" He reiterates.

Kinsey purses her lips, "Hmm." She kicks her feet playing down the importance.

"Yes, or no?"

She plays with one of her braids, "I'm debating."

"You know the answer, you're just stalling because you want to," Calix calls her out.

"Fine," she throws her braid back over her shoulder. "From the goodness of my heart, I'll go talk to your *little bird*." She frowns at the appalling furniture, "Can we finally leave this horrendous room. It's really giving me a headache." She puts the back of her hand to her forehead.

"Her name is Amiria. Kinsey, take this serious for once. Please get her to run, far, far away from here."

Leaping up from the chaise, Kinsey pauses next to her brother and side glances at him, "Oh, I'll *talk* to her all right."

Watching her saunter out of the room Calix waits until she closes the door. He reaches up and smooths his hair with a devious grin.

Forty-Six

With his trousers rolled up to his knees, Stirling wades through the tide pools along the coastal shelf jutting off parts of the island like a staircase leading to the depths. The early morning tide pulling out to sea exposes the pockets of miniature neighborhoods.

Disturbed, Ignis pulls his claws up and out of the water as a crab crawls around his toes. *"Eck!"* He spits. *"Can you please hurry up? I'm not too keen on this ocean life."*

Stirling squats down and adds another sea urchin to his bag filled with muscles, sea snails, kelp, and a sea cucumber, "I like the sea creatures." Stirling picks up a crab and watches its legs wriggling. It opens and closes its pincers, unable to reach Stirling's fingers.

Ignis makes an exaggerated gagging sound, *"You're holding it so close to your face."*

"We ate all this back in Leucasia. It's actually pretty good." Stirling sets the crab back in the water, it quickly scurries away slipping between rocks.

Continuing his gagging effects, Ignis coughs out, *"That's even worse. You eat the stuff. Oh, poor Amiria. You're going to poison her."*

"I am not! It's this or starve."

"I choose starve."

Stirling frowns down at his reflection in the pool. He reaches his hand back into the water and runs his finger along the back of a purple starfish. "She's not ready to leave, despite regaining her health. So, we have to make do."

"I'm surprised after yesterday you weren't able to convince her to come home with you." Ignis teases. Glancing down, he side steps away from another crab and continues talking, *"You still haven't told me, what took you and Amiria so long?"*

Stirling lowers his chin to his chest, his cheeks blushing.

Ignis pursues. *"Come on, it's just us guys now. You can tell me."*

Stirling throws his head back, annoyed. "Nothing, we just, you know, kissed." Stirling stands up, putting his hands on his hips. "I don't pester you for details every time you go off with your feathery friend."

Ignis' mind smiles slyly. "Do you want to know?"

"NO!" Stirling throws out his hand. "No! I don't!"

A tan dragon catches both of their attention. Ignis' head whips around to watch the wyvern cutting through the thin clouds.

"It's a wild one!" Stirling exclaims. Watching them soar free through the clouds never grows old to Stirling.

Since they've arrived, the dragons have kept their distance and have preferred to stay on the opposite side of the island as them, but now and then Stirling would catch a glimpse of one dipping in and out of the clouds.

He trails the dragon, watching it disappear around the backside of the island.

"Amiria." A voice like the sharp side of a blade cuts at her as she fumbles blindingly through the natural labyrinth of the island's fissures. The once light grey andesite stone is now black and porous, causing the fresh lava stone to shred her palms. But she doesn't stop. Further, she has to get further away.

"Amiria, my little Amiria," the voice assaults from every direction.

She slams into a dead end, her torn hands searching for a route, a step to climb out, any way to escape. Thick storm clouds pulse and swirl, peeling apart and revealing moonlight that fills the chasm.

"Amiria," she hears.

Reluctantly, she turns with the hairs on the back of her neck standing up. She stares down the straight black passage lit by the soft white light of the moon. The only color in the greyscale world is the pale blue of Calix's eyes. Their gaze is thrown across the distance and piercing through her like newly sharpened spears.

An abnormal smile stretches across his face as if hooks are pulling at the corners. His teeth reflect the light more than his dark armor.

"Come back to me, my little bird," he says with unblinking eyes. He holds up an iron birdcage. "I can keep you safe."

"Please." She falls to her knees with a hopeless whimper. "Don't."

With a cold sweat, Amiria's eyes open half-lidded, staring at the kelp-woven mat. It smells of low tide. She barely moves as Stirling shakes her shoulder.

"Were you having another nightmare?" he asks, kneeling beside her.

She turns her face toward the mat. Of course, she had another nightmare. All she has is nightmares. Nightmares that will play every time she closes her eyes. Nightmares that are telling her of her fate if she doesn't put an end to it permanently.

"Are you trying to sleep all day?" Stirling smiles lightheartedly and lowers his face to look at her.

Keeping her head on the ground, she finally makes eye contact with him. "Yes."

Stirling leans back on his heels. "Well, if you decide to get up, I've got some mollusks roasting on the fire."

Amiria scrunches her nose. "Oh, yay." She pushes herself halfway up. "Maybe I can shoot down a seagull."

Ignis interjects, "*I told you that sea life was gross.*"

"You eat fish, they come from the water." Stirling spins to him.

"*Creepy crawlers and a delicious mackerel are not the same.*" Ignis crosses his front legs.

"Your opinion means nothing." Stirling squints at him.

Amiria sighs at their typical banter, sitting cross legged. "What do you want to do today?"

Stirling turns his attention back to her. "Ask the same question I do every day, and my answer is always leave." Amiria faces away from him, unable to look him in the eye. "I'm going to take that as a no…" Stirling's voice trails off with the last word. He searches around, lost till he lands on the top of the island barely visible over the wall of their hideout. "I have an idea, let's go see the wild dragons.

Amiria gives a smug smile. "That sounds like a terribly good idea."

"*Amiria,*" Taika chimes in.

"Yes?" Amiria acknowledges.

"*Do you think it's a good idea to keep delaying?*" Taika lectures. "*Fight or run, Amiria. Those two choices are inevitable. You can't remain here in this delusional purgatory.*"

Amiria hangs her head casting her gaze to the dried green mat beneath her hand then raises it up to Stirling. Taika knows her, she can feel her well-being. Amiria is healthy enough to go on the journey back to Patu, but she is almost strong enough to march back into the castle and confront King Dietrich. *If* she can get there before Calix finds her here. It's a race of who will strike first. Two predators waiting in the tall grass.

"Help me up." Amiria smiles at the excuse to hold Stirling's hand.

She wants to spend these days with him. There is no way to know how many more there are, so she will cherish each smile, each touch, each moment beside him. To run with him? To have days like this for the rest of her life? It would be a dream, but she needs to fight. There are people dying because of the choices Stirling and she had made. There is no running, not anymore. Not without their ghosts following her forever.

Stirling wraps his hand around her, lifting her to her feet. Smiling up at him like a sunflower to the sun, Amiria cherishing his embrace, she still has here and now.

Forty-Seven

Perched on Stirling's shoulder, Amiria stands balancing as he holds her by the ankles. She reaches above her head and grasps the lip of the stone terrace, pulling herself up. Starting halfway up the island at their base and with now burning arm muscles they've scaled another fourth of the ancient volcano.

Amiria throws her leg onto the ledge and with nothing to grasp shimmies her stomach along the ground until she is away from the edge. Using the small amount of foot holds, Stirling scales the side of the wall and flops onto his stomach beside her, feeling the safety of the flat ground as he pulls his legs up.

Rolling over onto his back he sits up cross-legged looking down at the stairs of volcanic stone.

"Reminds me of Leucasia."

Amiria stands beside him, the ocean wind playing with the loose strands of her hair, "Yeah it kinda does."

Visions of the spectacular city unfold in front of her eyes. The grey stone stacks transform and shift into red-roofed homes. Each layer of the city is balanced atop of the other as it climbs the sea cliffs. She can almost hear the people talking and laughing at the entrance gate of the plaza. People who will never understand how free they are.

She steals a glance at Stirling, his curls lively in the breeze. Her mind and her heart argue and fight internally swaying her back and forth on what she should do. What is the right choice? Her instincts tell her she needs to fight but she sees a reason she wants to run.

Is she being selfish making Stirling stay here with her while she contemplates and slowly lets revenge rule her? While she lets King Dietrich and Calix live in her mind and the people of Wyverna in her heart rent-free. He has a new family and a home to return to. She is keeping him and Ignis from that.

If she truly desires to fight, she would have gone already but she stays here—afraid. She is afraid of making the wrong decision. She is afraid of giving up everything for nothing. She is afraid of bringing Stirling down with her and she is afraid of dying. This turmoil ravages her mind as she lies to Stirling about why she refuses to leave.

Stirling stands brushing the dust off his trousers, "Let's continue, we're almost there."

Amiria nods, still scanning the horizon. After the incident in the cave, they haven't seen any evidence they are still being pursued. If Calix hasn't found her yet on this barren wasteland of an island not far from the coast of Wyverna, maybe they aren't searching for her after all.

The gravel rolls beneath Stirling's sliding feet on the steep and narrow path sandwiched between two building-sized boulders. Barely fitting, he shimmies sideways through the last several steps. He clears the thin pass and stumbles out into an open area larger than their camp.

Without any time to process anything visually around him, Amiria leaps from behind tackling Stirling to the ground. Stirling can feel the rough ground tear at his sleeves and chin. Confused, he begins to lift his head.

Amiria pushes her weight down on him pushing his cheek into the dirt and screams, "STAY DOWN!"

A scaly mass recoils after its vicious strike. Its fanged mouth is unhinged and hissing, preparing for its next attack. Rising into a crouch, Amiria hollers, "Taika!" before diving to the side, avoiding the deadly snap of jaws. She rolls across her shoulders and pounces back up into a crouch, staring down the black dragon with spikes running from his head down his spine to the tip of his tail in his yellow eyes.

Like a cobra, the dragon charges again. With years of practice alongside Taika, Amiria dodges with ease. The boulder behind them quakes under Taika's weight as she lands from the sky like a meteor. Clumps of rock rip from her digging talons as she roars overhead with fire in her throat.

Stirling interlocks his fingers behind his neck protecting his head with his arms. The shadow-like dragon holds back its third strike, locking eyes with Taika. Spit sprays as he hisses with exposed fangs. Ignis flutters down, safely flanking Taika's right on the boulder.

He peers around Taika's wing at Stirling flat on his stomach with his face hiding, *"You're a goner."*

"Thanks," Stirling grumbles, his tongue tasting the dirt.

The dark dragon cocks his head, eyeing them suspiciously. He moves his leering gaze back to Amiria. He blows a strong breath out of his nostrils with a low growl rattling deep in his throat. With no sudden movements, Amiria keeps her head up as she drops to one knee. With her hands resting on her bent knee, she finally lowers her head into a bow.

Recoiling, the dragon pulls back his head with a startled expression in his eyes. Stirling uncovers his head looking back and forth at Amiria and the dragon in confusion, "Um…What?"

The wild dragon's pale sulfur-colored eyes flick back to Taika. They hold each other's gaze in an unspoken conversation. At the conclusion of their discussion, the dragon turns over his shoulder letting out a chirp-like bark. Facing back at his newcomers he nods his head and turns to crawl around the bouldering wall.

Hesitant to follow, Amiria asks Taika, "What did it say?"

"He understands we mean no harm. We aren't here to capture his family like they've done in the past. When you renounced your authority and gave him your respects, you earned his." Taika translates.

Stirling sits up on his knees, "I'm lost."

Ignis laughs, *"What's new?"*

Stirling shoots Ignis a look. Amiria offers out her hand, "He's okay with us being here and wants us to follow him."

Stirling takes Amiria's hand and stands up, "Yes, but why?"

Walking Amiria explains, "Have you ever put any thought into how I suddenly obtained the ability to converse with Taika?"

Stirling lifts his hands with a shrug, "Magic?"

"No"--she stares down at the hand still in hers—"Not magic. I think it's a vulnerability or weakness." She tugs on his hand, leading him in the direction of the wild dragon, "I think exposing raw human weakness to your dragon is the key. Like how you feared and cowered the first time you met Ignis. Dragons are prideful creatures."

Stirling frowns, the corners of his mouth pulling down to his chin, "Thanks."

Amiria continues, "I called out for Taika in desperate need of help. There's no other logical explanation."

"If that is the only factor then why haven't more people figured it out?" Stirling questions.

"Because the Cavalry will never let anyone, not even their dragons see them as weak."

They both stop in their tracks. "Wow." Stirling expresses, his mouth agape as they take in the sights before them.

Around the backside of the wall, it opens up to a half-moon crater, the remnants of an explosion only the gods remember. In the center of the crater is an aqua-blue tarn. Young fledglings safely prance around the shallows of the rainwater lake with the adults guarding the perimeter. Mothers and fathers lay beside clutches of eggs in the back of the crater, the younger sprightlier dragons perch on the tips of the crater wall and crowd the steep sides.

Stirling feels his hand being squeezed. He peels his eyes away from the sight to see Amiria's eyes glistening, dazzled by the scene no tapestry can capture the essence of.

She speaks to Stirling with her eyes still forward on the nesting ground. "Look at them. Wild and free."

Ignis hovers over Stirling's shoulder, his sphalerite eyes scanning the dragons, *"Do you think any of them knows anything about my past?"*

"Why don't you go and ask them?"

"Oh, I don't know." Ignis scratches at the ash-colored dust.

"Oh? NOW you're suddenly shy? Go on, introduce yourself," Stirling insists, stepping closer to Amiria allowing Ignis a direct route forward.

Disinclined, Ignis lowers his head. He drags his feet as he steps cautiously up to the black dragon who has opened the doors to his home but his eyes still watch vigilantly. Ignis twists his neck to look back at Stirling for reassurance. Stirling motions for him to continue. Turning back to the leader, Ignis bows his head.

Stirling watches as Ignis listens momentarily. Liking what he had heard, Ignis perks up, the feathers on his tail fanning out. With a new bounce in his step, he passes the black dragon and continues deeper into the crater.

Curious wyverns crawl their way down from the crater walls to approach the newcomer. They chirp and chatter all wanting to take a closer look at the peculiar orange dragon. Eating up the attention he has desired since leaving Patu, Ignis fans out his wings in a spectacle of sunset feathers.

Stirling's arms slip around Amiria, pulling her to stand in front of him and lowering his chin to rest on the top of her head. They stand in silence watching as Ignis integrates himself with the clan of dragons like proud parents.

She closes her eyes, letting his warmth blanket her. She can feel his chest move against her back as he breathes. Finally, she understands what Stirling had meant. Even if they live in constant fear of what is behind them at least they are together. Why throw yourself to the wolves when you can test their stamina? See who can run further—who can run longer. Each on a sprint to the new dawn. Every day the sun rises is more precious than the last.

Her heart is telling her to go, but her mind is filled with dread and guilt of abandoning the people of Wyverna. Stirling is right, she can't save them, not alone. Not when she is barely going to be able to save herself. One person can't make a difference, it's not as if she has anyone on her side that is willing to fight. She refuses to be controlled by Wyverna, by the king, by her upbringing anymore, this choice is hers.

"Stirling." She leans her cheek into his arm.

"Yeah?" His chin still rests on her head.

"Let's leave tomorrow morning."

Stirling holds her tighter and kisses her on the crown of her head and says with a breath of relief, "Okay."

Forty-Eight

Blue silk sheets tangle around Quilan's legs, barely covering him above his hips after another restless night. Sleeping on his stomach, Quilan blinks awake to persistent knocking on his front door. He holds the shimmering sheet around his waist as he sleepily stumbles across the room to the second-floor window and peers down at the entrance to his house.

"QUILAN, THERE YOU ARE!" Florence, his mother, yells up to him from his front step in her usual attire of rainbow silks. "IS YOUR LOCK BROKEN? MY KEY ISN'T WORKING!"

Without a reply, Quilan closes the shutters to his room.

Choosing to skip getting dressed, since he has no plans of leaving his house today, Quilan ties the sheet in place hanging low on his hips, and heads downstairs for an early morning snack before his cook prepares his usual late morning breakfast. Other than competition days, he never sees this time in the morning.

He passes the front door on the way to the kitchen and ignores his mother's constant voice through the painted wood panels.

"Quilan!" She shakes the door, "Is your door stuck? I can hear you walking. I'll tell you anyway." Rolling his eyes, Quilan leans against his counter and bites into the inside of a fig. "You've been getting lazy since that farm boy left. Just because your main competition is gone doesn't mean you can lay around all day. So I signed you up for a race in Ensam."

Fingers seizing up, the fig falls from his hand. Quilan doesn't know if his mother is still talking because the roaring of invisible crowds has punctured through the inside of his ears.

A race. He has to go to a race. He can't go to a race, not anymore, not alone. Quilan claws at his bare chest leaving behind five red trails. He can't breathe. His chest hurts. He can't breathe. Gasping for air, Quilan hugs his arms around his stomach and lowers down to his haunches.

He can't. He can't! HE CAN'T!

Eyes watching his every move, nothing he does is left unnoticed. Every movement, every word, every breath, every blink. Watching. Watching! WATCHING! They're reaching for him, hands extending out to touch him, to grab him. Hands on his arms, on his back, on his chest, other places—without his consent—everyone wanting to feel him as if that would solidify their proof he is real. He is real. He is alive. He is Quilan of Leucasia. He is a person.

Alone, alone, he is so *alone*. He is never more alone than when he is surrounded by people all declaring their love for a person they think he is, the person he will never truly be.

The person on stage with the perfect smile that they devote themselves to. That person is not a person. It is a handcrafted doll to fool you into a false state of adoration to follow its every command. Never will there be a day he is not acting when he is *that*.

The real him—he squeezes his arms tighter around his center—they would despise him like all of his exes. The people he let hang from his arm only enjoyed his company in the public's eye. Once they were alone they always became upset. They would complain to him that he is too quiet, too disassociated, too far lost into his thoughts. Over their short time together they would grow increasingly irritated with his behavior, calling him entitled and arrogant.

Why open yourself up, when opening a door is easier. In the end, he showed them all out.

They hate you, Pathetic trash,. Uselss, burden. Even Stirling has left you.
Stirling didn't leave him. Stirling cares about him. He left because he needed to help Amiria and not because of him. He's going to come back. He will be back and he won't have to face them alone. They'll be together. He promised. He promised. He promised.

You should have stepped off.
No. He's glad he is here. He wants to be here. He has finally made friends.

Who left you.
NO! He will be back, but he isn't his only friend. There is someone who is still here.

That's because she knows the quiet you, but she doesn't know you.
She won't walk away from him. She won't leave him. She can help him, she will help him. He is not alone. He is not *alone*. He *is not* alone.

Everyone hates you once you let them in.
No. She won't hate him. He is not alone. He has someone. He has her.

"Evelina."

Eve drops the hem of her apron, releasing the chicken feed to the ground as she startles to the sound of her name. She spins around to see Quilan standing at the corner of Stirling's house as she tends to his garden and animals first thing in the morning.

"Quilan, you scared me." She puts her hand to her chest. Her eyes fall to his fidgeting hands at his side then up to the unease in his eyes. She remembers this look from Stirling during his first games. "Quilan? What's wrong?" She steps forward.

Quilan dips his chin letting his pale hair fall in front of his face as he sways unsteadily on his feet, "I need—" His shoulder knocks into the stucco as he slumps against the wall.

"Quilan—" She has grown close to Quilan over this short period and has become used to carrying the conversations, but she could always tell something was wrong on a deeper level. There is a reason for his lack of verbal communication, she doesn't know why though. She can only guess it was something to do with fame, but she can't help him if he doesn't open up. She closes the distance between them and brushes back the hair from his face, "Talk to me."

Eyes as round as blueberries stare back at her. Pink lips open to speak but the words never fall out. Then in a swift movement, he's holding onto her. His arms had snuck under hers to curl around her back and pull himself to her. With his head buried in her neck, his body shudders with the tears he's been holding back.

"Hey—what's wrong?" she asks, surprised by the contact. Her arms curve over his shoulders putting up walls for him to hide behind.

His breath hitches but he doesn't reply. Ignoring the smell of spirits on his breath, Eve rests her hand on the back of his head and begins humming the tune she had used to comfort Stirling during the games.

The fingers that are clutching into the back of her gown begin to relax, but Quilan doesn't lift his head as he says, "Help."

She feels the pulse of dread through her body. It is not the fact she has to help him she fears, but it is that she was right with her observation that something is wrong. "I'm here for you."

Here. She *is* here. She is here for *him*.

His arms tighten once again around her as if putting pressure on her will keep *himself* together. He doesn't know how to begin. He knows he needs to tell someone but tell them what? Where does he begin? Does he start with how his thoughts about stepping off the cliff are returning or how maybe they never left? They just had a bandage covering them up while Stirling was around. But then he would have to explain to her after the closing ceremony he was one step away from never seeing the sunrise. If he tells her that he will have to tell her why, why he walked all the way up there and how long he's dreamed about it. Where does the why begin? Is it because he can't keep pretending to smile or because he's pretended to be someone for so long he's lost who he really is?   oes he tell her it wasn't his first attempt

"Help me," his voice is thick with tears.

"Of course, of course, I will. I need to know what though." Her heart is breaking at the sound of desperation in his voice.

He can do this. He can start with the most recent news that had set off the voices in his head that his drinks couldn't quiet.

Releasing her, Quilan takes a step back and slides down the wall to a sitting position, and buries his face in his knees. "I can't."

Eve squats down beside him, "Can't what?"

Life "Race."

Eve sits down beside him and takes his hand in hers, "Why is that?"

His fingers of his free hand grip his hair, "I haven't since he left. I—I—can't go alone." He begins trembling at the image of the mob pressing in on him. He's alone in a sea of people and he doesn't want to drown. Please someone, don't let him drown. "I can't anymore."

"You're not alone." She squeezes his hand.

Not alone. He lifts his face, stained pink with tears, to stare at his hand in hers, a hand that has pulled Stirling from the swirling eddies of the crowds. "Can you hum?"

"Of course." She stretches her legs out. "Rest your head." Hesitant, Quilan's eyes jump from her lap to her face. "It'll help you relax, trust me," she insists.

Nodding, he lowers himself until the back of his head rests on her thigh. Eve keeps her tears at bay as she sees his chest heave with heavy breaths. Taking his right hand in hers she notices the pale skin has a freckle that mirrors the one on her left. She slides her thumb down the outside of his hand over the matching dot.

The hairs on Quilan's arms rise and a small gasp escapes his lips as he feels Eve runs her fingers through his fine hair. His eyes slip closed as he is momentarily overtaken by a wonderful new sensation. In none of his relationships, no matter their gender, had any of them done something so intimate. They never once asked how he was doing. They were dating Quilan of Leucasia the number one elite racer, not Quilan who hates who he's become. When it became too exhausting to keep up his charade at home he would cut them loose. There was always another willing to fill his bed, to temporarily fill that void inside him.

Tears leak from the corners of his eyes and disappear into his straight pale hair. "Make it stop."

"Make what stop?"

"I don't know," he chokes out, his chest sputtering with tear thick breaths.

He's told he should be grateful for everything he has. A nice home, endless coin, and a barrage of people dedicating themselves to him every day. But they have hollowed him out until he was a beautiful, empty shell. His blood no longer runs and his heart no longer beats while they have control of his strings. His mind watches through the windows of his eyes, but no matter how loud it screams no one seems to hear it over themselves. They keep seeing the Quilan they want to see, it's easier to remain blind to the fact your idol is no more human than you are and is quickly deteriorating.

He's been so lonely for all of his life and he finally met someone who wanted to spend time with the real Quilan and he's lost him. He doesn't want to face those crowds anymore. He can't do it anymore.

She begins humming and his mind blanks. His thoughts stop tearing at the inside of his skull to listen to her voice. He is not alone. He is not alone because he still has her. She kept Stirling afloat and she can do the same for him.

"Help me," he whispers.

"Always," she brushes his tears with her thumb, "Always."

Forty-Nine

The setting sun dips beneath the ocean horizon, turning it a fiery gold. Beams of light spring from the end of the world striking the blanket of clouds moving in from the west in an array of orange and purple.

Ignis swoops down camouflaged in the amber light, taking a sharp turn the tips of his wings nearly clip the white caps of the choppy waters.

"Did you enjoy your day with the Wyverns?" Stirling asks. Ignis had spent the entire afternoon with the community as Stirling and Amiria headed back down the island to pack up any of the supplies they had and gave Ignis some space.

"Yeah, they aren't as scary as Taika," Ignis claims. Pumping his wings, he climbs the air up to the low-hanging clouds covering the top of the island.

Stirling ponders, chewing on his lip before saying, *"Well, they did try to kill Amiria and me, but if you get past the near-death situation they are a loving family."*

"I've been wondering what it would be like if they had raised me," Ignis refers to his upbringing as an orphan on his own.

During his day with the Wyverns, Ignis had been told tales by the elder wyverns that they recall a dragon resembling him. They remember her vividly because they had never seen a dragon with beautiful pale-yellow feathers before. She was accompanying a ship sailing far south of the island where no human trade routes run with flags they didn't recognize. The masts, they did recognize, were of the humans from the mainland who sailed in and raided the ship—sinking it and its occupants.

They found her injured in the mountains of the human's island but she succumbed to her injuries before she was able to tell them anything. They never knew she had a hatchling somewhere hidden.

"We wouldn't have met. You would have been living here instead of the forest," Stirling reaches up, his fingertips running through the belly of the bubbly mammatus clouds, *"And I would still be at the bakery."* Stirling touches the goggles Amiria had given him. Dropping his hand back down to the handle of Ignis' saddle he remembers creating with Bernard. *"You, Amiria, everyone in Patu, Aether. All of us oblivious of each other's existence."* Stirling lies back, watching the roof of clouds pass just above him and Ignis. He thinks back to laying on his bed in the bakery, staring at the ceiling of wood. He reached for the sky and felt it *"What a world that would have been."* Sadness hits him as he thinks of the boy he didn't say good bye to.

"Safer, but boring. I wouldn't have become the famous per'yanny svir that I am now." Ignis gloats, missing the glory of the annual games.

"That's all you got out of us meeting?" Stirling crosses his arms.

"No, of course not. I got to meet the love of my life, my beautiful Aether." Ignis smiles.

Stirling hangs his head in defeat. Distracted, they almost don't notice the silent descent of dragons lowering from the clouds in a synchronized air fleet.

"Umm," Stirling slowly glances three hundred and sixty degrees around at the dragons surrounding them. They've become an orange center to the formation of earthy tones. An orange mariposa lily standing out against the muted desert terrain.

The black dragon leading his flock tips his wings. In a wave of response, everyone repeats the movement following his wide banking turn. Struggling to keep his wings from clipping, Ignis plays along.

I think they are making us fly with them, Ignis realizes as he is given no choice but to stay in formation.

"Amazing," the word falls from Stirling's lips, and his jaw slacks with awe. The fleet of dragons plays with the clouds, bobbing in and out like a pod of dolphins in the ocean. Stirling grips the handles as the dragons begin to ascend, climbing vertically through the clouds until they break the top surface. Stirling glimpses the twilight sky with the stars blinking into existence as Ignis arches backward and dives back into the clouds with the rest of the group.

A whoop erupts from Stirling as he cheers in exhilaration. The formation begins to spiral downward, a massive twisting tornado of wings and scales. The vortex sprouts from the clouds reaching for the water. As if the ocean had a magnetic force field, the dragons bloom outwards, scattering across the surface in different directions.

Stirling punches at the sky, "WOOH! That's what I'm talking about!" He sits back in the saddle. If there was one way to spend his last night in this dreadful isle, this is it.

Shivering, Amiria pulls the blanket she shares with Stirling closer to her face. She scrunches her nose trying to keep her eyes closed but an unsettling feeling stirs her awake. Laying on her side, she and Stirling use the second blanket as a pillow. The warmth of his chest presses against her back as his arm drapes over her waistline. The hairs on the back of her head tickle as they move with Stirling's sleeping breaths.

She blinks the surrounding night into focus. The full moon shines down, turning the light gray stone into silver walls capped with a starry lid. She smiles at Ignis who is sprawled out, a splash of color on the grayscale backdrop. She tilts her head to look over at Taika.

Dread fills her heart.

Taika's eyes remain fixated on something behind Amiria, "*Someone's here.*"

Her mouth going dry and her hands beginning to tremble, she imagines Calix hovering over her with a wicked smile. Swallowing the lump in her throat, she props up on her elbow. Stirling remains undisturbed as his arm slides down to her hip. Careful not to wake him, Amiria sits up completely, and with a painstaking slowness hoping this is only another one of her nightmares, she turns around.

A girl in a pink cotehardie sits on the rim of their camp, her legs swinging as she looks down on them with a mischievous smile.

Amiria turns the color of the stone around her, "Kinsey."

"Amiria," Kinsey mocks Amiria's disbelief.

Amiria's eyes drift to the empty space on either side of Kinsey before snapping back to her in fear if she removes her from her sight she will disappear like a spider vanishing from the corner of your room.

"He's not here if that's what you're wondering," Kinsey says, still swinging her legs.

That was exactly what Amiria was wondering, but she doesn't tell Kinsey that. "How did you find us?" she questions instead.

Hearing the voices of a conversation, Stirling's eyes flutter open, his body goes cold as he sees Amiria's intense expression. She lays her hand on his shoulder keeping him from jumping up. He slowly twists his neck to see the unfamiliar girl with hair as dark as Amiria's but eyes as light as Eve's.

"So very Amiria to get straight to the point," she stops kicking her legs and throws her head back.

Amiria can hear Stirling's heart beginning to pound, "It was Calix, wasn't it?"

Rocking back, Kinsey kicks her legs up into the air before placing her hands on her knees and leaning forward, "Well of course. Did you *really* think my obsessive brother didn't know where you were this whole time?" She clicks her tongue. "Aw your false sense of security is so—" Her voice goes up an octave, "Cute!"

Amiria stares without saying a word. If Calix has known where she is this whole time, why hasn't he come for her himself? Why is Kinsey here instead?

Kinsey crosses her legs raising one shoulder to her cheek, "You're wondering why he hasn't come for you since he's known all along?"

Amiria holds her tongue. Calix had warned her about his sister's mind games. How she uses words to play with and ridicule her victims.

"Do you miss him?" She leans forward again nearly toppling over the edge, her eyes popping from her head, "Do you wish it was him that showed up! Because he sure misses you." She puts her hand to her heart. "You're all he thinks about."

Catching herself digging her nails into Stirling's shoulder, Amiria releases her tension but Stirling doesn't appear to notice as he stares petrified. With her hand still anchored to him for mental stability she questions, "Then why didn't he come himself?"

Spinning on the ball of her foot, Kinsey twirls to a standing position, "He wanted to, oh believe me he really did." She balances frivolously on the edge as she confesses to the moon, "Poor boy, poor lovesick boy. So sad, so painfully sad to bear witness." She sniffles, wiping an imaginary tear. "This heartbroken boy has gotten himself into quite a dilemma. You see. King Dietrich—" She looks Amiria dead in the eye "--he wants you dead. But Calix." She sucks on the tip of her finger then holds it out as if to determine the direction of the wind, she smiles finding the answer, "He *says* he wants you alive to run free."

Discreetly Amiria pulls her blades out from under her blanket pillow and stages them between her and Stirling.

Kinsey presses her forearm to her head as if she is about to faint, "Oh, what heartbreak does to some people." She drops her arm down to her side, her muscles going slack. "Tragic really. I could tell he was lying, he wants you dead too, but made up some facade to hide the fact he's too weak to do it himself." Her head rolls back to Amiria.

"And that's why he sent," Kinsey pirouettes and jumps out into a wide stance with her hands victoriously in the air, "ME!"

"If you're here to kill me, then why all this chatter?"

Kinsey clasps her hands together and presses her knuckles against her cheek, "Because I've missed you!" She tilts her head lowering her chin to her chest with a smile, her voice lowering, "My strong and empowered female counterpart." She throws her hands away, the momentum turning her parallel to the edge. She begins to sashay, exaggeratedly swinging her hips as she travels along the rim. She stops closer to above their heads.

Kelsea Koops

Cackling laughter fills their box-like campsite as Kinsey explodes, "And to think!" She throws herself to land perfectly on her back, in line with the edge and a single leg hanging off the side. She reaches to the sky, "We were almost sisters. I always wanted a sister." She drops her hand back to resting on her stomach, "Hard to grow up with only brothers." She pauses as a dark shadow crosses her eyes, she closes her eyes suppressing it, "Having to prove yourself."

She flips over resting her hand on her arm with her other hanging off the edge with her leg. She picks pebbles free from the rock face and tosses them mindlessly as she speaks, "Guess you wouldn't understand, being an only child," She rolls again turning perpendicular to the edge with her head hanging off, "No need to compete for recognition. You had your position guaranteed." Laughing it off she sits up with her back to them, "There I go rambling again." She twists her spine, poised like a model for a painting, "Feels good. I don't get to confess often. Have that girl-to-girl talk." She scoots, turning on her hip toward Amiria. Pouting, she lowers her cheek to her shoulder, "You know what it's like not having any friends." Picking up one of her long braids she flicks it as she talks, "What happened to you, Amiria? We used to be so much alike."

Remaining quiet during Kinsey's entire rant, Amiria treads lightly, "We are nothing alike."

An insidious smile creeps along Kinsey's face until all her teeth are exposed, "Oh, but we are." She stands in jerking movements like a doll being lifted by string, "Grew up in the harsh reality of the Cavalry, train until you collapse then train some more. A social outcast, liked neither by the Cavalry nor the citizens, too busy of a schedule to enjoy the subtleties in life. Well until--" Her eyes fall to Stirling for the first time. Her smile vanishes into a blank expression, her lips hanging partly open. Her eyes run their course over the entire length of his body as he lies propped up on his elbows beside Amiria. When she finally speaks, her words are pure. "Until you met him." Her eyes flick to Amiria, her words an icy bite. "Must be nice."

Amiria leaps to her feet furiously, both her swords in hand.

Kinsey spins giddily in a circle clapping that she finally found Amiria's trigger.

"Leave him out of it!" Amiria screams, stepping over Stirling's hip to stand on either side of him. "Come down here and fight! Or I'll come up there, whichever you prefer!"

Kinsey clicks her tongue. "Oh no. No, no, no," she says, wagging her finger. "We're not going to fight here."

"What do you mean?" Amiria demands. "Why not!"

"If I kill you here, what do I gain from that?" She puts her hands on her hips, "The answer is nothing. I gain nothing and Calix wins because he'll steal my credit." Kinsey crosses her arms, "and if Calix wins no one is happy. Not even him."

"Kinsey?" Amiria's voice warns.

"Amiria?" Kinsey imitates.

"What do you have planned?" Amiria asks but doesn't want to know the answer.

Kinsey jumps up and down excited to spill the confidential plan coordinated by her. Her volume increases with her enthusiasm, "The Reys are out Amiria! And the Gautiers are picking up the slack." She flexes her biceps. "I'm going to win it all, but I just need you to attack the castle first. I want everyone to bear witness to me killing you." She draws a line across her throat. "If you attack the king and I kill you, Calix fails, I win and then I will become Field Marshal. I will be the HERO!"

Amiria's knuckles turn white as she grips the handle of her short swords, "What have you done to my father?"

"Nothing…" She bites her lip as if holding back a secret.

"Kinsey, what have you done?" Amiria's voice a grave.

Unable to contain her laughter at Amiria's expense she bursts, "Nothing! I swear!" All her childish smiles and giggles vanish, her face dropping to a stoic expression with a cold voice, "Well, nothing yet."

Stirling looks from the devilish girl to the blades rattling in Amiria's hands as she replies through gritted teeth, "And what happens if I don't come to the castle."

"That's the fun option!" She skips a couple of steps before turning around. "I'll get to hunt you down and—" She holds her hand out, tapping her index to her fingers as if keeping tally. "Not only will I drag your barely living body to the king's feet—I'll also get to kill you." She points at Stirling. "And everyone you've ever come in contact with." Half her lips curl into a smile. "Like that little village you hid in. I heard farmhouses are extremely flammable."

"Taika!" Amiria commands.

With a hiss, Taika readies a flame in the back of her throat.

"Uh uh uh. I wouldn't do that if I were you," she scolds, her bone-white dragon revealing itself over her shoulder, "I'll turn this hole in the ground into an inferno. I guess I can't prove your death if there's nobody to find, oh well, then neither does Calix." Her face brightens as if she just thought of something funny, "Hey boy, you were a baker right? How ironic would it be if I turn this hideout into a giant oven."

She pauses waiting for her applause, "What? No sense of humor? Fine. You'll be dead soon anyways." She relocks eyes with Amiria, "Tomorrow night. We have a date at the castle." Nothing but Amiria and Stirling's lungs move as they stare up at Kinsey. Kinsey blows a kiss to the statue couple, "I'll see you soon, Amiria." She wiggles her fingers goodbye.

They say nothing. They think nothing. The only movement, the only sound is the gusts of wind created by Kinsey's dragon as it becomes a second moon in the sky.

Her weak knees buckling, Amiria drops her swords and collapses in place,

"Oomph." Stirling exhales as she lands on him. She sits there on his stomach, staring at the last place Kinsey was. Her loose hair tumbles around her in waves.

Though uncomfortable, Stirling doesn't make her move. He studies her, watching her flickering eyes replay everything that girl Kinsey had said. She doesn't say anything and he doesn't ask. She'll talk when she's done mulling it over in her mind. He has his own thoughts he needs to sort before they pile theirs together. He looks over at Ignis, who lowers his eyes to the ground, then over to Taika, whose eyes are sharp with fury.

They were so close. So close to being together even if they never had a permanent home. He hasn't forgotten his promise to Eve or how he didn't tell Quilan goodbye. Even on the run, he would stop by the village to see her, to see Quilan, hoping one day they could slow down. No longer running, he would take Amiria's hand in his and lead her up the staircase to the house he built where they can grow old together.

Why is it so hard for them to be happy? Why won't this kingdom let them be happy? They've let Wyverna go, why can't it do the same? They are two insignificant people in the world.

They *were* insignificant.

He deserted Wyverna, he wanted nothing to do with this kingdom. He didn't ask to become a household name. He was *free*. He still *is* free. He still is insignificant compared to her. If she is killed by Kinsey before the kingdom, any symbol they have become will be quashed. People will return to numbly following the kingdom's orders and return to the days when safety is more important than freedom.

Then he will go home. He and Ignis will finish living their days in Patu, Ignis will be reunited with Aether and he will be back with Eve and Quilan. He will live free.

He takes Amiria's hand in his. Could he ever smile if he let her sacrifice herself. Could he carry on like he had before imagining she was happy somewhere too? *I have, Stirling dreads. I was happy in Patu before--no.* Stirling pushes the negative thoughts away.

Amiria squeezes his hand back. Her night eyes become wet with an incoming storm. Staring into her face, he watches as the dark clouds begin to shroud her mind. He doesn't want her to go there, not the castle, but now-- whereever her mind is taking her. Already she is leaving him, he can feel it in his heart their seperation beginning. But how lonely will each crowd cheering his name be if he never hears the words "baker boy" again?

Leaning up on his elbow, he removes his hand from hers and cups her face. His fingers curl into the air and gently guide her down. She follows willingly. Her bottom lip parts his for briefly. Falling back, Stirling lays down with her head on his chest.

"Eh, hem. Do you need a moment?" Ignis blushes. Ignoring him, Stirling wraps his arms around her. He can't seem to hold her close enough. Amiria's body is caught in Taika's flames as her hands tangle into Stirling's curls; she buries her face into his neck. Her light frame rises and falls with his heavy breaths.

He lays there listening to her ragged breaths turn into the soft sounds of sleep. He stays on his back with her comforting weight on his chest as he stares up at the ancestral stars. He looks for his mother, he looks for someone to guide him. What is he supposed to do?

"What the—" Robert states, stopping dead in his tracks.

Following behind on the narrow pathway of the outer bailey walls, William bumps into him as they patrol the perimeter of the castle ground dressed in their soft, blue armor and chainmail. He rubs his nose, "What are you doing?"

Leaning back, Robert presses himself into William, who is barely tall enough to peer over his shoulder, as he asks from the corner of his mouth, "What is that?" He points to a figure moving about the spire of the northeastern tower.

Subconsciously grabbing Robert's elbow, William squints against the bright sun. A white dragon clings to the side of the steep rooftop with pearlescent horns casting rainbows in the light. Above the dragon is a figure of a girl in pink spinning around the pointed tip of the spire.

Raising his eyebrow, William questions, "Is there a girl dancing up there or have I lost my mind?"

"I'm glad you see it too," Robert sighs with relief, glad the hit he had taken several nights ago hadn't caused a late start on seeing hallucinations.

Clyde, their captain overseeing this section of patrol, approaches the two guards still standing together, "That *thing* you are looking at is Kinsey Gautier." Robert and William feel a shiver run down their spine as they hear the Gautier name. Clyde continues, "You haven't lost your mind but she has, in her defense losing your mind runs in the Gautier family."

All three pause and watch the girl play dangerously close to death's door. "Alright." Clyde claps his hands together, "You two need to talk less and patrol more. Go on back to work." He steps off to the side to allow them room to pass. "Oh by the way," he lowers his voice, "Do keep an eye on what she is doing."

"Yes sir." They answer in unison.

Fifty-One

The metallic sound reverberates in the small stone space as the broadsword bounces across the barren ground. Stirling breathes heavily, retracting his hand after throwing it.

"I'm not done!" Amiria screams at him, she in her dark metal armor and Stirling in the soft, blue armor and chainmail. She has been using him to practice most of the morning. Having him hold up the guard's broadsword as she repeats her movements, the muscle memory of fighting coming back with each swipe of her short sword.

She only has today to prepare. She has to make the most of it to ready herself.

Stirling's arms burn after deflecting her advances. He doesn't have to move to block; she is aiming for his sword, but the totality of her power behind each of the blows is already having a toll on him. They've been at it for hours, and he can barely hold up the sword anymore.

"BUT I AM!" he shouts back, infuriated. Sweat weighs down his knotting curls and drips in beads down his brow. He drops to a sitting position, exhausted, and groans, "I don't want to do this."

"You might not want to," Amiria snaps. Taking several steps forward, she hits her fist against her chest. "But I have to. I can't let you die."

"But I have to let you?" Stirling's teeth grind together as he clenches his jaw. It wasn't supposed to be like this. They were supposed to run together. The dawn of their escape has come and gone. He doesn't want her to fight. He doesn't want to lose her, but— He thinks of the unsuspecting villagers back home—the images of their homes set aflame by that girl as she doubles over in cackling laughter.

"This isn't a choice, Stirling," Amiria continues as Stirling dives deep into his thoughts. "You think I want to fight her?"

Stirling blurts, leaping back from the darkest parts of his mind and standing up, "YES!" Amiria pulls her head back as if Stirling has raised the back of his hand to her. Stirling throws his arms in the air, "I think you do want this. You've wanted to fight King Dietrich since you found me in Leucasia." He points his finger at her, calling her out. "I bet you're ecstatic to have an excuse to go fight."

Amiria crosses her arms. "That's uncalled for."

"No, it isn't. Because you live for the thrill of a fight. If you didn't, we would have left days ago." Stirling clamps his jaw shut, muting his words. He takes a step back as if he caught someone he trusted in a lie. "Do you even want to go back to Patu with me? Or did you just run out of reasons to stay here until that girl gave you a new incentive?"

"I do want to go with you! Stirling, believe me. I do want out of this." She motions to her armor. "I don't want this life, I don't think I've ever wanted it, especially not after I met you."

"I'll believe it when I see it," Stirling stabs. He grimaces at his words when he sees the impact on her face. His voice grows soft. "I'm sorry, Amiria, that—I—that came out wrong." He sighs. "I love you, Amiria, but sometimes I feel like you love that armor more than me." He hangs his head, unable to look her in the eye, unable to keep bearing witness to the pain he has caused written across her face. "I'll be up with the wyverns if you need me."

He turns to the silent Ignis, who is keeping himself out of the argument. Amiria humphs turning her back to him as he crawls onto Ignis' back and departs their camp.

She tosses her sword onto the blanket furiously. Stirling had called her a liar. She isn't lying, she did—does want to go back home with him. He is and always has been her center of focus. He only sees the path he is walking on. What he doesn't understand is the consequences it can have on others. He might kick a pebble down a hill but he'll never know that pebble became an avalanche on someone else's trail.

If she doesn't do this, everyone will die. Her father, Giles, everyone in the village. Mairead crosses Amiria's mind. She hopes the coin she had given her had gotten her far from the city. She hopes Kinsey will overlook a handmaiden.

"*Amiria.*" Taika's calming voice immediately cools Amiria's heated temper. "*He's just scared. He had given up his life in his village to risk saving you. Then after all that now he is looking at losing you forever.*"

"*Don't take his side.*"

"*I'm flying you into the fight aren't I? I believe you are making the right choice, but I understand the boy's opposition,*" Taika takes the middle ground.

Amiria begins loosening the straps of her armor, tossing each one to the ground at her feet, "*It's like what Clyde had told me back in the tower, I'm fighting a losing battle. But Stirling's also right, I would need...*" Amiria pauses, seeing the peak of the island reflecting on her pauldron. She turns to peer up at the ancient volcano. "An army."

Ignis trollops along the tarn's turquoise edge with fledglings skittering across the ground as they playfully try to keep up with their long-legged friend. With the chainmail disregarded to the side, Stirling leans back on a small boulder still in the soft armor with hatchlings the length of his arm, excluding their tails, crawling over him.

"*You know.*" Ignis slows to a stop holding his feathered tail out like a fishing line teasing the young fledglings, "*I'm still in the vote to go home.*"

"*Yeah, until our home is burned down by a lunatic,*" Stirling lets his head thump back against the hard stone. His neck bobs as he swallows.

"*That's only if Amiria runs too,*" Ignis draws a circle in the ashen ground with his claw, "*We could always, you know…*"

"*We're not leaving without her!*" Stirling holds the hatchling hanging onto his chest as he sits up straight.

"*But what if…*" Ignis drifts off, unable to complete his thought.

Stirling holds back the stress induced tears, "*But what if what? Ignis, what if what?*" He knows what Ignis was going to say. He just wants to hear someone else say it, the inevitable truth. Then what if she doesn't return? Stirling puts his hand to his throbbing head, covering his eyes, the evening light suddenly too bright.

"*Stirling, look who's here,*" Ignis mentally nudges him.

Peeking through his fingers, Stirling observes Taika land with Amiria on her back. She is down to her armor's soft base layers and he can see the dark glinting metal tied to Taika's saddle. Dropping his hand he fights through his headache to watch her leap from Taika with a grace only she possesses. He doesn't move from his seated position as she walks over to the black dragon with Taika as her translator. He watches from the sidelines as her arms wave through the air emphasizing her reasoning.

After most of their remaining daylight is gone, Amiria finally turns to Stirling, her wide eyes unreadable, a strange mixture of hopefulness and fear. Biting her lip she travels across empty space separating them.

"What is it?" His voice is still bitter from their prior argument as Amiria reaches him.

The resentment she felt earlier rises back to the surface. Pushing it down Amiria releases it out through her nostrils. "I'm sorry." Stirling peers up at her in confusion. "I'm sorry." She repeats. Sorry for how she yelled earlier. Sorry for not taking how he felt into consideration. Sorry for the position they are in. Sorry for what they will never be.

"I'm sorry too." A smile twitches on his lips but it doesn't stay. He pets the hatchling still clung to his chest with several more on his legs and beside him. "They seem to like me."

Careful not to startle the hatchlings, Amiria lowers herself down to her knees sitting back on her heels. She reaches out, running her hand down the ridge of a hatchling's back. It chirps crawling closer to her insisting on being pet more.

She doesn't look up from the hatchling as she speaks. "They are willing to fight with me. The adults that is."

"What?"

"The wild wyverns. I have to go tonight and I can't fight alone. Kinsey is only the start, my old squad will come as soon as I'm spotted. I can't fight the entire Cavalry on my own. I didn't want to admit it before but…" She meets his eyes. "I'm scared."

The hatchlings scatter as Stirling sits up on his knees and pulls Amiria into an embrace. He breathes her in as the sun counts down their time together. "Me too." He holds her in silence for a long slow breath. "Sit with me?" He pulls back from her. Taking her hand he scoots back against the rock guiding her to sit with him. She sits between his legs and leans back against his chest.

"But at least I'll have an army," Amiria says, scanning the wild wyverns. "Luckily, we have a mutual disdain for Wyverna."

"What do you mean?" Stirling questions, hoping Amiria is right that they will fight with her. Each dragon willing to fly with her will raise the odds of her returning to him.

"Wyverna has cast them away to this skeletal island from the lush lands of the main island. They stole their family and forced them into our own deadly wars. How can they not want vengeance? There's enough room in those mountains for the wyverns to live separately from the humans. They don't need to stay here in fear anymore. They just need to show Wyverna they shouldn't be reckoned with."

"I can't stop you, literally I can't, but even if the wyverns fight on your side," his mouth opens as he searches for how to say the words, "I'm afraid you'll go somewhere I can't follow."

Amiria pulls Stirling's arms around her and runs her fingers from his rough open palm to his calloused fingertips, "I won't."

He closes his hand around hers, "Do you promise?"

She doesn't answer right away, she stares down at her hand in his, "I can't."

Hunching forward, Stirling lifts his knees and brings his ankles closer together creating a capsule around her. She feels like a hatchling inside its egg with him around her. She breathes in his saltwater scent. Pine needles, rosemary, now salt water. Always adapting to what life throws at him.

She misses the days of the pine needles. Careless days of fun in the mountains and see you next week. If only she had known what would happen the day he asked her to run away.

She envisions a reality where she said yes. Where she disappeared into the night with him. She wouldn't show up for watch the next day and no one, not even Calix would know where to search for her. What a fragile timeline of events.

She remembers Stirling's friend Quilan, *It would be an honor,* he had told her. She could have been racing against them. She could have been the top racer, but she couldn't let go of her duties to Wyverna. She still can't.

All the innocent souls that were pulled from their bodies by braided rope, would they still have their lives if they never knew of the baker who flew. She closes her eyes, pressing a single tear free, and the soldier who said no more.

Their blood is on her hands. This is why she feels indebted to them. She has released this monster upon them. Now it's her job to rein it back in or die trying.

"It's not a you, it's a we. *We* caused this," Stirling whispers before settling back against the boulder. His arms still hold her tight.

"How did you—?" she begins.

"I can tell what you're thinking and it's destroying you. Don't take all this burden on your own shoulders. *We* didn't make those people do anything. They knew the repercussions but chose to do so of their own free will."

Her voice is thick with uncertainty, "Yeah."

"If you can't promise you'll come back, can you at least promise me you won't try and be Wyverna's hero?" Stirling pleads. "Do what you need to do, make your point, but please don't make it the last thing you do." He can taste the salt of the tears running down his cheeks, he dips his chin kissing the back of her head, "Please, please be the one who gets to go home at the end"

Warmth spreads from where he kissed her on her head to her toes then without a word, Amiria turns around in Stirling's lap to face him, her face streaming with tears.

"Amiria?" Stirling tilts his head with concern.

Her hands cup the sides of his face and she presses her lips to his. Caught off guard, Stirling's hands hang in midair, their lips interlocked. As Amiria sighs into him, Stirling rests his hands on her back pulling her closer until her body is lining his.

A small moan escapes Stirling's lips as Amiria's kiss intensifies. Her desire for him is as strong as a starving person with their last meal.

Amiria pulls back and calms her heavy breaths to whisper, "I love you."

His voice catches in his throat as he struggles to reply through his tears, "I—love you too."

Standing up, Amiria offers out her hand. Stirling, face still wet with tears, raises an eyebrow. Amiria points her eyes and tilts her head in the direction of the boulders leading them out of sight.

"Do you?" Amiria asks nervously, "Do you want to?"

Eyes widening with understanding Stirling squeaks, "Uh huh."

Taking Amiria's hand, Stirling is pulled to his feet.

Ignis' head whips around to witness Stirling following Amiria out of view. He calls out to Stirling hoping he could be heard over Stirling's pounding heart, *"Finally!"*

Around the corner of the boulder entrance to the top of the mountain where they first encountered the black wyvern and out of sight Amiria pulls Stirling's face to hers with a new sense of urgency. Without a single protest Stirling responds in kind, his hands splayed across her back to keep her close to him.

Amiria's roaming hands run across Stirling's chest, strong from years of manual labor, to grip the collar of his gambeson. She desperately pulls at the stiff fabric wishing it would come off easier. Stirling's feet stumble backward as Amiria pushes her weight into him until he is pinned against the gray stone.

Pulling their lips apart, Amiria fumbles with the ties of Stirling's gambeson. With his heart beating in his throat, Stirling's trembling hands find the other ties of his top and begin to help undo them.

The blue gambeson, half shrugged off by Stirling and half pulled off by Amiria, falls discarded at their feet. Free of the layer, Stirling's lips rediscover Amiria's and her hands slip under his tunic. Stirling shivers and releases a gasp at the sensation of her fingers running up his bare skin.

"Take it off," Amiria tells him as she kisses his throat.

Swallowing hard Stirling grabs the back of his tunic and tugs it over his head momentarily blocking his vision. The tunic is tossed to the ground as he blinks up to see Amiria undoing the ties of her dark blouse. His heart sputters at the image of her revealing skin and his body is lit on fire as he watches her top drop beside her.

Suddenly too nervous to move, Stirling is stuck petrified to the wall behind him. Amiria smiles and closes the gap between them. Taking his shaking hands with hers she places them on her body, she uses this break in the moment to tilt her head up and see into his eyes. Just as his hazel eyes are filled with different colors of brown, gold, and green, they are currently filled with an array of emotions. Fear, excitement, longing, and adoration.

Staring down at the woman he loves, Stirling can't help but wish this moment would last forever. That tonight there will be no goodbyes. They can stay here and now together forever. He pushes the thoughts of tonight and whatever will happen out of his mind and lets Amiria pull his face down to hers, her soft lips parting his. More, he needs more before there is no more. Amiria lets out a moan as he deepens the kiss. Her hands moving down to the rest of him.

Fifty-Two

The chill of the early night air prickles Amiria's skin. She awakes to the mental nudge of Taika letting her know what time it is. She doesn't want to move from her current place in Stirling's arms. She sits between his legs as he leans against the rock wall asleep. Their clothing is halfway put back on with none of the ties bothered to be closed. Stirling's gambeson hangs open with his bare chest exposed.

She turns, slipping her arms into his opened gambeson and around to his back. Hugging him, Amiria nuzzles her face against the warmth of his skin. The feeling of his gentle arms around her as they laid together earlier that evening still fresh on her body.

Stirling blinks awake and tilts his head down to Amiria cuddled to him. Running his fingers through her hair he leans his head back against the wall. No matter how much he wished it wouldn't arrive, the night is here. His eyes squeeze shut, forcing out a tear to slide down his cheek. With his chest constricting and his throat closing with longing and grief, Stirling wraps his arms around Amiria, his best friend, who he wants to spend the rest of his life with.

Then as if part of him is being ripped away, Amiria sits up. The cold air now blows between them and nips at the space on his skin she recently occupied. Amiria reaches over and squeezes his hand, a gesture that screams all the words she wants to say but doesn't.

I'm sorry. You'll be okay. I'll be back. I have to do this. I'll be fine. There's no other choice. I love you.

He squeezes back, but his says something different. *Don't go.*

Stirling watches numbly as his warrior prepares for battle. She slips her limbs through her bracers and tightens the straps in place. She holds her scabbard out in front of her. Pulling one of the blades halfway out she follows the swirling metal back to the moment Calix had given them to her—a time he was as warm as the fireplace they sat beside.

She shoves it back in with a significant click and attaches it around her chest and back.

Her hair has returned to her signature tied-back look but still flows down in waves free from the helm she lost long ago, when she had run for the free world. Now she will return to ensure her freedom and those she cares about.

She is stunning. The embodiment of a thunderstorm. A loud and majestic sight to behold but deadly when it decides to strike. Stirling slowly rises to his feet as she pulls on her last gauntlet. He stops an arm's length away, unsure if he's allowed any closer.

Reaching out, Amiria loops her fingers through the tied lacings of his gambeson and closes the gap. Her armor clinks as they wrap their arms around each other. Standing on her tiptoes, Amiria kisses him deeply. Stirling can feel his heart pick up in his chest, he wants to pick her up. He wants to take her and run. She pulls back, putting her weight on her heels but their lips only separate for a brief moment. He's not ready to let her go, he follows her as she moves, returning the kiss. He doesn't want the kiss to end. He knows as soon as he stops she will be gone, and he can't stomach this might be their last.

Amiria lowers her chin, breaking off the kiss first. She speaks to his collarbone, "If I'm not back by dawn, head to Patu without me."

His breath hitches but his lips remain glued together. There's nothing to say. The pangs in his chest grow as he holds back his emotions. The sensation of tears forming tickles the back of his throat.

Her eyes crawl up to his, "Don't do anything rash. Promise me." Stirling swallows back the tears and nods. "I'll see you later okay?" She musters a smile.

Stepping back from him she alone creates the distance between them as his feet grow roots planting him in place. He watches in agonizing silence as she turns away from him and walks to Taika. With each step, the tear in his heart rips further.

What should he say? What can he say? What does someone say in a situation like this? There is no combination of words that will change this scenario. There's no sentence he can stitch together to mend his breaking heart.

He doesn't see the world as she does. He sees a pinpoint view of what he wants. She sees the entirety of it, but she can also get lost in it. The good, the bad. The highlights, the shadows. The strengths, the flaws.

What he sees—Amiria grabs Taika's saddle and swoops up onto her back—is her. She sits glorious in her dark armor ready for battle. She lifts the horn to her lips. The same metal tip she refused to signal to her team the night she officially chose Stirling over her oath.

The sound emanating from the horn is a deep rich tone starting low with a sharp rise. The wild wyverns raise their heads. All eyes lock on the girl leading their command.

Amiria steals one final glance down at the boy she has fallen in love with, the one person she's opened up to in every way possible. Her eyes are unreadable. They shine with oncoming tears but are as sharp and alert as an alpha wolf.

She raises her horn to her lips one final time and lets out her howl. It's time to lead her pack on a hunt. With one thought from Amiria, Taika takes off into the sky. A storm cloud of ashen dust covers the half crater as a legion of dragons follows their commander into the colorless night.

His heart finally tearing into two, Stirling falls to his knees, the magnificent sight lost to the gales of dust around him.

Humming to herself, Kinsey rips another piece of her salted venison with her teeth. She bobs her head to her made-up tune and chews another piece of dried meat. Wearing her silver armor with a pink brigandine she had specially requested, she sits back comfortably in her saddle. Her ivory-colored dragon clings to the roof with its talons tearing the shingles and its tail coiled around the spire.

A white moth against charred bark.

Kinsey licks the salt from her claws as movement catches her predatory eyes. A thin smile stretches across her face, letting her fangs hang out.

The sirens they last heard almost a year ago ring out across the city once again.

Fifty-Three

Shoulder to shoulder, Robert and William lean against the parapet on the inner bailey wall beside an eastern-facing bastion. Propped up by the other, they keep each other from tipping over as they sit there against the short wall sound asleep. Robert's cheek is squished as it lays on top of William's head, which rests on Robert's shoulder. They spent the entire day watching Kinsey perched on the spire. She hasn't come down once, spending most of her time dancing and performing acrobatic stunts dangerously close to the edge. Growing bored of hoping she would fall, Robert and William fell asleep, slumping into each other as their unconscious bodies forgot they could be seen.

Alarms stationed in the bastion beside them are like knives in their ear drums. Ripped from his sleep, Robert leaps to his feet overwrought with fright and the bump still on his head now throbbing. He draws his sword and stands on defense while William curls up, covering his ears with his leather gloves, the ringing too loud for him to handle.

With the alarms ringing in his skull, Robert turns to search the sky. As he comes to face the eastern mountains, the broadsword slips from his stunned fingers. William, lying on his side, stares up apprehensively at his friend's unnerved expression.

Prolongedly, William gives into the inevitable. Still covering his ears, he sits up and faces the parapet he was leaning against. He rises up onto his knees and peaks over the lower section between the two raised defense walls. His eyes widen as he takes in the impending storm cloud of beating wings heading in their direction.

Robert's hands slide over William's, helping him block the noise. He mumbles his realization but barely comprehends as the alarms rattle his thoughts, "She's here, she's actually here. SHE'S HERE!" William's wide eyes turn up to him. Robert snags William by the back of his gambeson and yanks him to his feet, "WE HAVE TO FOLLOW THROUGH!"

Robert's hands return to help cover William's ears as they take off down the spiraling stairs inside the bastion where the alarm vibrates their bones.

As they start sprinting across the bailey, Robert drops his hands so they can run in a full sprint. William talks between his huffing breaths, "What happens if this doesn't work? It was only a gamble she would show up at all."

Robert keeps his eyes focused on the castle, his sprint never slowing, "Then we die."

"I don't want to die."

The pauldrons on Calix's shoulders clang against the stone as he throws himself to the window of the king's cabinet. He wears his official armor of light-colored metal and a red brigandine. The siren calling for wild dragons screams through the open window. Horns echo through every cavity of the castle and crevasse of the city telling people to seek shelter.

Shoulders hunched over the parchment, King Dietrich rubs his temples, the sound ricocheting in his skull, "Calix." He grumbles, "What do you see?"

Calix doesn't hear him. His focus is fixated on the impending storm of wyverns.

"CALIX!" King Dietrich snaps, "For god's sake, what do you see!"

He stares transfixed. What does he see? He sees her. The beige dragon sticking out against the dark sky and the cluster of dragons behind her.

"She's here," he says, barely loud enough for the king to hear. A pompous smile drags across his face. A white dragon the color of the moon launches from the dark tower. "Kinsey is after her."

The white ceramic bowl shatters on the kitchen ground. She isn't in the city but she can still hear the wailing alarms. The guardsmen howl to the Winged Cavalry for someone to save them. With trembling hands, Arietta looks over at her partner of over two decades with wide frantic eyes. His jaw is set, his face and body saying nothing, but his eyes are a window into his mind showing his deeply rooted fear.

This is the same alarm that changed Wyverna. After that night everything had shifted, it had started an unstoppable cataclysm. She knows the rumors of Amiria despite Derek keeping her in the dark. He kept his and Amiria's world separate from her for all these years, but their world has been leaking into hers. The two realities are swirling and mixing. She didn't need him to tell her to know about the baker who flew. She had seen him that dreadful night. People still talk about him now almost a year later.

She didn't know it at the time, but she learned later that it was Amiria's team who pursued him. Then she found out through the market streets what she had done for him. What her *daughter* had done.

When she met Amiria that day, she didn't know Amiria was planning on never coming home. That must have been the reason she revealed herself. It was always going to be a goodbye no matter how their conversation went.

She might have birthed Amiria, but she did not raise her. The girl who is out there changing the kingdom is not of her doing. Without anyone holding her hand, this is who Amiria became on her own.

Fifty-Four

Amiria sees the castle. She can hear the sirens. She has the power of a typhoon on her side.

Amiria barely has time to blink. Gripping the saddle, she hangs on as Taika dodges an attack from below. A seagull on the ocean's surface evades the snapping jaws of a shark.

"WEEEE!" Amiria hears Kinsey cheer as she dives up and over Taika.

"Keep your eyes on Kinsey, never lose sight of her!" Amiria instructs Taika. Her eyes scan the dark fortress below them. She can barely keep her vision focused in the dim light. Her head whipping to the side, they topple through the sky. She's being tormented and lured as Kinsey plays with her food.

Trying not to be distracted by the twisted girl nipping at her, she spots them. Five she counts. The shadowed figures emerge from the castle grounds. Calix isn't there. He isn't with them. He must be with King Dietrich.

Her vision flips again as Taika dodges Kinsey. Gathering her bearings, she checks over at the base. Another dozen enroute. She snaps her neck to where

Lumierna's unit, second to her team, is stationed outside the northwestern wall of the city limits. Another team of ten.

Twenty-seven against twenty-five excluding her and Kinsey. With generations of built-up anger towards the humans, the wyverns will distract the Cavalry long enough for her to defeat Kinsey and make her way into the castle. The Cavalry is forbidden to kill a wyvern, but harm, maim, or capture are still options in the playbook.

With Kinsey hovering above her, Amiria raises her horn and blows. "AHHH!" She hollers in triumph. Her battalion of dragons rush past her to the battlefield.

Waiting for the flood of scales and spikes to pass below, Kinsey descends upon Amiria. Taika barely has time to turn as the white dragon crashes into her. Wings, tails, and spikes tangle together as their talons rip and tear at armored skin.

Amiria ducks. A snapping jaw filled with razor teeth the size of her fingers closes on the space she occupied moments before. Kinsey's giggles turn into cackles, her dark braids whipping around in the wind.

"Taika, control its head."

Taika buries her teeth into the soft underside of the white dragon's throat. The creature roars, thrashing its massive body. The two wyverns are hooked together and somersault through the air. Their gnarled wings beat ferociously in a feeble attempt to keep the battered ship afloat.

Grace ignores the tingling sensation of cut-off circulation in her hand as Giles grips it. They stare wide-eyed and pale faced at the sky in the middle of the market road with the rest of the neighborhood.

A war has burst into life above them. Titans clash above their rooftops with roars thundering louder than the sirens.

Giles shields his eyes as the fires as bright as erupting volcanoes light the city streets.

Several of the Winged Cavalry spew flames across the sky, herding the wild dragons, who retreat far enough to dodge the flames before pursuing with savage attacks.

Giles' eyes frantically dart around the vicious scene. None of the dragons above match the description Stirling had given him of his orange dragon. The name of the creature already slipped from his memory.

His eyes finally land on a dragon he does recognize. His heart stops as he sees the two light-colored dragons rip at each other. He prays under his breath, 'Please don't be Amiria. Please let her be far away from here. Far away with Stirling in hand."

"AMIRIA, WATCH OUT!" Taika screams, her jaws still clamped around the dragon's throat.

Oxygen is forced out of Amiria's lungs as her back is slammed against the saddle's cantle. Her bent knees stuck in their holsters, she lays pinned beneath the giddy Kinsey. Straddling Amiria, Kinsey grabs the first attacking hand then the next, rendering Amiria's punches useless. Interlacing their fingers, Kinsey uses her downward weight to force Amiria's hands down above her head.

She lays her chest on hers, their noses practically kissing. Amiria can feel the warmth of Kinsey's heavy breaths.

She lowers her lips to Amiria's ear. Her seductive voice is barely audible over the howling wind, "I knew you wouldn't stand me up." Her lips brush Amiria's skin, "I'm really going to enjoy this."

Holding both of Amiria's hands in one, Kinsey slips a dagger from her weapons belt. Amiria's eyes dilate at the sight of the silver blade reflecting across her dark irises.

'Taika, flip over!" Amiria commands in a panic.

Releasing her locked jaws, Taika launches backward as if she was diving into the water, freeing herself from the ivory wyvern. Feeling the shift of gravity, Kinsey squeezes her knees into Amiria's sides, her gauntleted hands gripping Amiria's vambrace-covered wrists. Their bodies begin to lift from the solid matter of the saddle only to be stopped by Amiria's harness.

Hanging upside down by a single strap of leather, Kinsey wraps her legs around Amiria's waist. Amiria grimaces as the harness digs her armor into her skin, her legs slipping from the security of their holsters.

Seeing the sinister smile flash across her face, Amiria's voice is grim, "Kinsey don't"

With a flick of her wrist Kinsey slices the leather cord.

Fifty-Five

The sound of metal boots ricochets around the corridor like an impending stampede. King Dietrich marches, surrounded by his guards with a rushed sense of urgency. His cape billows out behind him like wings. Calix, with his helm low over his brow and his chin raised high, flanks King Dietrich matching his every step.

King Dietrich doesn't look back as he talks. His eyes locked on the future with Amiria at his beck and call, "You informed that *sister* of yours that Amiria must be captured *alive.*"

"Yes, Your Majesty." Calix holds his expression flat.

People, even his master of the games sister, are predictable. She fell for his trap, whether she believed him or not, the bait was too much for her greedy hands. He stares at the back of King Dietrich's head. The dim light from the wall torches glints off his crown as they pass each one. He has the King of Wyverna eating from his palm and has him trained to trust every word coming from his forked tongue.

They push through the doors to the throne room where King Dietrich will sit and wait for Amiria to be brought to him, or… a dangerous thought drags itself into existence. Or Amiria shows up on her own. What if Amiria defeats Kinsey? What will he do if she shows up standing before them? Will he be able to kill her and claim defense? Be the hero who slays the monster? Or will he perform as ordered and bring her to her knees, forced to surrender to the king? He will have come full circle back to a life of misery with Amiria alive and just out of reach.

Another thought dawns on him. What if she kills Kinsey, then proceeds to kill the king too? He could have the guards apprehend her and he would be able to keep her for himself. Everything will need to fall perfectly into place for that outcome. Either the guards will have to remain outside of the throne room and she manages to slip by them, all he would have to do is stand back as she killed the king. Then when she is tired from her second fight he would overpower her and finally, *finally*, she will be his. But if they are in the throne room he knows the doors will be locked stopping anyone else from entering. He could let her take out as many guards as she can on her own then he can finish off the king and the rest of the guards. By the time backup arrives he can claim she killed them all. They would believe it, she *is* the monster attacking the kingdom.

Feeling elevated with all the possibilities, Calix adds a skip to his step as they bound over to the throne.

The wind is a deafening roar in their ears. Their bodies are a silent stone as they plummet to the castle grounds at a screaming speed.

Kinsey's lips twist and curl, a wide smile from ear to ear. They are two teenagers jumping from the rocks into a swimming hole. Amiria isn't smiling. She can barely see the stars past Kinsey's crazed expression, but she knows the ground is coming to greet them soon.

Desperately ripping at Kinsey's latched fingers, Amiria attempts to pry her off her armor. Kinsey lets out a frenzied laugh and leans her body to one side, turning them. Starting slow, the speed of their roll picks up. Faster and faster they spin. Stars, mountains, castle, ground, city, stars, mountains, ground, stars, ground. It all blurs into one. Tumbling with no resistance, the air slides around their smooth armor like a hand on a silk sheet. Their hair caught in the whirlpool whips around wildly.

Unable to get a full swing, Amiria pulls her arm back and sends a weak blow to Kinsey's cheek. Her head snaps to the side but she doesn't let go. Amiria retracts her hand and jabs again. Kinsey's fingers begin to slip as her head is forced away by Amiria's punches and the pull of their spin.

Bringing her knees in tight, Amiria presses the soles of her boots into Kinsey and kicks. Kinsey tears free from Amiria, her hysterical laughing following her as the force rips her away. In a blink of wind-teared eyes, Taika is there snatching Amiria from the air like an eagle catching a fish from the water. Her talons wrap carefully around one of Amiria's arms and legs.

She strains her neck to see the bone dragon carrying its own rider to safety. Her lips curl in disgusted frustration. The fight continues.

The scene playing out around him is a perfect reenactment of ants on an ant hill. They march perfectly in line in unconditional servitude to their queen, but draw a line in their path and chaos erupts.

Clyde leisurely strolls the halls of the royal family's corridors. With his hands behind his back he drums his fingers on his hidden insignia. He might as well be whistling through a walk in the garden. His compatriots under his command stomp the halls like cattle dogs herding the nobles residing inside the castle back to their private chambers.

The plan the guards are executing as if they've trained the past year for was devised by Clyde after Amiria escaped. He had constructed it in secrecy under the brass and noble noses. He thought of it as a wish, a fable, the strategies you make up as a kid and will never enact. He thought Amiria had run for good and the opportunity would never arise until he saw Kinsey Gautier perched on the spire like a hawk watching for its prey.

The once peaceful halls clamber with the echoing sounds of armor and shouting guards.

"Get back to your room!" Robert commands.

A young woman with her head poking out of her doorway jumps at his authoritative voice. "Wh-what's going on?" she stammers.

Robert is at her door. "I said to return to your room!"

The woman's jaw hangs open, aghast. "You can't talk to me like that."

"Sure I can." Robert reaches out, placing the palm of his hand on the woman's forehead. With a not so gentle nudge, he forces her back into her room and slams her door shut. Holding onto the handle of the inwards swinging door to make sure she doesn't open it, he ties a rope then pulls it up to the closest metal sconce mounted to the wall and ties off the rope.

Directly across the hall, William ties another door closed and peers over at Robert. Clyde steps between them, "You two are in charge of this section." He tells them motioning to the royal quarters, "I'm leading the group to the throne room."

"And after?" William wonders out loud.

"That all depends on the outcome," Clyde tells them. Lifting his chin, he keeps his sophisticated manner and heads towards the throne room.

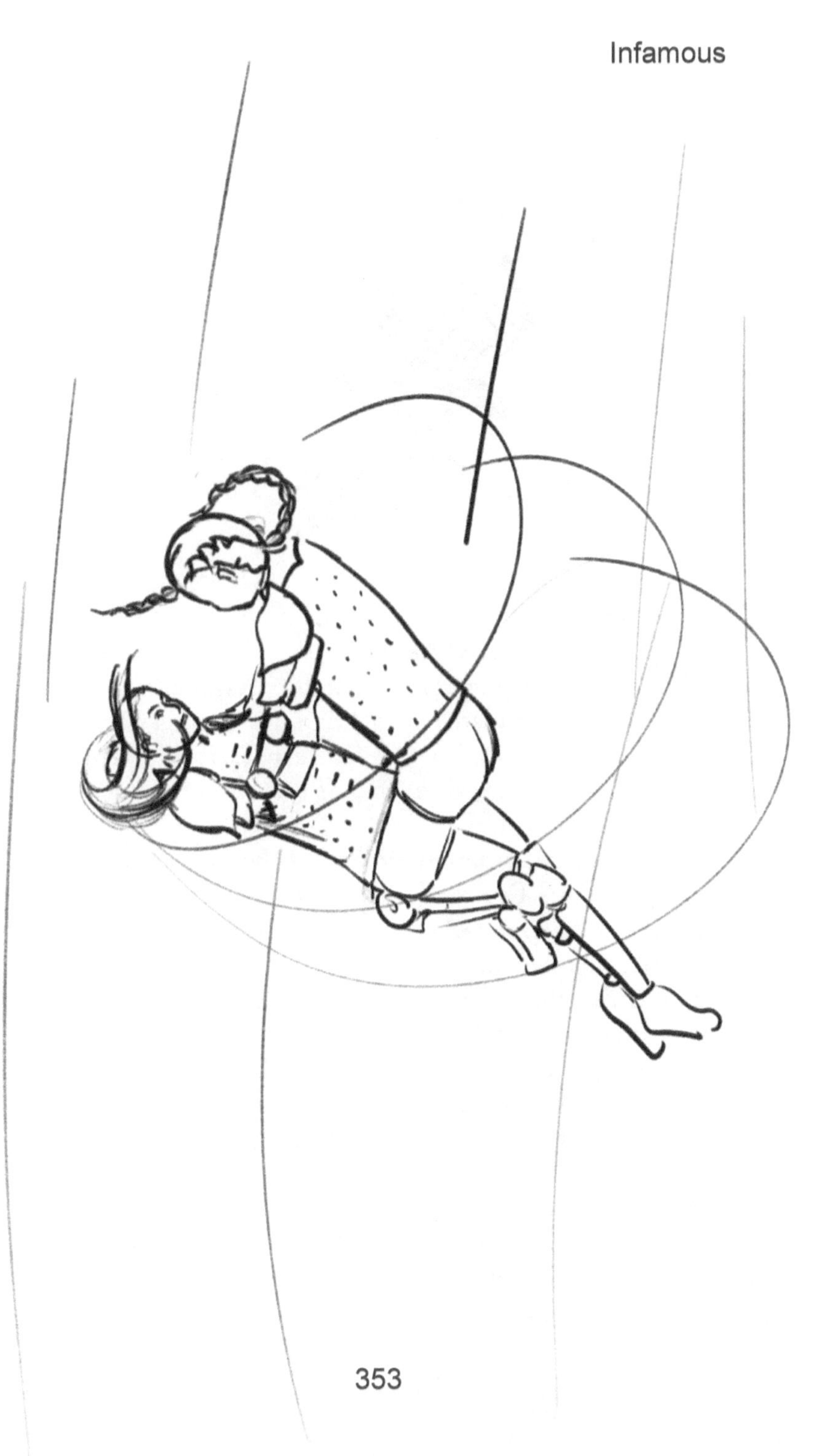

Fifty-Six

Lowering to a hover over at the tip of the slanted roof above the courtyard Amiria used to frequent, Taika releases her grip on Amiria's leg first. Amiria's body swings, still held by the arm up righting her. Amiria's toes barely touch the clay tiles before Taika releases her arm. Sliding several spaces down, she palms the smooth fixtures stopping herself.

Kinsey's dragon pounces down to the roof with a shuddering weight. The roof quakes beneath Amiria and she struggles to keep herself from sliding further. Beneath the wyvern's talons, tiles tear free from their slots and tumble down to the overhanging edge where they fall to shatter several stories below.

Standing up on her dragon's back Kinsey puts her hands up to the sky. Swinging them down and up again, she backflips. Without a misstep, she lands poised on the ridge of the roof with her hands up waiting for applause.

Her nimble body slinking, she curves her spine with a tilt of her head, "You chose poorly Amiria. This is my playground. Your clomping stance is more suited for level ground." For no reason but to show off, Kinsey straightens back up, and with a running start, she vaults into a handless cartwheel. Her feet arching over her like a silver rainbow. Spinning on one foot, she pulls out her longsword and points it down at Amiria, inviting her to fight.

Taika swoops back down from the sky, slashing her spiked tail at the white wyvern, her spikes striking the dragon's face. Hissing, it snaps at the retreating tail, the clamp of its jaws missing by a scale. Several more tiles rip free and fall as the furious dragon launches back into the sky.

Amiria crawls to a standing position, her feet struggling to find stability. She rolls her eyes at Kinsey's show. Why so much flaunting? This is a fight that either one or neither of them will fly away from, but she doesn't act like it. They are fighting to the death and she is acting like they are part of a choreographed performance.

She doesn't have time to play games. Amiria cracks her neck then locks her sights on Kinsey and charges. Their swords are a volley of pandemonium. The discordance of manifested claws and fangs for humans to satisfy their desire to kill.

The dark short swords are nearly invisible in the night. The only sign of their existence is the whirring sound as they cut the air and the sharp piercing sound of clashing metal.

"Still wielding my brother's engagement gift I see," Kinsey points out. She arches her back, avoiding the blade aimed at her throat. "Are there still some lingering feelings?"

Pulling her blade back, Amiria spins into a crouch, sweeping her leg with intentions to trip Kinsey who leaps over, landing perfectly on the balls of her feet. The muscles in Amiria's jaw twitch as she grinds her teeth. She bites back her tongue, the more she says the more weapons Kinsey will possess.

Like a battle axe coming down heavy, Kinsey brings down her sword on her crouching opponent. Amiria jumps to the side dodging the approaching guillotine. With her hands clasped around her ivory grips, she digs her fists and toes into the slippery slates. Halfway down the roof, she slows to a stop.

Kinsey makes a "tsk" sound and flirts, "You should have made it easier and slid all the way off for me." Leaping from her perch, she surfs down the roof.

Amiria, who is quick to her feet, readies her blades, "I don't think King Dietrich will appreciate having to scrape me up from his gardens."

Kinsey rolls her head along with her eyes, "He'll get over it. You're not the only pretty face in the kingdom."

Their minds and actions are in a concurrent state as they rush each other in another flurry of blades humming through the air. With each strike of metal, each dodge of sharpened edge, they step and slide closer to the edge. Amiria feints a strike to the head with one of her short swords. Kinsey raises her long sword to block, opening access to her plated armor stomach. Amiria thrusts the tip of her sword at the brigandine hoping to slip between the riveted plates.

Surprised, Amiria lets out a pained gasp. A blunt object hammers down on her forearm, knocking her trajectory off course. The pommel of Kinsey's sword makes a small dent in Amiria's vambrace. As Amiria stumbles a step forward, Kinsey hammers her fist into Amiria's shoulder blade. Amiria crumbles to her knees, the pain of the old injury that has never left overwhelms her.

Grinning like a madman, Kinsey raises her sword up preparing for execution. Time appears to stop as Amiria stares up at the blade raised above her head. She thinks of the promise she couldn't make to Stirling about returning. How she couldn't bring herself to say goodbye because she will do everything she can to make sure she is the one who leaves tonight. She thinks of the soul crumbling behind his hazel eyes as she left him behind.

She won't leave him behind like this. Not to her.

Surging with adrenaline, her body acts on its own. Her movements are quick and precise. Her dark swirling blade slices along the inside of Kinsey's lower knee where it is no longer protected by her cuisse and before the knee guard starts.

Kinsey lets out a screeching wail, her sword coming down to strike the empty space Amiria no longer occupies as she rolls and leaps up sideways. Amiria stops, teetering on the edge of the roof. She can feel the night air coming up and beckoning her down to the garden.

With her knee bleeding, Kinsey favors her good leg leaning heavily to one side. She grimaces as she attempts to take a step. She spits her words at Amiria, "I didn't take you for fighting dirty. Guess that's how you knocked my brother's tooth out."

"He deserved worse," she says between her heavy breaths, "None of this would be happening if he just let me be."

Kinsey jabs her finger accusingly as she speaks, "None of this would be happening if you stuck to your oath!" She shifts her weight again with a limp. Blood oozes from her wound, already beginning to soak her leg down to her boot.

Kinsey's eyes flit away for less than a single blink. Amiria swears she saw something behind their chestnut color. But it couldn't have been what she thought she saw. The brief glimpse of anguish was blown out as fast as a candle's flame.

With a guttural growl, Kinsey launches forward swinging her blade wildly. Her movements are sporadic and rampant. She bears her teeth snarling as if she has turned rabid.

Amiria doesn't have time to block and she feels the sword bounce off her pauldron. The twang of metal fills her ear over the sound of her rapidly beating heart. She frantically tries to keep up with the new manic style. The soles of her boots touch dangerously close to the lip of the roof with each defensive step backward. A trail of blood follows as they creep along the edge.

Kinsey's rage controls her. It pulls her limbs like a puppeteer. Her blade arcs above her head higher than necessary.

Amiria concentrates on steadying her breaths, keeping her mind focused on the task before her. With Kinsey's blade touching the star-lit sky, Amiria closes the distance once more.

The short blade designed by her brother hacks down into the inside of Kinsey's good leg, stopping at the bone. Kinsey falters in shock, the unbridled blade finally coming to a stop. She howls in pain as she collapses to the roof, her legs no longer able to support her. Amiria leaps back a step out of reach. Kinsey glares up at Amiria with the entire whites of her eyes showing.

She curses again and with pain-filled obscenities as she tries to push herself back up. A crimson waterfall flows from her leg down to the garden below.

"KINSEY STOP! It's not worth it!" Amiria shouts.

"Not worth it? NOT WORTH IT!" she shouts back, sitting up on the side of her hip. "Are you that ignorant?" She spits blood from a bite on the inside of her cheek splattering the space between them. "This will never stop." She is practically singing. "Never stop, never stop, we're disposable and this will never stop." She leans back laughing at the moon. Her laughing seizes, a crescent-shaped smile stuck on her lips. Her eyes roll down to Amiria with her head following behind. It falls to the side like a broken doll. "This is your life. We only stop when we're dead."

Amiria is repulsed. By the sight or the words, she doesn't know. "This is not the life I want."

"Doesn't matter what you want," Kinsey grunts out. She tries to lift herself up but is barely able to get to her knees before her leg gives out and she falls back to sitting on her hip. She continues, her words spiteful, "You think any of us want this? Some of us want to become a mother and take care of the home. Instead." She grips the sword still in her hand. "We are handed a blade and instructed, don't stop till you're at the top even if it kills you."

Picking up the sword, she drives the tip in between two of the tiles. The blade wobbles and bows as she uses it as a crutch to pull herself to a half stance. She speaks through the agony, giving no weight to her partially severed leg, "Let me tell you a sad fact about this life of yours. You—" She closes her eyes, her face puckering as she fights back the overbearing pain. "You will never be allowed to stop fighting. There will always be someone coming for you."

Amiria shakes her head. "No you can stop this. You can still be a mom, Kinsey."

Beads of sweat run down her graying face. "I can't. Think back, when has the general or field Marshal ever been a parent?"

"You're wrong, Kinsey, you can change that. We do have a life past all this. I've experienced it."

Kinsey sucks her teeth. "Wasn't playing pretend fun? Look where you still ended up. Now let's play family." Using her crutch and her good leg she throws herself at Amiria who had dropped her guard during their conversation.

Colliding together, Amiria falls backward, landing with a thud. Only half of her back makes contact with a solid surface. Her arm whips out to catch herself. Grabbing nothing but a handful of air, her heart spikes as they tumble off the roof.

Fifty-Seven

Major Gautier yanks on his dragon's reins as he dodges an incoming wyvern. "Where did all these wild dragons come from!" he exclaims with no one around to hear. Team Larua and the Winged Cavalry who have sprung into action at the call of the alarms are spread out across the sky above Lumierna. Each member is fighting an individual battle against their own wild wyvern.

With the reach of his long sword, he slashes at the black dragon that rears its head back. It strikes faster than Major Gautier can react. He screams out in white hot pain as teeth the length of fingers puncture through his armor and pierces the flesh of his thigh.

His field of vision is muddied by scales and talons that rip and claw at each other as his dragon attempts to fight off the invader. Another wail of pain escapes him as his leg is pulled from its socket by the dark beast. His harness strains against the mighty strength to hold him to the saddle. Refusing to succumb to the agony, Major Gautier slashes at the dragon. The tip of his sharpened blade skips over the armored scales, unable to find a soft spot to slip in.

He grinds his teeth in pain and frustration. He needs to embed the blade into the soft under skin of the dragon's neck before his leg is torn off. The wild wyvern hisses as Major Gautier's dragon pokes holes in its membranous wings with its horns.

Hearing the cries, Eda rushes to his aid; she can get there in time, she knows it. She needs to get the dragon off her leader. A few more beats of her dragon's wings and she will be there.

At the cracking of his femur, Major Gautier's hand opens and drops his sword with a blood-curdling scream. "I'm going to kill you, you wretched beast! I'M GOING TO KILL YOU!" He pulls his dagger from his hilt and presses it against the dragon's throat at the bottom of his jaw.

As the cool sharpened metal touches the vulnerable underside of its throat the black wyvern thrashes his head, ripping Major Gautier from the saddle.

"NO!" Eda keens as the shrieks coming from the two dragons mangled in the air are stopped short and she watches as her major falls. "No. No. No! NO!"

"EDA!" She hears Everard's voice call from a distance. She searches the sky around her but she sees nothing but chaos around her. Through flames that make her skin flush she catches a glimpse of Dicun struggling to hold his own against a wild wyvern. She turns in her seat seeking out Everard but before she can find him, Warrick pummels into her with fury in his eyes.

Garret spirals down from the sky to assist in the attack against the strong female Winged Rider but is cut off by Everard who sideswipes him defending Eda. Garret, outmatched by the older more experienced Rider, loses his barrens as they tumble through the sky. Garret's dragon is shoved back by Everard's separating them. The stars and city turn around him as they topple through the air above the castle. His dragon extends out its membrane wings, halting them in place. Turning his head back to Everard, Garret doesn't see the incoming arrow until it is protruding from his neck. Blood spits from his mouth as Garret chokes on his liquid filled breaths.

Everard lowers his short bow and uses one hand to yank on his reins, careening his dragon back to Eda who is holding her own against Warrick. With a snarl he charges.

Fifty-Eight

Watching her swords succumb to gravity, Amiria grips the roof suspended beside Kinsey, whose manic laughing pierces her ears. Amiria examines her situation. She kicks out her legs but can't reach the wall for a foothold. She strains her biceps in a desperate attempt to pull herself up but she is too tired and heavy with her armor on. If she lets go, she is too close to the wall and to the ground for Taika to effectively catch her. Maybe Taika can cling to the wall beside her or use her tail as a rescue rope. If she is able to arrive in time.

Amiria cranes her neck to see Taika still fighting airborne.

Feeling Amiria's thoughts, Taika calls out to her, *"HOLD ON!"*

"Not much of a choice!" Amiria calls back. Kinsey's laughing interrupts her thoughts. She finally snaps, "Why are you always laughing! We're about to die!"

"I KNOW!" Kinsey says in a state of delirium. "But we're going together!" She lets her head fall back. Peering around her arm, she locks eyes with Amiria. Her zealous grin fades and softens to heartbreak as she watches above Amiria.

Amiria follows the devastated gaze. She feels weightless, as if she can fly back to the safety of the roof.

If you're the hero, who will be yours?

Tears blur her eyes, distorting her vision as a boy with sandy curls kneels above her. Strong hands covered in scars wrap themselves around one of her arms, already making her feel secure.

"Isn't that nice?" Kinsey sneers. "So romantic." She watches as Amiria is whisked to safety by a person she disregarded. A person she calculated was weak and would run and hide as he's proven to do in the past. Maybe people can change when they find something to change for.

Her gauntlets, slick with her blood, start to slip. No one is coming to *her* aid. No one cares that she's a fingertip from death. *No one.* Her mother only cares that she will lose her heir, but she has her younger brother Keaton. "You just have it all don't you?"

Climbing into the safety of Stirling's arms, Amiria hears Kinsey's words. She turns to reply in time to see her gauntleted fingers let go. Stirling closes his eyes as he clutches Amiria to him but that doesn't block the sound. Bile rises in his throat, revolted by the idea of her body hitting the ground, but Amiria had watched the entire fall. She finally peels her eyes away from the garden below and buries herself into the curve of Stirling's neck and breathes in the scent of salt water.

Overtaken in gratitude, Amiria still finds it in her to chastise him. "You idiot." She clings to his gambeson as if letting go will place her beside Kinsey. "I told you not to come."

Stirling tightens his arms around her. "I'm kind of bad at doing what I'm told."

"Tell me about it," Ignis chimes. *"You don't know how many times I've told him let's go home, yet here we are back at the beginning."*

Amiria tugs on the rope tied around his waist to the saddle on Ignis' back, "Smart." She holds her gaze on the tether. "Thank you," she mumbles. "For not listening." Already sapped of energy, she reluctantly pushes herself out of his arms. "There's still more to be done. She was only the first hurdle."

Stirling frowns. "She wasn't just an obstacle, she was a person. Crazy, yes. But still a person." He can't convince himself to peek over the lip of the roof—where he saved Amiria and let the other girl fall.

"Yes," Amiria begins. She pauses, remembering the insight Kinsey let her have during her final moments.

She knew she was going to die when she admitted her deepest desires, the life she truly longed for. She hangs her head. Kinsey made her choices tonight. Her decisions and threats to end innocent lives brought her to that edge. Her actions brought her to that conclusion. There was no talking reason with her.

She lifts her chin, catching his eye. "You haven't had to fight to the death before. Showing mercy only gives your opponent an advantage, because believe me, in this world, they won't show you any in return."

Amiria is correct. Stirling thinks to himself as he sinks back into the roof tiles. Kinsey would have burned down the entire village without a single care, but it doesn't stop the remorse from settling deep inside him.

While Amiria catches her breath, Stirling watches the war of Wyverns above them. At the speed they are moving he can barely tell which have riders and which do not. The total doesn't add up. One side appears to be greatly outnumbered. He doesn't see any fatalities on the ground but that doesn't mean they aren't there. The wild wyverns were instructed to retreat if they are wounded, no need to sacrifice themselves for the cause.

Stirling blinks, doing a double take as two dragons fighting close to them catch his eye. He takes back his initial statement. He can tell which wyverns have riders and which do not, because he is watching wyverns with riders fighting against the Winged Cavalry. The Winged Cavalry is fighting the Winged Cavalry.

He touches Amiria's shoulder and points. She follows his finger and sucks in a breath of disbelief. Over half of the Cavalry were fighting against their own. Winged Rider against Winged Rider. She spots Dicun's dragon as he struggles to hold up against two riders.

"I'm going to retrieve my weapons and—" She stares at Stirling's gambeson.

"What?"

"You're not wearing the mail."

"It's heavy," Stirling shrugs.

"Oh, Stirling," Amiria frowns. Kinsey's armor will be too small and there isn't time to find him any chainmail. "I'm going to the throne room. I'd prefer if you'd hang back, for many reasons, but I can't stop you. Come with me or wait here. It's your choice."

His hazel eyes look back and forth between her dark as-night irises, "Okay."

Fifty-Nine

Standing at attention, guards line the doors to the throne room inside and out. The sounds of their drumming hearts are muffled by their gambesons and chainmail. Calix stands positioned at the bottom of the dais, eagerly waiting to see which route his plans will be taking. His eyes dance around the throne room, unable to stay fixated in a single direction. Door, door, window, door, door. Which one of these entry points will give a sign of his approaching Amiria? That is, if she isn't laying in a pool of her blood, hopefully with his sister staining the grass not too far away.

His gaze finally lands on King Dietrich slouching in his throne, his brown eyes hidden beneath the heavy shadow of his crowned head. His chin is lowered to rest on his silken robes. Calix's line of sight falls to the king's hands gripping the armrests, his knuckles turning the color of his throne.

The expansive room is lit by an abnormal amount of candles and the small hint of distorted moonlight casts a thin haze of light, then within a blink, the entire room is lit. Calix squints at the sudden burst of immense light engulfing the entirety of the mosaic windows. He raises his hand to shield his face from the attacking sun and the heat radiating from the molten light. The glass before him is on fire.

The once extravagant mosaic wall bubbles and melts, turning its array of spring colors into a hellish dystopia. Holes begin to form as the panes fall away, scouring the granite flooring, like droplets of lava seeping and oozing from the channel of volcanoes that created the Isle of Wyverna.

Calix grins madly. What a spectacular show. What a grand entrance, an entrance only she can perform. Why risk being shredded by shards of glass when you can merely melt the wall away? Stunning, elegant, a true masterpiece created by god. Sadly he must put an end to such a brilliant mind. She is too perfect for this messed-up world. An angel amongst the broken souls. They don't deserve such a divine creature. No one does.

King Dietrich pushes up slowly from his throne, his eyes wide with astonishment as the flames leak through the gaps in the glass licking the inside of the throne room. His golden crown reflects the blazing light like a mirror. The flames flicker and dance across his forehead. The King of Wyverna's mouth hangs agape.

Then everything stops. The room is a dark cave now as their eyes adjust. The air feels like a cold winter's night absent of the summer sun without the flames.

Calix, King Dietrich, and the guards of the room stare idly at the exposed wall, the mosaic now a gaping portal to the night. The only sound to be heard is the rustle of the leaves outside from a steady breeze.

Calix whips out his blade, seeing the beige dragon like a colliding moon. Taika dives through the open window and grapples onto the arches holding up the high ceiling. Plumes of dust and small fragments of ceiling fall speckling the floor and the onlookers. Her tail wraps around a pillar, holding her secure. Upside down, she roars a deathly call—her threat aimed at Calix and King Dietrich. The guards flinch, hiding their heads in their shoulders at the sight of the furious beast.

Dragons do not intimidate Calix, not when he slept as a child down the hall from the only monster he's ever known. He doesn't bother to look up at the wyvern when the girl standing on the remnants of the window sill holds his undivided attention.

He raises his arms up as if he is praying to the heavens. "Amiria it is so lovely to see you again!"

"That it is. I have such fond memories of our last meeting." She hops off the sill, her boots clicking across the cooled glass as she travels, blades in hand, halfway across the throne room. Her eyes target Calix with King Dietrich looming behind.

"Amiria!" King Dietrich's voice is a rumbling avalanche of rocks in the canyon. "Drop your weapons and return to us. Come to me willingly and there will be no need to place you back in the oubliette."

Amiria raises her chin.

Calix adds, his voice now soft and nurturing, "Amiria, please. I can protect you from this." He holds his hand to his heart. "I can keep you alive."

"Alive is not living. I refuse to be kept as a pet," she spits, raising her weapons.

King Dietrich's voice bellows over Calix, as if raising his voice will have an impact on her decisions, "I am your king! You do as I command!"

"No, I don't think I will," she smiles.

Unexpected to all but Amiria, an orange dragon hurdles over the window sill, landing on the smooth tiles. It slides tractionless across the floor, his claws creating screeching and grinding sounds as they drag uselessly, unable to stop him. Amiria slowly blinks as she resists acknowledging her awareness of Ignis' clumsy entrance.

Calix's face twists into an unsightly snarl at the sight of Stirling. Of course, her useless tagalong is here. The boy who started this mess to begin with. Every death is on his hands. This baker boy is solely to blame for everything wrong with Wyverna today. If Amiria had never met the boy, if he never existed, she would have been his. That short amount of time they had together. How they were together. He could have given her that for the rest of their lives, but *he* had to interfere. *He* had to ruin *everything*.

I guess it's his lucky day. He can distract himself with the boy, while Amiria takes out the guards and King Dietrich. His plans are falling into place even without his manipulation. He will get to dispose of the girl who consumes his mind and soul or get to keep her, either way, it's a win. Plus the worthless boy who is unworthy of her love and who stole her away from him will get what he deserves—bleeding out slowly and alone. If only they had killed him four years ago when he initially ran away. Well, better late than never.

King Dietrich shouts, commanding the guards, "Apprehend her! I don't care if she loses a limb, just keep her alive."

Sliding off Ignis' back Stirling holds out the guard's broadsword. He points it at Calix, the man whose name used to spark jealousy in him because he was once an option for a life Stirling could never offer Amiria. The man's broad shoulders square off to Stirling with narrowed eyes. Stirling gulps, his palms already coating the handle of the blade with sweat. What did these people do to invoke the nightmares plaguing the strongest person he knows?

"Guards!" King Dietrich snaps, the authority ringing louder than church bells.

The thin blade wobbles in Stirling's shaking hands. He's a deer confronting a wolf. "Oh no, oh no no," Stirling whimpers as Calix stalks closer to him.

Calix's breath sticks and catches in his throat as he is hit hard in the side by an armored shoulder. "I'm your opponent!" Amiria screams as they collide, knocking him sideways.

Caught off guard, Calix swings his muscled and armored arm, battering her away. Amiria bends backward, ducking beneath his arm and creates distance with her blades ready. Calix twirls around to see the guards who had been ordered to capture her standing idle at their posts. Confused, his eyes search out King Dietrich, who stands at the top of his dais seething.

Spit flies from his mouth as he barks, "I will have all of you hung for your transgression!" He turns to Calix. "Capture the girl, your team will be here soon enough. They will take care of these cowardly guards."

Backing up against Ignis, Stirling whispers, "The guards aren't fighting, why aren't the guards fighting?"

"Your guess is as good as mine. I can hear them fighting outside," Ignis replies.

His plans falling apart, Calix turns to his opponent Amiria, whose eyes flick up to Taika. "Now..." He tsks. "We can't have dragons distracting us, can we?" Calix states, bringing a whistle up to his lips.

Taika springs from her perch, pouncing on a brown dragon emerging through the open space where the mosaic wall once stood. Armor scales clash together as the brown dragon is exiled from the throne room. The massive bodies crash through an immaculate garden with flowers to decorate the throne room, a marble bench cracking beneath their rolling weight.

"Umm," Ignis starts, *"about that."* Vicious snarls of predators trying to devour their prey and the snapping of powerful jaws carry through the window along with the sound of a wooden structure collapsing.

Amiria side steps, circling Calix. Planted in place, he turns on a dial following her. His eyes latched on to her, he asks, "Tell me, what has become of my sister?"

The corners of Amiria's mouth twitch, "Go to where we first danced and find out."

He lets out a single breathy laugh and a grin spreads across his face showing off his missing tooth, "Fantastic."

"You're sick," she slaps.

He raises his shoulders with a tilt of his head, "Yes, but I'm not the one who killed her. Thank you for that."

He charges Amiria.

Nearly being nicked by the long sword, Amiria deflects Calix's blade. It's a sliver of silver light able to decapitate with a single swing. Moving to the side, she slices sidelong through the air aiming at the exposed fabric of his hips below his brigandine. Calix stabs towards the ground covering his side with his sword and blocking the impact. With one sword occupied, she stabs at his naval. Using his armored forearm, he knocks the thrusting blade off course.

With her arms winged out to the sides, he stomps into her space, his knee turning into a battering ram slamming into the gates of her chest and throwing her entire frame back. She lands hard on her tailbone, her body arching in pain. Already bowed back, Amiria uses the momentum in a single fluid motion to rock backward and throws her body up into a standing position. She widens her stance into a readied lunge, lifting her blades in time to catch a downward slash.

Stirling can't settle his agitated nerves; they wreak havoc through his body like a colony of fire ants. The sword he stole from the guard rattles in his hands. Past the point of the blade stands the King of Wyverna glaring at him from the top of his dais. He has never seen King Dietrich, or any of the royals, before this moment. He was nothing more than a boogie man in name, someone your parents will tell you will take you away if you don't finish your chores. But he isn't an invisible monster lurking in the tales of the night. He is worse. He is flesh and bone, he is real and he stands tall with the menacing look of murder in his eye.

King Dietrich purses his lips and whistles as if calling for a dog.

Confused, Stirling glances around the room for what King Dietrich could be whistling for. What appears to be shifting stone on the ceiling catches Stirling's eye. Yellow and red eyes blink awake like freshly lit torches as a wyvern speckled with various shades of gray shifts its camouflaged body above them.

Dread fills Stirling and his frightened gaze flicks to Amiria. He can barely see her, her body surrounded in a whirl of her blades deflecting Calix's strong and relentless attacks. Reluctantly, his eyes fall back to the king.

Reaching up to a wyvernite clasp matching his sparkling fingers, the king unclasps his robe, letting it fall to a pool around his feet. A claymore with a gold and wyvernite ivory hilt glints at his hip in a scabbard tied around his gambeson jacquard with an intricate floral diamond pattern of purple and gold. Flistoons of fabrics like decorative streamers hang out from the bottom of his gambeson around his thighs over matching chausses.

King Dietrich huffs. "You look like a surprised child. Did you think a king was supposed to be fat and lazy? Always hiding behind his guards?" He pauses as if waiting for Stirling to reply. Stirling, with a mouth full of cotton, can't even open his mouth. Step by step King Dietrich descends the stairs.

The frills that were lying flat against the dragon's neck shoot up with a thin layer of webbing stretching between them like hide on a tanners table as it unhinges its jaw with a hiss.

King Dietrich continues to taunt, "You aren't what I expected either. With all the trouble you've created for me, I expected someone less—boyish. You are nothing more than a foolish child who dove into a lake before learning how to swim. Now I can finally get rid of this blight that plagues my kingdom."

King Dietrich's wyvern bears down at Ignis with the power of a typhoon. *"Taika, help!"* Ignis shouts, his claws scraping on the slippery stone as he takes off through the open window.

"IGNIS!" Stirling cries as he watches his friend get swiped sideways. The floor quakes beneath his feet as the two dragons tumble across the granite.

"First rule of a fight, don't take your eyes off of your opponent." King Dietrich's voice crawls like spiders down Stirling's spine.

Rigid, Stirling turns around. He heaves, bending in half as a fist finds its way into his gut. He barely has a moment to look up before another fist pounds into his temple. Staggering, Stirling almost drops his sword in his futile attempt to stay steady on his feet. He won't go down on the first hit again.

He shakes away the throbbing pain and holds up his sword.

Amiria keeps Calix in the center of her line of sight, but she is still able to watch the room in her peripheral. Ignis has been violently chased out of the room, leaving Stirling vulnerable. He is already in over his head against the king. She's also noticed all of the guards have slipped out into the hallways where she can hear a commotion of people yelling.

Above.

Side.

Stab.

Side.

Above.

Amiria remains on the defensive. Block after block, the blades of dark swirling metal he had gifted her save her from his deadly touch. His moves are simple, he knows she has already been through an excruciating battle and is exploiting her weakness. She has already hit her threshold of exhaustion but he has only begun. He is wearing her down, slowly depleting her of any adrenaline she has in reserve. You don't win by playing fair in the game of life or death.

She needs to end this, and soon.

She catches his sword slashing down at her with the flat side of her blades. Keeping the pressure stable above her head she grinds her blades down the length of his, stepping into his personal space, too close for his long sword to properly work. Before he is able to step back away from her she drags her blade across the gut of his brigandine, the fabric curling open to reveal the metal plates sewn inside.

Calix lifts his sword high above her head and drives the pointed end down with the intention of impaling it through her and into the ground beneath her feet. With her face almost pressed to his chest, she throws her fist into the air aiming to drive her second blade through the bottom of Calix's jaw.

He shifts, pulling his head back. The scalpel-sharp edge of the blade he had custom forged slides up the soft tissue of his cheek. It catches his eyebrow, splitting it in half before finally, the tip lifts the helm from his head.

Stirling flinches at the sound of metal clattering against the granite. Taking full advantage of the subtle distraction, King Dietrich conducts a volley of fast blows. Stirling stumbles over his heel, blocking an overhead slash. With each half step Stirling takes back, his center of gravity is left behind. He struggles to hold the sword every time it shudders with expelled energy. Growing tired, Stirling can't stop his sword from being knocked away from his center and away from his body. He throws the sword back in front of him in time to block another attack before his arm windmills out again with the force of King Dietrich's sword.

In the midst of catching himself, Stirling is unable to block King Dietrich, who lunges forward swinging his blade at Stirling's chest. Letting himself fall back and having gravity pull him away, the point of King Dietrich's sword skims the surface of Stirling's gambeson. The tip barely tears through, drawing a line across Stirling's skin.

Outside Ignis takes to the air, fleeing King Dietrich's dragon that is snapping at his feathery tail.

"Oh thank the heavens." Ignis pumps his wings and takes shelter behind a wall of wild wyverns as they descend from above and surround the castle-colored dragon. Catching his breath, Ignis glances around.

Where did the Cavalry go?

Calix's eyes slam shut. Blood flows from his eyebrow, drowning the sight from his left eye. Reacting to the searing pain, he backhands Amiria. The sharp metal of his knuckles strike her across the face. Her head cracks to the side, throwing her light frame with it. Dazed, she crawls with swords in hand away from Calix before stumbling back to her feet. The room tilts and rocks with her blurred vision. She touches the back of her gauntlet to her cheek.

Blood decorates her dark armor, like a red cypress vine growing on the dank walls outside.

Regaining her vision, she turns back to Calix. A scarlet river runs down the left side of his face, flowing and blending into his red brigandine. He shakes his head. Blood splatters on the ground as his sweat-dampened hair flops back and forth before falling forward, disheveled. He takes an unstable step forward, his eye on the ground before him watching the blood paint his boots. Amiria shuffles her stance, sliding herself to his blind side.

He brings his sight up in search of her but is taken by surprise as she jams the pommel of her sword into the back of his knee, buckling it. He screams out in pain as the pommel touches the back of his kneecap. Not completely succumbing to her weakening of his leg, Amiria drives her shoulder into the back of Calix's hip. He crumples beneath the weight and falls forward, catching himself on all fours. His sword lands with a slap as his palm hits open-handed on the ground. Exhausted and with haggard and heavy breaths, he takes the moment to watch the blood running from his face quickly fill the empty space between his hands.

Wounded, he was wounded. She's brought him down. His hand curls into a fist around the grip of his sword. With a lunging step, Amiria doesn't hold back as she kicks Calix's hand. His hand flies into the air. The sound of skidding metal echoes in the hall but neither of them watches as the sword slides across the throne room.

His face is neutral as he drops his hand back to the ground and the cool metal of a blade taps the side of his neck. His diamond eye crawls up the woman he desires. The woman who has tortured him for four years. What a magnificent specimen she is.

Strong. Clever. Unpredictable on the battlefield. These are the attributes that made him fall in love with her. She is still stunning, even here and now. Blood and sweat trickles down her cheek. Blood, his blood splattered on her armor. Her left blade held to his throat and the right raised up by her left ear preparing to end their time together.

Methodically, he sits back on his heels. Amiria watches, cautiously keeping her blade close as a reminder. He releases a slow breath and runs his hand through his hair, using his blood to slick back the locks from his face, then wipes the blood from his eye. He opens it.

Amiria can't stop the skip of her heart when he opens his eyes and meets hers. His clear blue eyes, lighter than the sky. Eyes full of life, showing thoughts and emotions. His shoulders rise and fall with his breathing. A living breathing person.

A person she had shared intimate moments with, even if only for a brief time. What had led them to this moment? To this moment where she holds a sword to the throat of someone she once wanted to be around, to talk and laugh with. Someone she felt safe with.

He brought us to this moment, she reminds herself...*I brought us to this moment.* She adds on her eyes lingering on the on tied to his armor. The ribbon he had gave her.

She jumps slightly at his voice. His words are smooth and calm, "You won Amiria. You are the better fighter." Her panting breathing stirs at his words, becoming rapid and uneven. He tilts his chin up exposing the vulnerable vein of his neck, "Go on."

Her hands twitch, like stuck cogs of a mechanism trying to press forward but unable to complete their designed action. Her muscles are unwilling to cooperate, refusing to listen to her commands. Or—is it her mind instructing her hands to stand down?

She mentally pushes against her restraint. Her arms are frozen as if shackled in place. Why can't she go through with this? Why is she wasting time?

"Just do it already!" He cries out, his eyes never leaving hers.

Something catches in the back of her throat as she watches the tear form in the corner of his eyes. She has to do this. She needs to do this. She *wants* to do this. Does she want to do this? She thinks back to the man who was run through with a blade in the market streets.

His scream turns to a beg, "GET IT OVER WITH!"

She closes her eyes, breathing deeply through her nose and calming her mind. Her eyelids slide open and with a sharp intake of breath, and before she can change her mind, she hammers the pommel of her sword into Calix's temple. His body falls over limp into an unconscious pile on his side.

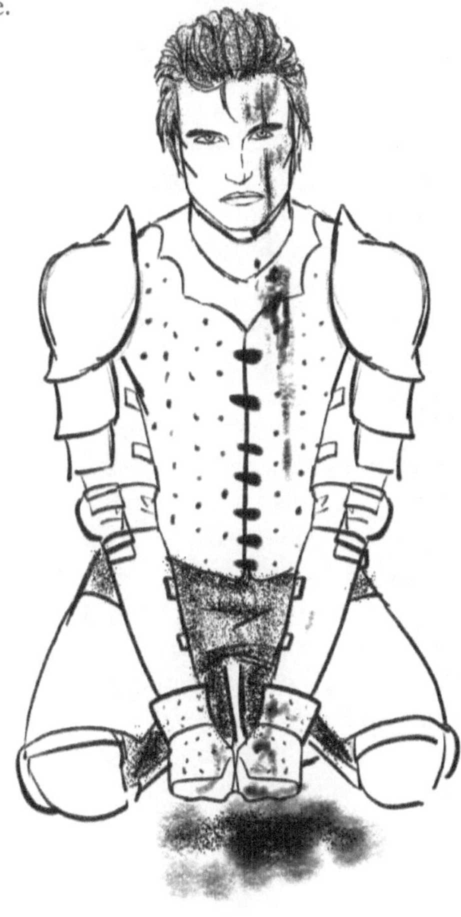

Sixty-One

Sweat drips from Stirling's brow and coats his palms as he fumbles to keep a tight grip on the sword. The handle slides and spins in his grip each time he swings it. King Dietrich stabs again. Stirling can only blink as his sword is knocked free from his hand. His mind watches absently as it falls to the granite. The world slows, but so does Stirling's reaction. He does nothing as King Dietrich's sword arches sidelong through the air.

The lids of his eyes disappear and reveal the white surrounding his hazel irises. With terror-filled eyes he watches as the tip of the blade cuts across his stomach, momentarily connecting a silver path from him to the king.

Stirling's jaw drops with a silent scream as King Dietrich's sword cuts through the thick fabric of the gambeson with ease and the blade separates his soft skin. The cool metal burns as it slices him open. He can feel each skin fiber tearing as they split apart. As soon as the intrusion began it was over. Standing there, he knows he had watched the blade cut him open but his brain has not caught up with the events to process the reality of it.

Then a sickening amount of pain begins. A guttural sound crawls out of him as his hands shoot to cover his stomach and his legs fall out from beneath him and he drops to his knees. This is an amount of pain he only thought he knew. This isn't like the scars on his arms, the bruises he once wore, or the mark on his brow. This is suffocating. Every nerve is screaming and vibrating through his body, making his body overwhelmed with the agonizing sensation. He lifts one of his hands to check.

Blood. His hand is covered in red liquid. The room tilts on its axis but the king does not slide, his feet firmly planted on the angled floor.

"Amiria," he whispers before hitting the ground. He lays half on his side staring up at the arched ceiling, his hands loosely clutching the wound across his middle. The sound is muffled but he believes he hears his name being shouted. Who is that?

"Amiria," his voice comes out weak as he grits through the pain. Every inhale of air moves his stomach, opening the slash across his middle. "Help."

I'm going to die. I'm going to die. I'm going to die. I don't want to die. I made a promise. I don't want to die. Please, I don't want to die. I never told him goodbye.

"Ignis, help me."

Amiria's voice tears a wound from her heart to her throat as she watches Stirling's body crumble. Blood drips from the end of King Dietrich's sword as he stands there over him. The room is a heated blur, she can see nothing but a tunnel view of Stirling laying broken and gasping in pain.

Grinding her teeth as her vision turns red, before her mind can control it, her feet propel her forward in a sprint towards King Dietrich, swords in hand.

Raising his claymore above his head, King Dietrich takes an ominous step forward shadowing the wretched boy at his feet. Holding one arm across his wound, Stirling reaches behind himself and begins palming the ground slick with his blood. He releases a desperate cry of pain and fear as he tries to drag his body. King Dietrich laughs at the worthless attempt to escape. He takes another step, immediately destroying the distance Stirling struggled so hard to make.

Stirling's grating calls of pain run through Amiria like a bull down the market streets. It terrorizes her cells and destroys everything in its path.

King Dietrich's eyes flick to the side as the new impending Amiria charges into view. Switching his target to the real threat in the room, he swings his sword as if swiping flat across a table top. The blade whipping towards her face, Amiria drops to her knees.

Sparks fly as she skids across the granite, arching back she slips under the blade. Once clear of the sword she leaps to her feet and strikes. King Dietrich turns in time. His knees bend as he absorbs the shock of the dual blades crashing into his claymore.

They hold their pose, two fighters posing for a tapestry. Amiria snarls up at the king. The man who she had sworn an oath to protect. Sworn her life to protect. She had been ready and willing to lay her life down to save his. The corner of her mouth curls up. No one is here to protect him now. No one to sacrifice themselves to save him. It's his turn to dance with silver ribbons.

Why the guards standing post at the doors are only assisting to keep them shut, she doesn't know. But she is grateful.

"Where is your Cavalry?" she asks with a sly smile.

"You should have taken my offer," he growls, ignoring her question and leaning his face in close.

Grinding her teeth, she takes a step back holding her balance as his weight overpowers their standoff. Her eyes flick to Stirling's weakening state at the sound of him groaning. A moment of clarity to refuel her rage, a reason to keep fighting.

"Oh?" King Dietrich purses his lips reading the anguish on her face.

With his claymore on top, King Dietrich presses down on Amiria, the blades creeping closer to her face. She slides her blades across his until the edge of his blade hooks on her guards. Holding his blade locked, she dips beneath them and snakes behind him.

King Dietrich stumbles forward without her support holding him up. Regaining his composure he spins around to confront her and with a yell of fury he closes the distance in two long strides. He swings, retracts, stabs, retracts, slashes. A volley of attacks always defaulting back to being in a guarded position before another attack, lessening any openings for Amiria to exploit.

She blocks using both of her blades to stop the heavy metal from hitting her. His claymore's reach keeps his body at too far of a distance for her to block and attack simultaneously. She has to remain on the defensive until she figures out an alternative or advantage.

Running out of adrenaline, her foot work begins to slip, her blocks begin to slow. She can no longer push back as she uses what she still has to knock his sword away.

"I've decided I don't want you as a servant," his voice is steady in between strikes.

"What?" she snaps with a raddled breath.

The flat side of his claymore hits her like a kick from a horse in the center of her chest, throwing her down onto her back. She heaves, desperately sucking in oxygen to keep her going. He stands above her like the castle towers above the city. Before Amiria is able to recover an anvil lands on her chest.

His knee staked to her ribcage, he snarls, "I will kill you." Using his knee to hold her in place, he takes his time observing what a disgrace she had turned out to be. He offered his right hand side to her and she spat at it. What a troublesome monster the Field Marshal Rey had raised. No normal human could have caused this much chaos in their own kingdom. She is the root to all the problems in Wyverna. She is the contamination and must be exterminated, her and the boy who is staining his beautiful throne room as he bleeds out behind him.

Amiria gasps, choking for a full breath. King Dietrich leans down close to her, his weight only crushing into her further, "But, not until after you hear the cries of all your criminal followers dying in your name."

Curling her hand firmly around the grip of her sword, Amiria can feel the cool stone through her sweat-dampened hair. She sees past King Dietrich to the arches above. Closing her eyes, she focuses on her breathing. There's a flash of light illuminating the back of her eyelids red.

Distracted by Ignis' flames, the king takes his eyes off Amiria. The shift of his weight lessens the pressure on her chest.

She moves in two rapid movements.

King Dietrich yowls in pain as he feels the tendon of his heel being sliced apart. Using the point of the blade that opened the back of his ankle, Amiria stabs it into the outside of the thigh anchoring down on her chest.

With the blade protruding from his thigh, King Dietrich drops his claymore and falls back from Amiria, releasing his restraint on her. She scrambles to flip herself over then launches to her feet. King Dietrich throws his hand out, snagging her by the ankle. She trips falling onto her stomach. She whips around with the one sword she has left and slices at the hand shackling her.

King Dietrich recoils, blood already dripping from his fingers. Amiria rolls across the ground away from him, her hand landing on the hilt of his claymore. He moves to stand, but grunts in pain as his ankle refuses to hold him.

He can get no higher than a kneel. Furious he rips the sword out from his thigh and holds it up in defense.

With his vision fading to black around the edges, Stirling watches lethargically as a girl raises a long sword above a king brought to his knees. He hears no words exchanged, not even a cry out as the blade with a golden hilt is a blur through the king.

Stirling lies with his face pressed to the floor in his pool of blood feeling the world grow colder around him with each pulse. He blinks, watching the head fall back before the body slumps in the opposite direction.

Sixty-Two

Her knees landing hard on the granite, Amiria is at Stirling's side in an instant and is tearing off her gauntlets. Her eyes are already glistening with tears as she rolls him onto his back.

"Hey—hey—look at me," Amiria says, her words a broken whisper, her hand resting in the dry half of his curls. "Look at me Stirling." Her breath hitches as she searches his distant eyes, "It's okay—you're going to be okay—please."

Refusing to acknowledge the puddle she is kneeling in, she removes a dagger from her boot, "We'll get this off of you and staunch the bleeding okay?" Her voice wavers and tears run down her face. "Okay!" she says with force.

Stirling, who is turning a shade of bluish gray, manages a nod. His shallow breathing slows to an extent Amiria sees a pause between each breath.

Her blade slices the ties down the front of the gambeson while she keeps her attention on Stirling's face. "Don't go to sleep Stirling—" she finishes cutting the last tie. "Please—don't go to sleep," she begs. His gambeson falls open revealing a gash across his stomach, burbling with blood. She covers her mouth, stifling her reaction to the sight.

Ignis crashes through the open window in a haste, "Stirling! Stirling!" His massive frame slides to a stop several steps from Stirling's fading body as Amiria, hands already stained crimson, presses a scrap of the gambeson to his stomach.

Ignis' shouting voice turns to a whimper. "*Stirling?*" Lying beside him, Ignis lowers his snout to gently press Stirling's shoulder. "*Stirling?*"

"Ignis," Stirling croaks. His hand struggles to lift as if fighting a restraint until it falls limply against the side of Ignis' face and slides back down to the floor.

Ignis' bounces from Amiria's face, flooding with tears, then back to Stirling with denial of what he is seeing.

"Oh, Ignis," Amiria weeps as their eyes meet. "It's my fault. It's all my fault." Her gaze falls to the red covering her hands like gloves.

BOOM

At the sound of the throne room door crashing open, Amiria throws herself over Stirling. *Boots.* She can hear men piling into the room. Picking up her dagger, as her blades lay tossed beside the king's body, she spins to a fighting stance. Her aching muscles cramp as she stands protectively over Stirling.

Castle guards march in the throne room filing into perfect formation facing her then they part in the middle. Clyde strolls down the center with his hands interlaced behind his back. He cocks his head at the gruesome scene displayed before him with no other indication of his thoughts. Taking a single step to the side, Clyde allows room for Derek Rey to step forward.

Amiria's heart drops at the sight of her father. His eyes are unreadable as he looks upon the death and carnage she left behind. His footsteps echo louder than the clashing blades moments before. He travels only part way across the room.

He stares unflinchingly down at the headless king. "What a pity."

Amiria's heart rattles in her chest as fast as a rabbit caught in a corner by a fox.

Derek studies his daughter's fleeting expression, but she will not leave the boy behind. He can see it in her, she has not begun to understand what she has done. Swept up in her revenge, she never saw how many people were caught up in her tidal wave. These guardsmen stand here loyal to *her*. Winged Riders of the Cavalry converted to fight alongside her and not against her. She believes she stands here alone but she is far from it.

"They are at your command." Derek tests his daughter.

"What?" She replies breathy and wiping at her face leaves behind streaks of Stirling's blood.

"They are at your command, Amiria Rey."

Amiria is dumbfounded. Orders? Commands? What does he mean?

Her father's stern eyes burrow into, "What are your orders?"

"I—I can't—"

Orders? Orders, she must give orders? She shouldn't be giving orders. Why would she be giving orders? She should be killed on site. Is this a test? A test to see if she was seeking out power? A test to see where her loyalty still stands? To see what side she stands on, if she is only fighting for herself or for the people. She doesn't have time to deal with her father and these guards. She needs to be trying to save Stirling's life. Stirling had saved her twice and now he lies fading on the ground behind her.

"He—." Her words stagger and trip. She twists her spine to look down at Stirling. His dulling eyes remain fixated on her as if she was the only thing he can see in the room. "He ne-needs aid."

Her father dips his chin holding his gaze on her. No one moves. Everyone is waiting for her command.

Amiria takes several deep breaths to steady her nerves. They are asking her to play the role she was born to be. If they want Amiria Rey next in line Field Marshal of the Winged Cavalry, she will give exactly that.

"R-render" Her voice shakes. She stops to compose herself. All of her emotions are filling her head and suffocating her mind. She catches them with a net of control and stuffs it into a chest.

Lifting her head, Amiria faces the guards and barks, "Render aid to Stirling Bakere. His survival is your top priority! Those who are not rendering aid will take post outside the royal family chambers. No one is to leave or enter until further notice. Do not inform the nobles in the castle what has conspired. They will be informed when the time comes. Guards and Winged Riders still loyal to the king shall not be killed. Use verbal tactics to get them to stand down." Derek Rey smiles at his daughter. "If they continue to refuse, apprehend them. I repeat do not kill. Result only to deadly force if your life is on the line. Finally take Calix—" Her words die on her lips. A pool of blood shows where Calix's body once lay. She follows the red prints to the window sill, "Find Calix Gautier! I repeat do not kill. Find and arrest, Calix Gautier!"

Clyde faces his men. "You heard Rey's orders. You three render aid. You five check the royal chambers. Guards should already be stationed outside the rooms. The rest of you join the Winged Cavalry in pursuing those who stand loyal to King Dietrich. Make finding Calix Gautier your top priority."

Taking a step back out of formation, the guards remove themselves from the throne room in a clattering jog.

Feeling like she has been hit with the weight of a dragon, Amiria collapses. She falls into a sitting position leaning heavily onto one hip. Her legs have become useless, every muscle fiber burning as if it's being ripped from her bones while she depends on her arms to pull herself closer until she is back against Stirling.

She takes his clammy hand in hers and pulls it into her lap. "It's okay." She brushes his curls, wet with his cold sweat, back from his forehead. Wiping away the tears, she forces a smile as she meets his half lidded hazel eyes.

"Amiria." The name comes out sluggish.

"Don't close your eyes. Stirling please don't go to sleep," she pleads, her words catching in her throat. She strokes his cheek with her thumb as the guards surround her.

"So tired." Stirling's voice is barely a whisper past his unmoving lips.

"Stirling please—" She presses the back of his hand to her cheek, choking back her tears, "Please don't fall asleep, I love you."

Those are the last words Stirling hears before his heavy eyelids close.

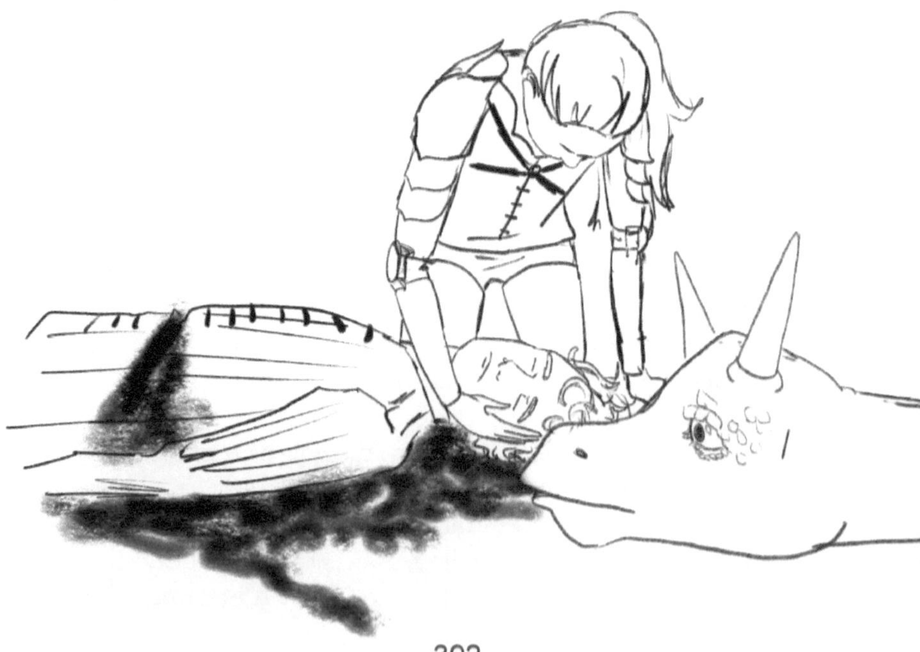

Sixty-Three

*I*t hurts, He thinks. *I can't move…it hurts.* He sees nothing but the back of his eyelids. He twitches his fingers. There is something in his hand and it squeezes.

"Amiria," Giles' voice is deep and sympathetic as he leans into the bedroom of his home above the bakery.

Amiria lifts her head from where it rests upon the bed beside Stirling. He lays on his back deep in sleep, his bandaged torso rising and falling with his faint breaths. Cleaned of dust for the first time in almost 4 years, the stool had been dragged from its imprints by the window to take its new place by the bedside.

They were able to cauterize the slash across his stomach that was only skin deep with the gambeson taking most of the blow. There was no major internal damage but death was breathing down his neck as he suffered from blood loss and shock. If King Dietrich was half a step closer, the result would have been devastatingly different. She held his limp hand as they sutured his skin and applied herbs and she refused to let go as he spent the night in the castle infirmary. Then at her request, Stirling was transported to the bakery so he was somewhere familiar when he finally opens his eyes.

Carted through the streets from the castle, then carried to the steps of the bakery by guards, Stirling lay unconscious on a canvas stretched between two bars. Amiria squeezed Stirling's hand as Giles opened the door with Grace, who caught him as he nearly collapsed at the sight.

Her hand finally slipped from his as the guards carried the stretcher up the staircase. She followed them up the stairs and into the bedroom where they transferred him to the bed. Then once she heard the front door close and she stood in the home with no one else but Giles and Grace to hear, she began to scream.

Blood, his blood was soaked through her clothing beneath her armor and coating her skin. Amiria wailed with hysteria, ripping her armor from her body she discarded the gear and clothing in a heap in the corner of the room. With blood still on her hands, she sobbed. Overtaken with guilt she threw herself onto the bed and shook with grief until sleep gained control of her salt stung eyes.

In the morning she had laid distraught beside Stirling and was barely able to give Giles a simplified tale of what led to this outcome.

Amiria sits up at the sound of Giles' caring voice. She had fallen asleep holding Stirling's hand again. It's late into the morning and he hasn't moved more than his fingers. She squints at Giles. The late morning sun pours in through the open window behind him as he leans his shoulder on the door frame.

"A guard by the name of Captain Mannering is here to accompany you to your meeting."

Amiria turns back to Stirling's soft featured face, her heart longing for his eyes to open, to see the beautiful hazel again. Struck in the heart at the sight, Giles sinks into the door frame as he is brought back to a scene that wasn't far off from this. When Stirling was the one who sat on the stool and another set of sandy curls laid sprawled on the pillow. He steps across the room letting his mind travel back in time. Stirling had learned at a young age what true heartache and loss was.

He reaches past Amiria and rests his hand on Stirling's curls. He keeps himself strong for Amiria now, but when he had opened the door and saw her in armor covered in blood he nearly fainted. How is a father supposed to react when their son is unconscious and bandaged on a stretcher? How many times can one father lose his only son?

"But what if he wakes while I'm gone?" Her eyes are as round as a button as she stares up at him.

Giles's face softens at the girl beside him. She isn't the warrior everyone has attached to her name. She is a human, a human with a heart that is crumbling. A heart with so many fractures, a single breeze can break it into pieces.

The news of King Dietrich has not been announced to the people yet. Not until they know which direction the kingdom will be going in, but there is no doubt the word will spread before that. The people of Lumierna saw the sky last night. Even he could see from the window of the bakery the glowing flames at the throne hall.

"If he wakes, I'll tell him to go back to sleep and wait for you," Giles says with a weak smile.

Amiria rolls her eyes, then hangs her head. "I just—" She squeezes his hand and tries to see through his closed eyelids. "Want to see them again."

"You will. We all will." Giles transfers his hand from Stirling's hair to Amiria's shoulder. "Just let him rest and he will wake up soon."

Dressed in a deep purple cotehardie, Amiria steps outside the bakery. She taps the orange tail extended out in front of the entrance stairs with her foot as she steps over it. Golden eyes open up and meet hers. Tilting her head to the heartbroken dragon, she gives him a fragile smile. Taika, with small abrasions from the battle, lies asleep taking up the entrance to the store beside the bakery. She lifts her head and reaches out to Amiria with a mental hug.

The street appears desolate compared to the packed crowds she is used to. Maybe having two dragons outside your shop after an aerial battle isn't the best sales tactic. There are two other people outside the bakery. Clyde stands beside a single horse drawn wagon with a driver.

Stepping up to him calmly, Amiria pushes up the sleeve on her right arm exposing her mostly healed brand over her insignia. "Good morning, Clyde. I've never got to repay you for this."

"Um—"

Smiling politely, Amiria drives her fist into Clyde's gut. He grunts and keeps a single hand holding onto the cart, stopping him from tipping over as he half hugs his middle and doubles over.

"I think you're underpaid but—" She leans in close to his ear for only him to hear, "thank you, for what you did in the end." She pushes past him and climbs into the back of the wagon.

Rubbing his stomach, Clyde hoists himself into the wagon and faces Amiria on the opposing bench. They stare eye to eye barely moving as the wagon begins to roll with the flick of the reins by the driver.

Amiria speaks first. "Are you going to brief me before we arrive on the current situation, or am I going into this ignorant?"

"Well, what's any different than when you devised a mutiny without even knowing you had people on your side?"

Amiria eyes him.

"I'm just saying. There was an unplanned uprising and it all started because of that boy in there." He points his thumb back at the bakery shrinking behind them. "Four years ago, he changed the way the lower class saw the world."

"That's the one thing I *am* aware of." She crosses her arms.

It's still hard to comprehend how they got to this moment. She went from hiding in a cave to sitting in a wagon on her way to the castle after she killed King Dietrich and is *not* in shackles. How did Wyverna turn upside down all because of one single night? Can she pin it all on the one event or was it something inevitable that was bound to happen regardless? If Stirling and she didn't ignite the flame, then was it only a matter of time before someone else did?

Clyde puts his hand up signaling her to hold on. "Let me finish, When people saw him fly, he opened the eyes of the lower class, but *you* opened the eyes of the entire Kingdom. The baker made sense, lower status wanting to rise up. But you—you were given life on a silver platter. You had title, power, money. People like me in the guards, people like—" He cuts himself short. "People like Nellie, in the Winged Cavalry. We saw you throw it all away and for what end goal?"

Nellie? What does Nellie have to do with this? Amiria cocks her head.

She picks at her teeth with her tongue as she thinks. Not even she knows why she did it. It started because she was raised to protect Wyverna's people and she needed to protect them from Wyverna herself. In the end that was no longer the reason. It was spite and vengeance. Saving the people of Wyverna was put to the back of her mind, she wanted to kill King Dietrich because of what he did to *her* and what he had planned to do to *her*. She is not the hero people are perceiving her to be.

Clyde continues, "We began to idolize you. The former king went mad with power and began to hang our own in an attempt to put an end to our new free way of thinking. He also made your father walk them through their own execution to slowly break him down. In the end, all of the threats and lives lost only added fuel to the fire. No one was safe anymore. We had a choice. Conform or die."

Wait. Amiria's face turns ashen as she puts the story together. She meets Clyde's eyes and can see the answer before she asks it. "Was Nellie—"

Clyde drops his gaze. Amiria's mouth forms the shape of, "Oh." It's her fault. It is her fault Nellie is dead. She swallows the lump in her throat. It is her fault all those innocent people died. They weren't just following Stirling, they were following her too.

They sit steeping in the heavy silence as they mourn the loss of not just a classmate but a person whose choices were led by Amiria's example. Amiria dares to meet the faces peering out at her from the market home windows. Faces who recognize her. Faces she recognizes from the years of walking these streets.

She never planned this far ahead. She never believed she would cause an entire insurrection. She was blinded by her revenge. There was no life past fighting King Dietrich, she honestly didn't think she was going to even make it to the throne. She foresaw herself dying as she reached the castle grounds by the same team, she once fought beside, and if they didn't get her Kinsey and Calix were lying in wait. When she told Stirling goodbye, she thought it was for the last time, but if it wasn't for him she would have watered the garden with her blood beside Kinsey.

Instead of being dead, she sits in this wagon on her way to a council meeting to determine the outcome of the kingdom. She doesn't want to do this. She doesn't want to suffer through a Winged Cavalry meeting. She wants to be beside Stirling but—but isn't this what she used to want? She remembers almost a year ago turning down Stirling's offer to run away because she wanted to protect the citizens. She remembers arguing with Stirling in Leucasia for him to come back to Wyverna and save the people. She has come full circle, she is not here to help everyone because she wants to, but because she is required to.

She can correct this. She can fix this. She can clean up her mess. Isn't that what heroes do? She stares down at her lap. She isn't a hero—she's a murderer.

The castle grows before her. Its dark stone is now covered in a new ominous layer. Despite the sun sitting high in the clear sky, the castle grounds lay abandoned. Keeping her eyes on her lap, Amiria can hear nothing but the rolling of the wagon wheels and the clopping of hooves, the castle as quiet as witching hour.

Servants stay hidden in their quarters as the castle remains on lockdown. Only several run the kitchen to bake and help the guards serve bread and cheese to each of the rooms. Those who are not on lock down have been too afraid to step out of their chambers after the violent overthrow of their beloved king.

Amiria hangs her head back until only the tops of the towers are in view.

She overthrew the king.

She. Overthrew. The king.

She killed King Dietrich.

She hugs herself as a prickle runs down her spine. She can still feel his eyes clinging to her all those years. Clyde hasn't said a word since he released the catapult of information on her. He watches her thoughts run across her face and her mind finally drifts to the sky.

He begins wringing his hands. How does one mentally accept they unknowingly started a revolution with their words and actions. People died walking in their footsteps.

He thinks back to the words Amiria had spoken to him in the main keep. *At least I'm fighting. Pathetic is someone who continues to follow orders to keep his life comfortable at the cost of others.*

When they started killing people for the crime of wanting self-identity he knew he was on the wrong side, but all he cared about was keeping himself from being the one with the noose around his throat. It wasn't until she was behind bars and she made him feel like the criminal outside the cage did he finally come to terms of who he had become and that is not who he wanted to die as. He spent that night reflecting on his choices and he only made one choice that benefited someone that wasn't himself and that was choosing Robert and William for his special detail. It was partially because he knew they were excellent guards and fit for the role, but another part of it was he wanted a way to protect them. No one should be killed for who they love, that is one thing he has *always* believed. He knows from experience you don't get to choose who your heart desires.

Plus, wasn't that what he was born for? To protect the innocent?

Clyde follows Amiria's lead and lets his head fall back to watch the wall of the inner bailey pass over them as they enter the center grounds. His thumb mindlessly rubs his insignia hidden beneath his sleeve. The best and worst Winged Riders in class, never would he have guessed they would both fly so far from the nest where they were cultivated to end up together on the same branch.

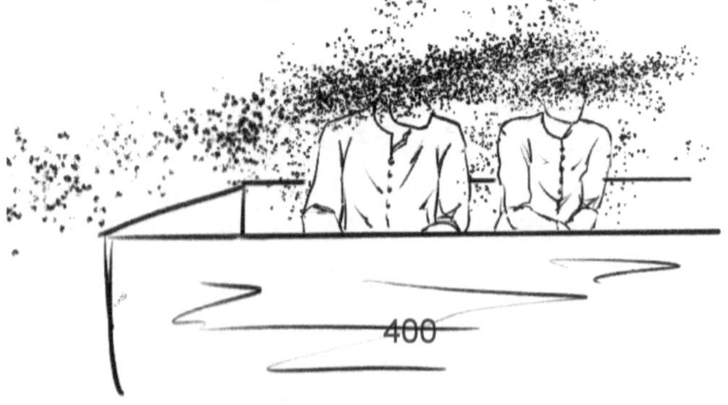

Sixty-Four

The tension in the air has more pressure than the stones in the arch ways as Amiria trails behind Clyde through the Castle corridors. He had filled her in with the mayhem that followed the former king's assassination.

A small select few of the Winged Riders had refused to follow the new orders, holding faithful to King Dietrich over the Field Marshal. They were brought to the main keep to be stripped of their status as a Winged Rider. Many had lost their lives during the war with the wild wyverns and the rebellion of the guards. Major Gautier, Dicun, Armundus, and Kinsey were listed on the fatality report, but so were others that Amiria knew. Warrick and Garret had made that frightful count, leaving only Amiria and Clyde left from their original class. Then a list of Winged Riders who have been unaccounted for has been drafted and several warrants have been enacted. Calix, Eda, Everard and General Gautier are several of those on the warrants list.

Winged Riders and guards weren't the only ones who had lost their lives. Several dragons, Major Gautier's and

Warrick's being two of them, had given up their lives trying to defend their riders. A majority of the survivors fled with the wild dragons but some were captured and returned to the Winged Cavalry's breeding grounds.

Clyde and Amiria approach the antechamber that not even a year ago she sat at the table with her team while they listened to King Dietrich assemble a reconnaissance party to capture Stirling. In the end King Dietrich didn't have any need for Stirling, not when she was a much better example to make of. She lied to the king that day and Calix had seen right through it.

Her blood turns cold as she imagines Calix on the other side of the elaborate wooden door. He will be sitting leaned back in his chair beside hers. Then his pale eyes will pop up to her from the table and he'll smile knowingly at her as if he could read every line of her soul. He had the nails to her coffin in his hand ready to punch each one through, but in the end it wasn't her coffin being lowered into the ground. A queasy feeling washes over her, unsure if it's from the image of Calix behind the door or the reminder of the innocent lives lost due to her insubordination. She pauses outside the door to take several deep breaths.

Shaking his head, Clyde steps around her and pushes the door open. The clamor of voices comes to an abrupt stop as they step into the room. The quiet is as heavy as if no one was speaking to begin with. The eyes in the over-capacitated room follow Clyde and Amiria, but Amiria's gaze is on the collar of her father's golden gambeson as she is unable to meet his eye. Derek Rey, not yet seated, stands at the head of the large yew wood table with the purple and red Winged Cavalry coat of arms runner cutting down the center.

The brass of the Winged Cavalry and Lumierna's Guardsmen sit shoulder to shoulder around the table and line the walls of the room. Disgruntled faces of the men and women in charge stare at her with excruciating critique of each breath she takes.

"Our last members have finally arrived," Derek says to the room, "the meeting may now commence." His expression closed, he turns his chin to Clyde and Amiria, "Have a seat," and gestures to two empty chairs on to the right of him.

Clyde pulls back his chair triumphantly and plops down into his much deserved seat. Amiria's eyes never lift from the grains of the table as she slides into her chair beside her father.

"We, those in leadership of the Winged Cavalry and the Guards of Lumierna have gathered to this chamber to discuss the matters of the events that conspired two nights ago," Derek Rey announces to the room. "An unplanned revolution erupted and the former King of Wyverna, King Dietrich, was beheaded in the throne room. He was one of the many fatalities. We must now work in unity to stitch this Kingdom back together before someone else or another empire does."

Brigadier Terrowin speaks up. "You excluded a fact. We know it was *your* daughter who beheaded the king. We wouldn't be in this situation if *she* followed orders."

Major Puttock jabs their fingers at Terrowin. "You mean the king who hung your niece because she spoke only of admiration towards Amiria Rey?"

Brigadier Terrowin crosses his arms. "And the blame still falls back on her."

Amiria shifts in her seat unable to meet their eyes.

Clyde speaks up in defense. "If not her, then it would have been someone else. Many were motivated by the baker who flew. Many of us already had the idea that changes needed to be made before that. We were on a slippery slope and it was only a matter of time before someone else took the plunge." His eyes shift around Derek to Amiria's hanging head. "We should be thankful she ended this quickly, putting a halt to the civilian, guard, and *Cavalry* fatalities. We cannot be a strong kingdom if we are killing our own people."

"Well said, Captain Mannering," Derek approves. "Anyone else have opinions they want to get off their chest?"

"The Royal family," Lt General Ward starts. "They will not be so keen on handing over what is rightfully theirs."

"His heir is nothing more than a small child and his daughters only know how to stand and smile," Major Puttock replies dismissively.

"There's the regent."

Derek Rey retorts, "The boy can be trained in new laws if it need be. The laws must be changed no matter who is next in line and we will deal with the regent, appoint a new one if need be."

"What if the dignitaries refuse to comply?"

"We are the military," Derek Rey says bluntly. "Who is going to tell us no?"

Amiria disconnects herself from the conversation. This is a meeting about a shift of power from one dynamic to another. She picks at the small scabs on her face where Calix's gauntlet had struck her. They had not found any trace of where he had gone, but she knows he is far away by now. He is familiar with Uviktiland and what lies beyond it, Tillfalya. He wasn't flying off into the unknown when he escaped.

Why couldn't she kill him? Now he is out there, around any corner waiting for her. He wouldn't have even hesitated if the roles were reversed. Her blade was touching his throat, but she couldn't go through with it. When he looked up at her, all she saw was a human. Stupid, she's so stupid. Stupid and weak. The fingers of her hand scratching at her face dig, clenching up and dragging her nails roughly down her face.

Grimacing, she drops her hand to the table exposing the blood of the scab she picked free. A flash of embarrassment heats her face, she covers the side of her face with her hand while never removing her eyes from the table. Like the scar on his face she will live with a constant reminder that he is out there. Is she destined to live in fear for the rest of her life, afraid to turn every corner, afraid of what is lurking in the shadows.

"Amiria, is everything all right?" Clyde asks in a hushed tone as the dignitaries continue to argue, each of them having their own side.

Amiria looks through her hand at him. "I don't know how to answer that."

"Understandable." He shrugs.

The chatter of the room cuts in and out of her mind, she overhears a woman's voice say, "No matter our point it always comes back to who will replace the king. Not much of a monarchy without a family lineage."

Derek places his palms on the table and leans forward. "I've been thinking during this, who says we need a monarchy."

"King, emperor, ruler. They are all the same except by name."

Derek shakes his head, "Seeing all of you in discussion has given me an idea." He scans the room, "The Winged Cavalry will run Wyverna. We will use the leadership we already have. A system of steps. Not one person who holds all of the power, but several. There will still be a primary role of the Field Marshal."

"Are you electing yourself in charge?" a snippy voice calls out.

"No. I suggest we speak about the new Field Marshal and make a decision as a military council. If I need to step down then so be it. I'd rather have someone suited for the job be voted in instead of being born into it."

Amiria can't fill in the gap of the conversation she missed. She doesn't understand how it went from training the king's heir to the Winged Cavalry running the entire kingdom in a tiered system. She looks about the room at the strong majority nodding.

Lt General Ward hits her fist lightly on the table, "I agree with this. Those who are interested in the position raise your hand." Majority of the hands rise into the air above their heads.

Derek Rey's lips pull into a line, "Who wants to run for the position of Field Marshal?" Several hands pop up. "Those who raised their hands are not to be voted for. Those who want power shall not possess it. People those naturally follow are the ones who make the best leaders. They lead out of instinct and not desire to control. They do not force people to follow but let the people choose."

"Swaying the vote already, Rey? Fine, who do you nominate?" Brigadier Terrowin waves his hand.

"I nominate Amiria Rey."

Amiria's face turns as hot as Taika's flames, if it were not for her tanned olive skin she would be as red as a poppy.

"Any other nominations?" Derek addresses the room, "You can add the name anonymously when we vote, but if you want to nominate someone for others to decide upon, speak now."

Major Puttock speaks up, "I have someone to nominate, Clyde Mannering." Clyde sits up stiff in his chair. "He was able to coordinate all of the castle and city guards without a single noble catching on. When the revolution began, it was Captain Mannering they followed and not King Dietrich."

Smiling, Derek Rey nods his head in approval, "Valid point, Major. Any others?" He pauses, "No? Then we shall cast an anonymous vote."

Scraps of pressed paper are passed around the room and each person in the room scribbles their vote. They fold their votes and place them in a bowl that are then tallied and counted by three people in the room at random.

Derek had seated himself during the voting process. He sits up straight as the last counter sets down the final paper and makes their mark. He motions his hand to the three asking, "What is the result? Who shall be the new Field Marshal?"

Colonel Aimar stands up and announces, "Amiria Rey."

Her heart drops, breaking through the sturdy chair and through the granite floor. Her lips fall slightly parted but she is unable to push any air out to form words. She blinks at the room wide eyed. She can't be Field Marshal. She doesn't want to run the Cavalry, let alone an entire kingdom.

She shakes her head.

Everything she has done these past years in defiance of who she was born to be led her to an even higher seat of power. How can that be right? She almost lost her life—Stirling's life. People *had* lost their lives for her and now she has been elected to rule them? Her stomach knots with the guilty feeling she had paid for her spot with their blood. If she had played the loyal soldier she would have been Field Marshal of the Winged Cavalry and no one would have died. She spills their blood now she is Field Marshal of the Isles of Wyverna.

She continues to shake her head slowly picking up speed until the movement is about to fling her out of her chair, "I cannot accept the proposal."

Shocked, Derek Rey raises an eyebrow and peers over the side of his shoulder at the daughter he had trained her whole life to be Field Marshal. This is everything they wanted and more, how can she not accept? He reevaluates his thoughts. She had not only trained her whole life, but he had forced her to sacrifice her childhood. He forced—forced. "Why is that? The room says otherwise."

Amiria hangs her head. "I want to help rebuild, but I want to work alongside the new Field Marshal and fix this Kingdom. I do not want to lead it. A good leader has to also be happy in their role or they will turn cruel and bitter."

Derek nods his head with disappointment hidden beneath his tough top layer, "We appreciate the honesty. Colonel, who is the second place vote?"

"It is you sir."

"Pardon me?" He blinks.

"There were only three people voted for. Amiria Rey, Captain Mannering, and you, sir."

Derek adjusts his collar. "Just because I already possess the title doesn't make me a suitable candidate."

"We are in disagreement, Sir Rey," Colonel Aimar says. "Those who voted for you know you are more than a title. You've shown that to us, especially these recent days. If anyone can reestablish Wyverna in a new light it is you."

Amiria peaks up at her blushing father. He has turned a shade she never expected to see on him, the shade of light red different from his purplish tint of anger. She turns her head to look at Clyde beside her. He stares past her to her father with admiration. It's obvious on his face he must have voted for her father too.

Her father pushes his chair back and stands with his shoulders pulled back, "I accept the responsibility." He bows at the waist, "We as a team will make this kingdom safe for all its people. I believe now is a good time to take a break for lunch. What has been discussed in the antechamber shall not be spoken past this door until we are all in agreement that our format is ready."

"What is the rush?" Clyde huffs, catching up to Amiria who is practically running out the entrance of the castle. They have completed a long day of dry governmental talk and Amiria desperately wants to return to Stirling's side in case he wakes up.

Taika had been her saving grace, keeping her from nodding off during policies and keeping a constant tab on the Bakere's household.

Clyde stops as she turns to him. Her irises are the corners of your room where the light doesn't reach and blackened by your dark thoughts and memories. Staring into them, he's back standing in the throne room; her lamenting voice cracking as she cries out the boy's name, while he stands by watching her spirit crumple beside his diminishing body. A love developed slowly over time between two friends.

She will never know how well he understands her. He has experienced what it's like to be stripped of your title in the Winged Cavalry. He has felt the utter despair as you helplessly watch the light die from someone you love. What Amiria will never know is why he commanded the guards to turn against the kingdom. She will never know because she will never ask. They were two parts in different stories and hers isn't over yet.

"Alright." He answers without Amiria uttering a word, "I'll drop you off."

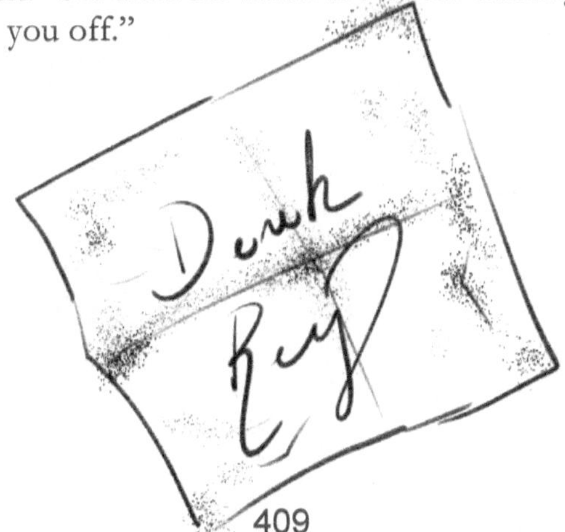

Sixty-Five

There are no goodbyes when Clyde departs. Amiria is out of the wagon before the wheels stop turning. With the horses slowing, the drivers turn to Clyde. He leans back against his seat and waves for the driver to carry on. No point in stopping when she is already almost to the front door.

Ignoring the bystanders ogling Taika and Ignis, Amiria pauses long enough to pat Ignis' head, resting by the front door, between his horns.

He closes his eyes, enjoying it. *"Taika, tell Amiria to try and wake Stirling up with a kiss."*

"I'm not asking that," Taika snaps, her head jerking in Ignis' direction.

Amiria raises an eyebrow. *"Taika? What did he say?"*

Taika mentally rolls her eyes. *"He wants you to wake Stirling with a kiss."*

Amiria's heart sputters, sending a pulse through her body as she remembers their last evening together before the battle. Composing herself, she looks back at Ignis and scolds, "It doesn't work like that."

Ignis sings, *"But you wish it did."*

"Amiria you should be glad you can't hear him," Taika says sincerely.

The door to the bakery opens. Giles smiles down at her. "I thought I heard someone out here." He turns his frame, opening a path for Amiria to step inside. "Come on in, Grace and I are about to get ready for supper."

Amiria scrunches her nose at Ignis and hops up the steps.

A fair skinned woman with red hair stands timidly by the table. She has not spoken to the Winged Rider Amiria Rey yet. She watched speechless as a girl in blood covered armor roared throughout the night until exhaustion took her consciousness. After witnessing an explosion such as that, Grace has given Amiria a wide berth of space.

Amiria crosses her arms sheepishly, "I'm sorry about last night. It's nice to meet you."

Grace softens at the sight, a Winged Rider can be shy? No, a young girl. A young girl who has been through more than she can imagine. "You have nothing to apologize for. It is nice to officially meet you too." It had never occurred to her before last night that Winged Riders are human too. Many of them, like Amiria, are barely older than children.

Stepping up behind Grace, Giles places his hands on her shoulders, "See I told you."

Grace leans back into him whispering over her shoulder, "If I didn't see her armor, I would never have guessed she is the one who—you know."

Amiria only hugs herself tighter, "I want to thank you, Grace."

Confusion rolls over her face as she straightens up, "Thank me?"

"Thank you for being here for Mr. Bakere when I could not. It makes me feel better knowing he wasn't alone through these times. He's like a father to me."

"Oh—um—it is my pleasure. I love Giles, what is important to him, is important to me," She stammers.

"Good, that's good." Amiria's smile reveals sadness of an aching heart. The words "*I love…*" bringing her mind directly to the boy sleeping upstairs.

Giles steps away from Grace and turns Amiria to face the stairs, "Go on. I'll bring supper up to you." With a nudge from Giles, Amiria sprints up the stairs.

Using only her fingertips, Amiria taps the door open. It swings open effortlessly revealing the slumbering boy exactly how she had left him this morning. He has survived the initial wound and blood loss, but she dreads blood poisoning. If only he would open his eyes and let her know he is okay.

Before entering the room, she glances over her shoulders at Ignis who is standing on his hind legs and poking his head through the window. Amiria leaves the door open for Ignis to see his best friend then she drags her heavy feet across the room. With his hand resting on top of the covers, she slips her fingers into his and collapses onto the stool. Shuddering with incoming tears she presses the back of his hand, clasped in hers, to her cheek.

Please wake up.

His light eyelashes lay resting on his cheekbones as he continues his endless slumber. The blanket pulled up to his bare chest hides the bandages wrapped around his middle, but because you can't see them, doesn't mean they aren't there. With her cheek stuck to his hand, she watches him breathe, the only sign he is still with her. She presses her lips to the back of his knuckles, she can taste the salt left behind from her tears.

Making sure Stirling is the last thing she sees, Amiria rests her head on the bed and closes her eyes.

Giles holds a bowl of roasted carrots and potatoes with a chunk of barley bread as he stops in the threshold of the bedroom.

Grace touches his arm, "Let her sleep."

Quietly, Giles crosses the room and sets the bowl on the bed beside her.

The room comes into view, blurred like an oil painting ruined by the rain. His body feels heavy and he can barely lift his arms. His sluggish eyes fall to the object weighing down his hand. His fingers lay curled around something tan. A blurry purple figure with dark extensions lays attached to it.

Amiria.

Her hand falls free from his as he fights against the invisible restraints trying to stop him from lifting his hand high enough to run along the top of her head. His hand slides down her hair and drops limply to his side.

His eyes slip back shut.

His vision cracks open. It must be morning. Light raining in from the open door stings his sensitive eyes. He curls and uncurls his empty hand, longing for the small fingers to intertwine with his.

"*Stirling?*" He hears Ignis' voice before he falls back under.

Without opening his eyes he can tell it is night. The chill air of the room is a relief to his fevering skin. He curls his fingers closed. The soft hand is there again.

He feels the pressure of something cradled against him. The light floods his eyes as his vision returns. His head lobs to the side lethargically. The curvature of Amiria's back is pressed to his side and her arms wrap around his, cradling it to her chest. Her face is nuzzled against his bicep as she sleeps.

He takes in his surroundings, the day is unknown to him, the time is unknown to him. It can be dusk or dawn, he doesn't know.

His body still feels too heavy to move but even if he could, he doesn't want to. He doesn't want to disturb Amiria, he doesn't know how long she has been asleep.

"Stirling?" Ignis' voice pipes into his slowly awakening mind. Ignis's head pops through the window in the other room. *"Good morning, sleepyhead."*

"Morning?" Stirling replies, his head still feeling cloudy.

"Boy do I have a lot to fill you in on."

"I was cut," Stirling points out.

"More than cut, I didn't know humans had that much blood," Ignis replies insensitively.

"I'm not dead?"

"Not unless I'm your guardian angel," Ignis teases.

Stirling groans in reply. He looks back down at Amiria still snuggled against him. He closes his eyes, reliving the last moments he can remember. He had watched her kill King Dietrich. He watched as the king's head fell separate from his body. Squeezing his eyes he tries not to think about what he saw on the castle roof. Her face showed nothing when she watched Kinsey fall to her death. He has always known death was part of being a member of the Winged Cavalry, but witnessing her—his eyelids lift, letting his hazel eyes search the ceiling beams—witnessing her take the life of someone good or bad feels different in his mind. After all this, is she still Amiria? Is he still Stirling?

"So," Ignis begins his tale, *"you were there dying."*

Amiria pushes open the door to her old bed chamber. A weak line of light from the corridor draws a divide across the room. His dazzling smile is luminated as the light strikes it. Amiria turns to run but finds herself in the center of the room, out of reach of the door. She reaches out with a silent shout for help as it slams close.

He's behind her. The warmth of his breath kisses the back of her neck. She can't move, her body snagged in his entrapment as his elongated fingers curl around her arms. He dips his head pressing his mouth to her ear.

She can feel his lips move against her skin as he speaks. "I'm sorry, Amiria, but you made me do this." His hand crawls across her until she is wrapped up in his arms, and her back cracks against his chest. "I'm sorry. I love you too much. I'm sorry."

He continues to crawl, his fingertips run over her collar bone. "I'm so sorry." His fingers encase her neck. Her head slams back against his chest. Choking, she grapples at the claws trying to pry them off.

"I'm sorry. I'm so sorry. I have to. I'm sorry. I love you." The grip is tightening. Amiria coughs and chokes as she desperately tries to drink the air around her. Her mouth gaping open, unable to call out as her jugular is crushed within his ever-tightening grip.

"You made me do this. I'm sorry. This is your fault." A dying wheeze escapes her lips.

"Are you okay?" She hears through the rushing of her ears The presence is gone, and she stands alone in the chamber. "Amiria?" The disembodied voice asks again.

Rolling over, Amiria's arm slings over Stirling's stomach. Her fingers curling around his side, she pulls herself closer to him, pressing her face against the warmth of his chest, stealing his heat. Her eyes move rapidly behind her eyelids as she stirs.

"Amiria?" Stirling brushes her hair back from her face.

Her eyes flutter open. She feels the blood in her veins make a final pulse as her heart stops. The world is put on hold as she looks into Stirling's hazel eyes.

"Good morning," he says weakly with a lopsided grin.

The air catches in her lungs as she leaps up. Grabbing Stirling's head, she gives him a dozen tiny kisses over his entire face.

Stirling winces between his rasping laugh. I m in ured, remember

She sits back to take all of him in. "Sorry." She wipes her eyes. "You're awake." She lets out a single breathy laugh. "You're really awake." Curling her fingers through his curls she leans in, placing a soft kiss on his lips then presses her forehead to his. "I love you, baker boy."

Stirling's heavy arms find their way up to her frame. Running his hands from the small of her back to her shoulder blades, he pulls her into him kissing her harder. A soft moan resonates deep in his throat as they meld together.

"*Whistle whistle,*" Ignis interrupts.

Breaking off his kiss with Amiria, Stirling throws his head back on the pillow. "Why Ignis? Why?"

Amiria looks out the door to see the orange dragon struggling to keep his head through the window as he stands on his hind legs. Enveloped in Stirling's arms, she lowers herself to gently rest her head on his chest. "When did you wake up?"

"Just before sunrise. Ignis filled me in on the past few days."

Amiria sits up abruptly. Stirling winces as his hands fall limply to the side.

"Sorry," she apologizes. "I didn't realize how late in the morning it was. I didn't wake up for my meeting."

She has been on a strict schedule. Giles helps wake her up. Clyde arrives by wagon and escorts her to meeting after meeting running laws, policies, systems, and structures. They have been making the finalized decisions on the royal family to keep their status as a high noble house and will be able to keep their careers as dukes and lords. They will be allowed to keep their current living quarters due to the leaders of the Winged Cavalry opting to stay in their family manors outside of the castle.

"My father came by earlier, he said he told a guy named Captain Mannering that you needed the day off."

She collapses back to the bed beside Stirling. "Sometimes I think this is all a dream and I'm going to wake up in the oubliette. But yet, knowing this isn't a dream is terrifying too." She covers her face with her arm.

"What do you mean?"

She keeps her eyes hidden as she talks. "I killed a king, Stirling. Killed him. I wasn't dragged through the streets for regicide. I was made second in command. It's stressful rebuilding a Kingdom after that. Trying to not miss a step, the fear of a second rebellion or a foreign attack. If it's been done once, it can be done again."

"What do you mean second in command?" Stirling asks.

Amiria rolls over, turning away from Stirling. "I'm no longer the daughter of the Field Marshal of the Winged Cavalry. I'm General Amiria Rey of the Isles of Wyverna."

Stirling is taken back, unsure of what to think. "G-General? You're in the Cavalry again?"

She sits up but she looks at her shoulder instead. "Not only the Cavalry, but over all of Wyverna. It's only for the time being. I owe it to the people."

"And how long is *for the time being?*"

Amiria doesn't answer.

"Amiria, you don't owe them anything." His voice is gentle. "You've done more than enough for them." He leans his head forward, unable to sit up, he wants to look her in the eye. "When I'm fit to leave, I will be heading back to Patu, I made a promise and Patu is my home. Not Wyverna, it has tried to kill me too many times. I want to know Amiria, will you be coming back with me or are you staying here?"

"I—let me get you something to eat." She removes herself from the bed. "You must be starving." She drops the subject and Stirling watches her leave the room with a frown.

Sixty-Six

Faces blend together like grains of sand on the beach, each a speckle contributing to something greater. Insignificant on their own but together they create something moving, a true sight to behold. They stand in a mass coating the grounds surrounding the entrance gate to the castle.

Amiria stands at the ready with her hands behind her back in line with Lt General Ward, Major Puttock, and Brigadier Terrowin. They stand in matching uniforms atop the gate—silver chain mail below a quartered red tabard, the color of military strength. Removing the color purple signifying royalty and power from the Cavalry's coat of arms, they replaced it with light blue for loyalty and honesty.

Derek Rey, Field Marshal of Isles of Wyverna, stands in front of his people.

The citizens of Lumierna stare up at him with curious minds, anxiously waiting on what kind of news will be delivered that warranted them all to be brought to the castle instead of their market squares.

Taking in a deep breath, Derek Rey's voice projects over the crowd, "A few of you might recognize me, many of you recognize my daughter Amiria Rey." He turns his over his shoulder to her then returns to the audience, "I've walked these streets amongst you for over twenty years. I feel like a neighbor when I look out over your faces—I am your neighbor, but I am also your Field Marshal, no longer only in command over the Winged Cavalry but over the entirety of Wyverna. I stand here today to serve you, the people, with my daughter Amiria Rey—" He motions his hand to her with a proud smile, "as your General."

Amiria is stunned, for the first time in her life her father gave her the look of approval. He smiled with fulfillment as if she finally finished putting herself together and no longer needed improvement.

"I speculate you've heard rumors of our former king's demise." The crowd breaks out into a murmur. "He has been laid to rest and the royal family's lineage has been concluded. Your kingdom will no longer be ruled by a monarch. It will be run by the Cavalry. The leadership rolls you see standing here will no longer be by birthright, but instead earned. If it takes a team to run a military, it should take a team to run a kingdom. Criers will be dispatched to repeat this message for the next several days for those who did not attend today. They will then make their way to all cities across Wyverna. Many of the laws will remain the same. To keep everyone employed you will still be assigned a trade. By default it will be the trade of your family, though if you can prove significant talent in another trade you can request permission to change. Which leads to how a few laws have changed. The age of marking an insignia will be raised to adulthood at sixteen to reassure it is the correct career path. Then the practice of another trade will be decriminalized as long as it is nonprofit. That concludes the end of my announcement. Any further updates will be carried out by a crier. It is our honor to serve the people of

Wyverna." Derek Rey bows to his citizens. Straightening out, he takes a step back to join the rest of the council beside her.

Amiria blinks. She sat at the table when these laws were decided but hearing them spoken has brought written fiction into reality. She can hear the indistinguishable words of the crowd as they speak to their neighbors, but she can't pick out what they are talking about. They sound like the wind in her ears as she dives from the clouds. They will still be assigned trades but they have a choice to change, they had agreed this was the best way to keep the unemployment at bay and Wyverna successful while still giving the people a freedom of choice.

The cord of the citole hums faint sounds as Stirling's pale thumb strums down on the wire, pushing it down until his thumb passes, letting the wire snap back into place.

"Good," Grace encourages, "Now use your finger tip to basically pull up on the cord letting it slip away.

She sits on the foot of the bed instructing the still feverish Stirling who hasn't found the strength to get out of bed. Giles sits on the stool stationed against the wall. He leans back relaxed as he watches his son, alive and recovering, strum another cord.

He scans the bandage around Stirling's stomach. This place had almost stolen his son from the world again but like every time before he planted his feet in the soil and refused to leave. Like a sunflower he smiles towards the sun brightening up each day it rises. Its long stalks appear weak and unstable but when surrounded by its peers, it is resilient against the strongest of winds.

He would love for Stirling to stay here in Wyverna, in this bakery. He can now with the new laws and Amiria as General. If he wanted he could join the Cavalry, but Giles can see it in Stirling's eyes. Wyverna is not his home. It never was. He always belonged somewhere else and he had finally found it. For the sake of his son's happiness, Giles will watch his son leave one more time. Stirling is meant to be in Patu, not here.

Stirling peers up from the citole as Amiria shuffles through the open bedroom door. Exhausted she nods at Giles before walking to the other side of the bed and collapsing beside Stirling.

"Long day?" he asks, setting the citole on his lap and pats Amiria's head. She nuzzles her face into his thigh nodding. "Anything exciting?"

She shakes her head. "How's citole lessons?" she mumbles, barely audible.

"Good, it's really fun." Stirling plucks a cord aimlessly. He had asked Grace to teach him to help pass the time, but he has also used it as an excuse to get to know her, and to apologize for the way he behaved the first time they had met. He had grown to like Grace over the day he had spent with her. She cares about his father and the things he cares about. Seeing the way she makes him smile soothes Stirling's own peace and mind. He's become grateful to her. He knows he no longer needs to worry about his father.

Grace smiles like a proud mother. "He's actually picking it up quite quickly."

Amiria rolls onto her back as she rolls her eyes. "Of course, he is." Other than combat she knows Stirling has a lucky gift at learning any trade he tries.

She's still jealous of his multi trade talent. She had tried mundane chores in Patu, but could barely manage cracking an egg. Will she ever be able to learn the qualities to live outside the castle? Will she be able to grow and prepare her food, build and create everyday items, or mend clothing? Or, will all she ever manage to be is a Winged Rider, no matter where she lives?

"Supper should be done stewing," Giles states from his place against the wall. With a groan, he pushes off his knees and stands up. "Stirling, I'll help you get to the table."

Sliding off the bed, Amiria's now vacant space is replaced by the citole as Stirling sets it aside. Grimacing, he steadily shimmies his legs off the bed, careful not to move his torso too much.

Amiria frowns at his discomfort. "You can stay in the bed, you know. I can bring you the food."

Grasping his father's arm, Stirling weakly stands. "No. I want to be at the table," is all he tells her but never expands on why.

Amiria doesn't argue. Flanking his side, she walks beside him as his supportive father acts as a crutch walking him to the dining table. Sitting down as gently as he can, Stirling grips his bandaged wound, his teeth grinding as he holds back an exasperated sound of pain. He gives Amiria a promising smile, but the look of concern on her face doesn't waver.

Giles dishes out a hearty barley stew in wooden bowls then hands them to Grace to set before Amiria and Stirling. Tearing a loaf of leftover rye bread that is beginning to stale into four pieces, Giles distributes them out. Amiria thanks Giles and dips her portion halfway into her stew to soak. A shadow darkens the room. She can see Stirling's lips curl up with delight, that can only mean one thing.

With a mouthful of bread, Giles grumbles, "That dragon of yours better not scratch the outside of my bakery."

Amiria turns on the bench seat to see Ignis once again nosing his way through the window. She eyes Ignis as she speaks to Giles. "Don't worry, Mr. Bakere. I can compensate for any structural damage caused by Stirling's discourteous dragon."

The orange dragon huffs. *"I'm not breaking anything."* Something can be heard cracking. *"Except for that. Ignore that. I just miss you Stirling."*

"I miss you too," Stirling says for everyone to hear, his heart reaching out through his mind to Ignis.

Amiria chuckles, after all these years she can feel as if she could read Ignis' mind through his mannerisms, "Let me guess, he stated I'm not breaking anything as he broke something."

"Precisely." Stirling grins.

Giles shakes his head, "I never thought it possible to talk to a dragon, if you told me a year ago I would have thought you two were mad, but here we are with a dragon's head through my window."

"I only recently discovered the secret, but Stirling unknowingly discovered it ten years ago." Amiria playfully pokes his arm, "He managed to figure out what others spend their entire lives searching for and still die never knowing."

He holds his hand up turning down Amiria's gloating, "Except the secret is being weak, so it's nothing to be proud of."

Amiria clicks her tongue, "Showing weakness and being weak are different."

Ignis snorts, *"Unless you're, Stirling."*

"Shut up, Ignis," Stirling jokes.

Amiria raises a dark eyebrow and Stirling fills her in, granting a laugh from the entire table.

"You're far from being weak." She lowers her chin bashfully, "A weak person would never have done what you did." Sucking in his lower lip, Stirling tries to hide his coy smile. "You've saved me twice now." Amiria bumps her shoulder with his, "My hero."

Giles laughs silently beside Grace as he watches his son turn redder than a beet. The conversation takes a lighter turn and Amiria listens in on the mindless topics. Now and then Stirling refers to Patu, the villagers, Eve, and Quilan, while Giles and Grace tell stories of the neighbors and her grown children.

This is what Amiria used to dream about when she visited Giles. Sitting at this table conversing over a meal about their days like a family.

A family.

Nibbling on her now soggy bread, she watches Stirling out of the corner of her eye. The way his jaw moves as he chews, his neck bobbing as he swallows and immediately begins to talk again. She lowers her eyes to his hand resting on the table. She has to make a decision soon. She knows this perfect scene won't last forever. Stirling is anxious to return to Patu. The only thing holding him back is—she looks at the wound beneath the bandage. He isn't here still because he wants to be. Why can't she have both worlds, why does she have to choose.

Stirling stops chewing mid bite. He stares down at his hand now occupied by Amiria's. With a mouthful of food, he smiles at her.

Sixty-Seven

Wearing a lavender brigandine over a golden tunic, Amiria leans over a map of Wyverna. Her dark blades are displayed upon her back. Her father, wearing his usual golden brigandine with a new red cape over one shoulder, paces their private cabinet.

She couldn't take King Dietrich's old cabinet. Even with a new set of furniture she couldn't remove his prying eyes from her mind whenever she entered the room. So they made a new one, a new cabinet for a new leadership. No center point desk for a single man to sit at but a massive table for a group to conjure around. Shelves line the walls with enough scrolls and books to be considered a library.

Her father doesn't stop pacing as he speaks, "If we truly want the citizens to follow our leadership we will have to visit every town of significant size. A crier will not suffice in the long run. We need to connect to the people, meet face to face. Show them we are human too and not a name to fear. We will keep our people in the light. We have to tread carefully though. We will not rule by fear but we don't want people to hold their own revolt. We need to gain their respect."

Amiria nods, running her finger over the port town where Nellie was stationed. "You are correct Field Marshal, we have lost too many of our own already."

"Cavalry or citizens?" He stops pacing, now locked on her.

"Yes," she answers, blinking up at him.

"Correct, we need to unify." He nods, returning to his pacing.

A knock raps on the door followed by a voice, "Field Marshal, I have the maps you requested."

"You may enter."

Amiria doesn't raise her head as she hears the click of the door handle, but she feels something familiar triggering a promise she made several weeks ago when the guard respectfully enters. He holds out the rolled map in the direction of the Field Marshal. Dropping the map he ducks, dodging a book aimed at his head. The pages flutter as it slides out into the corridor.

"ROBERT!" Amiria shouts. "Don't you think I forgot about the promise I made!" She steps around the table drawing her blades.

Cowering, Robert steps backwards towards the door. "Excuse me, sir." Robert bows to Derek Rey still taking retreating steps backward. He reaches the door frame as Amiria charges. He skitters and takes off down the hall.

Blades in hand Amiria slides into the hall, shouting threats to his retreating form. "Go run to William!"

"General," her father drawls.

"Sir?" Amiria turns back to him.

His eyes crinkle as he smiles saying in a joking tone, "Didn't I just say we won't rule by fear."

"Yes, you did, sir, my apologies. But I made a promise. and Reys always keep their word."

Derek Rey's grin widens. "Good, General. Now where were we."

A line of people snake out of the throne room and through the castle, with everyone waiting to speak their grievances to the new council. Amiria nods as the man standing before them's words go in one ear and out the other. A scribe's quill scratches at his parchment as he takes down what Derek Rey declares as a solution to the man.

Amiria's head crashes onto the pillow exhausted after a long day.

Parchment after parchment is slid across Amiria's desk as she and the rest of the council read over the current taxes per city in Wyverna. Amiria sighs, her eyes going cross as they fail to focus on yet another paragraph of dry legal matter.

Her eyes close as her head makes contact with her pillow.

The council sits at the table in their cabinet. "We need your decision, General?"
Amiria brings her eyes up from where she was scratching at the table, "Yeah—What was the question again?"
"The new trade agreements with Uviktiland."

Her head hits the pillow.

"General, we need you to sign—"

Head to pillow.

"General, the issue still needs to be resolved."

Stirling rolls over, awakening to the sound of boots clunking to the ground. He speaks through a yawn, "You're getting back later each time." His eyes follow Amiria's shadowy figure in the nearly lightless room as it moves across to the bed.

"Yeah." Her voice is a whisper.

"Did you eat?"

"Yeah." She lays down with her back to him.

"Anything interesting happen?"

He can feel her shrug, "Not really."

"Oh." He doesn't reach for her as he sinks back into the bed. He lies on his back awake, watching the imaginary shapes swirling about in the dark room as he waits for breathing to change to the soft rhythm of sleep. If there is one thing he can do for her, is comfort her when the nightmares begin—and they always arrive.

Amiria stirs with a whimper pulling herself into a ball. Stirling rolls onto his side, curling his body around her and soothingly rubs her arm. Still asleep, Amiria unfurls and turns into his chest seeking refuge. Her body relaxes as he settles his arm protectively around her.

It's not until he hears her breathing patterns return to normal before he closes his eyes.

"I'm late," Amiria vocalizes as she bounds down the steps of the bakery. She finishes tightening the straps of her double scabbard over her new brigandine. Maybe she should start sleeping at the castle. It's been three weeks of this commute and it has cost her tardiness on several accounts. Clyde stopped escorting her after the first week when Stirling woke up. No need to watch over *her* anymore. He is now in command of the whole Guard and has too much on his plate to worry about to chauffeur her around. He isn't her nanny.

Stirling stands beside Ignis, fixing a cart to his harness to help his father run errands and pick up a month's supplies. His coin is worthless here but he packed items of value he can bargain with, like silver cloak pins and new leather gloves.

"Morning," Stirling says with a sunny smile. Amiria doesn't acknowledge him as she fusses with the straps of her back scabbard. She passes by him without a glance. "Amiria?" he calls to her.

"What!" she snaps, spinning around to him. Stirling shrinks back, unable to speak. "What is it, Stirling? I'm already late."

"I just—" Stirling fumbles with his words. "Well—I'm leaving tomorrow—I want to know if you're coming?"

Amiria blinks twice before finding herself facing away from him towards the castle. "I'm late," is all she replies.

"*What's her deal?*" Ignis scrunches his snout. "*She's been more temperamental than normal, and that's saying a lot for her.*"

Stirling shrugs off the encounter. Ignis is right. She used to come back to the bakery exhausted but she was still the Amiria he loved, nevertheless. The same girl he fell in love with back in the cave, but the past week she has been changing into someone he doesn't recognize. In the past he has seen her yell and threaten other people with harm. He has seen her kill—he pushes the memory away. But when it came to the true her, she was warm and loving, an Amiria only reserved for people she was comfortable to let her guard down around. Now, she only speaks to him as if they were only acquaintances.

"It must be the stress of the job. Being a General over an entire Kingdom can't be easy." Stirling defends her behavior.

"*Does she still lay beside you?*" Ignis asks as they head towards the market grocer.

"Yes and no. It's more like it's somewhere she crashes at the end of the day. The most I hear from her is from the nightmares I know still plague her. She mumbles and stirs most of the night, but won't let me comfort her or tell me what they are about."

"*That can't be healthy,*" Ignis comments.

"No, won't do her any good if she can't sleep well. All this, this is why she needs to leave this place, this place will be the death of us. In one form" He looks up towards the castle, then touches his side. "Or another, and I really don't want to die in Wyverna."

"*Is that why you keep surviving each deadly encounter? Pure stubbornness?*" Ignis teases.

"Yep."

"*Would you rather die in Patu?*"

"I'd rather live in Patu."

Amiria curls her knees into her chest. "*He's leaving tomorrow. He keeps asking me to go with him. Asking me to be with him.*" Amiria sits on the slanted roof top of the courtyard. This is where she had killed Kinsey. This is where Calix had kissed her, and she had kissed him back.

"*What have you told him?*" Taika asks, her body laying out across the tiles, taking in the sun.

Amiria hides her face between her knees. "*Nothing. I've given him nothing but short answers and diverting the topic.*" Just like the Cavalry had taught her. You can't get hurt if you hold no one close.

"*I think you owe him at least an answer,*" Taika says like a stern mother.

Amiria shrugs. "*I can't answer what I don't know. I don't know why this decision is so hard.*"

"*You only have tonight to decide. Pull him aside and speak to him alone. Don't think about your answer beforehand. Just say what comes to mind first when you look at him.*"

Falling back on the slates, she stares numbly as the clouds float far above her reach. She might have danced with Calix in the courtyard below her, but the clouds were reserved for her and Stirling. A place where worries didn't exist and they only had each other. She closes her eyes, holding the memories close.

Sixty-Eight

"Are you sure you're well enough?" Giles pesters as Stirling packs the last of the items he had brought to Wyverna, tools, spare clothing, blankets, and restocked provisions in the leather bags ready to be hooked onto Ignis' hips. "You can rest another week."

Stirling stuffs another worn out linen tunic he had traded his father for with his quality cotton into the bag. Being the father of the baker who flew, Giles is no longer in dire need of coin. His signature cheese stuffed bread has been flying off the shelves. Amiria had offered Giles a position in the castle's kitchen but Giles only stated he would sit on it. He can't see himself ever leaving his bakery, especially now since Grace has officially unofficially moved in. Maybe he will take on an apprentice to pass it on to, one of Grace's daughters had shown interest in learning how to bake.

"Father, it's been almost a month since the incident. Flying won't be a problem, and I don't plan on fighting—ever." Stirling leaves the bag and sits on the bed. He looks over at the few items belonging to Amiria sitting packed in a bag in the corner of the room. Her black armor and the underclothing she had worn that night remain in a heap where she tossed them. His blood still coats the metal, now dried and stained on her once soaked garments.

She had packed her stuff last night without saying a word to him.

He lies back on the bed with his legs hanging off, he talks to the rafters, "She still hasn't told me what she is doing. Every time I bring up leaving, she gets quiet or changes the topic."

Giles leans back against the wall. He glances over at Amiria's belongings then back to Stirling. Sensing that Stirling already has an inkling of what the answer might be, Giles holds back and remains silent.

"*Stirling, I have a message.*" Ignis mentally pushes through.

Stirling sits up, "*From Amiria?*"

"*Yes. Taika says to meet them at the plateau.*"

"*Right now?*"

"*Right now.*"

Stirling meets his father's gaze, "Amiria wants me to meet with her." He pauses, letting the unsettled feeling in stomach grow and begin to eat away at him. "I'm scared of what she has to say."

Giles crosses the room and rests his hand on his son's shoulder offering him a gentle squeeze. "Better to hear an answer you don't like than to leave without one." Biting his lip, Stirling looks down at his lap. Giles tussles his hair. "I'll save you supper."

Her dark red and light blue tabard with the Winged Cavalry's coat of arms billows around her legs as she stands at the edge of the plateau overlooking the ocean. The chain mail fitted to her small frame glows fiery with the setting sun. Amiria crosses her arms behind her back. This is where she met Stirling, she sat down beside him and learned about what events brought him to that moment as the sun rose on their new day.

The sun gave a new light to Wyverna that morning as Stirling enlightened her on a world of possibilities. There is more to life than duty and responsibility to the Cavalry. He taught her about freedom. How to have fun and develop trust through friendship. He had shown her what it is like to truly love someone. He was the first person who hadn't tried to control her. He just wants her to be happy. Even if that means he's not involved.

With her hands still clasped behind her back she turns only her head to watch Ignis land on the pads of his feet. He lowers his belly to the ground to help Stirling with an easier departure.

Stirling plants his feet firmly on the ground then almost crumples as he locks eyes with Amiria. His stomach twists and his heart flips no matter how many times he sees her. He thinks back to the first day he saw her. They were only children and she didn't know he existed. He thought of her as a prude with her nose in the air, too good for the rest of the class. How he unknowingly developed a crush on the talented girl. Then he finds out she's just as lonely and outcasted as he was. That's the woman he fell in love with. She's strong and incredible, but she laid her armor down and became his friend. It's not the warrior he loves, it's his best friend he wants to be with...or so he thought. Now...he is unsure.

Her shoulders follow her head and squares off to him with her chin held high. A General stands before him now.

His fingers curl around Ignis' harness, keeping himself from running to her, stopping himself from scooping her into his arms and kissing her until the sun disappears. Letting go he walks toward her at a steady pace.

"Hey." Her voice is strong but her smile is weak. His feet stop on the gritty earth just out of reach.

Struggling to hold his face neutral, he asks, "Why all the way out here?"

Shrugging Amiria's eyes fall to the canyon, "I don't know."

Stirling sets his jaw waiting for her to talk. To finally speak the words she's had on her tongue but refused to say this past week. To tell him what she had brought him all the way out here for, but she stands there idly staring at the canyon where they had both trained under different circumstances.

"Amiria?" Her name said with his voice snaps her back. Her head turns to him with her eyes lingering on the canyon. Still, she can't meet his eyes, she peers past his shoulder to Ignis who responds by lowering his head.

"Ignis must be excited." The words are muddied, something to fill the silence and delay the inevitable.

Stirling is short, "He is."

"Stirling," she says to the ties of his tunic. She pictures reaching out to the strands, mindlessly fiddling with his clothing as she talks. How she would run her hand up to his neck and pull him down to her and they will share the same space, breathing put on hold as their lips interlock. How is she supposed to talk if she can barely catch her breath?

"You're staying, aren't you?" Stirling concedes for her. It's not the first time she's made this decision but this time it hurts differently, as if the *I love yous* or the intimate evening they shared didn't mean anything in the end.

Her glistening eyes trail up his body to meet his, "I didn't—"

He cuts her off. "You don't need to. You've shown it. If you were coming back to Patu with me, we would be sharing a laugh over supper in the bakery. Not—" He raises his hands to the plateau. "Be here."

"You need to understand, It's just I can't. I can't leave them. I owe them," Amiria defends.

"Amiria." Stirling doesn't want to hear her excuses. Even if it hurts, he wants her to say it plain and simple to him, *I want to stay.*

"They need me," she says with pleading eyes.

"I need you!" His voice begins to rise but he drops it back down, "but it's always the same—I will always come second to Wyverna."

Amiria shakes her head, "It's not like—" she starts.

"But it is." Stirling's face twists with his breaking heart. "Tell me. What has Wyverna ever done for you?" He steps closer to her, "Take your time and really think about it. What has it *ever* done for you?" Amiria's eyes search the marigold clouds for the answer yet she finds nothing but empty air. Stirling continues, "You can't stop yourself from serving Wyverna unconditionally. You are ready to give your life for them and they—and they expect you to. How many of them would do the same for you?"

Amiria opens her mouth but doesn't answer.

"Those guards, they stood by as we almost *died.* They *would* have let us die if you didn't kill King Dietrich. Then they march in when all is safe and say they are at your command. They used you Amiria and they are still using you. You were merely a tool to do a chore they didn't want to. You were a scapegoat in case it all went awry."

Stirling's head snaps to the side. He stares at the shadowing canyon with his cheek stinging with a thousand needles. Amiria's open hand still hanging in the air, her face a new shade of red.

"SHUT UP!" she screams.

Stirling slowly raises his hand to touch his cheek already reddened with broken blood vessels. With his hand on his face he turns to her with a shattered heart. Amiria retracts her hand as she reads his pained face, a deep hurt not caused by physical pain.

"Stirling—I'm so sorry—" She reaches for him, "I didn't mean—"

He bats her hand away, "Don't." He takes a fearful step back.

"Stirling." Her voice is a broken whisper. She takes half a step forward but he only retreats another full step back.

"No—no Amiria. You've made it clear. I—I meant what I said because I care about you. I truly thought you saw a life outside the Cavalry, but I guess you had us both fooled." Tears are whelming up in his eyes, distorting his vision.

She doesn't try to close the distance, "Stirling, I need to stay. You can stay too, please, it's just a little longer."

"What's a little longer? A week? A month? *A year?* I never wanted to return here in the first place." He grimaces and jabs his finger at the ground.

"Please, Stirling." She can feel the tickle in the back of her throat. She won't cry. She can't cry. She pushes it back down watching him take another half a step away from her.

"My life is no longer here. Ignis' life is no longer here." He wipes away a tear that had escaped, "So if staying here makes you happy then stay. Otherwise I'll wait for you until sunrise." With a stake in his chest he catches her eye, "but no longer."

He waits a moment for her to reply. She says nothing, she mouths words she can't seem to form, her fingers twitching at her side. They long to intertwine with his, to feel his callouses against hers, but she can't watch him recoil from her again. What has she done?

With the sound of gravel beneath his foot Stirling turns back to Ignis. He wipes away the tears beginning to flow down his cheeks.

An anvil sits on her chest, breaking through her ribcage and obliterating her heart. With blurring vision she looks down at her trembling hands. What has she become? She wanted to tell him she was staying, he had guessed right, but she didn't want it to turn into this. How did it turn into this?

After all they've been through, the happiness and the sorrow they experienced together, this is the memory he is leaving with. She's just another one of Wyverna's monsters. She thinks of her old teammates, Kinsey…Calix. Time after time they let Wyverna and the Cavalry consume every ounce humanity in them until they are a soulless shell functioning on a life of orders.

She watches Stirling's back. He doesn't turn around as he slowly approaches Ignis. She clenches her fist biting, *Come back,* as he mounts the orange dragon. But there are no words to undo the damage she's done to him. She hurt him with her actions, her words, and—she lifts her hand—physically.

Why had his words caused her to react like that? Was she upset he was spilling out lies to coax her into leaving with him, or is it because deep down she knew what he was saying was true?

Feeling the gales of wind, she watches her hero return to the sky. She is finally seen as perfect in her father's eyes. Standing strong and powerful at the top. Squeezing her eyes shut she fights a losing battle of holding back the tears. Here she is, standing at the top like she, no *he*, always wanted, but it is a lonely place to be.

She wants to scream, she wants to hit.

Collect yourself, compose yourself.

She crosses her arms behind her back and takes in a deep breath letting it out slowly. Turning about face, she returns to Taika.

"You sure you made the right choice?" Taika asks.

"I hope so. Otherwise I gave up everything for nothing."

On Ignis' back, Stirling doubles over from the pain deeper than the slash across his stomach. These scars on his skin are nothing more than physical reminders of why he wants nothing to do with Wyverna. But their pain is shallow. They heal and disappear over time. The pain deep in his soul is here to stay. Like the insignia on his arm, his heart will forever be scarred.

Who was the girl on the plateau?

"You okay? Like your face is it okay? I'm gonna guess emotionally no," Ignis asks.

Stirling touches the sensitive skin of his red cheek, *"Yeah, just took me by surprise."*

Giles and Grace's heads turn from their places at the table in the bakery. Their conversing smiles drop as they see Stirling's tear blotched face. He passes them by without granting them a nod hello and storms up the stairs to the bedroom.

Sharing a glance with Grace, Giles pushes back from the table and stands up, "I'm going to go talk to him."

Stomping across the room, Stirling throws himself stomach down onto the bed and hides his face in his arms. He can feel the bed frame shift as his father sits beside him.

Giles sighs, "Do you want to talk about it?" Stirling shakes his head without removing his face from its hiding place. "Do you want me to leave?" Giles asks, looking at the sand colored curls. They flop back and forth as Stirling shakes his head.

"Stay." His voice is muffled by the blanket.

Waiting patiently, Giles watches the dust float through the dimming light, the last streams of natural light before settling down for the night.

Stirling finally lifts his head, unable to look at his father he speaks to the wall, "How did you know you wanted to marry mum? Like how did you know you wanted forever?" Stirling crinkles his face as he thinks, "How did you do it all over again with Grace?"

Facing the opposing wall of the room as Stirling, Giles sighs, "No one really knows. Love is weird, something you can't control. One day you just see them and you just, well, you just know."

Bringing his knees up, Stirling sits up cross legged in the center of the bed. He moves his hands grasping for the words, "I—" He hangs his head, "I wanted forever, but—not anymore." He wipes his eyes damp with new tears, "I thought we were in love." He drops his hands to play with the hem of his pants, "But now—I don't know who she is."

Giles reaches over to lift Stirling's chin to meet his red rimmed eyes, "You did love her." Stirling pulls his chin away, diverting his gaze. Giles continues, "You *did*. But listen, people change, especially after—after what you two have experienced. I love Amiria too, like a daughter except—" Giles sighs. "I think you should go home to…"

"Patu."

"Go home to Patu. Be with your new friends. Live your life. Fall in love again."

Eve and Quilan are waiting for me. Stirling wipes the last remnants of his tears. He belongs in Patu. He is happy in Patu. He is happy with them. He belongs with *them*.

Giles squeezes Stirling's knee. "You can go home knowing you saved your friend's life and a whole kingdom of people. She's alive and successful all because of you." He points at Stirling's chest. "Now." He opens his arms pulling Stirling into an embrace, "It's time for you to focus on yourself."

Sixty-Nine

The door to her old chamber swings open on dry hinges with a groan. Standing in the threshold of the doorway she stares at the cold and empty room. Her purple painted furniture, tapestries, and furs all given away or sold. She holds her oil light out, only her arm entering the room casting heavy shadows behind the replaced furniture.

Her body spasms, almost dropping her light as she sees a tall figure in the corner of her room. Swinging the light, she casts it upon the threat. Her body relaxes as she sees her silver armor glowing with the reflection of the candlelight. They had moved her armor from the stand in their private armory to her room in preparation for her.

With a prickle down her spine, she grabs the handle of the door and slams it shut, retreating to the safety of the corridor.

Derek Rey laughs as he sucks the duck grease from his fingers. Arietta sits across from him at the dinner table as she holds a strand of her long dark hair over her lips mimicking a mustache.

Swirling the wine in her pewter chalice she raises it to her nose and inhales it, "I say."

The house is warm with a steady fire and lit by the laughter of the loving couple. Derek shakes his head, slowing his laugh. He can't help but smile as he looks over at her. The ear-to-ear grin fades as a knock on the door stills them both.

"Stay here," he tells Arietta motioning with his hand for her to remain seated. He travels across the entrance room as another soft knock echoes in the home.

"Hold on!" he shouts back, already irritated that someone is knocking on his door at this hour. There were several reasons he too chose to remain in his home rather than move into his castle and one was to spend normal nights with Arietta.

Slicking his hair back, he opens the door about head width with his foot planted behind it as a door jamb to keep it from being pushed open. Amiria's soft onyx eyes stare up at him. Taika's light-colored figure can be seen behind her in the yard.

"Ami—Correction, General?" He says, stunned at her sudden appearance.

"Father." She searches his confused face, "Can I stay here?"

Derek's shoulders soften, he doesn't see the General of a nation, he doesn't see a member of the Winged Cavalry. What he sees standing before him is a little girl. Who he sees is his daughter. Derek smiles warmly and opens the door.

The sun pokes over the mountains as Stirling's fingers tap nervously at his side. Streams of light break through the pointed peaks Stirling once called home, bringing color to the cold valley. His hazel eyes that match the sunlight of the forest are brought down from the sparsely clouded sky.

Ignis nudges Stirling's shoulder with the tip of his snout.

Popping his jaw, Stirling forces a small smile at Ignis. "Yeah, it's time to go." Blinking back the liquid forming in his eyes he faces his father. "I'll come back to visit in a year. If you change your mind, Patu can always use a baker…and a citole player." He smiles at Grace.

Giles' lip quivers. "We'll see you in a year's time." He grabs Stirling by the shoulders and pulls him into a tight embrace. "I'm going to miss you." He kisses his cheek. "Keep doing great things you hear. I'm immensely proud of you. More than I ever thought possible." He holds Stirling out at arm's length. "Even after all the scares you've given this old man."

"I'll miss you too, pa." Stirling's shoulders rise and fall as he takes a shuddering breath. Using the heel of his hand he wipes his eye and laughs off his tears.

Giles' breath hitches, "Go on now, your friends have been waiting for you for too long."

"Y-yeah, they have." Stirling turns to Ignis. "Ready?"

Ignis begins to bounce. *"More than ever!"*

"Okay, okay calm down and help me up." Stirling motions with his hands.

"Can't—too—excited," he says in-between bounces.

"The sooner you lay down the sooner you can see Aether." Stirling puts his hands on his hips.

He can feel the vibration beneath his feet as Ignis drops his mass to the ground. Giles laughs freely at their brotherly antics. Stirling grabs the handles of the saddle he made with Bernard and pulls himself up. He waves his last goodbyes and peers out at the spectators watching from the market streets. Their faces no longer stricken with fear. They smile as children wave their hands goodbye.

Turning to the sky, he no longer cares about all the eyes of the market.

The folks of Milleoaks watch as the parade of Wyverns land in the empty field on the outskirts of town. The towering peaks of the mountain rim of the land are only blue shapes on the horizon from the farm lands. Standing amongst the people, Mairead shields her eyes wondering if she had run far enough and for what reason has the Winged Cavalry flown out to this insignificant town.

She watches curiously as the men and women in red and blue tabards dismount their dragons. All of them match except for one with an opposite pattern. She squints in the burning sunlight. Her jaw drops with disbelief. She begins to push her way to the front of the crowd.

Sergeant Gautier, a dark haired man with a significantly crooked nose, holds his hand to greet the new Field Marshal of the nation. The Sergeant's wife and kids standing supportively by. He had received the letter about their arrival, and the news of his family, a family only by name. He holds his hand out to the young woman beside the Field Marshal. She must be the new General. The acclaimed Amiria Rey. The woman holds herself with a form of elegance that beautifully emanates vigorous authority.

With a strong grip she takes his hand shaking it but her eyes are caught by a girl emerging to the front of the crowd. She drops Sergeant Gautier's hand and breaks out into a childish grin.

"Mairead!"

Two buckets of water drop to the packed earth saturating the ground around her feet. The weather is warm as always with the sun shining clear without a cloud in the sky. Eve stands idly staring.

"Evelina?" Quilan tilts his head, a pail of water in each of his hands.

Her hand shoots to the air, pointing to the sky. Her mouth hangs open, unable to form the name. With a quizzical expression, Quilan turns to see what has ensnared her. His dark blue eyes widen and his buckets join Eve's watering the dry earth.

A wide smile stretches across Quilan's face reaching all the way to his eyes, brightening their color.

At a table outside the alehouse, Bernard lifts his tankard to his lips. Raising an eyebrow at Eve's unhinged jaw. He follows her and Quilan's gaze to the sky. His ale sprays from his lips and covers Edward the miller who is sitting across from him.

Eve's body is vibrating with ecstasy and with a squeal she grabs Quilan's hand and takes off into a sprint to the fields. Her heart races, pounding so hard in her ears it is all she can hear. Her vision tunneling, pinpointing on the only thing important at this moment, blocking out all unnecessary objects besides the hand in hers.

She can't hear Bernard running behind her, all she sees is the curly haired boy sitting on the back of an orange dragon.

The sole of Stirling's shoes barely touch the soft soil of the grassy fields before Eve leaps into him. Her arms curl around his neck forcing a grunt out of Stirling from the impact. Using her momentum, he swoops his arms around her waist spinning her. He holds her close as they twirl. Slowing to a stop he sets Eve back on to her feet but he doesn't let go, he raises his hand cupping the back of her head as her face fits perfectly in the curve of his neck.

"You're back," she says breathy, with incoming sobs, "You're actually back."

"Yeah," he whispers, nuzzling his cheek against her ringlet curls, "I really am."

Large arms scoop them both up and off their feet. Bernard's bellowing laugh rings in their ears, "STIRLING!" He cries squeezing both him and Eve.

"Yep," Stirling squeaks as he's crushed.

"AETHER!" Ignis hollers and begins galloping towards the blue Quetzalcoatl who had been napping by the alehouse stable. "AETHER, AETHER, AETHER!"

At the sight of Ignis, they spring from their coiled position and half-fly half-slither to him with excited adoration. The two dragons collide in a twisting embrace as Aether wraps themselves around Ignis and nuzzles their face to his with a cooing song.

Stirling is dropped back to his feet as Bernard releases him. Quilan stands before him with his arms shyly folded across his chest. Without a word, Stirling grabs Quilan by the shoulder and pulls him in for a hug. Quilan sighs into him with the corners of his lips turning up. Fitting together perfectly they stand there for several breaths holding the other up. ith his face resting on Quilan's head, Stirling breathes in the scent of home before finally pulling back. He keeps one arm around Quilan and throws the other around Eve's shoulders pulling the three of them in tight.

Breathing in deep, Stirling says, "Let's go to the ale house, I've got quite the tale to tell."

The cave in the mountains is distorted around them as Amiria stands before Stirling, their toes nearlyt touching. Swilring night tendrils crawl into the cave and latch on to the shadows darkening them further. The stars hanging outside wink like thousands of blinking eyes.

"Stirling," Amiria says, holding onto the hem of his tunic, "I'm so sorry." She tries to see his face but she can't make it out. It seems wrong and out of focus. "Please, hear me. I'm sorry. I take it back. I take everything back." She tugs on his tunic but his body is as still as a marble statue.

Her fingers curl into the fabric, threatening to tear holes with her nails. She leans in defeated, pressing her forehead to his chest, "I'm sorry." She whispers.

Toned arms encase her. She lets them wrap around her and pull her tight against his chest. She sighs with relief.

"Stirling, Stirling you're hurting me." Her eyes widen as the arms around her begin to crush her spine. Drops of thick liquid drip onto her and slide down her face. Her voice comes out a croak as her lungs cave in, "Stirling?"

"I accept your apology."

It isn't Stirling's voice. Her head shoots up to see Calix's face still split and bloodied staring down at her. Leaning down, he gives her a kiss on the forehead. He pulls back leaving a crimson mark behind.

Amiria's eyes burst open. She's panting, her body in a cold sweat. Her covers have been thrown, lost to the floor of the midnight room. Pupils dilated, they search the ceiling for the map of her surroundings.

She's awake, it was just another nightmare. Every night they haunt her in a place where no one can help her. No one but—she reaches out to touch him, to provide herself with a comfort only he has to offer. A supportive touch that can lift all of her problems. The palm of her hand lands on the empty fabric of her bed in her childhood room.

"Oh, yeah," she mumbles curling up into a ball, numbly twirling the leather bracelet around her wrist.

The small nocturnal bird, nightjar, lands on her open window sill. It hangs on the cusps of the walled in world and the freedom of the open sky. Its small brown head tilts side to side observing its surroundings.

Amiria watches the bird hop on the sill with tears leaking from her eyes. Finding nothing of interest, the nightjar takes off back into the wild. She closes her eyes but sleep never returns.

"Here's something to snack on." Stirling sets a wooden plate stacked high with fried battered apple rings.

Stirling has been settled back home in Patu for about two and a half months with Leucasia's Skylit Endeavor being only a week away. It's already been a year since he first arrived in Patu. A year he would rather not repeat. While Stirling was gone, he discovered Quilan had been— still is—using his loft with Aether sleeping in Stirling and Ignis' room. Quilan brought up the idea of purchasing land on the hillside overlooking Patu but the two boys growing fond of the other's constant presence, no plans of moving out have been made. The first night Stirling returned was the first night he slept without Ignis, besides his time in recovery at the bakery, in 10 years. He saw Ignis cuddled up with Aether in the room and decided to give them their space. With Quilan in his loft and Aether in his room, Stirling has set up his bed space in the main room in front of the hearth.

"Don't mind if I do." Eve reaches across the table snatching several right away.

Stirling smiles. Other than competing, he enjoys the quiet life in Patu. This, here and now, spending time with his friends is all he wants from here on out.

"Who ended up buying your place?" Stirling asks Quilan

Quilan, sitting beside Eve, watches her for the verdict as she chews. She dances in her seat with delight and shoves a second in her mouth. "Sister." He finally answers.

Satisfied with Eve's response, Quilan reaches over and picks one up for himself.

"Oh, she's married to Peyton, right?" Stirling takes a seat across from them as Quilan nods and nibbles at the piece of fried apple. "Just eat it," Stirling teases, popping an entire ring into his mouth. He grins wildly as he chews.

Quilan's dark blue eyes look through his light eyelashes as the corner of his mouth curls up. "Savoring it."

Stirling chuckles. "If you keep that pace up, Eve will eat all of them."

"Hey!" She scoffs with a mouthful of fried apple.

All heads turn to a knock on the front door.

Eve swallows her apple and asks, "Expecting someone?"

Quilan raises his eyebrow and takes another small bite.

Stirling shakes his head, unsure of who is at the door. "No. Not anyone that I know of." Placing his palms on the table Stirling goes to stand up. He pauses. Memories of Calix surface. He subconsciously touches the newest scar on his stomach. Hiding his nerves, Stirling composes himself and removes himself from the table.

The short walk from the table to the door lasts an entirety. He passes the hole where his bedroom door used to be, now covered with a canvas curtain. He steps over where his blood is stained into the wood flooring and stops where Calix had stood gloating when he took Amiria. Reaching out, Stirling takes hold of the door handle that had once opened up to a nightmare chapter of his life.

With butterflies in his stomach, he pulls it open.

"Hey, baker boy."

Warning:
The follow short story portrays depictions of child
abuse.

Like light through a prism, butterflies of varying colors flutter about the spring flowers in the garden behind the Gautier's manor, a stone structure a few rooms short of a castle. The lavish garden with trimmed rose bushes, morning glory covered arches and an herbal garden is not for use. There will be no family outings or walks through the blooming flowers. It was designed for one purpose in mind, an appealing scenery outside General Gautier's office so she can open the windows and smell the floral scents wafting in.

"Kinsey! Oh, Kinsey!" Sixteen year old Emil, the oldest Gautier son, calls out from the edge of the garden. Shielding his eyes from the sun with his hand he stands on his toes peering over the hedges for any sign. With no visuals he ventures into the garden.

Sneaking through the maze of hedges, he calls, "Kinsey? Oh Kinsey. Where are you?" He crouches down and crawls to scan under the bushes. A sound catches his attention. Pausing, he tilts his ear to the sound of giggling, and with a sly smile, he hops up and heads in the direction of a willow tree at the edge of the garden.

"Hmmm, I wonder where Kinsey can be?" He spins as he walks with his hands behind his back. "Oh where, oh where, can my baby sister be?"

Stopping outside the thick willow beside a small pond, he smiles knowingly and pushes through the curtain of leaves and strolls across the room created by the tree.

"If I was Kinsey, I would be—" He jumps around to the backside of the willow's trunk. "Here!"

Kinsey lets out a high pitch squeal that turns into giggles as Emil scoops her up with a tickle attack. Throwing her small body over his shoulder he says, "Shall we go for a swim?"

"NO!" she screams with a grin.

Emil strolls over to the pond's edge where the willow tree hangs over and drops her back into his arms and begins to swing her, "One. Two—"

"No! No!" She squirms while laughing.

"Okay, okay. You've got a foolproof argument." Giving in he sets his five-year-old sister back on her feet. "You'll make a great general one day." He lays his hand on top of her dark hair tied into two long braids.

"I don't want to be general. You're supposed to be general. Stay so we can keep playing," Kinsey whines.

"Because, I have to go protect another part of the kingdom." He kneels beside her.

"Will you come back to visit?" Kinsey's almond-colored eyes are saucers filled with hope.

"If father allows it, but you'll still have Calix and soon Keaton will be big enough to play." Emil forces a smile.

"Calix never wants to play. He's always frowny anyways," she mopes, crossing her arms.

Emil's smile drops. "Well Kinsey, don't turn into Calix. Don't stop playing no matter what our parents do. Here—" He reaches into a satchel strung across him. "I've got a present for you."

Kinsey's pupils dilate as she leans in expectantly, "What is it! What is it!"

He reveals a doll wearing a pink dress sewn together with linen fabric and stuffed with sawdust. "Don't let father see it okay?"

Giddy, Kinsey's hands shoot up and snatch up the doll, pulling it close to her chest, "What will he do?"

A darkness falls over Emil's face before he quickly hides it away with a toothy grin, "Just don't let anyone see it okay? It's our secret." He puts his finger to his lips.

"Oh okay!" Kinsey mimics him, excited to be sharing a secret with her oldest brother.

"What are you going to name her?" Emil asks.

"Ummm, Anina."

"That's a beautiful name." Standing up, Emil offers out his hand. "Want to show Anina around the garden?"

"YEAH!" She smiles with delight. Taking her brother's hand, she walks with him out of the willow.

With the sun setting and the doll safely hidden by the willow tree Emil escorts his only sister back to their home as the candles are beginning to be lit.

"Get behind me." Emil pushes Kinsey into his shadow as they step over the threshold from outside into the secondary drawing room that faces the back gardens.

"A Gautier does not get disarmed!"

Kinsey flinches at the sound of their father's voice, there has never been a positive outcome when she hears the Captain. Terrified of being spotted, she stays tucked behind Emil as they shuffle along the wall toward the hall.

As they traverse, Kinsey catches sight of Calix. Thin and gangly, at eleven years old Calix has already mastered holding his composure. His stoic face says nothing as their father's hand encircles his bicep, but his calculating eyes tell an entire tale as their father continues to lecture him.

"No child of mine gets disarmed," Major Gautier growls and begins dragging the still silent Calix toward the door. "Start running," he demands as he throws Calix's light body down the back steps.

Calix barely winces as the rough dirt scrapes his palms, brushing the dust off his clothing he turns back to the open doorway and spots Kinsey and Emil. His mouth pulls back into a thin line as anger reflects across his eyes like golden light from the lowering sun.

"If you don't start now, you'll be running in the dark." Their father's figure almost fills up the entire door.

Calix's eyes dart back to the man leering over him, with an aggravated exhale of breath through his nose, he stands up and begins running his laps.

Spinning around, Major Gautier turns his sights on Emil, "What are you still doing here!"

"I'm departing tomorrow morning, sir." Emil motions behind his back to Kinsey for her to keep moving.

"You useless being, waste of air and resources." Emil's father advances on him, his hand pointing accusingly. "You are an embarrassment to this name and don't deserve to take it with you."

"I'd rather leave it here too," Emil remarks.

Within a blink a strong and practiced hand strikes out and grabs Emil by the roots of his hair pulling his head down to off balance him, "I might not be your father any more but I am still a Captain."

The muscled arm as immovable as the stone around them holds Emil's head in place at a hunched level. "I don't care." Emil sweeps his leg, kicking his father's ankle out from under him, sending them both toppling to the ground.

Kinsey, hiding around the corner of the room, jumps at the sound of the two men hitting the ground. A colorful berate of words she has never heard before fly from her father's mouth.

A small gasp escapes her lips at the sound of knuckles striking and cartilage crunching. That sound *is* a sound she has heard before. Unable to help her older brother, Kinsey takes off down the hall, seeking the false safety of her bedroom.

At the creaking of her door opening, Kinsey ducks beneath her covers. The last light of the day is hitting the tops of her bedroom wall, but Genevieve has already lit the oil lamp in her room.

"It's me," Emil announces with a gruff voice. Kinsey begins to pull down her covers, "Don't. Let me sit down first."

Kinsey listens to his tired footfalls across her room then the slump of his body as he sits on the floor beside her bed.

"Okay," he tells her.

Pulling down her covers, Kinsey sees the back of her brother's head as he rests it against her feather mattress.

"Emil?" She reaches out and touches the top of his dark brown hair. She can see his hand touch his face but he doesn't turn around.

"I'll be okay, Kinsey. He just got me good this time." His voice slowly becomes thick as tears begin to form.

"Are you crying?" Kinsey sits up.

"Yeah—Yeah I am." He almost laughs as if the idea is absurd.

"I thought we weren't allowed to cry."

"Kinsey, I need you to listen to me and remember everything I'm about to tell you."

Leaning forward on the bed, Kinsey tries to peek around and see her brother's face, but he turns his head, obscuring her view of him.

With his head tilted away, he begins talking, "Whatever the Cavalry tells you, it's okay to be sad and cry. You're allowed to feel and be afraid. You are human, you can act like it. Please—please Kinsey, don't stop playing."

Kinsey climbs to the foot of her bed and hops off. Coming around to the side she finally sees what her brother was hiding. Blood from his crooked and purple nose spills down his face and onto his shirt. His high cheekbone and lip are split and there is swelling beginning around his eye.

His almond colored eyes, filled with sorrow, find hers, "I'm sorry, Kinsey." Kinsey lays on the ground beside him and rests her head on his lap without saying anything. He rests his hand on her shoulder, "I love you."

To those words, she closes her eyes and falls asleep.

"Don't cry, don't cry, Cavalry doesn't cry," Kinsey tells herself. *Emil says it's normal to cry though.*

Barefoot and still in her night shirt, Kinsey stands on the stoop to the entrance door of the Gautier manor. She sniffs, wishing she could be holding her new doll that is hidden in the willow tree as she watches her oldest brother tie the last of his belongings to his dragon. Her eyes shine with the incoming tears. Her heart is telling her to run to him, hug him one last time as she begs him not to go, not to leave her here alone. He had disappeared from her room before she awoke and she found herself tucked into her bed as if he was never there.

Her father had given her direct orders not to bid Emil farewell. According to him, Emil is no longer her brother and should be treated as such. There will be no send offs to a stranger even if they share the same last name.

She digs her fingernails into the palms, biting back the tears. *Don't cry, don't cry. Calix will tease you if you cry.*

His face battered and bruised from the previous night, Emil turns back to the house he grew up in. It isn't his home now and it wasn't before. A home isn't somewhere you feared going to. He needed to escape. It was a selfish choice, he knows it, and it's already begun to eat at him. He purposefully botched his evaluation to keep his marks below the adequate level to become General or even a Captain.

I'm sorry, Kinsey, he thinks. His baby sister is holding herself together the best she can at the top of the stairs. He knows it is wrong to leave her behind but it was the one form of control he could take in his life. In no world will he let himself fall into either his mother's or father's footsteps.

He made it through his childhood without breaking and he was the first to learn their father's *lessons.* She is a strong girl, it won't be easy but she will overcome this.

A figure in the upstairs window catches his eye. His younger brother stands in the large window of the family's solar room. A room none of them were ever in at the same time.

Calix scowls as Emil nods his goodbye. Genevieve, their housemaid, appears beside Calix with a damp cloth. She gently pinches Calix's chin and turns his head so she can inspect his split lip. With a sympathetic smile she presses the cloth to his face resulting in a grimace of pain. Remembering that he could be seen, Calix pulls away from Genevieve and disappears from the window.

Emil frowns. Being five years apart, Calix and he were children together. He loves his little brother and remembers the days Calix used to smile as they played games. Emil didn't care about the reprimands he would get from their father. Words don't hurt and bruises fade. Each strike from his father only implanted his decision further into his mind. He hoped Calix would be the same, but the first time he was caught playing after the age of five he was ripped from the gardens and thrown into a closet. When he was finally released he was no longer a child.

It's pointless in this household to do as their father instructs. He will find another reason to take out his stress on the first one he sees.

His eyes fall back to Kinsey, Emil wishes he could take her with him and raise her himself. She would be able to grow up without fearing every misstep. The world would be a bright place where she is allowed to be a kid, to be herself.

Hanging his head, Emil climbs onto the back of his dragon. There is one thing he fears now.

The next time he sees Kinsey, it will be too late.

Like a shadow stuck to his heels, Kinsey trails behind Calix through the halls of the manor. She has attached herself to his orbit as soon as he passed through the entrance gate after his training, all the way up to the second floor.

Calix stops outside the door to his room. Turning his head over his shoulder, Calix glowers down at her. "Do you need something?"

With her hands clasped behind her back, Kinsey hides her head in her shoulders shyly, "Well—it—I—well."

"Don't be weak," Calix says crudely. "Come on, speak up. What is it? You obviously want something."

"Do you want to pla—" Kinsey's words are cut off as Calix slaps his hand over her mouth.

He leans down closer to her. He is a spitting image of their father and Kinsey is finding it hard to not stare at the yellow and purple coloring beneath his eye. "Why father hasn't caught you yet bewilders me, but you need to cut this childish stuff out."

"But why?" She asks through his fingers still over his mouth.

Calix releases her with a shove. "Show father your doll and find out."

Standing on the balls of her feet, Kinsey balances on the far end of a willow branch. She clings to the leaves around her for support with her doll, Anina, strapped to her chest. Each step she takes the solid branch beneath her feet grows thinner and weaker.

She had begun balance training in her Winged Rider tutoring and has taken an immediate liking to it. The act of walking where your feet are not meant to go is thrilling. She will climb higher and higher until she is out of reach of everyone.

This isn't playing, this is training. She is training—not playing. Not playing—training.

The thinning branch holding up her weight begins to bow. With a yelp of surprise Kinsey dangles in the air gripping the willow leaves as the branch she was standing on falls to the grassy ground far below her.

Giggling, she kicks her feet through the open air and begins to swing her body. She stretches her toes out and on the third try is able to grab hold of the still attached branch. Bending her back, she uses all of her muscles to pull herself back up onto the branch.

"That was a close one." She pats her baby on the head. "But don't worry, Momma kept you safe."

Walking back toward the trunk, Kinsey playfully bounces with the buoyancy of the branch and spins her way across. As if she was raised in the tree, she gracefully swings down the branches until she is back at the roots.

"Bed time," Kinsey tells her doll and kneels down beside a raised root creating a doll-sized room in the ground. Removing her from the carrier, Kinsey gives her a kiss on the head.

Then with a loving smile from Kinsey, Anina is placed on a chunk of bark and tucked into bed with a scrap of cloth for a blanket.

"Momma will be back tomorrow." Kinsey hops up and skips back to the manor.

A tan woman with curly dark hair pulled back into a top knot whacks Kinsey's shins with a leather crop, "Tighten your core."

Kinsey struggles to keep the pain off her face as the skin where the crop continuously hits begins to split. Her father saw her natural gift in balance and has begun to exploit it by having her private tutor, Petronella, conduct all of her lessons on wooden beams of various widths and slopes.

For the past two years they have stripped the joy out of one of the few things she enjoys.

Relentless hours, blistered feet, and bleeding shins, Kinsey spins, parries, advances, blocks, and strikes all while on the beams.

Sweat dripping onto the beam and overwrought with exhaustion, Kinsey's legs wobble beneath her.

"BACK! BACK! BACK!" Petronella instructs Kinsey to retreat on the beam as if her opponent was advancing on her.

Kinsey's feet nimbly find the beam no thicker than they are behind her in a quick rapid succession. Off by a toe,

Kinsey topples off the beam that is hip height with Petronella, who stands with her arms crossed making no movement to catch her. A sharp pain shoots up and down Kinsey's arm as her elbow lands first on the gritty ground. She cries out instinctively and curls in around her injury.

Whack There's pain of a new welt on her shoulder blades.

"Get up," Petronella demands.

Struggling to keep the tears at bay, Kinsey bites her lip. Even with all of her forces up one tear slips through and runs down her cheek.

Whack The crop strikes her on the back. "Winged Riders do not cry. Now get up."

Kinsey moves to stand but the pain in her arm brings a whimper out in her.

Whack

The force of the crop sends her back down, defeating any progress she made in standing. Hurts. Hurts. Everything hurts. She has to stand, she has to get up. Her elbow, her shins, her back. Everything hurts.

Don't cry, can't cry, smile, this is fun, this is fun, smile and tell yourself this is fun. Kinsey uses all her will to pull back the corners of her lips and slowly rises to her feet, cradling her injured elbow.

Petronella's face pinches with a disconcerting expression as she stares down at the small girl smiling up at her. Raising her lip she dismisses Kinsey, "See to Genevieve to have her tend to your arm. Training will resume tomorrow morning whether you splinted or not."

"Yes Ma'am." Kinsey's smile stretches further but never reaches her still damp eyes.

"Oh, it's already swelling," Genevieve says as she inspects Kinsey's elbow. They sit in the drawing room with Genevieve knelt before the young girl swinging her legs still smiling. Scrapes, bruises, and sprains, Genevieve has tended to everything on the Gautier children. She has been specialized to handle everything in manor from cooking, to cleaning, to lighting the oil lamps, but her primary focus is taking care of the next in charge of the Winged Cavalry.

It wasn't their father who taught Emil how to walk. Their mother wasn't there for Calix's first words. It was she who trained Kinsey to use the privy. Only she gets up when the youngest Keaton cries.

Despite all that, these are not her children. She cannot stop the hands that harm them. She can only do her best at being there for them when they do.

"Kinsey, doesn't it hurt?"

"Yes, very much." Kinsey doesn't break her new gleeful character.

"Then why are you so happy?"

"Because, maybe if I smile long enough it will stop." Kinsey closes her eyes with a proud smile as if she had discovered a secret.

Genevieve's body deflates. "Oh, Kinsey."

Around the corner, peering into the room, pale eyes narrow.

The setting sun glows through the bright green streamers of leaves hanging from the willow tree. Pushing through the curtain the smile Kinsey held up all afternoon finally drops. This is her small world, in here she can be herself, Kinsey a seven-year-old girl and not Kinsey Gautier next in line for General of the Winged Cavalry.

Limping from the bruises and wounds on her legs, Kinsey hurries across the open space under the tree until she falls to her knees at the base. In here she doesn't have to hide her tears, she's allowed to cry, she can cry. In here it is okay to be sad and cry. She is allowed to feel and be afraid. Emil told her so.

With her good arm she picks up Anina and cradles her against her chest. Tears without restraints flood her face streaking it red. She wipes snot with the back of her sleeve and falls to her side curled up around her doll.

It's okay to cry. She is sad, she's allowed to cry. It's okay, it's okay, it's okay. Here she can be the Kinsey she wants to be. In here she is Kinsey, a future mother who will love her children with her entire heart like she loves Anina. In here she is only a little girl.

But even here, she is lonely. She is so alone. Sad, sad, she is sad. It's okay to be sad. It's okay to cry. She is always sad, always always sad.

She misses Emil, she misses having someone who loved her back. She begins to weep for what she will never have. There will never be another sibling to hold her hand and guide her. No one to be her friend. She will never have a father who tells her she's doing a good job or a mother who tells her good night.

Her weeps turn to a broken laugh as she continues to cry, fetal position around her doll.

Kinsey Gautier will never have a family.

Her laughter grows as she hugs Anina closer, but one day she can create one, a real one. All she has to do is put on a smile. Smile and it will get better. Smile and tell them you're happy. Smile, laugh, and dance around. Everyone will see you as happy. Smile and never, ever, *EVER* stop playing.

Kinsey's eyelids shoot open. The moonlight shimmers in through her window, casting a glow across her bed as she lays with the covers pulled up to her chin. Holding her breath so she can hear better, she doesn't move as she waits and listens, too afraid that the ruffling of her fabrics will block the sound she is searching for.

There is no light coming from under the door, the candles being snuffed out by the caretakers hours before.

A creak in the floorboards sends a sharp intake of breath through her.

He isn't supposed to be home this week. He was sent out. He is supposed to be at the harbor. Kinsey's breathing begins to pick up in pace with each footfall drawing steadily closer.

Pulling the blanket over her head, Kinsey squeezes her eyes shut. *Stop at Calix's. Stop at Calix's. Stop at Calix's.*

They don't stop.

Throwing off the blanket, Kinsey dives for underneath her bed as the door to her room bursts open. It hits the wall, cracking the wood as the metal door handle bounces off the stone wall. He is across her room in two strides. Fear restrains Kinsey's movements, her hands uselessly slap the ground failing to pull her body forward and scramble beneath her bed in time.

She screams as a large hand encases her ankle. Her nails scrape across the floor as it drags her back out into the open. Instantly regretting letting the sound slip, she clamps her hand over her mouth. He hates it when she screams, only babies cry. Winged Riders fear nothing, but it's not true. Not true. Not true. Not true. Not true. NOT TRUE!

There is one thing she fears.

He is leaning over her and she can feel the sudden hot sting of pain on her cheek where he had slapped her. Blinking back tears she stares up into the void of his shadowed face in the dim moonlight.

Only one *person* she fears.

With a silent gasp of pain, Kinsey grabs the hand clenching her braid by the root pulling her to her feet and out into the dark hallway. Her small legs catch and trip over the other's ankle as they struggle to keep up with her father's stride. Liquid wells up in the corner of her eyes from the pain in her scalp. *Don't cry. Don't cry. Don't cry.* Crying will only make it worse. *Only babies cry.*

Calix stands in his doorway. Straight faced, only the gears in his eyes turn as they track Kinsey struggling to keep up with their father while they pass him. He stands as still as the portraits on the wall but doesn't dare lift his eyes from Kinsey to their father.

Kinsey doesn't look to him for help. How many times has she hid under her bed when it was his room their father stopped at. She would hum and plug her ears when it was his feet stumbling as he was dragged down the hallway. She can't count high enough for the number of times she was playing out of view in the safety of the willow tree while Calix was taking the blows of their father's full attention.

She has been lucky, always staying out of her father's sight. If it wasn't for her brutal tutoring she was close to believing that her father forgot she existed.

But how could he forget a daughter who is next in line for General.

Thump

Her feet fail her as they meet the stairs.

Thump. Thump. Thump.

Unable to get her footing she is dragged down each step.

Thump. Thump. Thump.

Her hands still clenching the wrist of the hand locked around her braid.

Thump.

Her knees hit the cold flooring of the first level. Down the hall she can see the fire burning bright in the hearth of the main drawing room. Without waiting for her to get up, her father drags her light body into the room. Elongated shadows of the furniture move in time of the daunting fire along the surrounding walls. They dance and wave like an audience celebrating her hanging.

The hand finally releases her, dropping her hard on the rug in the center of the room. On her hands and knees the hellish light is reflected in Kinsey's wet eyes as she blinks at it. Why is the hearth lit in the middle of a summer night?

She follows his movements from the corner of her eye as he steps to stand beside the raging fire. She doesn't know what drives her to slide her eyes from the fire up to father but they move on their own accord to see what it is he had grabbed off the mantle and is holding on display by the neck.

Anina.

Her eyes shake with her quivering body, but she doesn't dare raise her gaze further than the doll hanging suspended in air at chest height. She can't meet the eyes of the monster standing in front of her, they remain locked to the doll. Following the doll her eyes drag along the short distance as the clawed hand moves it above the hungry flames that reach up eager for their next meal.

NO! She screams inside her skull. *NOOOO!* Her eyes plead for the safety of her baby but she is powerless against the monster who has her. How had he found her? How, how, how, how—Calix. He had known about her. Tears begin to well up again at the thought of her brother's betrayal.

She doesn't care anymore that she will be punished further for appearing weak as the tears tear free and flow down her face. She can't save her baby, but at least Anina can see she loved her. That's what everyone needs, right?

To be cared about, to have a parent who loves you—to have *someone* who loves you.

Tiny hands curl into fists that will never be thrown. The light of the fire turns the trails of her tears into yellow streams of fury flowing past her snarling lips. Then the site before her shatters her face into a blank canvas.

She watches uselessly as Anina is released from the monster's grip and descends silently through the air to land on the burning logs. In a blink, the sawdust stuffed inside the linen body catches on fire and flames ravage the small doll. Staring blankly, Kinsey can't remove her eyes from the only thing she had left that she loved disintegrating into ash.

Long after her father has left, Kinsey continues to sit there numbly in the center of the room until each coal has gone out.

Lying on his side, Calix's nose scrunches as he is pulled from his dreams and stirs awake to the feeling of someone watching him.

"WHAT!" he yelps as he finds Kinsey standing over him, a foot on either side of his torso. She tilts her head smiling as he scampers back to sit up against the wall. "What are you doing!"

She falls to her knees sending smoky plumes of dust into the air and throws her arms around his neck. "Calix!"

Calix coughs, "What is that?"

"One day, what you love will be taken away too," Kinsey whispers into his ear. Before Calix can respond she leaps off the bed and spins across the room. "Good night, big brother."

Calix's eyes knit together as she closes the door leaving him alone in his dark room. Blindly, Calix runs his hands over the top of his blanket brushing a layer of unknown substance. Feeling the silken dust between his fingers he brings it up to his nose and sniffs.

His eyes the color of the moonlight widen then dart back to the door.

Twelve Years Later

A single pair of male boots step along the gravel path through the once beloved garden now beginning to be overrun with weeds and untamed hedges.

Emil, now a thirty-year-old man, pulls back the leaf barrier of the willow tree and steps inside the green room letting the entrance swing closed behind him. In over a decade it hasn't changed. With the view of the manor, the mountains and the castle obscured, it's as if this circumference of space will never be touched by time. A safe haven you can slip into when you need a break from reality.

But— Emil adjusts a wooden object under his arm—*it's only pretend in the end.* He stumbles across the moss-covered world he once escaped to.

Barely able to pick up his feet under the weight of his sorrow, Emil reaches the base of the trunk and finally collapses under the strain of a broken heart. His face contorts from the pain in his chest as he pulls the cross out from under his arm and presses it into the soft dirt.

His fingers linger on the wood as his head drops to hang, "I'm so sorry." Tears begin to drip, "I'm so sorry." Tipping forward, he hides his face in his hands and lets them rest against the ground, "I should have come back for you. I shouldn't have left you."

Kinsey and the others who fought on the side of King Dietrich and perished that day were burned, leaving Emil without a sister to bury. With knees sinking into the damp earth, he kneels in front of her memorial as the only person in the kingdom mourning her.

He weeps for the little girl who was once full of love and happiness, the little sister he adored. He cries for the woman—the mother—she never got to grow up to be because he had failed her.

There were stories of the young female Gautier, nightmarish tales he refused to accept. How could he believe his baby sister's gleeful smile turned twisted and devious. If only he had listened and gone back to her, but maybe it would have still been too late to help her. Maybe the broken pieces of her would no longer fit back together after being warped for so long.

"Papa?" a little girl around the age of four says behind him. Her small hand rests on the back of his shuddering shoulders. "Papa, are you crying?"

Emil sits up and turns to his daughter. With his voice catching in his throat he croaks, "Yeah." Reaching out with a fluttering smile he tucks a loose strand of dark hair behind her ears, "Papa is sad."

Throwing her arms around his neck, Emil's daughter asks, "Why is papa sad?"

"He lost someone very dear to him," he answers, returning the embrace.

She pulls back to look at her father, "Where did they go?"

"Somewhere very far away. A place where they can never come back, but it's a place where nothing will hurt them anymore."

"Will we go there?"

"Not for a very very long time." He kisses the top of her head, "I love you, Anina."

Anina beams, "I love you too, Papa!"

Using the tree to help him stand, he reaches back down and pulls Anina up into his arms, "Ready to go?" Anina nods. "Say goodbye, Kinsey."

"Goodbye, Kinsey." Anina waves at the cross.

Emil wipes a stray tear from his eye and smiles, "Goodbye, Kinsey."

Turning away from the willow tree, Emil holds his daughter in his arms. One day she will choose if she wants to join the Winged Cavalry. She has the bloodline to make it easy to form a bond with a dragon, the laws have changed and the future is for her to decide. He knows no matter what she chooses he will support her all the same.

At the edge of the willow tree, Emil stops before the swaying green wall and turns back to the cross. He opens his mouth to speak but closes it and dips through the leaves.

Keaton stands on the top step of the manor entrance. His chestnut eyes leer down at the strangers who share his last name. With a stiff posture he crosses his arms. From the pointed features of his face to his every demeanor, he is his mother's son.

The person who had stated to Keaton that he was his older brother, Emil, holds his hand up in a friendly gesture.

Keaton's eyes narrow further, "You said your goodbyes to my sister. Now vacate my property."

Emil's face drops with his hand as he stares up at the boy who has barely turned sixteen and now stands alone on the stoop of a manor. He doesn't know this boy, the last time he had seen him he was only a toddler. Keaton lost everyone that night. Kinsey and their father both lost their lives and Calix and their mother disappeared.

He wishes he could begin their relationship as brothers. Even though Keaton is a legal adult it isn't too late for him to show Keaton compassion and what it is like to be part of a *real* family. Not all of the Gautiers are gone, Keaton doesn't have to be alone. He still has a brother, but there is also an extended family out there they can reinstate connections with. There are uncles, aunts, and cousins who had been cut off after they didn't inherit the general or captain position.

Keaton, the last remaining of his immediate family, remains in a hard and stoic stance in front of the manor that has nothing left but the ghosts to keep him company.

"Papa, who is that?" Kinsey whispers into Emil's ear.

"My brother, your uncle."

Anina waves her goodbye, but Keaton only turns his back on the father and daughter who strikingly resemble his older sister and slams the manor door shut behind him. For the second time, Emil walks away from the Gautier manor leaving behind a sibling in need.

Acknowledgments

I'll start with the obvious, my family and my husband. My mom, for showing excitement for me by making a reusable bottle with pages from my book. My sister, for letting me read to her my roughest drafts and knitting me a stuffed Ignis. My dad, for taking the time to read the rough drafts, the final product, and being my number one fan. My husband, for dealing with me constantly talking about my book, hounding him with questions, and hovering over my laptop. I will, of course, love to thank my in-laws, who love my book no matter what.

I have to give a special shout out to some of my best friends. Taylor who helped me name my protagonist, Jessica who helped proofread, and Sophi who helped edit my book. That girl would sit in the cold, raining PNW forest with me while camping as we took turns reading the book out loud and making adjustments.

I'm also going to give thanks to my editor Belle Manuel. She was the one who helped change my book and characters for the better.

Then I'm going back to the roots, where it all started. I will not mention the place I had worked but let me say graveyard was so dull that I started writing this book. I will never forget those I worked with at the place that shall not be named. They supported me when the book was nothing but scribbles in a journal. They listened to me as I told them my idea and encouraged me to go for it. Four and half years later and its finally done because of their initial support.

Now I won't neglect to thank the later years. I had left that initial job and began somewhere else. My coworkers and supervisor watched me write furiously in my rough draft notebooks and type on the computer during down times. Instead of my supervisor telling me to put the notebook away and my coworkers getting upset that I was distracted at work, they supported me. Constantly asking me how my progress was going and putting positive vibes that I will one day finally complete it. Here it is guys. Except, I will still be typing at work because there's no stopping me now. So, you're stuck with me still click-clacking away, but after all these of watching me type, you must be used to it now. Thank you, everyone.

Kelsea Koops

About the Author

Born and raised in Thousand Oaks, California, I had changed what I wanted to be when I grew up numerous times like any child. Looking back through all my schoolwork and old notebooks, I loved story writing. The evidence was there, but I just ignored it. End of high school, I took that interest, believing I wanted to be a screenwriter. I wrote a full-length movie, but I didn't enjoy the lack of detail. I love writing detail, really building a mental picture of the world. I dropped out of college before gaining an associate degree and went straight into the workforce. I attempted to write another movie for the fun of it but never finished it. Looking back now, I don't know why I didn't just write those as books.

At 21, I had entirely given up on the idea of being a screenwriter but still liked writing as a hobby. I wrote a short story for only me to read, and it wasn't until I was 25 that it occurred to me to turn it into a full-length novel. Scars of Lumierna is the result.

When I'm not at my full-time job hovering over a computer, or at home sitting on the couch with my computer. I'm out camping, with my computer. With a rooftop tent mounted to my four-wheel drive Toyota, I love taking long drives through the Olympic Mountain's logging roads, even some roads that my car shouldn't be going on, and I had to do the sketchy backup and turn around. At the end of the day, my friend Sophi and I would pick a spot, make a fire and work on my book. There is no better place to work than in the middle of the forest with no one around except your best friend, some dogs, and the sound of the crackling fire.

Connect with me online at
Tiktok kelseakoops author
Instagram kelseakoops_author
kelseakoops.com